DAY FOR NIGHT

Also by FREDERICK REIKEN

The Odd Sea

The Lost Legends of New Jersey

DAY FOR NIGHT

FREDERICK REIKEN

A REAGAN ARTHUR BOOK

LITTLE, BROWN AND COMPANY

NEW YORK   BOSTON   LONDON

Reagan Arthur Books / Little, Brown and Company
Hachette Book Group
237 Park Avenue, New York, NY 10017
www.hachettebookgroup.com

First Edition: April 2010

Reagan Arthur Books is an imprint of Little, Brown and Company, a
division of Hachette Book Group, Inc. The Reagan Arthur Books name
and logo are trademarks of Hachette Book Group, Inc.

The characters and events in this book are fictitious.
Any similarity to real persons, living or dead, is coincidental and
not intended by the author.

Portions of this book have appeared previously, in
slightly different form, in *The New Yorker* ("The Ocean"),
Western Humanities Review ("Yesterday's Day" as "Carousel"),
and *Glimmer Train* ("Shadow").

Library of Congress Cataloging-in-Publication Data
Reiken, Frederick.
    Day for night / Frederick Reiken. — 1st ed.
        p. cm.
    ISBN 978-0-316-07756-9
    I. Title.
    PS3568.E483D39 2010
    813'.54 — dc22   2009038597

              10 9 8 7 6 5 4 3 2 1

                           RRD-IN

                Printed in the United States of America

To Cailin

This web of time — the strands of which approach one another, bifurcate, intersect, or ignore each other through the centuries — embraces *every* possibility. We do not exist in most of them. In some you exist and not I, while in others I do, and you do not, and in yet others both of us exist.

—*Jorge Luis Borges*

DAY FOR NIGHT

1

Yesterday's Day

"THEY'RE AROUND HERE," said our guide, as we slowly motored up the Homosassa River. It was late afternoon, a mildly sunny day in midwinter. My boyfriend David, his son Jordan, and I wore wetsuits, which we had rented along with snorkeling equipment. We'd been assured that a group of five overwintering manatees had been grazing all day in the oxbow.

"Look!" Jordan yelled, and pointed. Across the river, a pair of seal-like heads had surfaced.

"Well, thar she blows," said the guide, and let the motor die. He tossed a small metal anchor into the blue-gray water.

We'd been in Tampa for one of David's conferences. We had heard about the Homosassa River, an hour's drive north and one of just a few places on earth where it was possible to swim with wild manatees. I had mixed feelings about the venture, but we had Jordan, who was thirteen, with us, and he had been extremely bored and brooding for the three days of the conference.

Since the proximate cause of Jordan's moodiness was not apparent, I chalked it up to the obvious, larger issue we were facing. Six months before, David had been diagnosed with leukemia. He had recently gone into remission, but the odds were that the remission would not last more than a year. Though Jordan had not been briefed yet on the prognosis, his father's bald head and skinny frame were enough to suggest that something was vastly different. This three-day trip also marked the first time either Jordan or I had gone with David to a conference. Perhaps it had not been a waste of money, though Jordan and I had spent most of the time playing backgammon in our motel room while David agonized about his presentation.

In our rented car we'd driven up to the town of Homosassa right after David finally gave his talk about the latest trends in the population dynamics of the long-spined black sea urchin. During the ride I offered David my impressions of the talk while Jordan tuned us both out with his Sony Walkman. He was thirteen, after all. Somehow he'd managed it. His mother died when he was six, but he'd come through it more or less okay. I attributed this to David's good and loving nature, and I reluctantly gave some credit to the two twentysomething budding marine biologists whose thesis committees David had more than chaired. That was during the years between his wife Deborah's death and our first meeting, on the occasion of his bringing Jordan into my office with tonsillitis. It took three years before we started discussing marriage, but then his diagnosis came, and so instead we discussed my plans to adopt Jordan, if David died.

I thought about this as Jordan jumped into the river. He liked me now but I wondered if he would still like me as his mother. I guessed the grad students were more sisterly than maternal, and that maybe this had been a safer enterprise. I also guessed I wasn't anything like Deborah. She was a dancer. David once told me she had a habit of getting extremely lost while she was driving. Sometimes she went to the store for milk and took an hour to get home.

Jordan swam calmly up to the nearest manatee and dove down, as if to take a few bites of whatever species of aquatic grass was growing on the river bottom. When he resurfaced, the nearby manatee approached and seemed to nuzzle him. Within seconds, he appeared to have been approved as a new member of the herd.

David followed Jordan in. With the same unlearned skill Jordan had inherited, he too was quickly welcomed by the manatees. For twenty minutes or so, I watched the two of them swim around with these floating teddy bears, one of whom seemed to be continually demanding that David tickle him. "Go on," said our guide, a tall, skinny young man who looked to be in his early twenties. He had blond hair and a very bad complexion, and I had noticed that he kept glancing at my chest.

I said, "I don't know that I want to."

He said, "Why not?"

I didn't answer. I almost told him that as a young girl I had lived in a small village in eastern Poland, that we didn't have any marine mammals, and that I'd once seen a dead man floating facedown in the river Bug. But that would have been melodramatic. The truth was I was afraid that I would not be made as welcome by these manatees. That they would sense a certain problematic energy in me — or worse, I would find that I was terrified of them. As rationalization, I was reviewing various environmentalist arguments against fostering interaction with wild animals. These ranged from ethical problems related to ecotourism to the dangers these manatees might face thanks to their willingness to tolerate human presence. Of course, it also occurred to me that they'd been tamed long ago, that their nature was genuinely docile in the first place, and finally, that I had never seen creatures more beautiful in my life.

So I went in with my rented mask, fins, snorkel, and too-small wetsuit. I swam toward them with far less ease than David or Jordan, veering away, then toward, then back away, and at last choosing to swim in the general direction of a single manatee on the periphery. It was the wrong choice, I quickly realized. This manatee was the only member of the group that appeared to be the least bit skittish. I stopped swimming when it drew back from me. I prepared to face unprecedented manatee rejection, but thankfully, it did not turn its whiskered snout away. With the most placid, unearthly face, it watched me. Its tiny eyes looked to me like stars. It let its tail fluke sink until its body was almost vertical. When I looked down I saw that the tail was horribly disfigured, sliced into several leaflike segments by the blades of an outboard motor.

I knew what to do, somehow. I swam away from the manatee and it followed. I took a few more gentle strokes, let myself glide, and did not look back. When the creature swam up beside me, I kept going. It stayed with me for a minute or so, once even nuzzling me, and finally I turned toward it. I saw more scars on its back, including one that was shaped like the letter Z. It moved up close and pressed the side of its long body against my shoulder. Then it drew back again, submerged, swam under me, and was gone.

Our guide had told us that if you stay where you are and do not try to follow, the manatee will usually return in a few minutes. I treaded water until its head popped up near the main group. It stayed away and submerged again when Jordan swam out toward it. I didn't see its head resurface, although I waited ten more minutes. Then I swam back to the boat and felt as if my heart would burst.

I pulled myself up the rope ladder that our guide had hung down the boat's side.

"That one, she likes you," he said.

"She swam away from me."

"She's just a shy one. See any markings?"

"What kind of markings?"

"Propeller scars," he said, and glanced down at my chest again. Fixed action pattern, David would say. All part of preprogrammed neurophysiology. He'd claimed his attraction to the second of the two grad students, a top-heavy girl named Stacy Bennett, could be blamed on the phenomenon of "supernormal stimuli." Just like the oversized claw of the fiddler crab or the inflatable red neck of the magnificent frigatebird. David conveniently ignored the fact that these and other supernormally stimulating appendages typically cited in college textbooks were, almost exclusively, traits that occurred in males.

"Oh, those markings," I said. "Yeah, her tail was mangled. She also had a scar shaped like a big Z along her back."

"That's what I figured," he said. "Zelda. She's a real shy one, like I said."

"Do you have names for all the manatees?"

He nodded and said, "We get to know them."

"And this is all you do? Take people out to see manatees?"

"No, ma'am," he said.

"What else?"

"I work on boats."

"You're a mechanic?"

He said, "Yes, ma'am."

"What's all this *ma'am* stuff?" I asked.

"Being polite."

"Did you grow up around here?"

"Born and raised in Homosassa." With a twinkly smile he added, "Ma'am."

"That's very nice," I said, and stared at his vaguely Germanic features.

"I also play the guitar," he said. "We have a band. We're called Dee Luxe. That's because Dee, she's the lead singer and she started the band with her boyfriend. He plays the drums."

"Is his name Luxe?" I asked.

He smiled again and said, "It's Jerry."

Jordan and David were swimming up. By then they'd been in the water close to an hour.

"Hey, Beverly, did you see us?" Jordan said, as he climbed up the rope ladder.

I said, "Yes. You turned into a manatee."

"Maybe I did," he said, and appeared to be assessing the possibility. He reached behind himself to unzip his wetsuit. I helped him peel it down off his shoulders and draped a towel around his neck. Jordan was wearing a little necklace he'd won last summer playing Skee-Ball at an arcade in Cape May, New Jersey. He and Rocky, my younger daughter, had each cashed in their win tickets for a pendant of polished light green stone that hung from a thin black cord. They called them "wonder stones," which, apparently, was how they had been marketed.

"We saw you swimming," Jordan said. "With that one manatee who wouldn't go near me and Dad. It had a messed-up tail, from all the boats."

I said, "Our guide said her name's Zelda. She has a Z-shaped scar across her back."

"What about that one with three scars on its head? What's his name?"

"That must be June," said the guide. "The others were Lana, Kate, and Francie."

"How do you know?" Jordan asked.

He said, "I came here with another group this morning. They swam right up to the boat, so I got a good look at their scars."

"Can you tell who they are without the scars?" I asked.

"Not really."

Jordan said, "Dad," and looked at David, who had just climbed up the ladder. "We were with Lana, Kate, and Francie."

"That's good to know," David said softly, and pushed his mask up to his forehead. He'd started growing a new mustache, which made him look like a big, wet seal.

On the ride back, I sat with David, pulling him close with my arm around his shoulder. For the first time in a long while, he seemed relaxed, even serene. I recognized his mood. He'd been this way after a whale-watching trip we'd taken during the past fall. For all his scientific deconstruction of wild habitats, for all the academic bureaucracy and political maneuvering he had weathered, David had somehow preserved his fundamental love of nature. For me it was long gone, beaten out of me in my twenties, during med school, when I was taught to recognize the many horrors that nature can bestow. This was a problem, I later realized, and maybe one I'd hoped to remedy by falling in love with David.

But in the three years since we'd met, I hadn't healed much or gotten any softer. And in the months since David's diagnosis, I'd often felt — more than he — that I wanted to give up trying.

— — —

When we got back to the dive shop, our fearless guide gave me a flyer for his gig that night at some local bar. I thanked him, folded the flyer up, and stuck it in my pocket. I wanted to tell him there were drugs that he could take for his bad acne, but I didn't. It didn't really seem appropriate.

We ate pizza and then returned to our motel room. The plan was to wake at six, drive back to Tampa, and catch a nine-thirty flight to Newark. I made phone calls — checked with my answering service, called two patients, and then called Jennifer and Rocky, my two daughters. Rocky was short for Roxanne, a name I'd once been keen on, God knows why. As expected, I got the answering machine. I left the number of our motel. I said we'd swum today with manatees and were staying in a town called Homosassa. I said to call if either one of them got home that night before ten o'clock.

As had become our nightly ritual, Jordan and I played backgammon. He rolled doubles on three straight moves and went on to achieve a gammon. Because David no longer had his presentation to obsess about, he'd been coaching me and suggesting moves, and after this thorough beating, I let David take my spot.

I went downstairs and found the motel lobby. I bought three root beers from a soda machine. As I walked back up, I encountered David, who had run down to find me. He said that Rocky was on the telephone, that it was urgent. *"Nu?"* I said — Yiddish for "So?" or "Well?" — which had become our little joke. My mother said it all the time, and for a year David had thought she was always asking about my clothes. "So is my house burning down?" I asked, when he didn't answer. Then he explained that my older daughter, Jennifer, was about to spend the night in jail.

I assumed that whatever happened had involved alcohol. I was wrong, as it turned out. She'd been arrested with a girlfriend of hers, Alison Belle, for blowing up a mailbox in East Brunswick. They'd used M-80s, Rocky said, which I inferred was some kind of explosive. The owner of the exploded mailbox was Mildred Turner, a hated history teacher. Still it seemed strange to me since Jennifer's midterm grade in history that trimester had been, as usual, an A.

To make matters more complex, Rocky had Jennifer on hold, calling from the police station, and had called me since, in theory, Jennifer was only allowed one phone call. I guessed she might have been granted two, but, in truth, I didn't want to talk to her.

I let Rocky tell me that Jennifer needed a lawyer, that she was going to be transferred to the Middlesex County juvenile detention center, that she would need to be bailed out in the morning, and that somehow I was supposed to make all of this happen despite the fact that it was 10:20 p.m. and my plane would not be landing in New Jersey until almost 2:00 p.m. the next day. What little I knew was this: (1) being two months shy of eighteen, Jennifer was still a minor and would most likely get off easy; (2) I would have to call Mel Blumenthal, my pediatrics practice partner, and get him to bail her out. I told Rocky to tell Jennifer these two things and that I'd see her when I got back. I stayed on hold after that for about five minutes, until Rocky returned and explained that Jennifer was crying.

"What is she crying about?" I asked.

"She keeps on saying it's a mistake, that she shouldn't be there."

"Well, was she present for the explosion of Mrs. Turner's mailbox?" I asked Rocky.

"Yes, but Alison Belle is evil," she said, as if this clarified everything.

"What does she want?" I asked, and realized I was shaking.

"She blew up her teacher's mailbox, and now she's feeling bad because she happened to get caught."

"She's crying," Rocky said. "She's all hysterical."

I took a breath and tried to suppress my anger, not to mention the surge of empathic terror I was feeling for my daughter.

I said, "Okay, Rocky. Listen. This is what I want you to tell Jennifer. Tell her she's going to be fine and that Mel will bail her out first thing tomorrow. Tell her I love her, and that you love her, and that one night in a county lockup won't kill her. Send her a hug for me and tell her to be brave. Then ask her to take a deep breath and hang up."

I sat on hold again while Rocky relayed this message. It took another five minutes before Rocky's voice returned. She said, "I told her. She won't hang up."

Somehow I'd guessed this would be the case.

I said, "Then I will. I'll call home from the airport in the morning. Tell Jennifer that I said good-bye, okay? I'm hanging up now. Here I go."

"Wait," Rocky said, but I went through with it. She may have tried to call me back, but the line was busy since I immediately called the East Brunswick Police.

I pleaded with two officers, begged them to let Jennifer out that night on the pretense that she was fragile and might have a mental breakdown. A Sergeant Jones informed me that the lockup facility would be quite comfortable and that Jennifer and her friend had both seemed hardy. Furthermore, he said my daughter had committed a very serious and disturbing crime and that maybe a night in jail would be enough set her fragile soul straight. Barely resisting the urge to respond rudely, I hung up on him. I quickly got in touch with Mel, who promised he'd be there to bail out Jennifer at 7:00 a.m. sharp. I also called my lawyer friend, Lynn Burdman, who said she'd come with me to Jennifer's arraignment Monday morning. David and Jordan sat there listening to everything. I hung the phone up after the last of an hour's worth of calls and said, "Root beer, anyone?"

"Are you okay?" David asked.

I said, "Not really."

"I'll have a root beer," Jordan said, and smiled at me. I smiled back at him—Jordan could elicit this—and tossed him one of the three cans I had put down on the bed. I agreed to play one more game of backgammon, during which I explained the situation. He again beat me badly and apologized. I assured him it was okay.

Jordan said, "Why don't you take the wonder stone tonight?" and lifted the black cord off of his neck.

"Thanks," I said, and slipped it on over my T-shirt.

We turned off the light so Jordan could get some sleep. It was almost midnight. David and I went outside to take a walk. There wasn't much to do but wander around the parking lot. After we'd walked the full perimeter, we got into the rented car. Illogically, I began kissing him, which lasted twenty seconds or so, at which point I started crying. Then David held me against his chest and continued telling me how brilliantly I'd handled things. I calmed down after a bit and asked him whether he thought Jennifer would be okay in jail.

"She should be fine," David said. "She's tough, like you."

I said, "But I'm not fine."

"I think you'll be calmer in the morning."

"Do kids go to jail a lot these days?" I asked. "Is this a normal thing?"

He said, "It's probably more common than it used to be."

I still felt negligent, guilty of raising a precocious and pretty girl who blew up mailboxes. And Jennifer was the honor student, whereas Rocky was dyslexic and God only knew what I might get with Jordan.

We went inside and got in bed. Jordan was snoring away, and although David rubbed my back under the covers for a few minutes, he soon nodded off as well. I counted sheep and other things I never do. I tried filling my body, part by part, with a gold mist, but this old remedy also didn't work. So I got up, slipped on my jeans, walked outside, and leaned over the second-story rail. The bending caused me to feel the piece of paper in my back pocket. I pulled it out. Dee Luxe at the Blue Ox. 10 p.m. One free drink with $5 admission. The address was on a main road, the name of which I recognized. I went inside and found the car keys. I flipped the light on and quickly scribbled a note for David, although I guessed that I would be back in an hour.

— — —

The Blue Ox was as grungy as I'd expected it to be. A sedimentary layer of beer coated the floor and the ventilation system seemed not to be working. Two steps inside and a cloud of cigarette smoke and body odor enveloped me, though the place wasn't really all that crowded.

The stage was near the entrance, and I immediately saw our young manatee guide. He was wearing ripped jeans and a white button-down, sweating profusely, his electric guitar dangling above his thighs. I found the bar, ordered my free beer, and then sat down in the small section of the Blue Ox that had tables. From where I sat, I couldn't see the stage well. The sound system was terrible, but the music I found tolerable. Mr. Manatee Guide knew how to play guitar, and the lead singer, Dee, clearly had charisma. She was a hefty and sexy girl whose crass expression and haughty presence contrasted nicely with the soft, sweet quality of her voice. She had once been in a church choir, I suspected. Now she was doing the angry and rebellious thing, wearing sheer tights, platform sandals, and hot pink miniskirt. She strutted around the stage while Mr. Manatee Guide stepped up to play a fast, bluesy, and altogether skillful lead. When he'd stepped back, Dee shouted, "Tim the Slim-Jim Birdsey on guitar!"

Tim Birdsey. His name seemed to fit him perfectly. They played one more song and thanked the twenty people or so who were standing around in front of them. They put their instruments down and turned the amps off, and it was clear that they were finished for the night.

I was about to leave when a young pixie-haired waitress came to my table, placed a Bud Light down in front of me, and said, "Timmy asked me to bring this." I thanked her and looked toward Tim, who had been breaking down the stage setup with the other members of Dee Luxe. A waitress brought all of the band members tequila shots and they downed the shots in unison. Tim had a lime wedge in his mouth when he caught me looking. He pulled it out and called, "Hey, I'm glad you made it. I'll be done here in a minute." I was relieved to feel myself detaching from the night's debacle regarding Jennifer, but I still wondered why I'd wait for a redneck boy who'd spent the afternoon staring at my chest.

"So how'd we sound?" were his first words when he joined me at the table. He had a beer in his hand and had just put on a Miami Dolphins cap.

I told him, "Pretty good, though maybe not quite ready for the big time."

"We'll get there," he said, and then laughed amiably. He seemed different, much more confident and grounded.

He said, "The funny thing is, I thought you'd come tonight."

"Are you a psychic?"

He said, "I just had a strong feeling."

"I had some trouble falling asleep."

He asked, "Did you and your husband fight?"

"No," I said, and didn't bother telling him David was not my husband.

He said, "My mother used to stay up the whole night after she fought with my crazy daddy. He always threatened to smash her skull in with a shovel while she was sleeping."

Thankfully, the waitress appeared just then. She had another shot of tequila on her tray.

Tim said, "You want one?"

I said, "No."

He took the shot glass in his hand and this time drank it without the salt or lime.

"It's a tradition," he said. "After we play. But two's my limit. Dee and Jerry can both drink me under the table."

"Dee has a nice voice," I said.

"I know. We could make it big because of her. So why aren't you sleeping? Are you one of those insomniacs?"

I said, "My daughter got arrested."

He seemed unsure of whether or not to believe me.

"For vandalism," I said. "Back in New Jersey, where I live. She and her friend blew up their history teacher's mailbox. You ever do that? Blow up a mailbox?"

After a moment's hesitation, he said, "Sure, once or twice. Though it was more fun to just drive around and knock them down with baseball bats. Mailbox polo is what that's called. You sort of hang out of the passenger-side window..."

"I get it," I said, and forced myself not to imagine the other crimes Jennifer may or may not have committed.

"That's a nice necklace," Tim said.

I was still wearing the wonder stone.

"Is it jade or something? Malachite?"

"No," I said, surprised by Tim the Slim-Jim Birdsey's knowledge of semiprecious stones.

"Tourmaline?"

"It's a wonder stone."

"A wonder stone?"

I said, "Yes. I have to go."

"But what's a wonder stone?" Tim asked.

I took the stone between my fingers and held it toward him.

"I have no idea," I said.

Tim said, "Actually, it looks more like aventurine."

I asked him how he knew so much about green stones.

He said, "My pop was a big rock hound. Guess I became one too. And you know, Dee, she knows things about gemstones, like that jade is good for calming the nerves and ridding yourself of negativity. She has a necklace with jade and rose quartz. Rose quartz is good for creativity. She keeps a bunch of stones in our practice room. Aventurine is one of them. She said it helps the imagination. Maybe that's why whoever gave it to you said it's a wonder stone."

"It's my son's," I said. "He won it at an arcade in New Jersey."

"Well, it looks pretty."

I said, "Thank you."

"Your name is Beverly, right?" he said.

I said it was.

"That's a nice name," he said. "I knew a Beverly Dupont back in high school. In ninth grade we were partners in biology lab. We once dissected a fetal pig. She didn't look anything like you, though. The funny thing is I feel like I just *know* you. Maybe we've met somewhere, a past life or whatever. Dee's always talking about past lives. Says she was once the servant of a wizard somewhere in England. You seem familiar is what I'm saying. I bet that maybe you're like me in certain ways."

"I bet that maybe you're drunk," I said.

He shook his head and said, "Trust me, you would know if I was drunk."

"How would I know?"

He said, "I'd probably be telling you all about my crazy family."

I said, "Okay then, Mr. Psychic. Why don't you tell me all the ways that I'm like you?"

"Well, off of the top of my head, I'd say you think too much," he said. "That's not so bad, really. It just gets tiring. I'd also say that way down deep inside, you're sad. Did both your parents die when you were really young or something?"

"No," I said, although my father was believed to have been murdered in World War II. But this was after my mother and I escaped from eastern Europe, and all we'd ever heard were stories. All we could ever truly know was that we had never seen him again.

"Well, both my grandfather and father blew their brains out," he said. "My grandfather did it seven years before I was born. I never knew him. My dad did it when I was sixteen. Right in our yard. I think it's why I became the way I am."

"Which is what way?" I asked, not unaware that he was telling me all about his crazy family.

He said, "Oh, lots of ways. But *worried* is the word I always come to. I'm sort of worried all the time, though I doubt anyone who knows me would even think it. I worry about my grandma and my mother, who I barely ever see, and about Dee because we slept together a few times, more like a few dozen times actually, maybe like five dozen, and even though we told Jerry, I still feel guilty because I'm pretty sure I'll sleep with her again. I worry about other people and right now I'm even worrying about you because your husband, he looks like he's pretty sick. But like I said, I doubt I even look like I'm worried about anything. Maybe it's wary, more than worried. Maybe that's it. I'm always *wary*. Maybe wary is what you look like when you're secretly always worried. Does this make any sense at all?"

I said, "A little," though I think I was being charitable.

"I want to take you somewhere," he said.

I said, "I'm sorry. It's getting late."

"It won't take long."

I said, "I'm sorry."

He said, "It also might help you sleep."

I concentrated on his face and I sensed earnestness. Strangely enough, his intent seemed pure.

"I'll tell you what," Tim said. "You can just follow me in your car. When we get to what I have to show you, you can just leave if you don't want to get out."

"How far is it?"

"Five minutes up the river."

It was one-thirty, possibly later.

I said, "Okay."

— — —

I was surprised by the bright light of the moon. A day or so past full, it had emerged from a patch of clouds. Its glow had turned the Blue Ox into stone. I got into the rental car and Tim walked across the parking lot to his pickup. He placed his guitar down on the rear bed, wedging it in beside some boxes. He climbed inside, rolled down the window, and said, "Okay, just follow me."

I was still not sure if I'd really follow. I thought of Jennifer and hoped that she had managed to fall asleep. I also found myself thinking about my mother, who had lamented, more than once, that my appearance of perfect assimilation often led me into "extremely stupid American situations." She was referring to my two daughters and my ex-husband, Richard, who I'd been married to for less than four years before he left to pursue his acting career in Hollywood. We'd tied the knot in 1964. I had wanted a child immediately, and after eight nerve-racking months of trying, I became pregnant with Jennifer, who was just two years old when Richard and I separated. A little more than a year after we'd signed divorce papers, Richard was spending a few days in New Jersey. We made a plan to meet and talk, got very drunk, and after a single night of unremarkable sex, I was pregnant again, which to me seemed so miraculous that I did nothing except watch my belly grow. I didn't tell him for six months, at which point, as expected, Richard *plotzed* and for some reason I just laughed at him. "Funny how easy it was," I said, and he said, "You are a fucking cunt." When I told my mother, she moaned and groaned and said my father did not save our lives so that I could become a fallen woman. I suggested she might at least feign happiness for the fact that she would soon have a second grandchild. She called back later to apologize, but, as expected, the conversation ended with her moaning again.

"Well, are you coming, Bev?" said Tim, having already sensed my hesitation.

He didn't scare me, but clearly something made me nervous. "Don't call me Bev," I shouted back. I put the car into gear and pulled behind him.

"Just follow me," he said once more, and we drove off.

He led me back to the road that ran along the river. For a mile or so we drove beside the water. We passed the shop with the SWIM WITH MANATEES! sign, which was where we'd first encountered Tim that afternoon. The road turned south and the river vanished. We passed by citrus orchards and several herds of cattle. Given the alcohol he'd consumed, Tim drove commendably. Soon we veered back and drove again along the Homosassa River. In certain places the road ran right above the levee. I wondered whether the thing he'd brought me to see was simply this river glowing in the moonlight. It would have been enough, I thought, to see the river against this night, which was almost day.

At a sharp curve in the road, Tim pulled his truck onto the shoulder. He turned his engine and his lights off. I pulled over and did likewise. "Look there," he said, and held his head out of the window. He pointed to a missing section of the guardrail. He said, "It happened a few days ago. Truck crashed right through. Look in the water."

Beyond the bank and almost right in front of us, a pair of manatees lay resting on the surface of an oddly inclined island or peninsula. My eyes adjusted to the strangely illumined darkness. Then I was gazing, most unexpectedly, at the roof of a sunken carousel. It had come to rest along the river's bottom, which sloped enough that, in the section nearest the shoreline, the top portion of several poles and a few horse heads had broken the water's surface. Except for the corresponding section of the roof, the rest of the carousel was submerged.

"They got the truck out," Tim said. "It landed down on its side, but they dragged it out. I don't know why they haven't picked the carousel up yet. The water can't be doing it any good."

I spotted a third manatee, most of its body underwater, bearing its weight on the sunken portion of the roof. Then the head of a fourth popped up behind the others, in the water.

"How did you know they were here?" I asked.

"They were here last night."

Something was rising up inside me, something uncanny. I was starting to feel an overwhelming sense of déjà vu.

He said, "Those manatees must like having something to rest on while still being in the water."

"Maybe," I said.

"Want to get out?"

I said, "I think so."

He pushed his door open and stepped out.

I said, "Hey Tim, can you tell me why you brought me here?"

He said, "Just thought you could use a little wonder."

I smiled at the cleverness of his answer and pushed my door open. As I stepped out onto the glowing roadside, I considered how I might explain all this to David and to Jordan. It struck me that I'd probably choose not to.

"You coming down?" Tim asked.

I said, "Yes," and followed after him. I had that feeling of being stupid but also knowing that what seemed stupid would be okay. Somewhat incongruously, I also found myself trying to recall the Seven Wonders of the Ancient World. I could get three — the Great Pyramid of Giza, the Hanging Gardens, and the Colossus. We reached a sand shoal that glowed hazily in the moonlight. "Do you know the Seven Ancient Wonders?" I asked Tim. He said,

"The what?" and I said, "The Seven Ancient Wonders. Like the Great Pyramid." He said, "Nope."

We walked out farther, to the water's edge, where less than fifteen feet of river lay between us and the portion of the carousel that was visible. One of the manatees began moving, awkwardly sidling along the submerged roof until it reached water deep enough to swim. The creature's movements suddenly turned graceful. The water rippled in its wake, seemed to fluoresce. And then it vanished, leaving its momentary, perfectly smooth footprint on the surface. I stood there feeling the small weight of the wonder stone. I thought of Jordan and it struck me that this part of his life was going to seem wondrous, and that my Herculean task, if David died, would be to keep this sense of wonder from imploding, turning inward, and reshaping itself as longing and despair. Or perhaps such a task was futile. Perhaps it wasn't my task at all. What would my task be then and what was wonder anyway?

A nechtiger tog, I thought, and then a door inside my brain opened.

This was a phrase my father used. Biblical in origin, it was Yiddish for "a yesterday's day," by which he meant something absurd, silly, or impossible. Often sarcastic, sometimes not, the words could substitute for "Don't bother even thinking about it." It's what he'd say if I worried that the friendly talking ravens in a story I loved got angry when I finished the book and closed it. It's what he'd say each time my mother expressed her wish that we leave Poland and cross the ocean to America.

On a summer night two months before we fled from Poland to Lithuania, he woke me up and took me out to see the glow of the full moon over the Bug floodplain. We'd come to live with his brother, Lejb, after my father left his job at a gymnasium in Warsaw. He'd been a science teacher there. Now he helped Lejb run his small farm and in the evenings he read books. He held my hand as we walked.

The moon was casting its glow over the fields that ran beside the river. I had the sense that the bright light was clinging desperately to the earth. And for one purpose—to remake yesterday's day, which, with a five-year-old's capacity for literalization, I believed might happen if the full moon glowed bright enough. That night as we walked along the river, I kept waiting, hoping the light would reach its threshold, so that *a nechtiger tog* would actually appear.

The manatee's head popped up again. Its fist-size muzzle floated on the surface of a deep pool right in front of us. I could hear its exhalations. Raspy, stertorous breaths. As if the river itself were drawing air through its enormous river-lungs and using this lone manatee as its mouth. I turned to Tim and said, "Are we anywhere near the place we swam today?"

"Maybe a quarter mile upriver."

I said, "How come you didn't take us to see this carousel?"

"Boss said not to," he said. "Whoever owns it called him up and asked him to keep tourists away. Anyway, the manatees were downriver, where we found them."

"You think it's Zelda," I said, "right here in front of us?"

Tim said, "Who knows. We'd need to see her scar."

"Or else her tail," I said, and crouched so that my knees were sticking out over the water.

"Are you okay?" Tim asked.

I said, "I'm tired."

As I spoke, the manatee ducked under again. Another smooth, still print appeared on the water's surface. Five seconds later the manatee's head popped up downriver. Then it submerged again and did not reappear.

"Well, that's like Zelda anyway," said Tim. "She's not too social."

I said, "She's wary," and stood back up.

We stayed there maybe another minute. The water shimmered, and some reckless, erratic part of me was longing to dive in. To become part of that glowing river. Somehow to enter its ghostly province. It seemed within my reach, a day beyond all days, its wonder. But it would wait, I understood. Possibly it would wait for a long time.

"Ready to go?" Tim said.

I nodded. I had the silly thought that I should kiss him. I refrained, knowing the gesture would be foolish and misleading. I also refrained once more from telling him he should see a dermatologist. In the end, I hooked my arm in his and asked him whether he would guide me to my vehicle. He said, "Yes, ma'am," and we headed up the levee.

— — —

On the plane ride home, David slept while I held his bald head in my lap. I had the window and I watched the eastern seaboard, trying to figure out which states we were flying over. At one point David woke disoriented, sat up stiffly, and looked around. He sometimes woke like this, in terror. He'd once explained that sometimes when he woke he would feel certain, for a moment, that he had died.

"We're in a plane," I said. "We're over one of the Carolinas."

He seemed relieved as he registered the interior of the airplane. "Hi," he said, and then leaned over, kissed my cheek, and said, "I'm back."

I took his head in my arms again. Jordan sat listening to his Walkman with his eyes closed, now and then mumbling a snippet of a song. I felt happy, in a way, or at least peaceful, despite the impending drama that was sure to ensue with Jennifer. It was a feeling I wasn't used to. It seemed to have to do with balance. I guessed it also had to do with manatees, and I told David I was glad we had gone to see them. I fell asleep soon after that and didn't wake until we hit the runway.

2

Close You Are

THERE WAS A part of Dee I loved, and that part of her was sitting by the window as we huddled close together in the third-to-last row of a red-eye flight from Tampa to Salt Lake City. Both of her hands had found their way under the thin Delta Air Lines blanket I had covered myself up with. I had been meaning to try and sleep, but she had worked open my jeans, slid down the zipper, and started whispering all sorts of arousing things.

She said, "Sometimes when we're onstage and you're playing leads I have the urge to turn and face you, shake my ass for whoever's watching, and French kiss you."

This despite the fact that her longtime boyfriend, Jerry, who she lived with, was our drummer.

Dee always knew exactly what to say to get me going, so while it certainly was possible she could imagine something like this, I didn't really believe that she would think it while we were performing. I assumed she mostly thought about the songs and the words and the fact that if by some colossal bit of luck we could all manage not to break up for a few more years, there was a chance that someone might discover us.

She could get wild onstage, but still, the things you think about are whether the band is tight and whether there are more than fifteen people in the audience. At least, that's what I thought about and the fact that our potential was way, way beyond the circuit of college bars we'd been stuck playing in western Florida. What I am saying is that I thought we should be famous. I say this not because of me or Jerry or our bass player, Bill, or because

I dreamed the same things every member of every rock band since the Beatles has ever dreamed of, but because it was impossible not to recognize the virtuosic talent that was Dee.

She said, "Hey, Timmy. Timmy Bird. Gonna sing your bird-song?"

My name's Tim Birdsey.

She said, "Hey, Timmy, you play a mean guitar and always eat in the Steak Bar and love to drive your Jaguar."

These were words from a song by Pink Floyd that we covered, a spacy tune from the mid-seventies, which Dee had transposed into her sweet and sultry voice.

"Bathroom," she said, and took her hands away.

I said, "You need to use the bathroom?"

"You too," Dee said. "You need to use the bathroom."

I thought about what Dee had just proposed, which included thinking about the person on my left, an attractive dark-haired woman who looked to be in her late forties or early fifties, who hadn't said a word or acted like she knew what we were doing. But I felt sure the woman knew what we were doing, and I wondered whether, on an airplane at two-thirty in the morning, I should stand up and parade by her with Dee. Of course, I did it. I zipped my pants up and moved the Delta Air Lines blanket. We both stood up and I said, "Excuse us," and then the woman stood to let us by. She wasn't sleeping or really doing much of anything, though it seemed that she was as wide awake as we were. I told her, "Sorry," and the woman said, "It's okay." Meanwhile Dee, in catlike fashion, ducked underneath my elbow and after two quick strides slipped into the bathroom. I looked around to see if anyone was watching, but everyone I could see was sleeping with the same blue Delta Air Lines blanket draped around them. I followed Dee, counted to ten, and then went in.

She had her sweater off already, her silver cross necklace hanging in the crevice between her breasts. As always, she wore one of those push-up bras and smelled like lavender. That was the scent she liked, although it was not perfume. It was some kind of special oil. She had a mole on her right breast and the last time we were in bed I'd made some comment, and she said, "Why don't you think of Marilyn Monroe and lick it?" So far as I knew, Marilyn Monroe's mole was on her face, but I got the point. What I had not been sure of was whether Dee had meant for me to think of her as Marilyn Monroe or just to imagine Marilyn Monroe. I was remembering this whole conversation as Dee shoved me against the sink in that little cubicle of a bathroom. I saw the mole when I took her bra off, and I licked it.

We were inside the airplane bathroom for fifteen or twenty minutes. There was that smell you always smell in an airplane bathroom. Sort of like shit and piss and something else. There was some turbulence and Dee laughed. She said, "Rough ride," although by then we were done and Dee was putting on her sweater. She went out first and I waited a few minutes, smelled the smell, and washed my face with the lukewarm water from the sink. As I stepped out I was already feeling guilty that I would have to make that woman in our row stand up again. But when I got there, she was already standing and waiting. She was tall. "Your friend's upset," she said, and when I looked at Dee I saw that she had her face pressed against the plastic window so she could muffle her sobs, and this was working.

The woman next to me wasn't asking questions, but as I sat down I turned to the woman anyway and said, "Her brother got in an accident. Crashed his motorcycle and now he's in a coma. That's where we're going, going to see him." The woman nodded and said, "I'm sorry." Then she sat back and I watched Dee and I wondered whether the woman next to me had thought that I was lying. I didn't think so, because why would you make something like that up?

It took five minutes but Dee calmed down and told me that

she needed to get some sleep. She wrapped herself up in the thin blue Delta Air Lines blanket. She closed her eyes and I took out the in-flight magazine. I turned the reading light on and did the crossword puzzle, which was easy. Doing those in-flight magazine puzzles always made me feel smarter than I am. From time to time I watched Dee sleeping, and meanwhile the woman on my left stayed wide awake and stared at nothing and did not move. I wondered why I had told her about Dee's brother. I also wanted to tell her more. I said, "So where are you from?" but the woman shook her head and made it clear that she did not want to engage in conversation.

Instead I read an article about an actress who was deaf and had three children. Still, it was hard to resist speaking to this woman. She seemed to be the kind of woman who had seen things, who was wise, or who could warn you about the future. Probably this was just me *inventing* her. Dee says I do this all the time.

But this is what I could have told the woman. Assuming that she had been willing to listen, I could have told her all about our band and how the girl I'd obviously just had sex with in the bathroom was our lead singer, that she was Chrissie Hynde with some Stevie Nicks and a splash of Michael Stipe or maybe Sting. I could have told her that I had been sleeping with Dee a few weeks ago while her boyfriend, Jerry, was off visiting his daughter in Atlanta, that Dee had woken up from her usual restless sleep and sat bolt upright. It was so sudden that the mattress shook and I woke up and said, "What's going on?"

Dee had said, "Beltane."

I said, "What?"

Then Dee repeated the word and explained to me that Beltane was a Celtic holiday, and that the people who invented it performed rituals that were meant to ensure that the passage between the spirit world and our world was barred, and that these spirits would seek instead to be reborn through the bodies of the living.

It was in spring and it divided the Celtic year up, along with Samhain, which took place during the fall. Samhain was the opposite. On Samhain you opened up the passage between our world and the spirit world. You let the spirits roam around, so they'd be happy and not pissed off when the passage closed back up on Beltane. Dee said that Beltane was coming soon. I found this interesting but suggested that we talk about it in the morning. Dee had said, "Not till you understand." Then she explained that in Celtic times there would be bonfires. Cattle were driven through the flames, which was supposed to preserve the fertility of the herd. And there was lots of unlicensed sex, by which Dee meant, as she explained, sex between people who were not legally married. All of this sex would provide the doorway through which spirits could be reborn into the bodies of the living.

I said, "You want a beer?"

Dee had said, "Jesus, Timmy. No."

I said, "I think I'd like a beer. Is that okay?"

Dee had said, "Fine. Go get a beer."

I said, "I'm not trying to be rude, but if you want to talk about mystical things, it would be nice to have a Heineken."

She said, "I'm talking about me, and about Dillon. If you'd just let me."

I said, "I'll be right back," and I went downstairs to get a beer.

Dee's real name is Gwendine. Her brother, Dillon, had crashed his motorcycle at high speed on a road in Israel. He had been driving along the shores of the Dead Sea. It had taken several weeks for his and Dee's extremely wealthy parents to move him back to Utah from the hospital he'd been staying at in Jerusalem. Dillon was hooked up to a bunch of wires at a hospital near the saltbox colonial–style house where he and Dee grew up. I had known all this because one evening before a gig, Dee sat us all down and explained it. I'd thought it strange when I had recognized the parallels — the Dead Sea and Salt Lake City and saltbox house. When I had mentioned this to Dee, she rolled her eyes at me and told me to shut up.

But when I came back to the bedroom with a beer that night, she told it all to me again and this time I didn't comment on the parallels. She turned the light on and she kept on saying, "Beltane." She kept on saying, "Jerry wouldn't understand."

"Understand what?" I had asked.

She said, "I have to go and see him. I haven't seen him for five years, not since I ran away after high school. I never thought I'd go, and now I have to do it, go and see him. I have to help him."

"Help him with what?"

She said, "You wouldn't understand."

I said, "I might."

She said, "It's ugly."

I said, "Does it have to do with your history of childhood trauma?"

Dee nodded. We had one song that was secretly all about what she referred to as her history of childhood trauma. It was called "Down in the Sea of Me," but it was cryptic. You might just think it was a song about the ocean. Dee once told me we're alike in certain ways because my father was a raging alcoholic who got violent when he was drunk and would scream all sorts of things we didn't understand because he usually screamed in German. My father killed himself when I was still in high school. That was right after my mother ran off to Mobile, Alabama, with some businessman who drove a Cadillac. My father's father (who also killed himself, way back in 1954) moved from Düsseldorf to Florida right after World War II, and Dee said probably my grandfather was a Nazi, though I have no way of knowing. Once or twice I searched through photographs to see if there were any of my grandfather wearing a swastika armband or maybe shaking hands with Hitler. I never found anything other than the usual shots of people sitting in chairs while holding cigarettes or standing in front of lakes.

When Dee got up from the bed where she'd been sitting, she was still naked. I saw the mole on her breast. I sipped my beer. She said, "Hey, Timmy, I'm going downstairs. I'm going to write you a little note. I'm going to seal it up, and then I'll give it to you in Utah if you're willing to come with me."

"Go to Utah when?" I asked.

She said, "We need to get there before Beltane."

"Which is when?"

She said, "About two weeks."

"What about Jerry?"

She said, "Jerry won't understand, like I've been saying. He'll have to trust me, or forget me."

"Will Jerry know that I'm going with you?"

She said, "No."

"Will he see the letter too?"

Dee told me, "No."

Then she said, "Timmy, look. You need to understand that what I went through, my history of childhood trauma, it wasn't normal. It wasn't typical abuse is what I mean. I was, like, messed with." She sighed and then said, "Well, I suppose anyone who calls herself a Survivor has been messed with. I think I'd better just go write it in this letter."

She left the room and went downstairs to write the letter. While I was there, drinking the beer, I had the feeling that this whole thing with Dee was going to wreck our band. There was no Yoko factor or dead drummer or band member who was turning into a junkie, and so it struck me that the person who would be most to blame if our band broke up was me. Then I was thinking of the painting Dee had painted a few years ago when she took a summer art class. Jerry didn't like it, so he wouldn't let her hang it on their wall. Dee had offered it to me, but I didn't like the painting either. It was a picture of a girl with a giant, multicolored belly, like she was pregnant with all these geometric shapes in all different colors, and the girl's mouth was a big wide circle, which made it look like she was screaming. I accepted the gift because I didn't want to insult Dee or her painting. I never hung it, and I just told her that my grandmother didn't like me making holes in the walls.

When the plane landed in Salt Lake City, I woke Dee and she said, "Sorry about the crying. It was fun before that, especially in the bathroom. I just wanted to, you know, have some fun."

As we deplaned Dee touched my back and I walked behind the woman who'd been sitting next to us. She must have been about five ten or five eleven—not quite as tall as me, but she towered over Dee. We went to baggage claim and Dee said she wanted coffee, so I stood waiting at the carousel. I watched the woman walk out through the automatic doors. She had no luggage other than what she'd taken with her on the plane, and as I saw her go I really had the sense that there was some important message she could have told me. More likely, it was just this thing I sometimes have for older women. Show me a poised, fifty-year-old woman with a tired, pretty face that has some love in it and, really, I will get an instant hard-on.

When Dee returned, I had our bags and she put her arm around my shoulder. It was five-thirty in the morning. She said, "Let's rent a car and go to a motel and get some sleep. Then I'll start figuring out how to see my brother." I began thinking about our last gig, just four days before, how each of Jerry's drumsticks broke within a span of about three minutes. Then I was thinking about my shell collection, which for some reason I have never thrown away. Then I was hoping we might run into that woman from the plane again. I suppose my brain was making these strange jumps due to lack of sleep.

We got a piece-of-crap economy-model Ford from Avis Rental Cars. Then we found a Sleep Six, and in our room I ate the complimentary bite-size chocolates while Dee showered. I was thinking again about my seashells. For instance, where I'd found that

perfect little tulip shell (Sanibel Island). Then I had thoughts
about my job as a boat tour guide for an outfit that runs skiffs out
to see manatees in the winter as well as larger boats for fishing
expeditions. The pay was shit, but I liked it better than my job fix-
ing boats for crazy Dennis in his repair shop that I think is more
of a front for all the drugs he sells to people who own boats. Then
Dee walked in with her hair up in a towel and her breasts bounc-
ing, and she said things like she had when we were sitting on the
plane. She said, "You know, when we're onstage I sometimes think
I'd like to straddle your guitar and let you blast me with those
power chords." Then she was pushing me down onto the bed and
she said, "Timmy, I'm a monster," and I said, "No, Dee, you're
a genius." Then she was on me, saying, "Timmy, you don't even
know who I am." Saying, "You have no idea, really. Timmy, you
don't even know who *you* are."

When I say Dee is restless in her sleep, I'm not exaggerating.
She doesn't toss and turn so much as tremble and twitch and gasp
and sometimes yell things. She grinds her teeth a lot as well, and
it's so loud that I sometimes wake her up because I'm worried about
her jaw. But when I do, she will just tell me to get used to it. So
what I try to do with Dee is just get used to things that normally I
wouldn't want to get used to.

She slept her twitching, jaw-grinding sleep at the Sleep Six
motel while I lay staring at the plaster ceiling and noticing that
even after twenty-four hours there was no way I could let go.
Before she ran off with the businessman, my mother used to say
that to summon sleep you have to let yourself stop breathing and
be *breathed* by the giant lungs of God himself, who will protect you
for the time that you surrender to the sea of the divine. This was
supposed to make me calm, but it always creeped me out to think
of myself as being breathed. You hear something like this when
you're young and the impression it makes never really leaves you.
Add to all this the things that Dee had said about the spirit world

and this holiday called Beltane. I didn't really believe in things like spirits or God's lungs, but I'd been up all night, and sex with Dee tends to make me loopy anyway, so as I lay there it was easy to start worrying.

We have a song, which Dee wrote—she's written all of our songs—called "Close You Are," and unlike "Down in the Sea of Me," it isn't cryptic and it isn't about Dee's history of childhood trauma. What it's about is the idea that we're much closer than we think to the random people we see on any given day, that everyone in this world carves out a little groove and that although you may think your world is large you rarely venture far outside this groove. That there are other people in these grooves with you, that grooving, at least in this song, means to be dancing with all the people in your groove. The chorus of the song— *Close you are, grooving!*—might sound dumb just to say (especially since most people hear it as "groovy" and not "grooving"), but it sounds good when you hear Dee sing it. She jumps around a lot when she sings this song and it's fun to watch her. It's like she's two different people singing, one who sings "Close you are" and another who chimes in "grooving!" She seems so happy and clear, unlike in "Down in the Sea of Me." When she sings that song, you get scared because it's like she's turned into this big black hole and you're sucked right in. Her face turns mean and you would think a person with a face like that could kill you. A face like that you will keep on seeing in your mind and you'll feel relief when you drive home and know that face is just a memory. The problem is that when you're far enough away you'll want to see it again, this face that is cruel and luscious and arousing. You think you really might be willing to go down into that sea.

It was noon when Dee woke up again, put her clothes on, and made the coffee that was in the plastic coffeemaker in our room. Then she picked up the motel phone, but before she dialed, she said, "The people in my family call me Gwen."

She made a call to the office of her aunt Julia, who taught marine biology at the University of Utah and who she'd spoken to by phone the week before. When her aunt picked up, Dee said, "Hi, Julia. It's Gwen. I'm right here now, in a motel." Then she was listening to whatever her aunt Julia was saying. It took me that long just to get it. Gwen. Gwendine.

"So he's at Lakeview, up in Bountiful?" Dee said, and listened.

She said, "No one will be there tonight, you're sure?"

Again she listened and I drank some of the coffee. Inside my head I started singing "Close You Are." Then she was off the phone, pouring coffee, and saying, "We have to go meet my aunt Julia. She has an I.D. I can use to see my brother at the hospital."

"When are we leaving?"

She said, "Soon."

I watched her sipping her cup of coffee. Watched her full lips and suddenly, for the first time since leaving Tampa, I remembered about the letter.

I said, "That note."

Dee looked right at me.

I said, "The note you wrote the night you asked me to come with you. You told me that you would give it to me in Utah."

Dee said, "Yeah. I have the note, but I changed my mind when I was writing it. I didn't write the note to you. Instead I wrote it to my brother. It's what I'm going to do at the hospital. I'll sit down next to him and read him the whole note. I don't know whether you'll be able to get in and anyway I'm not so sure I want you hearing it. You might decide I'm crazy. Most people would."

"That's okay," I said, because it's what I always say to Dee.

"Maybe I *am* crazy," she said.

I said, "How long is the note?"

"Long," she said. "Like ten or eleven pages. And listen, Timmy, I also brought a xeroxed copy that I made of the whole thing. I was thinking you could hold it, that you could keep it, and then maybe there would be a time, after we're home, when you should read it. But what I'm thinking now is maybe I should give the extra copy to my aunt."

"To your aunt Julia?"

Dee nodded. She said, "Aunt Julia's a bitch, but I still trust her. Do you trust me?"

I said, "Trust you about what?"

"Look, Timmy," she said. "I left another copy at home. It's in the top drawer of my dresser, in a sealed envelope. Now you can find it, if you want, if something happens."

"What would *happen?*"

She said, "Don't worry. We'll be fine. Julia says my parents won't be visiting the hospital tonight."

"Why am I here then?" I said. "Can I just ask that? Not that I'm saying it isn't fine. Not that it's been much of a problem, even if I wind up staying awake for forty hours. But I'm just wondering if maybe you could tell me."

She said, "You're being passive-aggressive."

I said, "Oh, really?"

"You would do better to just try being aggressive."

"Fine," I said.

But then I didn't really know what I could do to be aggressive. I thought about throwing the Styrofoam cup of coffee across the room or about going through Dee's bag, taking the letter, locking myself in the bathroom, and then reading it. Or, I could say something like "Fuck you, Dee." Instead I sipped the coffee and I said, "Maybe you could just explain it, so I understand. It would help me to have more of an explanation of why I'm here."

Dee looked into my eyes, but it was as if she was looking through them, into my brain, scanning the gray matter or whatever would be the logical part to scan. It was a look I didn't think I had ever seen, as if some part of her was trying to speak and

40

another part was saying not to speak and another part was saying, "This guy's an idiot," and another part was wanting to sing "Down in the Sea of Me." Finally she said, "Timmy, you're here to hold me. To be my anchor. You're here to be someone I can recognize. I have a job for you. One job. I'm going to tell it to you now. If I look empty, at any time—and I mean empty, like my mind has been sucked out—if I start to look or sound like that, I need you to just grab me and get me back here to this room, or to the airport, or back to Florida."

"Or to your aunt, who you trust?"

As this came out of my mouth I realized I was being passive-aggressive. Dee didn't call me on it this time. She just said, "Not if I'm like that." Then she said, "By the way, you stink. Before we go, please take a shower."

I took a shower and then we drove our rental car to the university. We walked across the campus to the student center, picked a table in a corner, and waited for Dee's aunt. Eventually a slim, blond-haired woman appeared. She looked to be about thirty-five. She was petite, unlike Dee, which made me suspect that they were not related by blood. Then I was sure of it. The woman seemed to me more narrow. By this I mean her range, her possibilities, were narrow. Maybe I mean that she lived in a narrow "groove," even though Dee had said her aunt had conducted research in many parts of the world, that she could scuba dive, and that she had once been part of an expedition where they'd discovered a new species of octopus. Dee had said men often got hung up on her aunt Julia, but as I watched her approach, I thought, Not me. Give me that woman on the plane. Or give me Dee.

When her aunt Julia sat down at the table, Dee introduced us. She said, "This is my friend Tim. We're in a band."

Her aunt said, "Hi, Tim," and smiled. She pulled a wallet from her bag. She said, "It's here," and produced a Utah driver's license with a photo. Julia Wilson. I saw the photo. I was surprised that in the photo she looked like Dee. At least the blond hair and feline eyes. Maybe the shape of her aunt's nose was roughly similar. Julia was also close to the same height as Dee, and so it didn't matter that their bodies were so different. People can always put on weight.

"You don't have any plans to kill him, right?" said Julia. "No tab of cyanide in your pocket?"

Dee said, "You know I'm not that reckless."

"You're pretty reckless," Julia said. "From what I've heard."

"I want to see him, that's all," said Dee. "And spend some time with him. I wrote a note. I want to read it to my brother. They say that people can sometimes hear you even if they're in a coma. People who come out of comas say they remember things. They can remember where they were, and they can remember certain things that people said."

"A lot of fuss just to read a note," Julia said.

"I guess I'm fussy."

She said, "He's been in a coma for just about two months now. The good and surprising news is that he hasn't passed into what they call the vegetative state. That's a deeper coma. Odds of recovery are less likely."

"I know what a vegetative state is," Dee said curtly. "I read a book."

"Well, anyway, you can keep the license," said Aunt Julia. "After you called last week I went to the DMV, told them I lost it, so they're sending me a new one. As for your parents, they're going to a gathering down in Provo this afternoon, and from there they plan on heading to the house up in the mountains. They're having a big party out there tomorrow. I talked to your mom to tell her I wasn't coming. Not that I ever go to their parties. Visiting hours at the hospital end at seven, but you can probably stay later if you sweet-talk the security guard."

She looked at me and said, "Your girlfriend could sweet-talk anyone."

I didn't answer. Then Dee reached down into her bag and pulled out a sealed white envelope.

She said, "Aunt Julia, I want you to hold on to this. This is a copy of the note I wrote to Dillon. It's actually more of a letter. After I leave, it would be good if you could read it. I know you're smart and that you understand that certain things are *mysterious.* That even when people know certain things are *possible,* they prefer thinking that these things don't really happen. I kind of doubt that you'll ever see me again, so if it's not entirely clear, I like you. You're the only sane person in this family. If I were you, I'd get away."

Julia squinted. She said, "Gwen, I know your parents..."

"No, you don't."

She took the copy of the letter.

"I'm working late tonight," Julia said. "I'll be crunching data in my office if you need me." She slipped the letter into her bag. Then she said, "Bye, Tim. Nice to meet you." As she rose to leave, she looked at Dee and said, "I've always liked you too."

Back in the piece-of-crap Ford, Dee closed her eyes before she turned the key. She sat there for a moment. When she reopened them, she told me that her brother was in a private room and that to see him during visiting hours your name had to be on a special list. She had learned this back in Tampa, in her first phone call with Aunt Julia. That was why she needed Julia's I.D.

We drove north on the highway to the hospital, which, as it turned out, was not in Salt Lake City but in a suburban town called Bountiful. I had heard Dee say the name when she was on the phone in our hotel room. I hadn't realized that it was a town or that, in fact, it was the town where Dee grew up. Apparently, her brother had been moved from a hospital in Salt Lake City to a hospital that was closer to where her parents lived. But as Dee noted, repeatedly—she had said this at least five times—her parents were down in Provo. I must have really been messed up from lack of sleep by this point, since I remember at least three signs for the Lakeview Hospital but have no recollection of having viewed, even once, the Great Salt Lake.

We parked the car in a lot and headed in through the hospital's front entrance. Dee seemed calm and almost happy, but I felt strange, kind of unstable. My brain was racing from thought to thought. I thought of Julia wearing scuba gear and of Dee wearing a leather miniskirt. I thought of Jerry watching football, cursing a lot at Dan Marino, the Dolphins' quarterback. I thought of dolphins, I mean the animal. I thought of manatees and then all I could think about was Dee onstage, performing. We really could, I thought, be famous.

Dee's brother's room was on the third floor of the hospital. As we stepped into an elevator, I started singing the chorus of "Close You Are." Dee shook her head at me, then smiled, then she joined in with her voice soft, and together we sang:

Close you are, grooving!
Close you are, groo-ooooving
Find the groove and you can fall into the groove or
leave the groove and there you are
so close you are, groo-ooooving

I sang the three chords that would follow and played air guitar, but when it was time to go back to the chorus, Dee made a stop sign with her hand, gave me a weary smile, and looked up at the elevator's numbers.

"No one's around," she said again. "They're all in Provo, at a party. Let's all remember that."

It was as if she was addressing a group of people.

She said, "Let's just go in there and be calm, do what we came to do. Anyone who is not okay with this is free to leave."

Then she said, "Are we on board?"—though not to me, and anyway, at that moment I was thinking about the stop sign she had made with her hand, which was the gesture she'd always made when we performed our slowed-down version of "Stop! In the Name of Love," though we'd stopped doing "Stop" in recent months because our bass player, Bill, had said that playing Diana Ross songs, even one, always made him want to puke his guts out. He'd said, "It's goddamn fucking *pandering,* that's what it is," and later I'd asked Jerry what Bill meant, and Jerry shrugged and just said, "Dee says we're done playing that song forever."

The elevator doors opened. Dee and I walked down a hall. We passed the wing to the critical care unit and kept on looking straight ahead. "Maybe I'll be able to get you in," said Dee, and I said, "Me?" and she said, "Yes. I'd think you'd want to meet my brother."

"I guess I would," I said, but my head was spinning. Something about singing that song and the way Dee had made her stop sign made it spin.

We found the room and, as expected, a guard was posted outside the door. Dee showed the I.D. her aunt Julia had given her. She told the guard, "This is my husband." She said, "You look like you've had a bit of a long day."

The guard said, "*Long* isn't the word."

Dee flashed her clearest, brightest smile, and I half-expected her to launch into a verse of "Close You Are." Then it was easier than it should have been. He pushed the door open. We both walked past the guard and into Dee's brother's room. There were three chairs next to the bed and we took two of them. Her brother sat on the bed, propped upright. She told him, "Dillon, it's me. It's Gwen."

There was a scar across his face from what had probably been thirty or forty stitches. There was another scar across his head, which had been shaved but was starting to grow the hair back. His cheeks were sunken. So was his body. He might have weighed a little more than a hundred pounds. He was hooked up to a machine that showed his heartbeat.

Dee looked at me and said, "I think that you should go soon and sit outside with the guard while I read the letter. I'll be connecting with Dillon, telling him things I've wanted to explain for a long time. Maybe he'll never wake up, but if he does, then possibly he'll have heard what I want to tell him. Timmy, I'm sorry, this is already very hard. But if you really want to read this letter, I'd prefer, like I said, that you read it when we get back home."

"And there's a copy in your dresser?"

She said, "Right."

Then Dillon moved his arm, which startled me. He began mumbling. What he said sounded like "Azalea."

"What's going on?" I asked. "Is Dillon waking up?"

Dee pinched her brother's arm. There was no response. She shook her head. "People in comas sometimes move or talk," she said. "Sometimes they can even walk, but they're not conscious. They don't respond to pain, or not externally, and technically they can't hear."

"You're going to read the note right now?"

"In a few minutes," Dee said. "First I just want Dilly to get used to my being here. You should probably say hello to him yourself. Why don't you do it now?"

I said, "Hello, Dillon."

She told him, "Dillon, this is Tim. He's a good man. We're in a band. He plays guitar and I'm the singer. Some of our songs are pretty good. Our amps are bad, though. We could really use new amps. It's a big problem."

I said, "One Peavey, though, is good. It's our one good amp but our bass player always hogs it."

I looked at Dee and she seemed okay with what I'd just said to her brother.

I said, "Hey, Dillon. I'm going to step out now. I'm going to leave you with...Gwen while I go out and get a Coke."

He moved his arm again. He seemed uncomfortable.

I said, "I hope they have Coke because I like it more than Pepsi. I hope to God it isn't RC Cola. Then I would probably opt out and go for the grape soda."

Dee nodded and I said, "Bye, Dillon. Maybe I'll catch up with you later."

I stood to leave and Dee said, "Timmy's going now. He's a good man. We can trust him."

I looked at Dee before I left, just to make sure she did not look empty. She stared at Dillon and she was smiling her weary smile. So I stepped out.

The security guard was, of course, still standing there. I said hello and he said, "Hello, Mr. Wilson." I asked him where I might find vending machines and get a can of Coke. "Go down those stairs," he said, and pointed to a doorway. "Go to the second floor, turn left." I asked him if the machine had Coke and he said, "Coke or maybe Pepsi." I said, "I really hope it's Coke," and the man said, "Well, if it isn't Coke, I'm sure it's Pepsi."

I thanked the man, and at this point I most likely became delirious. I went down to the second floor, turned left, and I looked all around but couldn't find the vending machines. There was a man who walked by pushing an empty gurney. I asked whether he knew where I could get a Coke, but instead of directing me to the vending machines, he explained how to get to the hospital's snack bar and cafeteria. He said the snack bar would be open. It was down on the first floor near the hospital's side entrance. I thanked him and took the steps again, but what had seemed to be one flight down brought me out not to the first floor but to the basement. I walked around, searched for an elevator. I passed some file rooms and a laundry room. I passed an X-ray room and a room with some other very large machines.

Finally I found the elevator. I took it up to the first floor, but I was far away from any entrance. I walked around until I found the information desk. A volunteer directed me to the snack bar. I passed a room that was full of people who were listening to someone who held a plastic doll and I figured that it was either CPR or else a class about having babies. I found the snack bar, which was closed.

There was a sign on the door, however. The sign said SNACK BAR WILL REOPEN AT 6:30. I looked at my watch. It was six-twenty. I was surprised it was still so early. It felt as if it could have been past midnight. I waited ten minutes. Fifteen. Twenty. No one came, so I walked back to the information desk. There I was told that I could find vending machines on the second floor. I took the elevator up, and this time I located the machines easily. By then, I probably knew the entire blueprint of the hospital. I got a Coke and returned to Dillon's room.

The guard was still there. He said hello to me. He went to open up the door but I waved him off. I said, "She wants to be alone with him. It's her brother." The man nodded and I realized I'd slipped up since Dee supposedly was Julia. He didn't catch it. I said, "It was Coke and not Pepsi, after all."

As I was going to sit down on a nearby chair and drink my Coke, another man appeared. He walked down the hall and stared right at me. He looked confused. He wore tan slacks, a blue shirt, and a nice tie. He was short and had blond hair and was slightly balding, and he looked like he could be anyone. Then he was shouting at me. "Who are you? What are you doing here? That's a private room." I didn't answer. When he had reached the door, he glared at the guard and said, "Who is this person?" The guard glared back at him and said, "He's on the list."

"No, he is *not* on the list," the man said.

Then a woman came down the hall. Much more than Julia, this woman resembled Dee — same light blond hair, same chunky figure — although the woman's hair was long and straight and hung below her shoulders. She wore a silky white dress patterned with blue flowers. She said, "What's happening, Ed? What's going on here?" The man pushed open the door, walked in, and with a tone of what was clearly great surprise, he said, "Gwendine?"

And then the woman was skipping by me, wearing high heels that were making little taps on the smooth floor. She said, "You're kidding, is it Gwen? Who is this boy? Is it Gwendine?"

The strange thing was that, at this moment, I felt sleepy. I mean so sleepy that I could have lain down on the granite floor, closed my eyes, and been asleep in an instant. I had to fight, of all things, this desire to curl up and just sleep. It didn't last long, not more than about ten seconds. Then I was trembling. It was as if I'd started shivering. That also lasted about ten seconds. Then I was clear again and trying to decipher the situation.

According to Dee, her parents were as merciless as Darth Vader and as demented as Caligula (I'd seen the movie). What I could see of them, however, looked pretty normal. They appeared to be your standard upper-class couple, a well-dressed husband and wife heading to a party, but who had stopped off at the hospital to check up on their unconscious son. Based on what Julia had said, they were supposed to be in Provo. But, of course, Julia could have been wrong. Dee's parents could have been home all this time in Bountiful. If there could be a town named Bountiful in the first place, then why couldn't there be people who were there instead of being at someone's lake house down in Provo? None of it added up to much.

Before the guard could think to keep me out, I decided to go into the room after them. The man, Dee's father, was saying, "Gwen, what are you doing here? You could have let us know that you were coming." Then Dee was looking right at me and I thought at first that she looked mean. But then she opened her mouth and she looked to me like a startled little girl. I called out, "Dee?" She looked away, as if she did not know where my voice had come from. "Who is this boy?" the woman asked once more. She turned to face me and said, "Who are you?" Her eyes seemed vicious, all of a sudden. I placed the unopened can of Coke on a nearby table. I met the woman's gaze and I said, "Gwendine is with me."

You have to do this sometimes, make fast decisions. You do it not because you're sure that what you might be doing is right or wrong but because the decision seems so obvious, and if it really is that obvious then how could it be wrong? I should add that this line of thinking will work best if what it is that you're deciding on doesn't have to do with sex or, for that matter, fighting in a bar, because with those two things you have to factor in your hormones, and so it may not be a case of simply acting from your heart. I've never known what faith is. I've never had much, which is probably why I tend to be nervous, even when I seem to be relaxed and calm. I once told Dee that the only time I feel at peace is when I'm playing guitar onstage, making all sorts of jerky motions, letting my fingers fly around the frets, and doing everything at high speed. What happens is that inside this motion, inside this feeling, I will slow down. I'll feel my fingers taking over and I can watch myself, almost. I'll feel like something that is outside of me is doing it, not me, and it feels like everyone who's watching is a part of it. It feels like this is the closest I can ever come to being *breathed*.

I grabbed Dee. I still don't understand exactly how I got the guts to do it. I threw her up over my shoulder. I grabbed the letter from her hand and stuffed it in her bag. I slipped an arm through the bag, and as Dee's mother yelled, "What is this boy doing?" I sprang beyond them. I was part fireman and part fullback and part maniac and part me.

I ran out past the guard and through the door he'd indicated an hour before when I began my complicated search for a can of Coke. This time I didn't have a problem. I ran down three flights of steps. Directly across the stairwell on the first floor was the snack bar, which was now open, and beyond it was the side door of the hospital. I ran outside. I could feel Dee breathing hard and

I could hear her gasping. It took a moment to get my bearings, to trace the features of the lot to where the car should be. Then I was running again, not looking to see if anyone was following.

I found the piece-of-crap Ford and then, in what proved to be a complicated maneuver, I slid Dee down off of my shoulder, pressed her against the door, and held her there with my body. I let the bag slide down my arm and sifted through it until I found the car keys. She'd gone so limp that I had to hold her with one hand as I unlocked the door. I laid her down in the backseat, and when I looked at her I knew I had been right, that she was empty. Soon I was driving, calmly handing a few dollars to an attendant at the parking gate. I looked around for the man and woman, or for security guards running at me with their guns. But there was nothing. It was all dreamlike. In my head I began singing "Close You Are." I found the highway, headed south, and I followed signs toward the airport. Once I was close enough, I knew which turns to take to the motel. This seemed a better plan than going to the airport.

By the time we got there Dee was sitting up and crying, pressing her mouth against the back of the seat, so that her sobs were muffled almost into silence. Then we were back in the room and suddenly she wasn't empty. She began talking. Her voice seemed normal, and then I couldn't really be sure what had happened. I also felt as if I might pass out. "I'm lying down, okay?" I said. She said, "That's fine. You could use some sleep." As I lay down on the bed she stroked my head and she said, "Timmy, it's okay. What you did back there was okay. They won't come looking, I don't think. There is no reason they would come looking." She placed her hand along my cheek, leaned down, and kissed me on my forehead. Then I could almost feel myself surrendering, slipping under, being breathed.

3

Monster

For the purpose of this debriefing, I have agreed to answer questions regarding the recent encounter with fugitive Katherine Clay Goldman in order to review and expand upon the details of my written report filed on May 6 of this year in reference to the events of April 30. I am Special Agent Leopold Sachs, U.S. Federal Bureau of Investigation, badge number 2663.

Agent Sachs, will you please describe the interview that took place on the morning of April 30, 1984, in Salt Lake City, Utah?

My partner, Special Agent Scott Witherspoon, and I questioned a young man and woman, Timothy Birdsey and Gwendine Morley, both age twenty-three, at a Sleep Six motel several miles from the Salt Lake City International Airport.

Your purpose in doing so?

We believed there was a possible connection between the young man and woman and Katherine Clay Goldman, whose case I have been assigned to since 1971.

What led you to believe this?

The young man and woman sat with Katherine Clay Goldman in row twenty-six, seats A, B, and C, of a flight that departed Tampa, Florida, on April 29, 1984, at 12:22 a.m. and arrived at Salt Lake

City at 5:04 a.m. of the same morning. Goldman was in aisle seat C. Birdsey was in seat B. Morley was in seat A, next to the window. There were a total of twenty-eight rows on Delta Air Lines nonstop flight number 603.

Was Goldman traveling under an alias?

Yes, she was traveling under the name Tess Eldridge. She also used this name on a previous flight from Orly International Airport in Paris to Tampa, Florida, on April 28, 1984. We believe that her stop in France was logistical rather than purposeful, but we have been unable to trace her route to any earlier point of origin.

Do you know of other aliases used by Katherine Clay Goldman?

She has used many. We have confirmed the following: Lynette Templeton, Lynette Elson, Christine Lofgren, Anthea Horwitz, Rose Emmett-Browne, Rosalyn Emmett, Miranda Emmett, Joelle Beals, Jessica Beals, Joanna Glassman, River, Leah Silver, Ursula Wilcox, Brotislawa Szerkowszcyzna, Aviva Luria, Sima Perlman. There are undoubtedly many others.

Please describe the origin of the Goldman case and your involvement.

I was assigned to the case in February 1971, seven months after the bombing of an abandoned warehouse in Reno, Nevada. The home-made bomb was detonated at 4:36 p.m. on July 22, 1970. For reasons that remain unknown, two men and one woman, all three of them accountants for a state agency, were inside the warehouse at the time of the blast. All three were killed and identification required matching teeth to the dental records of the victims. Five months later, two sixties-era radicals, Gloria Eads and Daniel Helmuth, were apprehended and each confessed to a role in the bombing, which they alleged was arranged by Katherine Clay Goldman, with whom they claimed to have been part of an independent radical collective since January of 1970. In exchange for milder sentences, Eads and Helmuth provided information that should have helped us locate Goldman. Either they played us or Goldman knew them well enough to anticipate the information they provided. I guessed the latter. The end result was that the information did not help at all. Additionally, Eads and Helmuth each alleged that the deaths that had resulted from the bombing were accidental, and that the intention was simply to blow up a warehouse that had at times been used as a storage area for governmental weapon stock. We still do not have any conclusive ideas as to why the three accountants were inside the warehouse at the time of the blast. Theories range from happenstance to conspiracy to sexual liaison.

Was Goldman affiliated with any particular radical faction during the sixties?

She was thought at first to be a founding member of Weatherman, known colloquially as the Weathermen, a revolutionary group that was formed in 1969 as a subfaction of a larger organization known as Students for a Democratic Society. As the years went by, however, various leaders of Weatherman, which then became the Weather Underground Organization, surfaced and none acknowledged affiliation with or an awareness of Katherine Clay Goldman. It was then determined that she had been acting of her own volition and had quite possibly never been part of Weatherman at all. The fact that the three deaths were allegedly accidental led us to believe that Goldman, like many Weather Underground Organization members, would eventually come out of hiding. Of course, the Weather Underground had managed not to kill anyone despite the numerous bombings they took credit for between 1970 and 1974.

Still, I expected that we'd eventually receive a call from Goldman, a proposed deal, or at least a query. It never happened.

Has Goldman been a suspect in any other crimes since the bombing of the Reno, Nevada, warehouse?

She is a primary suspect in the unsolved 1975 disappearance of two Klansmen from the town of Selma, North Carolina. These disappearances occurred in late April of that year, after which she fell off the radar until a tall, masked woman was seen in three separate videos taken by surveillance cameras during the robberies of banks in Tucson, Arizona; Colorado Springs, Colorado; and Austin, Texas. All of the robberies took place within an eight-month interval in 1978. In each robbery there were five assailants, and in each case the robbery was accomplished without incident, save the loss of a few bank vaults' worth of cash. I viewed the surveillance tapes and was not able to confirm that the tall, masked woman was indeed Goldman.

Do you have sworn testimony tying her to the two abductions in Selma, North Carolina?

We have one signed affidavit stating that a woman fitting Goldman's description was seen at a convenience store in Selma that same evening.

Are you asserting that, except for the bombing of the Reno, Nevada, warehouse, nothing has been conclusively tied to Goldman?

I am. But the warehouse bombing and the reports of her continued revolutionary activity have been sufficient to maintain her status as a threat to national security.

Do you have any explanation for why it has proven so difficult to locate Goldman?

I do not. What I can tell you is that I have discovered roughly fifty different places where she has been at some prior time, that twice I missed her by a matter of hours, and once by minutes. And on one occasion of random chance in Portland, Oregon, I saw her crossing the street no more than a half a block ahead of me. I sprinted after her so reflexively that I was almost hit by a moving vehicle, but by the time I reached the spot where I should have logically intercepted her, she was gone. That was three years ago, in June of 1981, at which time I filed report of the incident, the result of which seemed to be an enhancement of the mythos surrounding Goldman.

Describe this mythos that you allude to.

There are stories, some of which seem so far-out that all I can do is shake my head. For instance, one is that she herself is deep-cover FBI. That even though I have been legitimately assigned to this case, it is all just an elaborate fabrication to ensure that her allegiances are not questioned within whatever framework she has infiltrated. Another is that she is the descendant of the famous anarchist Emma Goldman, who died in 1940. I researched this and found that there is no possibility that she and Emma Goldman are related, although I did discover that Katherine Clay Goldman's ancestry dates back to Colonial-era settlers in Virginia. As a point of interest, perhaps, it has been confirmed that she is related by blood to the well-known 1800s politician Henry Clay, known as "The Great Compromiser" for his roles in brokering the Compromise of 1850, widely believed to have delayed the onset of the Civil War for eleven years. It is assumed that the Clay in Katherine Clay Goldman has been passed down through this lineage. Another amusing fact that I came upon was that a man named Alexander Berkman, who had been Emma Goldman's lover, was convicted in 1892 of the attempted assassination of a factory boss named Henry Clay Frick. I do not ascribe any significance to this but note it here and will add that coincidence tends to be the mainstay of the conspiracy theorist.

Will you elaborate on this last idea?

If you look hard enough into the history of anything, you will discover things that seem to be connected but are not. A case in point would be all the parallels that have been made between Lincoln and Kennedy. Eerie as these may seem at first, it is easy to find what seem like parallels or correlations between any marginally related sets of data, as debunkers as well as statisticians frequently note. The case has been humorously presented that there are parallels to be made between the deaths of JFK and Jesus Christ, through which we might conclude that JFK was a myth invented to embody Christian ideology. An earnest example of this same desire to forge meaning from coincidence might be attributed to a group of Orthodox Jews residing in Jerusalem who demonstrate that if they use what they refer to as the codes on the Old Testament—a simplified, modernized version of certain principles of an ancient Talmudic practice called gematria— they are capable of irrefutably proving the existence of God. Using the codes is the practice of choosing a certain biblical text and counting out letters at fixed intervals, which will yield certain phonetically precise names such as Dayan, Sadat, Einstein, Hitler, Munich. Recently a math professor from the U.S. demonstrated that he was able to find most of these proper names using the same technique applied to *Moby-Dick*. His point was to show that certain patterns or combinations will be found as a matter of probability.

In your report you allude to the legends of the *tzaddikim nistarim* as well as the golem of Prague Ghetto. Please explain how these pertain to the Goldman mythos.

The *tzaddikim nistarim,* or "concealed righteous ones," are more commonly known as the *lamed vavniks* of Hasidic Jewish lore. In more than one instance, the suggestion has been made that Goldman is a member of this sect, or something like it, as technically a woman could not be one of the *lamed vavniks,* which translates to "the thirty-six" and refers to thirty-six holy men that the existence of the world depends on. According to one Talmudic interpretation, there are always thirty-six in the world at a single time, and if even one were missing, the world would come to an end. They are said to justify the purpose of mankind in God's eyes, and for the sake of these humble servants, God will preserve the world even if the rest of humanity has degenerated into barbarism and ruin. It is said that if the identity and true purpose of any one of the thirty-six is discovered, that *lamed vavnik* will instantly die or disappear, at which time the role is transferred automatically to someone else, which helps to illustrate the absurdity of this notion as pertains to Katherine Clay Goldman, since according to legend, mere speculation that she might be part of the sect would, if true, cause her to vanish in an instant. As I noted in my report, there are many fantastic ideas floating around with regard to Goldman, which go so far as to include the suggestion that her last name may be considered a perversion of the word *golem,* as in the fabled golems of the Middle Ages, animate creatures created from inanimate material, the favored golem-sculpting material of that era being—you guessed it—clay. The idea is that Goldman is either metaphorical or literal kin to the legendary Golem of Prague, which was said to have been created by a famous rabbi for the purpose of defending oppressed Jews in the sixteenth century. Our files suggest that Goldman is aware of this particular absurdity and finds it funny. In short, if I had to seriously consider every tall tale I've ever heard regarding Gold-man, then I would also have to reflect on the suggestion that she has located a place outside of time, a hidden Shangri-la or Avalon she returns to whenever it proves necessary—in other words, that when the Clay Monster needs to avoid capture, she simply finds her little portal and leaves the world.

The Clay Monster?

This is a nickname coined by Agent Witherspoon and myself. When dealing with as befuddling a case as this, one naturally resorts to irony. We have only used this name amongst ourselves.

Returning now to the incident on April 30, 1984, will you describe the sequence of your actions on that morning? Specifically, please describe your establishment of verbal contact with the young man and woman who had been seated beside Goldman on the plane.

After landing in Salt Lake City late the night before, we woke early. We had received word from an anonymous source the previous afternoon that the woman traveling as Tess Eldridge was most likely Katherine Clay Goldman and we had learned that she had been seated in row twenty-six, as mentioned, with Timothy Birdsey and Gwendine Morley. Once we commenced our search, it took less than four hours to find the young man and woman. We were able to track them by the license plate of their rental car. We made sweeps of parking lots of nine motels and found the car in the parking lot of the Sleep Six near the airport's access road. We consulted with the front desk and determined that their room was on the second floor. We knocked on the door but no one answered, so I went back down to the front desk and procured a room key. While Agent Witherspoon covered me with his sidearm, I inserted the key, pushed the door open, and stood clear. All was quiet except for the sound of water running in the bathroom. We saw that Timothy Birdsey was sleeping soundly and we determined that Gwendine Morley was in the shower. Almost incredibly, Birdsey still did not wake up once we had entered. It was ten-thirty in the morning. While Agent Witherspoon stood in the room's entrance, his gun still drawn, I went and knocked on the bathroom door. The young woman called out, "Hey, Sleeping Beauty, you're awake," and I told her that I was not her friend and then announced the presence of Agent Witherspoon and myself. A moment later, the woman appeared wearing a long T-shirt and her underpants. I estimated her height at five foot two and her weight at about a hundred thirty pounds. She had blond hair and green eyes. She was the type of girl my father would have called *zaftig*, meaning that she was robust and voluptuous. Definitely she was a girl who many people would consider to be attractive as well as sexually provocative. Still what I saw mostly was a kid, although she also seemed to have that old-soul quality you sometimes see in the most unlikely people. My daughter, Renée, was like that. When she was five I would take one look at her each morning and I would think to myself that this little girl had seen it all. She's a good litigator now, the kind you'd rather not be facing in a courtroom. All this is to say that looking at Gwendine Morley caused me to think about my daughter and that I miss her. Whether this had any effect on my later actions, I do not know.

What happened in the motel room after you established contact with Gwendine Morley?

I showed her my badge and she immediately asked Agent Witherspoon to show his badge as well. After he did so she asked if her parents had sent us, which was confusing. I told her no, her parents had not sent us, and she reiterated the question several times.

Then finally the young man, Timothy Birdsey, woke up. All of this banging around and until that point he had not stirred. I guessed the obvious. He was on drugs. He was a lanky young man with acne, shoulder-length wavy hair, and a big nose. It seemed to me, and Scotty said as much later, almost unfathomable that these two were together. Birdsey yelled, "You let her go!" and with surprising quickness he sprang up, lunged from the bed in his Jockey underwear, and went for Agent Witherspoon, who is a longtime black belt in aikido and was able to turn, absorb the weight of the flying young man, then in one motion land him facedown and pin him with an elbow to his neck. For a minute or so, Birdsey continued to attempt to break free, and the image that comes to mind is that of a six-foot shark that has just been landed on someone's boat deck. A plucky young man, I must say, but not too bright under the circumstances. Finally he went limp and Agent Witherspoon informed both him and the young woman that we had simply come to ask them a few questions. At this point Gwendine Morley changed her tack and asked if we had come to *investigate* her parents. I found this question as confusing as the first one. I took a hard look at the girl. Her eyes were big and, as mentioned, seemed to contain multitudes. Once again, I told her that our presence was not in any way related to her parents, whose names are Edward and Delilah Morley. Her father is a high-powered corporate attorney and her mother is a realtor. They're very wealthy, having inherited approximately ten million dollars' worth of stocks and real estate from Delilah Morley's late grandfather Otis Wilson, and when the woman's father dies they are likely to inherit a great deal more. I was surprised to learn that they are not Mormons, nor do they appear to have strong ties with the Lutheran Church, which they belong to. They live in a suburban town called Bountiful, about twenty miles north of Salt Lake City. When the young woman appeared to be convinced that we knew nothing of her parents save the information I have just provided, we commenced our questioning.

Did you determine any linkage between Katherine Clay Goldman and the young man and woman?

Not at first.

Be more specific.

Our interview with Timothy Birdsey and Gwendine Morley suggested that they had no knowledge of who Goldman was and that their proximity to Goldman on Delta flight 603 was accidental.

Please describe relevant details of the interview that pertain to Katherine Clay Goldman.

Birdsey and Morley confirmed that they had been sitting next to a tall woman with dyed black hair. Each alleged that the woman was not very talkative. Birdsey, who said he did not sleep during the flight, alleged that the woman also did not sleep, nor did she read or do anything at all. I asked him what he was doing and he rubbed his nose in a manner that suggested a subconscious tic, so I pressed him, and he attempted to deflect my question until Morley started laughing and said that Timmy, as she called him, was the worst liar she knew, and that what he was hiding was simply the fact that the two of them had gotten up from their seats at a certain point and "done the mile-high-club thing," by which I confirmed that she meant that they'd engaged in sexual intercourse in a bathroom three rows behind their seats. Goldman stood up, they said, to let them by, and Birdsey said that when they returned he was feeling guilty about disturbing her but that she was pleasant and polite about it. My sense was that Birdsey, like many others, fell for the charismatic charm and odd compassion that never seems to be lacking in Katherine Clay Goldman. That's part of how she protects herself. She plays the confidence game as well as any con who's ever lived. So I was not surprised at all when Birdsey went on to explain that he had tried to start a conversation after Gwendine Morley fell asleep, that Katherine Clay Goldman had just shaken her head and chosen not to answer, and that after this exchange she remained silent for the duration of the flight. Birdsey said he had seen her leave the terminal alone, that she had only a single carry-on bag, which he described as being navy blue. To sum up, it appeared as though this couple, who for five hours were at various times either sitting beside or blithely having sex in a bathroom three rows behind the fugitive I have tracked for the better part of thirteen years, were able to provide only two useful details, that her hair was black and her bag was blue. It seems that Goldman, as per usual, expertly ignored them and was able to do so without revealing even one minutely telling detail, as both her hair and bag would undoubtedly change color again soon. It was all so astoundingly unnoteworthy that afterward I could not help but wonder if these two kids knew more than they were telling, if possibly there was a brilliant bit of conspiracy being played. But half an hour of grilling the two of them, of feeling the presence of one old soul and one so young that it was almost as affecting, was adequate to convince us that they were on the level and that, as mentioned, neither one of them had even the faintest inkling of who she was.

You mentioned in your written report that there was a 1949 file, now declassified, regarding Birdsey's grandfather George Gunther Birdsey. Will you summarize the relevant facts in that case file?

George Gunther Birdsey was questioned twice, in 1946 and 1948, on grounds of being a suspected Nazi and former SS officer who fled Germany in 1945. The bureau's interest in him was tied to the possibility that he knew where Josef Mengele could be located. He denied this, and not only could no one prove he had been part of the SS, the man claimed to have hidden Jews in his basement for more than three full years during the war. "I hided Jews" is a quote that appears over and over in the transcript of his two interrogations. In 1954, George Gunther Birdsey put a shotgun into his mouth and pulled the trigger. His son, James Birdsey, also committed suicide. The suicide took place in 1978, shortly after his wife, Cecile Birdsey, left him for a man named Leonard Hutchinson, who owns a chain of convenience stores in and around Mobile, Alabama, where he and Cecile Birdsey both still live. James Birdsey's suicide was accomplished with a .38 caliber handgun, which he fired into the right side of his head. Timothy Birdsey lives in Homosassa, Florida, with his grandmother Alicia Birdsey.

You also mentioned in your report that Gwendine Morley gave you a copy of a letter she wrote and read to her younger brother, Dillon Morley, who lay in a coma in a hospital in the town of Bountiful. You explained that the reading of this letter to her brother was Gwendine Morley's sole explanation for her visit to Salt Lake City.

That is correct.

Please describe the circumstances under which she handed you the letter.

Toward the end of our questioning, she handed it to me and stated that if I wanted to do something worthwhile, I'd read the letter and then go after her parents. I said I would read the letter and contact her if we felt any action was appropriate. I slipped the letter into my pocket and at the time considered this to be a small act of diplomacy, nothing more. She let me know that her aunt, Julia Wilson, a professor of marine biology at University of Utah, had also been given a copy of the letter prior to Gwendine Morley's visit to her brother at the hospital in Bountiful, which took place in the evening on the day before our interview. We asked Gwendine Morley when she had returned from the hospital and she claimed to have been back at the motel room by 7:30 p.m. or slightly later. Then she noted, for our records, that Timothy Birdsey was not her boyfriend. Apparently, I had used the words "your boyfriend" in my conversation with her. She stated that she and Timmy were in a band and that Timmy was her guitarist. We checked this out and it appears to be true. Gwendine Morley's boyfriend is the band's drummer, Jerry Flanagan, with whom she resides in Homosassa, Florida.

In your report you noted that Gwendine Morley's letter had been written in a style that you described as "polyphonic" and "intra-conversational." Do you still consider these words to be accurate descriptors?

Yes.

For the sake of this interview and this document, we will presently read the Morley letter aloud. Is there anything else you wish to qualify?

Not at this time.

The following is the full text of the Morley letter, filed by Agent Sachs as an attachment to his May 6, 1984, report of incidents that occurred on April 30, 1984.

Dearest Dillon,

Five years have passed since I last saw you. I was glad to hear from Aunt Julia that you went someplace far away. I hoped you'd call when I gave Julia my number. But I was worried too because I didn't know what to say. Even with you being in a coma now, I don't know where to begin or end. I'll start by saying that if all has gone as planned and I am reading this to you in person it means tomorrow will be May's Eve, the beginning of the Celtic holiday known as Beltane, one of the two primary ritual days that divide the Celtic year. There is a lot that I could say of what I've learned about the history of Beltane, but right now what is relevant is this. For both of us, it's a bad day, although what we experienced, as I will try to describe, was not confined to Beltane. These things were happening all the time, on every holiday as well as other days. There is logic to the madness and there is no logic. The only thing I can say with certainty is that Beltane was when some of the worst things happened.

Lately I've tried to think of ways to wake you. I think a lot about silly television commercials we used to sing. I thought if I sang you the Super Smelling Pretty Color Finger Paint That Turns to Bubblebath jingle it might wake you. But if I'm reading this it means that you have not woken during the time I've been here despite my singing and all the times I've told you that I love you. I am hoping that despite not waking you'll still hear me, in some part of your brain. What I am going to say now is important. I want to suggest that if you can't wake up and run far away again it will be much better for you to die.

Now I have to do something that will seem strange and this is why I wrote this down. I want to allow certain parts of me to speak to you, and I mean this literally. So far I can only get in direct contact with these parts when I am writing or when I am in a room with my psychotherapist in Florida whose name I won't write here but will give to you if ever we speak again. The things these parts will say will seem impossible and you won't want to believe them. Even reading this will be hard for me because you need to understand that I've been taught never to say these things. I have been taught never to think of them. I have been taught not to know them. But I've been able, as you'll see, to say and know them. So far I've only said these things to my therapist, although now I am saying them to you and whoever else may read this letter.

Hello. It's like experiments or like programming a machine. In a ritual something happens to you, but it's not you, it's another you split off each time you need to. You go to bed but you wake up and something's done to you that cannot be remembered, because if it was, then you could not be you. Each holiday and there are many holidays you go to a dark place with lots of candles. People you thought you knew will talk in different-sounding voices.

Each of these parts has a certain age, Dillon. I can interject, as I am doing here, because I am co-conscious with these parts. The part that spoke about the ritual is thirteen.

The goal is to make us live in a secret world. The power comes and passes down fertility and strength which serve the battle goddess Morrigu even if you are afraid you do not have to be you're hidden in a place that can't be seen we're very lucky this way I do feel lucky.

That part is ten, Dillon. In other words, I was ten years old when she split off from me.

There are ways that punish you and other ways where you become the punisher. We were forced to give poison tablets to two girls whose arms were tied and who wore blindfolds which were shiny and maroon. I was told if I did not put the tablet on her tongue and touch her throat and hold her mouth it would be given to you and I would be responsible. You were told the same and we gave the tablets. The girls were taken from the room and you said maybe the tablets are really candy and I said shhhhh because I thought it too. Then we were told we'll be protected because it serves the greater good and after that we were embraced by many people. I do not *want to think it was really poison and I am hoping what we saw later was really cat guts. Sometimes if you can't feel your feet it's cat guts.*

What she means, Dillon, is that sometimes her feet go numb. She was once made to wear spiked boots and kick a cat until it was dead and mutilated. Afterward the remains were draped around her head and shoulders. She is seven. I will cease interrupting now and let a number of parts speak in succession. Most of these parts are aware of other parts, which enables them to address each other.

You follow the ball around the room with your eyes and hope it doesn't go to you 'cause then it's your turn and this is just how it goes, it's no one's fault, that's how the ball bounces, we understand this.

They prefer to use words like "holiday gathering" and "visitors" and "serious time" and "fun time" and "go to bed." Splitting. This is easy because if she's very young you can form her. This becomes a special thing and safe because no one believes it. Watch the basketball.

Hello. She's referring to a published study in which subjects were asked to watch a videotaped basketball game and count the passes. Follow-up questioning shows that a significant percentage of people tested are so focused on counting passes that they don't notice that a man with a gorilla suit has walked onto the court. We are not making any of this up.

There was a shriveled ball of Blood and Mucous. It came early and was taken and sacrificed by a High Priestess. Priestess was the Ascendant Morrigu Diana. She is not the Highest Priestess but she is third in the Hierarchy of Power passed down through the Female Lineage. One of us was going to become the next High Priestess.

Hello, I am the one who knows what really happens. I will tell you that when a child is overwhelmed with physical and mental trauma she either dies or learns to split off and create other selves that hold (1) pain, (2) horror, (3) secrets, (4) love. Of course, there is love. There is always love. Why wouldn't you think there is love? I read a book all about this. A mental hospital calls it multiple personality disorder. Most doctors would say these are false memories. Something bad happened but not the things I say and definitely there is no high priestess.

The best word is "multiplicity." We have co-conscious multiplicity, which means that we can switch without it being like Dr. Jekyll and Mr. Hyde. Each of us has a job like being sexy or being hurt or knowing the beginning of a ritual. Multiplicity is always a response to childhood trauma. It is not a genetically determined condition like schizophrenia. There are people who switch and are not co-conscious and they are said to lose time or have amnesia. Those who are not co-conscious stay this way because they are blocked from recognizing or believing they are like this, or because it was not done with intentional and systematic programming.

No, it's not like that. It's not intentional, even if it is a program. No one has any idea what's going on. You are aware, in a far-off part of your brain, of what you're doing. You are incapable of movement out of what you've been locked into so you describe it another way or else you hide by going into a tunnel.

I want to remind you of the person in the gorilla suit, like you mentioned.

We have been told we are very happy!

In a ritual, a young child can be used as a kind of battery.

Hello, I am the one who knows what really happens. In the Korean War the Chinese practiced the art of brainwashing and there is a book written about it and it was discussed in the trial for Patty Hearst and the technique used is outlined in the book. This can work, but if you brainwash an adult it only lasts for a short time. It's very different if you do it to a one-year-old. The neural pathways are wide open, primed for anything. If you spoke Latin, a small child would learn Latin. Can you imagine a small child speaking Latin?

I'm going to stop this discussion now, Dillon. As I've said, it may not make much sense, although perhaps some part of you will understand it. All people have different parts and can change moods in an instant, but for me it is very different. Everything inside me is compartmentalized. It's like I am a manager of all the parts and that I have delegated responsibilities to many different employees including some who I have never met. This is why I am not insane. Though it all happened it was hidden from me by these ingenious parts. In other words, the only time I have ever lost was the time during the abuse. I might have become insane eventually but I was able to detect the problem once I ran away and realized that certain things were not right. For instance, it was discovered that I have damage to one of my retinas, which is evidence of a serious head trauma that I do not remember. Some nights I would start trembling or a certain limb would hurt in ways that made no sense or I would start feeling as if I was suffocating or being strangled, though in the morning these feelings would be gone and for a long time I assumed these were bad dreams. Eventually, with the help of my therapist, I learned that these were memories stored in my body. After a while, when I integrated certain parts, I would discover the origin of certain bodily memories. Although I feel farther away when a part comes out I can still listen to what the part is saying and, as I have indicated in this note, I can return at any time. I continue to integrate these different parts and I am forming what my therapist refers to as the constellation of my core self, although sometimes it is not clear what is me. I do it slowly. I learn whatever I am ready for. It is not as if everything is solved and I have problems and sometimes I fall apart and sometimes I act like a nymphomaniac and sometimes when I'm singing parts will come out onstage though no one ever seems to notice. People tend to think it has to do with being talented. I think that maybe you were smart to go to Israel and all those other places. Part of you knew and maybe you meant to die when you were there and everything that is occurring now is strange for you, unlucky. If you decide to try again, do something simpler. Take a pill. That's all I can think to say right now though I am sure I will think of a lot more later. Don't sleep too long, my dearest Dilly. My dill pickle. Try to go one way or the other and do it soon. There is a chance I will not ever see you again although parting the two of us will be impossible. They made sure of this. There are some parts of you in me. They'll still be with me no matter what you do.

What is your professional opinion of the claims made by Gwendine Morley and her alleged co-conscious multiplicity?

What she is saying, though undocumented, does seem possible. I have read a fair amount about this. The second book she alludes to in the letter is, I believe, *Thought Reform and the Psychology of Totalism* by Robert Jay Lifton. It was published in 1961. It is widely known.

And you do not regard Gwendine Morley as being potentially delusional or psychotic or of having a disorganized mind?

There is nothing in her letter, nor anything I witnessed during our interactions, that would suggest she is delusional or psychotic. As for having a disorganized mind, this is a matter of perspective. What is abnormal to us, and therefore perhaps capable of the improbable "multiplicity" demonstrated by the alleged chorus of so-called parts in the letter, might also be considered a higher form of organization, one molded out of extreme circumstances and necessary for survival under these circumstances.

You say this and at the same time you align yourself with the debunkers regarding Katherine Clay Goldman?

I align myself with the debunkers of the stories I have heard. But I do not have a coherent theory of my own regarding Katherine Clay Goldman's activities or motivations or, for that matter, her true identity. In her case, even after thirteen years, I simply do not have enough to go on.

In your report you mention experience in dealing with cult activities. Will you elaborate?

In 1965 a previous partner and I broke up a cult that was operating in the panhandle region of West Virginia. That was my one success in this arena. In two other instances, one in Rhode Island and one in Southern California, I was unsuccessful. These are always difficult cases. Cults can take many forms, ranging from religious and/or ritualistic, to those that have a primary function of systemizing some form of persecution and/or violation of human rights, to those with larger sociopolitical intentions, to those that appear to have the sole objective of preserving wealth and power. These categories are not mutually exclusive. It should be noted that not all cults engage in criminal activities, though many do. It can take months or years to sting these people and usually you need someone on the inside. You need eyewitnesses and photographs and hard evidence. No one believes in this stuff and no one wants to. You see these things in a pulp novel or a bad movie. You tend to file it away somewhere along with the Creature from the Black Lagoon. No one wanted to believe us about the cult in West Virginia and we had mountains of hard evidence. There were murders, torture, rape, and incest. Among those involved in the cult's activities were elected town officials, local businessmen, lawyers, doctors, police officers, and former military personnel. Many appeared to be upstanding citizens. In the end, all we got to stick were the narcotics-related charges. Five men and women identified as the cult's leaders served prison terms ranging from four to seven years. Given the tendency toward disbelief and resistance to the idea of violent ritual cult activity among otherwise normal-seeming people in the good old U.S.A., this was considered a good result.

Please describe your activities immediately following your questioning of Timothy Birdsey and Gwendine Morley.

Agent Witherspoon and I ate lunch at a diner, during which we discussed our next steps. I figured we would stay in Salt Lake City another day, that we would monitor bus stations as well as the airport, though I assumed that if the elusive Katherine Clay Goldman was up to her old tricks, she was long gone. We outlined a basic plan of action. We ate burgers. When we were finished with lunch, we each read Gwendine Morley's letter. As I alluded to earlier, I had accepted the letter written by Gwendine Morley with the assumption that its text would prove insignificant. Needless to say, neither Agent Witherspoon nor I expected it to be the thing it was. I read the letter first. When Agent Witherspoon read it, he asked me what I knew about this stuff. I told him most of what I've just told you. I also told him that I thought we'd have to leave this alone for now, that this was not our case and even if it was we were not equipped to deal with it. Agent Witherspoon counterargued that it was our case, given that we had spent the morning questioning Gwendine Morley, who had been sitting in the same row as Katherine Clay Goldman on a plane. He was right, of course. Except I knew that what he secretly wanted was for us to show up during Beltane and break this alleged cult. Secretly I wished this too, although I knew it would be impossible. I agreed to pursue things insofar as we maintained the perspective that we were searching for information that might help us to locate Katherine Clay Goldman. Then we decided that our first move would be to speak with the aunt, Julia Wilson, who had also received a copy of the letter. We had her name and address right in our file. We went to see Julia Wilson at her home near the university. We matched the plate on a red Toyota station wagon parked in her driveway to the license plate on file. Together Agent Witherspoon and I knocked on the door, which was answered by a teenage girl, her daughter. Then Julia Wilson appeared and sent the daughter, Dara Wilson, age fourteen, to her room. We explained that we were on our way to check up on the status of Dillon Morley. We also told her that we had spoken with Gwendine and that she'd informed us that a copy of the letter she had written to her brother had been entrusted to her aunt. Julia Wilson confirmed that she had received a copy of the letter and that the reading of this letter to Dillon Morley was indeed her niece's stated purpose in coming to Salt Lake City. We asked her if she had read the letter. Julia Wilson replied that she had not. I asked her whether she would describe Gwendine as a stable woman, and she said "stable enough" but also mentioned that she'd run away after high school, cut her hair, and picked up, in Julia Wilson's words, "that whole trampy look." She asked us if we had met her latest boyfriend. We said we had and we did not bother to clarify. Julia Wilson claimed that she had no other information to offer and that she needed to prepare a lecture. I asked her what the lecture was on, and she said it was on the waggle dance in bees. I said I thought she taught marine biology, and she said that she also taught a survey course in ethology. I gave her my card and she immediately shut the door. As we drove away I explained to Agent Witherspoon what the waggle dance in bees was, at his request. Then Agent Witherspoon suggested that Julia Wilson had been hiding something and I agreed. Yet my instincts told me that while Julia Wilson was a handful, her niece was smart enough to know who she could trust.

Is Julia Wilson a direct blood relation to Gwendine and Dillon Morley?

No. Her husband, Paul, is the direct blood relation. He is the youngest of three siblings, one deceased, and Julia Wilson is his second wife. There were some immediate question marks regarding this marriage, however. Our sources at the bureau informed us that Paul Wilson had recently been spending a lot of time in Houston.

You called the bureau in Washington, D.C., for information after leaving Julia Wilson. What else did you learn at this juncture?

That Dillon Morley was twenty-one and had crashed a motorbike two months before while living in southern Israel. After the accident, he spent nearly three weeks at a hospital in Jerusalem and then was transported back to Utah in a private plane chartered by his parents, who live two miles away from the hospital in Bountiful. They also own a second home in the Wasatch Mountains, within an area known as the Mount Olympus Wilderness, outside the city limits of a town called East Millcreek. Dillon Morley had lived in Israel for ten months and before that he lived for six months in Greece, on different islands including Mykonos and Crete. Prior to that, he spent close to a year living in the Netherlands.

What did you do next?

We drove up to the hospital in Bountiful to check on the status of Dillon Morley.

And you discovered something surprising?

Yes. We discovered that the visitation of Dillon Morley was restricted to eight names on a list held by the front desk and security that was posted outside Dillon Morley's room. The names included Julia Wilson as well as her husband and daughter. Also listed were, of course, Edward and Delilah Morley. There were another three names I did not recognize. At least, these names did not ring any bells at first. I looked toward Agent Witherspoon and was about to say the names aloud, but before I spoke, one of the names registered. I looked again. The three names were John Myerson, Kitty Myerson, and Tess Eldridge. Tess Eldridge was the Clay Monster's current alias. It didn't make any sense. Or did it? I handed the list to Agent Witherspoon and watched his jaw drop. Then we walked briskly down the hospital's main corridor. We took an elevator to the third floor and made our way down a hallway. We found the room with a guard posted at the door. We told the guard that we were here to see Dillon Morley, and he informed us that we could not unless our names were on the list. "Do you mean this list?" said Agent Witherspoon and held it up, after which the guard grew nervous and amended his previous statement, explaining that his current instruction was to allow no visitors whatsoever, even if the visitor was someone whose name was on the list. Agent Witherspoon showed his badge, and the man said, "Sorry, can't let you in." Agent Witherspoon took the man by the arm and turned him around and pressed him against the wall and told him, "Son, I would advise you to comply with our request." At that point the security guard whimpered that Dillon Morley was not inside the hospital room. "Open the door, son," Agent Witherspoon said, and the guard, who looked to be about thirty-five, produced a key. They'd had some trouble the night before, the guard explained to us. A girl had come, his sister, using an I.D. belonging to an aunt whose name was on the list. We pressed him for information, but he claimed that a different guard had been on duty. All that he knew was that there had been a chase. The sister had run away and the parents worried she had come to hurt her brother, so they moved him. I asked where the patient had been moved to, and the guard said he did not know.

Then you went back to the main floor and called the aunt, Julia Wilson?

That is correct. It seemed the only logical thing to do. The teen-age daughter answered the phone. She recognized my voice and said, "Oh, you're the fed." Then there was shuffling and the phone dropped and then Julia Wilson was on the line. She informed me that I had one minute to speak before she would hang up on me. I said, "They moved him. They moved Dillon. Has he been moved before?" After a pause she said she did not know. I asked where they would move him and she suggested the two obvious places, their estate in Bountiful or their second home in the Wasatch Mountains. I asked for directions to both residences and after another pause and a long sigh she gave them slowly, double-checking that I had everything down correctly. When she was finished she asked me why they moved him and I suggested that her guess was as good as mine, possibly better. She did not speak. I asked her where her husband, Paul, was at the moment and she said Paul was in Hous-ton with his latest girlfriend. Had she and her husband separated? I asked, and she said, "Yes, you could say that." Then I asked what his relationship was like with his sister, Delilah Morley. "Hates Lila's guts," Wilson said. I asked her why, in that case, was his name on the visitors' list. Julia Wilson said she did not know. I asked why her name and her daughter's were on the list as well, and she said, "Dillon liked me a lot and so they probably thought it best to put our names down, though I'm the only one of the three of us who's gone to see him. And yes, I gave Gwen my I.D. Anything else?" I asked her if she could identify the other names on the list. She claimed she did not know which other names were on the list, and so I asked her who John and Kitty Myerson were. She said, "Kitty's a first cousin of Gwen and Dillon's father, Edward Morley. John is her husband, a corporate lawyer. He and Ed used to be partners. I haven't spoken to either one of them in years." I asked her if the Myersons lived in Salt

Lake City and she said no, they lived in the town of Logan, an hour north. Then I asked if she could also tell me who Tess Eldridge was. She said, "Tess Eldridge?" I said yes, and she said, "Tess Eldridge's name was on the list?" I said it was and she said, "Well, that's kind of strange." I asked her why, and she explained that Tess Eldridge was married briefly to Arthur Wilson, Paul and Delilah's deceased older brother, but that Tess Eldridge had all but disappeared in March of 1957, a little more than a year after the marriage, when she was twenty-two years old. She was believed to have become a beatnik in San Francisco. Arthur Wilson was able to annul the marriage or divorce her. Julia Wilson was not sure which. He remarried and moved to western Canada, where he died while helicopter skiing in the Bugaboos. Julia Wilson had never met him, as the skiing accident took place several years before she had met Paul. I asked her whether Tess Eldridge had therefore been, briefly, Tess Wilson, but she said Eldridge had never legally changed her surname. She added that all this should be double-checked, as this was information she'd heard years ago. I asked her if there were any other insights she could offer about Tess Eldridge, any snippet about her childhood, for instance, and she said no. I concluded my line of questioning by asking if she had ever heard of Beltane. She asked if this was someone's name. I told her no and I suggested that she read her niece's letter.

What else have you been able to learn about Tess Eldridge?

Not very much. We have confirmed Julia Wilson's information regarding Eldridge's marriage to Arthur Wilson, which was subsequently annulled. We also located someone in San Francisco, a former stage manager, Arnold Milano, age sixty-seven, who claims Tess Eldridge was a stage actress and that she performed in the Mummers of San Francisco summer Shakespeare festivals in 1960 and 1961. He alleged that Eldridge died of an overdose of heroin in 1964, but we were not able to confirm this with any form of official document. We have weighed the notion that Tess Eldridge was merely an alias against the possibility that Goldman actually is or was Tess Eldridge, but have yet to discover any factual evidence that would corroborate the latter. Nor do we understand how or why her name appeared on the restricted visitors' list. Our best guess is that this was a ruse manipulated by Goldman herself, quite possibly for the purpose of leading Agent Witherspoon and myself to the Morley home in the Wasatch Mountains.

You made a copy of this list?

Yes. It was submitted with my report. At the hospital, we also made copies of Gwendine Morley's letter. I wasn't sure what would happen at the Morley home, so I wanted to safeguard facsimiles of each.

Then you proceeded to the house in the Wasatch Mountains?

First we stopped at the estate in Bountiful. There was an unmanned gate and I was able to climb over it and approach the large saltbox colonial–style home, which was empty. Shortly thereafter it was dusk and I was driving at high speed in our rented Buick over a winding mountain road. With every sharp curve the car buckled, and I worried that if we didn't reach the house soon one of the wheels was going to fall off. But Julia Wilson's directions were precise and soon we located the Morleys' second home. We blocked the long and winding driveway with our car at a point before we could see the house. Then we got out and walked the remainder of the driveway.

What did you see when you reached the house?

We counted cars in a parking area adjacent to a large freestanding garage. There were nine vehicles in all. Six cars, two pickup trucks, and one van. We recorded the plates on each. Then we proceeded around back. There was a deck with a modest swimming pool and a cabana house. Except for a light outside the cabana house, the patio was dark. While Agent Witherspoon kept me covered, I crawled to a patch of bushes behind a back window, and when Agent Witherspoon signaled that it was clear, I crouched and looked inside the house. I half-expected to see medieval torture implements, cages, whips and chains, a pillory, or at least some sign of a cult ritual in progress. What I saw was a group of people holding drinks. There were wine glasses and plates of cheese and crackers. There were raw carrots, broccoli, and sliced red peppers arranged around a bowl of bleu cheese dip. I looked around for an unconscious boy but did not see one. It occurred to me that a cult ritual would be more likely to take place in the basement. I scanned the areas beyond the deck for a basement window or a bulkhead, but from where I crouched I saw nothing other than the cement foundation. I gazed inside once more at all those people holding drinks and searched the room for a tall, poised, black-haired woman. As of yet, I had not formulated any theory that might explain the relationship between this situation and Katherine Clay Goldman. All I could tell was that she was not there in the room before me or, at least, that I had not yet seen through her disguise.

Describe your entrance to the party and what took place afterward.

We went around to the front door, knocked, and were greeted by a woman who asked us if we'd gotten lost. We announced that we were with the FBI and that we'd like, if possible, to speak with either Edward or Delilah Morley. She said that she was Delilah Morley, and Agent Witherspoon asked her where her son was. I added that the hospital in Bountiful had reported that her son, Dillon, had been removed from his private room. "My son is here," the woman said. I asked if we might see him, and she told us that her son was in a coma. We asked her why her son was there, and she explained that from time to time they liked to give him a change of scenery, that it was good to take him places, shift his weight around, things like this. I asked her if there had been any trouble at the hospital. "None that we know of," she said, her first mistake.

There were a total of two mistakes?

Yes.

Describe the second mistake that compromised her story.

I explained that our report indicated that her daughter, Gwendine, had been to see Dillon at the hospital. Delilah Morley's response was "Well, why wouldn't she? She's his sister." I pointed out that Gwendine's name had not been on the list.

What happened then?

The woman crossed her arms. She did not seem flustered. She said her son was in the room by the pool and that if I wished to see him she could take me there. I thanked her and said I would prefer to go alone and leave her inside the house with Agent Witherspoon. At this point the other guests at the party began to stare at us and whisper. Delilah Morley showed me through the house, to a back door that led out onto the pool deck. When I'd been looking through the window, I had been standing roughly ten feet from that door. I saw the pool house with the light outside, and it seemed stupid that we hadn't bothered to look in there. But no matter. Nothing had changed in the last five minutes. I left the woman at her back door and said I'd take it myself from there.

The pool house was dark inside?

Correct.

Please describe precisely what occurred when you went in.

As I entered the cabana, I tried to come up with ideas regarding why they would be keeping Dillon Morley there. The most obvious reason seemed to be that it was the only first-floor room where he would not be in the way of the party. The other thoughts I had were more troubling, as was the fact that he was there in total darkness. I rationalized that a dark room was nothing to be excessively concerned about, given that he was in a coma. I pushed the door open and felt around for a light switch. I glanced back once and saw that Delilah Morley was still watching me through the window of the door. I turned the light on and saw Dillon there, propped up in an expensive leather wheelchair, held in place by a nylon seat belt. The floor was smooth ceramic tile. The walls were stucco. The room had one of those drop-down panel ceilings. The boy was sitting there, eyes closed, his inert face bisected by two long and curving seams of stitches, making him look to my eyes like a more clean-cut and nongreen version of Frankenstein. Although his eyes stayed closed, I wondered briefly if he was aware of me in some subtle or subconscious way. But then these thoughts were interrupted. I heard rustling. I drew my gun and turned. I thought I'd see his mother or his father standing outside the cabana door. No one was there, so I looked back at Dillon Morley. I looked to see if perhaps his arm or leg had moved. I wondered what I would do if he chose this moment to wake up. I heard the rustle again and stared at the boy. Dillon Morley had not moved at all. Then the impossible occurred, although it wasn't Dillon Morley rising out of a two-month coma. One of the panels began to shift in the drop-down ceiling just behind him. Then two long legs appeared. Maybe I should have seen it coming. I raised my gun and took a step back. Her body slithered out from the ceiling. She hardly made a sound as she allowed herself to free-fall to the cabana's floor and looked at me, her blue eyes unmistakable, her small upturned nose just as it is always pictured, her hair dyed black. After the soft thud of her landing, she seemed as quiet as light falling on a meadow. She made no sound with her breath until she spoke. She said, "Hello, Agent Sachs." I said hello, my voice as low as hers, though nowhere as clear or resonant. Hers was a practiced way of speaking, a necessity. What did I plan to do? she asked. I said I planned to take her to jail. "You didn't come for me," she said. I said, "But here you are. Sometimes that's just the way it goes." She smiled wearily. She said, "No." I waited for her to qualify this negation. She said, "So what's your first name, Sachs? I've never learned it in all these years. I know you live in Bethesda, Maryland. I know your ex-wife lives in South Orange, New Jersey. I know your daughter is a liberal-minded lawyer in San Diego." I asked her if she was threatening my ex-wife and daughter. She said, "Of course not." Then I told her my first name.

Do you believe that she was threatening your ex-wife or your daughter?

At the time, I considered it. In hindsight, I do not.

Please continue with your description of the encounter.

She said to leave him. Leave Dillon Morley. To go inside and wait there with my partner until both she and the comatose boy were gone. I pointed out that I was holding a loaded gun and asked her whether she was too. She said she might be, and I told her that I'd caught her. I said that there were no circumstances under which her unimpeded departure would be possible. "Let me rephrase this," she said. "Either I'll have to run away from you, in which case I'll go alone. Or you can leave me here and I might be able to save this boy from things you can't imagine." Was this her game now? I asked. Doing good deeds? She claimed that what she was doing was no game. "Who are you really?" I asked. "Are you Tess Eldridge?" In her unflappable way, she deflected the question. She said, "Who I am is a complicated matter and not something you would easily comprehend." I was still pointing my gun at Goldman's face when I suggested that my partner and I could easily take Dillon Morley out of there. She asserted that we had no legal grounds to do this, that even if we did we had no recourse that would help him. I asked her whether she was under the impression that she herself could help Dillon Morley wake from his coma. She said she could not be sure of anything. She said, "You'll need to make your mind up quickly or I'll have to do it for you." I said, "Unfortunately, there's nothing to decide." Almost before these words passed through my lips, she had burst forward. But even this seems like exaggeration. It was as if in the time it took to blink, she hit my torso with the force of a seasoned linebacker. In an instant I was flat out on my back. I had not known previously that Goldman had proficiency with any form of martial art, and though I'd like to describe her skill as being demonstrative of a particular discipline, she moved with such speed that her maneuver was less a movement and more like a flicker of a thought. Except that I was lying on my back and she held my gun in her hand and one of her knees was pressed against my wind-pipe. She explained to me that she was not going to kill me, but that if I made one wrong move, this offer would immediately be rescinded. She took her knee away, stood, and removed the ammunition clip from my gun. She said I'd find it in the driveway, beside my car, when she was gone. Then she instructed me to go inside the house and count to sixty. Once I reached sixty, she said, I was free to do whatever I pleased. For all she cared, I could chase her to the ends of the earth and back, but for sixty seconds following my departure from the cabana, I would need to do exactly what she said if I wished to live. I looked hard at Katherine Clay Goldman. She looked much older than she did in all the photos we had on file. I thought to tell her that I hated her. I thought to tell her she looked good. I thought to tell her that I would track her down again eventually, no matter how long this might take. What I did instead was ask permission to reach inside my jacket pocket with my free hand and pull out a piece of paper. She agreed to this and I pulled out a xeroxed copy of the letter. I held it up and said that it might help, that it was written by the comatose boy's sister, Gwendine Morley, and that she had read it to her brother the night before. Goldman folded the letter up and thanked me, although I had the strange impression that there was nothing in this letter she did not know.

Is it true that you could have shot her at almost any point prior to her attack?

Yes. Theoretically.

Did you consider it?

I did not.

Why?

Because I had no reason to believe she would escape. I still cannot account for the success or speed of the assault.

At any moment did you have the sense that your mind was being actively controlled?

That's a strange question. No, I did not.

Describe for us what passed through your mind after she released you.

Goldman tossed me my unloaded gun, and as I stood up, I became aware that I might have one final chance to take her down. I calculated that, if I was successful, it would take roughly three seconds to disable her. The sequence raced across my brain, as it had thousands of times, but as it dared me to enact it, I understood that I'd lost whatever jump I might have had and that now Goldman, who took a cautious step back, had recognized exactly what I was thinking.

Please conclude the summary of events.

I left the cabana. I walked back into the main house from the pool deck, looked at Scotty, and gave a nod. Delilah Morley approached. She said that sometimes Dillon spoke. Sometimes he moved. The doctors said this was normal but that still he was not conscious. He had not spoken or moved, I told her. Inside my head I was counting. I'd reached twenty. I asked Delilah Morley if it might be possible to get a scotch with a little ice. The woman nodded, went to the bar. I gazed out through the back window. I saw the dark silhouette of Katherine Clay Goldman wheeling the boy across the patio. Wheeling him over to what was undoubtedly another pair or two of helping hands. There was a vehicle there now. It had crept up in the dark with its headlights off. I could hear the engine purring, but no one noticed until the headlights went on suddenly, at which point the vehicle could be seen moving across the grass of the backyard. Agent Witherspoon yelled, "What the hell?" and looked at me. Then I myself yelled, "What the hell is going on here?" The woman stared at me with hatred, and Agent Witherspoon called out, "Who is the owner of the van?" No one answered, of course. We followed several people who were running to the front of the house to see. The van had made its way onto the driveway. It navigated the small labyrinth created by parked cars. Then I could see her. She had the window down. Agent Witherspoon recognized her immediately and claimed later to have realized just as quickly what had transpired inside the cabana room. She raced past and Agent Witherspoon ran after the van with his gun drawn. He did not get close enough to fire a shot. A minute later he was back with a report that she had crashed through and totaled our rented Buick. From the house he telephoned the bureau in D.C., put an alert out regarding Katherine Clay Goldman, though I was sure it would be quite some time before anyone sighted her again. Then we took statements from eyewitnesses, none of whom claimed to have recognized the woman driving the van. We pressed Delilah Morley about her role in what we referred to several times as a conspiracy regarding her son, which she denied, as did her husband. We promised that we'd return with a warrant to search the premises, but the Morleys did not make attempts to placate us, and more than once Ed Morley looked at me severely and said, "Why in the hell did you take our boy?" When we had finished gathering statements, we called a taxi, and we had waited outside for approximately twenty minutes when it arrived. The driver asked if that was our wrecked Buick. I had already gone to look at it. As promised, I found my ammunition clip on the ground next to the vehicle, which was on its side and angled up against a steep embankment. Clearly Goldman knew how to use the laws of physics in situations that involved ramming a parked car. I told the driver yes, the wrecked Buick had been ours. I heard the rumble of another car. A second car was coming down the driveway and momentarily I feared we'd called two taxis. But a dark-colored Mercedes-Benz appeared, with quartz-iodine high beams. For a second or two, as it moved toward us, the bright headlights were almost blinding. When the car stopped, a woman stepped out of the passenger seat. She wore a dark skirt, leather boots, a maroon top, and a small bejeweled crown. "Are you Kitty Myerson?" I called out, and she looked up at me. Her lips were painted with scarlet lipstick. Before she answered, the car's headlights were extinguished. The silhouette of this woman said, "I am," and then walked past. She was followed by a larger silhouette, which I assumed to be her husband. I caught a glimpse of his face under the porch light as he whispered to his wife, glanced once at me, and placed his arm across her back. "May I help you?" I called out, and the man said, "We'll be just fine without your help today." Kitty Myerson pursed her lips. She gripped the doorknob and said, "Good night." It was conjecture or possibly it was intuition, but I sensed that I was watching what the boy had just escaped from as this couple made their way through the front door.

4

All Along the Ruins

I. Four letters

My name is Jennifer. I have been told that most Jennifers are not "nice," that if I were more cheerful and bubbly I'd be called Jenny, and that if my presence were warm and comforting I'd be Jen. But I have always been called Jennifer, and while I don't espouse idiotic generalizations—these in particular were made by a boy I dated for five months in eleventh grade—I am definitely not someone you'd call nice.

The following is a chronicle of the spring of 1984, my senior year of high school, and while there are many things that seem relevant, I suppose that I should start with my mother's letters. There were four in all. I discovered them in late March in the drawer of her bedside table. I had just finished an essay on *Brave New World* and, as it was Wednesday, I knew she would be home late because it was her night to do evening pediatric rounds at the hospital. Possibly because my mother is so reserved—my father, who is an actor, once called her "luminously demure"—I periodically found myself in her bedroom, rifling through drawers, looking at papers on her desk, searching for clues that she was secretly someone other than the woman I thought she was.

She had told my younger sister Rocky and me, once, how she escaped from Soviet-occupied eastern Poland in fall of 1939 with her mother and father by running across beet fields under the glow of moonlight. They had been hiding in a barn when Red Army soldiers came and took her father's brother Lejb and his wife away. They had Lejb's dogs, two great big hounds, with them. The dogs had followed even though my grandmother had been shooing them away. As my mother and her parents ran across those beet fields, the dogs ran with them. Finally they lost the dogs and at some point hid themselves within a stack of hay so they could rest. Soon they were running once more, and as the sun rose they saw the two big hounds again, as if they'd never been apart from them. They ran and ran for their lives, and the dogs kept vanishing and reappearing. My mother claimed that every sighting of those two hound dogs reassured her that she and her parents would escape.

There was a train somewhere—my version of all this is clearly very impressionistic—and the plan was to climb inside one of the cars that was far back from the station where the train had stopped. Somehow they did it. They climbed into a car that was filled with bags of grain and hid between the bags as the train sped northeast toward Lithuania, at which point the two big hounds, quite obviously, were never seen again. I was twelve when my mother first recalled for us the details of her escape, and I have often wondered how much she omitted as well as which parts of her story were embellished. Mainly, I've wondered whether the inclusion of those two almost-magical hound dogs was just a way to tell the story so that we would remember it. The problem is that I sometimes dream about those dogs, and in my dreams they are enormous and beatific, kind of like Aslan in the Chronicles of Narnia, except in this case the dogs, just out of sight, are tearing unseen soldiers limb from limb. And I mean shredding them, devouring them, mutilating their bodies beyond forms that can be recognized. Then they come back into sight and they're just happy-go-lucky, ground-snuffling, oafish hound dogs, barking and making those explosive low-pitched yodeling sounds that hound dogs always make.

Anyway, the letters. All four were recent, postmarked on various dates in February and March. Two were from the Netherlands. One was from the Soviet Socialist Republic of Lithuania. One was from Israel. They'd each been mailed in those lightweight onionskin envelopes, which as a young girl I had thought were really made of the skin of onions. They'd all been opened and the most recent one, from Israel, had arrived three days before. As I began to read, I determined very quickly that my mother had contacted representatives at several European agencies in hopes of digging up information about her father. It also seemed that whatever she had written to these people was directed toward the remote possibility that her father had survived, though she'd told Rocky and me, long ago, that he'd been murdered in 1941.

There was a story about five hundred Jewish men that was continually alluded to in these letters sent by people from agencies that thirty-nine years after the end of World War II were still attempting to help others confirm the exact fates of family members who had vanished. I didn't know what the story was, and at the time I did not think that I was going to ask my mother. She was a good mother, angry at her as I was on most days, but when it came to talking about the war, she and my grandmother were at best idiosyncratic and at worst freakish. Just having heard the story of their escape from Poland seemed like a windfall. There was also the story of her exit visa from Lithuania, although that was less a story and more a catalogue of logistics. The only member of my family who spoke openly about the Holocaust was Aunt Doris, my grandmother's younger sister, who'd been a prisoner in a Lithuanian ghetto and then at Auschwitz and therefore was not simply an escapee but a full-fledged Survivor. She'd immigrated in 1945 and had lived since then in the northern part of New Jersey, but her story was not my mother's, and anyway, what I knew of my aunt's story was more like what I'd seen in the documentary we watched in class during my final year of Hebrew school, shortly before my excruciating bat mitzvah.

These are the four letters, word for word, as copied by me into a diary that I will soon describe. The first letter I read was dated

February 26 and was from Amsterdam. A man named Hans-Willem had written:

Dear Dr. Rabinowitz,

We have sort through census topic dating from 1939 and see no telling of Polish or Lithuanian man Jonah Rabinowitz. We have consult with Anne Frank House trustee Jacob van Vanderhoek and no telling in this respect as well. We have some coffee drink with Yitzchak Buchman from Haifa Institute and he is suggest you seek record of transport from his brother Zvi who work at Yad Vashem Holocaust memorial in Jerusalem. There is names on transport record to camps from different town and for Kovno, Lithuiania most is in three years 1942–1944 and we are glad for your hoping and not happy for your unknowing. We do not hear of this story of five hundred Jewish men but we tell someone on Anne Frank House trustee and none have hear this story or one like it. We tell you it is happy if you will come to Amsterdam when you seem to and need only on short notice if you are seeking us to meet.

Yours regretful,
Hans-Willem Schoonhoven

The second letter was from the town of Delft, Holland, dated March 8, and from a woman who spoke English with perfect fluency. She wrote:

Dear Dr. Rabinowitz,

I have investigated two addresses on Plein Delfzicht and have spoken to the landlord and several residents of an apartment complex there. There is no one with a memory of your father, Jonah Rabinowitz, nor has anyone ever heard the

story of the five hundred Jewish men. I will just say that there
are many stories such as these.

Sincerely,
Annemieke Voorhees

The third letter, postmarked *Vilnius, Lietuvos TSR*, was dated
March 18 and had several lines that had been crossed out, I assumed,
by governmentally employed censors. The letter was unsigned and
its anonymous author wrote:

To Mrs. Doctor Beverly Rabinowitz:

It is not so much for me to say what is or not and in such
case as this I find you will not see what you go look for. This
country is different place now than was for brief period then
and always this will be how change becomes with time. (crossed
out sentence) I am not so glad of what is happen and must only
say that yes I do know of some group with intellectual from
Kaunas in 1941 and all must be killed because no one were seen
again. This is long ago and there can be many place to hide but
none so many when you are standing beside trench you have
dig by Fourth Fort and then be shot to fall into these trench
as you say it is not likely scenario. (crossed out sentence) Once
woman who is called Olga say to me that lucky ones are ones
who die fast and unfortunate ones survive in case like these and
as you see these case continue to happen in places in the world
and though some people I know in Israel will say many time
to "never we forget" it is in many place forget though we look
all along (crossed out words) today is why I feel what Olga say
is true enough. Do not be so sad that one such as your father
have no survive because is better for him that way and for you.
I did have known in cases where person does survive and in
some cases there is suicide and always there is misery like what

*you can imagine though it also become possible in case like you
describe to imagine the thing you want. (crossed out sentence) I
am old man and I talk to people because this become my passion
and I write letters but I am always speaking my heart and
decide to see this must be best. I have read these words again to
find my spelling is correct but I am sorry that my English is no
better so all of this will be more sounding like a friend. Though
I do not know you this my hope in this world to sound like
friend.*

This was by far my favorite letter. I only wished I knew the
name of the man who'd written it.

The final letter was from Jerusalem and dated March 25. It
was from Zvi Buchman, the brother of the man mentioned in the
letter from the Dutch man. He wrote:

Dear Dr. Rabinowitz,

*I have read your letter with great interest. It is my
business to track down cases such as this and to seek evidence
that may document historical events that may shed light on
the lives or deaths of any one of the six million who were lost.
I have, as you requested, searched through archival material
at Yad Vashem. These include passenger logs for trains from
Kovno, Lithuania, as well as records pertaining to Treblinka,
Chelmno, Sobibor, and Auschwitz–Birkenau camps. I have
found no record of your father, Yonah (Jonah, Jojna, Janas,
Jonas) Rabinowitz, in any of these documents. Of course, there
is a great deal more archival material at Yad Vashem and a
thorough review of all of it would take months, possibly years.
I have looked in the obvious places, but always in cases such as
yours the places you will find anything of value are not obvious.
As for the instance of the five hundred Jewish men you have*

described, I have consulted with the historian Shlomo Weisgold at the Hebrew University in Jerusalem and he has shared testimony regarding 534 Jewish intellectuals who believed themselves to have been selected for archival work in Kovno but were taken to the nineteenth-century Russian fortress known as the Fourth Fort outside the city in early August of 1941 and shot. There is no testimony regarding other details of your story nor evidence that some may have survived the massacre, but he has filed a copy of your letter with a note to contact me in the event that he discovers a cross-reference. Please let me know if there is any other way I can be of service.

Tiheyeh briah (be well),
Zvi Buchman

And what to make of these letters? Clearly my mother had made very precise inquiries, with instructions regarding certain concentration camps, etc. She had made them sometime during that winter, most likely following the unfortunate matter of my arrest with Alison Belle for blowing up a teacher's mailbox. My mother had seemed oddly serene about the mailbox incident, which occurred in January, while she was down in Florida with her marine biologist boyfriend. Even now, I ask myself this question. How was it that reading these four letters made things worse for me than they were already?

II. War Is Peace

In Mr. Kananbaum's Utopian literature class, we were about to begin reading *1984*. He'd probably taught the novel every year since he'd started teaching high school English in the seventies, but he was acting like the whole thing was profound because the year was, as I have mentioned, 1984. He had just handed back our *Brave New World* essays, and although they had been, in his words, stunningly mediocre, he informed us that there would be no paper assigned for Mr. Orwell and that instead our assignment would be to keep a diary filled with impressions—some to be written during class and some at home—about *1984*.

"And not just the book," he added. "About the book and the world we live in. The book and your lives, our lives, now."

He pulled out two twelve-packs of lined composition notebooks. Each twelve-pack was sealed in plastic, which he removed, crumpled up, and dropped into a wastebasket. He passed the notebooks out and asked us all to write the date on the top of the first page. I wrote the date—April 4, 1984—and quickly reread his comment on my essay. He'd written: *Jennifer, as usual your intelligence is far beyond the level of most high school seniors. I wish you'd take a little more time developing your insights, such as why Soma, in a dystopia such as this one, is imperative. Still, your insights are exceptional. Grade = A.*

"Let's try an exercise," said Mr. Kananbaum, a stocky man with short blond hair and smart-looking rectangular-shaped eyeglasses. "Please take ten minutes to reflect on the last movie that you've seen."

A few people looked up, confused, and Mr. Kananbaum said, "What's wrong? I assume that every one of you watches movies. Please go ahead and write about whatever movie you've seen most recently."

As it turned out, the last movie I had seen was *Dressed to Kill*, which had been on HBO a lot in the last month. Some of the boys I knew in the senior class had already seen it five or six times or at least the opening scene where Angie Dickinson soaps her breasts up and caresses herself in the shower, though apparently they used a stunt double for the close-ups. In my new diary I wrote that I watched this movie because for some reason I'm fascinated with Angie Dickinson. I wrote that she died fairly quickly in the movie, that she gets brutally murdered by a preoperative transvestite who turns out to have been the therapist treating her sex addiction, that the movie's not-so-subtle subtext seemed to be that she deserved what she got for being so promiscuous. I wrote that she also died at the end of *Big Bad Mama* and that her movies always feature people dying and lots of nudity. I wrote that Angie Dickinson is not afraid to play these sexually objectifying roles and seems to like it. Same with the movie *Pretty Maids All in a Row*, where she has sex with a college boy who's half her age, though in that movie the subtext seemed to be that this was a good thing for the student. I wrote that Angie Dickinson is sort of weird, that all her movies are trash, but that for me it's hard not to be fascinated. I wrote that Meryl Streep is a better actress and that she has a hooked nose and uneven cheekbones, which goes to show that you don't have to have a perfect face to be pretty. I wrote that Meryl Streep is the opposite of Angie Dickinson and that sometimes I wonder which of them I'd choose to be if I had the choice. I wrote that Meryl Streep will keep starring in movies until she's eighty because there will always be roles for a good actress and that Angie Dickinson will star in movies only as long as they can make her face look like it doesn't have any wrinkles. I wondered what all this could possibly have to do with *1984* but didn't write that. Then Mr. Kananbaum called time and asked for volunteers to read their entries.

Three people had written about *Footloose*, two about *Splash*, and two about *Romancing the Stone*. Those movies were still playing in theaters. Then there were all the random movies people had seen on HBO or Showtime, entries on *Rocky III*, *Risky Business*, *Apocalypse Now*, and *National Lampoon's Vacation*. Just when I thought I had slipped by without having to read, Mr. Kananbaum said, "Jennifer, how about you?"

I lied and said I had also written about *Splash* and that the movie seemed to have been covered. Kananbaum insisted that I read my entry anyway, so I made something up about how mermaids were male fantasies and that in ten years *Splash* would seem extremely trite, even though one could reasonably argue the theme was similar to "The Wife of Bath's Tale," which I'd read sophomore year and at which time I had not agreed that Chaucer was a genius just because he had been able to write a story that compensated for his own raving misogyny. I made it seem like I was reading from the diary, but I guessed Kananbaum could tell I was just babbling. When I was finished he nodded gravely and described my thoughts as interesting and insightful. Two rows behind me, my former friend, fellow criminal, and now arch-enemy Alison Belle whispered, "The girl's either a genius or she's insane."

Then Mr. Kananbaum said, "The exercise we have just completed will make more sense tonight when you read chapter one, pages one through twenty." He wrote three sentences in block letters and explained that these were the slogans of the Party in *1984*. He had us copy them in our journals and said our written assignment would be to record our impressions regarding WAR IS PEACE, FREEDOM IS SLAVERY, IGNORANCE IS TRUTH. "Ask yourselves this," he said. "Is it possible that a thing can also be its opposite?" A boy named Peter Stamey raised his hand and said, "Do you mean just ask ourselves, or do we have to write it?" A girl named Lissette Willis said, "Duh," and someone laughed, and Mr. Kananbaum said, "Everyone's job for the next six weeks is to fill a diary. As long as what you write pertains to 1984, you can fill the pages any way you want."

At home that night I read the chapter and saw how clever Mr. Kananbaum had been. April 4, 1984, is the exact date that the book's protagonist, Winston, begins the subversive act of starting *his* diary, the result of which is, of course, that he's eventually imprisoned and re-educated by means of torture. Even more clever, Winston's first entry in his diary is a reflection about a movie he had seen the night before. I kept on reading past chapter one. I got as far as the end of chapter three, then took my diary out and stared at the three slogans. I asked myself if a thing could also be its opposite and decided I didn't care.

I wrote: *My mother escaped from war-torn Poland when she was five. She escaped from Soviet-occupied Lithuania, before the Nazis arrived, when she was six. She was born in 1934 and next November she will be fifty. All of this business in chapter one about the traitor Goldstein and the obvious parallels to the Nazis are not news to me and neither are the slogans. In fact, I read this book as well as Animal Farm when I was twelve. I had forgotten about Winston's diary and his description of the war film, though I remembered the dark-haired girl from the Anti-Sex League and the scene of Two Minutes Hate. I have to say that it seems like a good idea, in certain ways, to take two minutes each day and hate things.*

Then I went into my mother's room and got the letters. It was a Wednesday. Rocky was downstairs on the couch, alternating between her math homework and giggly phone calls. The letters hadn't been touched. I knew this because I had taken two long strands of my hair and laid them perpendicular to each other across the topmost letter. If anyone had picked the letters up, the unseen hairs would have been moved. I began to reread the letters and was overcome by an irrational compulsion. I wanted to steal the letters. Instead what I did was copy them in my diary. I introduced them in the diary by writing *These are four letters that my mother received in 1984.* It took me close to an hour to transcribe them, especially with all the broken English. Underneath the final letter, I wrote: *What do you think, Mr. Bruce Kananbaum? These people all suggest that my mother's wasting her time looking. Is this what Orwell meant by IGNORANCE IS TRUTH?*

The next day Alison Belle was called on to read her diary entry regarding the three slogans of the Party. She was wearing her creamy leather bomber jacket, and, as usual, most of the boys in our class were staring at her whenever the opportunity presented itself. Chances were that Alison was just winging it, but that unlike my extemporizing of the day before, Alison probably had not written anything at all.

Alison cleared her throat and either read or said, "I finished this chapter and all I could think about was MTV, and silly me, I began to wonder whether this could be a part of the author's vision. All I could think was hey, is Big Brother really J. J. Jackson or that dork goofball VJ Alan Hunter because, really, watching those waitresses turn all pretty in the ZZ Top videos or seeing Michael Jackson do his moonwalk doesn't seem the least bit totalitarian, it just seems dumb."

"MTV," said Mr. Kananbaum. "Any thoughts on whether this J. J. Jackson is like Big Brother?"

Peter Stamey said, "He's the second smartest of the VJs. First is Mark Goodman. I agree that Alan Hunter is a dork."

"What about MTV?" said Mr. Kananbaum. "Could we say that it's like the telescreen in the novel?"

"For my ex-boyfriend it is," said Alison, and half the class erupted into laughter. I had no idea why this was considered funny.

"It's like a telescreen for me," said Peter Stamey, who was, sadly, the most uninhibited member of the class. "I mean, I'm glued to it *all the time*. I mean, those ZZ Top videos are awesome, *especially* when those waitresses turn all hot. And then those geezers with the beards, I mean, who are they?"

"They're ZZ Top," someone said. "That's why they're holding guitars and singing."

At that moment, I half-wished Kananbaum had the guts to nail us all with a pop quiz or revoke outright the plan of assigning us the diary instead of a final essay. I also wasn't optimistic that the results of this curricular innovation would get much better. There was not likely to be a climactic turnaround, no great moment where Mr. Kananbaum gave a valiant speech and inspired us all to become more reflective human beings.

He said, "Let's move on from MTV then. Shall we consider something else?"

He looked at me and made what probably was his biggest mistake that day.

He said, "Jennifer, will you please read to us what you *actually* wrote last night?"

I said, "I'm not really sure I want to do that."

"Why?"

"It may offend you."

"I guess we'll see," Kananbaum said. With an exaggerated hand gesture, he indicated that I should go ahead. I read my entry, including the entire texts of the four letters. The only thing I omitted was his first name in the final sentence. When I had finished, he said, "Well, that was quite interesting. And quite relevant."

"I'm glad you think so," I said.

Behind me, Peter Stamey yawned.

III. Mailboxes, wallets, etc.

Part of Kananbaum's problem was that he seemed to have a dual crush going. One of his crushes was on me and, of course, the other crush was Alison. And, of course, he knew that back in January, Alison and I, supposedly, had blown up our U.S. history teacher Mildred Turner's mailbox. It wasn't far from the truth, although it wasn't the whole story.

Alison's twenty-six-year-old former boyfriend Raymond was the one who had produced, lit, and placed an M-80, the equivalent of a quarter stick of dynamite, inside the mailbox. Then he ran back to the car. He hopped into the driver's seat and slammed the door. For reasons that now seem inexplicable, Alison and I had gotten out of Raymond's car to watch him. An instant after the explosion we saw the flashing lights and heard the sound of an approaching siren. The cop car must have been a half a block away. With instinctive cowardice, Raymond put the car into gear and floored it, leaving both Alison and me standing on someone's lawn across the street from Mrs. Turner's house. We didn't bother to run. We had tight clothes on. Soon Mr. Turner came out and an hour later I was calling my sister, Rocky, from the East Brunswick police station. When it had become apparent that I would have to spend a night in the county juvenile prison, I had turned into a whining idiot.

The cops eventually caught up with Raymond, but he hired a good lawyer and lied his ass off. He claimed that I had lit the fuse and Alison had placed the M-80 in the mailbox. He said that he had been the driver, but that he hadn't even known where we were taking him. We knew the game that he was playing. Though nothing serious, Raymond already had a record. He knew that Alison and I would most likely get off with a hundred hours of community service. He might have even guessed that Mrs. Turner would see through the whole thing and drop the charges, which she did.

To make a statement, in a twisted sort of way, of her integrity, Mrs. Turner spoke to our parents and volunteered to waive all charges on the condition that Alison and I agreed to help clean out her basement. She also insisted that both Alison and I remain in her history class. For five straight Saturdays we went over there, sorted through boxes, swept, carried things out to the curb, and listened as Mrs. Turner stated, once each visit, that we would thank her someday for this lesson in forgiveness. We played along well, I thought, though on the final Saturday of our indentured servantry, when I stayed for an extra fifteen minutes to help Mrs. Turner hang a new mirror, she said, "There's no hope for your friend. Are you aware of that?" I told her no, although I was. She said, "Your friend has what Aristotle called the malicious temperament. He divided temperament into four types—virtuous, competent, incompetent, and malicious. Would you like to understand the four Aristotelian temperaments?" I knew exactly what they were, but it was obvious she wanted to explain them, so I indulged her.

She gave the wallet example, which is simply—What do you do if you find a wallet on the street? The *virtuous* temperament, without reflection, returns the wallet to its owner. The *competent* temperament thinks to herself, "Gee, I'd really like to keep this wallet and all the money," but knows the right thing is to return it and overcomes the moral quandary and does just that. The *incompetent* thinks the same thing but cannot resist keeping the money and tossing all the rest into a Dumpster behind the nearest fast-food restaurant. The *malicious* temperament, of course, keeps the wallet without thinking twice and may even try to use the credit cards.

"And which are you?" asked Mrs. Turner. "In my mind, you're either competent or incompetent. Obviously, there are choices you can make here. I don't expect you to turn virtuous, but you're so smart that I would hate to see you make a mess of things."

I said, "This whole thing was a really big mistake, and I'm really sorry."

"I'm glad to hear it, at least from one of you," said Mrs. Turner. She walked me to the door and said, "You know, I find it quite surprising that you'd be friends with a girl like her. Of course, it's obvious that you aren't really friends anymore. The question is— Would you still want to be?"

She had me there. She wasn't stupid, even if she thought the world of William Jennings Bryan. Would I still want to be friends with Alison, who, following our night in prison, had dropped me like a hot potato? Before I left, I looked directly into Mrs. Turner's eyes and said, "Some days I do. Some days I don't."

Who would have imagined it, though? Honestly. One sunny afternoon in mid-December I'm outside in the senior garden, wearing my fingerless gloves and standing there with Alison. We're both smoking so we've been talking and then we're laughing about something we both saw on *Saturday Night Live* and the next day after school we're with her twenty-six-year-old boyfriend and Alison's driving his car all around the fancy town of Bernardsville, a place I'd never even heard of, and Raymond's hanging out the passenger-seat window with a baseball bat, smashing up mailboxes by the dozens. We looked for nice ones with pretty pictures of birds, curlicue numbers, or in one case a mailbox that was covered with mosaic tiles. I'd been afraid of Alison for years, but suddenly, as of roughly Thanksgiving, we're the only two seniors in Mrs. Turner's class, and within weeks it's like we're pals.

Alison Belle. She's had at least five different boyfriends since ninth grade. Alison smokes in her own house. She's on the pill. Once last year Alison told chronic boyfriend-stealer Nina Fowler that she was going to spraypaint *cunt* on her driveway and had scared Nina so much that Nina didn't even say she knew who did it when one morning her father discovered the four giant neon green letters painted across the driveway as well as the garage doors. Something was wrong with me, clearly, for liking Alison. Something was wrong with me for liking that she liked me. She'd say "You're *brilliant*" or sometimes call me the Bored Girl Genius because I *was* bored, clearly bored enough to hang around with her and Raymond. Then one day Alison says, "Hey, Bored Girl, any idea what you want to do today?" From Mrs. Turner I had recently received a B plus on what was clearly an A paper about how awful a president Woodrow Wilson actually was, and I said, "I'd like to blow up our teacher's mailbox."

I didn't mean it, although maybe I did. Who knows? There's no point explicating the surprising events that followed. Or, perhaps, I've already explicated them well enough. The only relevant thing I seem not to have explicated is whether I thought Mrs. Turner had been right in her assessment of my temperament. Had I answered, I would have told her the four Aristotelian temperaments might have still made sense as recently as a thousand years ago, but that by now they seemed excessively reductive. I would have told her that briefly, in sixth grade, when I was really, really nerdy, I'd played Dungeons & Dragons with three equally nerdy boys who were in my gifted-students math class. I would have told her that all the creatures in Dungeons & Dragons are categorized according to their two-part "alignments." Creatures are designated *ethically* as being lawful, neutral, or chaotic, as well as *morally* as good, neutral, or evil. So, for instance, vampires tend to be "lawful evil." Orcs are "chaotic evil." Unicorns are "lawful good." Goblins are "lawful neutral." Gelatinous cubes are "neutral neutral." Likewise, the characters whose roles you play in the adventure can have alignments. My best and most beloved character was a fourteenth-level thief I'd named Cassandra and whose alignment was "chaotic good." But then she read some scroll that changed her. Everyone had to leave the room while the dungeon master, Kevin, explained to me that the scroll contained a curse and that now Cassandra had become "chaotic evil." I asked him how I could change her back. He said she needed to find another scroll. The problem was that, at this point, she was too busy betraying and endangering the other characters. The two other boys—one had an eighteenth-level wizard and the other had a fifteenth-level fighter—figured things out pretty fast and killed her. They asked me if I wanted to create another character. I told them no and I went home that day and cried and then stopped playing Dungeons & Dragons. If I had managed to tell all this to Mrs. Turner, I would have told her that chaotic good is what I seem to be, what I want to be, but sometimes it is like there is a spell on me. Sometimes I want to be something that is worse than chaotic evil or malicious. But luckily these spells usually do not last long.

IV. There are connections to be made

I began ignoring Kananbaum's assigned response questions as well as what I was reading in the novel. In my diary, instead, I wrote about the Five Hundred Jewish Men.

On April 14, I wrote: *Maybe the Five Hundred Jewish Men were like one of those organisms we learned about in AP Bio who at some point in their life cycle metamorphose from individuals into a single collective body. Maybe that tricked the people who were shooting them. Maybe the men turned into a giant puddle of goop, oozed down into the trench, and seeped away.*

On April 18, I wrote: *I had a boyfriend last year named Derek Hottel, who some people called Derek Hotshot and other people called Hotel. Things ended badly, but I still think of him and sometimes want to talk to him. I wonder if by now he's managed to decipher all the lyrics to the five songs he was obsessed with on the R.E.M. EP Chronic Town. I once suggested that the lyrics were just nonsense but Derek said, and I quote, "There are connections to be made." He asked me if I'd ever heard the lines from King Lear that are spoken at the end of the song "I Am the Walrus." I told him no. I said, "So what? What's the connection to be made?" Derek said knowing the origin of those words was the connection and I suggested that this wasn't a connection. It's a tautology, I explained, not a connection, but Mr. Hotshot had failed geometry and had no aptitude for concepts of formal logic.*

On April 23, I wrote: *Five hundred men is a lot of men. It's a lot more men than there are California condors in the world. It's more than the combined total of existent works of art by Michelangelo and Da Vinci. It's as many men as there are students in my high school. You would think one of them, at least, could have survived.*

On April 25, I wrote: *Why am I writing this? I had a dream that there were five hundred Jewish men in my living room. They were all shot and they were bleeding on the furniture and the carpet. So much can happen that a mother is not aware of. Not only in school but in a living room. Once I almost had sex with Derek in the same place where all those Jewish men were bleeding in my dream. But Derek didn't have a condom and shortly after this his family moved to Ohio. Lately I've had to resist the urge to call him up and scream at him. He knew my mother would be out at her boyfriend's and my sister would be sleeping at a friend's house. What kind of idiot doesn't bring a condom?*

On April 26, I wrote: *According to a book I read, 200,000 Jews were killed in Lithuania once it came under Nazi rule and in many cases these Jews were killed by Lithuanians who cooperated with the Einzatzgruppen, which means "Action Groups" in German, a clever euphemism for "murder squads," some of which were headed by German officers with Ph.D.'s and the sole task of which was to arrange barbaric massacres of Jewish men, women, and children. Of these 200,000, five hundred were, apparently, a group of hoodwinked Jewish intellectuals living in Kovno, which I've determined is this city's name in Polish, since on every map I've looked at I see Kaunas and no Kovno.*

On April 27, I wrote: *My mother left Kovno in the fall of 1940, so apparently she was not there on Five Hundred Jewish Men Day, as I might as well refer to it. My mother and her mother escaped on a train across Siberia because her father had been able to get visas to the Dutch island of Curacao. If this sounds strange, it is. Apparently the Dutch consulate in Kovno had figured out that a visa was not technically required for entry to Curacao, although this was because entry had to be personally approved by the Dutch governor there, and this governor rarely approved entry for anyone, much less Polish-Jewish refugees. So, it was a loophole, a bogus visa to Curacao, which then required a bogus transit visa through Japan, and it was thanks to Japanese consul Chiune Sugihara, for whom I was able to find sixty-seven different magazine and newspaper articles in the periodicals listings at the library, as well as twenty-three book references, that something like six thousand Jews obtained transit visas through Japan and were able to escape Lithuania before the Nazi occupation. He wrote out these bogus transit visas day and night for Polish-Jewish refugees, now thought of collectively as the "Sugihara Jews," of all idiotic labels, not to take anything away from the heroic actions of this man who barely slept for a month in order to be able to do this and was apparently still throwing visas out the window of the train as it left Kovno when the Soviets forced him to leave. However, not all recipients of these visas got to use them. The cost was two hundred American dollars for a single ticket on the trans-Siberian railway. If you didn't have the money, you had to apply for funding from one of several charitable organizations that were stationed there. As you'd expect, there was not much funding. Although my grandfather had obtained a family visa, the American Jewish Joint Distribution Committee (which my grandmother called "the Joint") could only underwrite two train tickets, which was why my grandfather stayed behind. My mother's voyage by land and sea to the U.S. took more than a month and the sole nonlogistic detail I'm aware of is that my grandmother cried nonstop for the first two days, assumedly because my grandfather had not been able to go with them. In other words, he stayed in Kovno and instead of becoming one of the Sugihara Jews (really, this phrase annoys me to no end) he became one of the Five Hundred Jewish Men (this phrase is also starting to annoy me).*

On May 1, I wrote: *Jesus Christ, Mr. Kananbaum, you're planning to collect these? Isn't that being a little totalitarian? Are you Big Brother here or what? You could have told us this three weeks ago. I have appreciated your not calling on me in class lately, but I am going to say right here that you are really not entitled to read this. Still, if you're reading this now, it means you are (see "tautology" in Apr. 18 entry), and if it's not clear, I've been feeling rather confused in recent days. Not only that, I'm waiting to hear from colleges that I don't even know if I want to go to. Would you go to Yale? To Brown? Do you think anyone there could tell me any more than what I know? My mother went to Barnard and she's a doctor. My grandmother thinks she should have found a husband she could stay with. My grandfather was most likely shot by Nazis and then buried along with four hundred ninety-nine other bleeding men. Incidentally, Alison Belle is telling everyone I'm crazy and it's possible that I am having an anxiety disorder and that this class is what is making me so anxious. Because I think about Big Brother and I think maybe it would be nice to love Big Brother. Certainly Peter Stamey would, so long as ZZ Top videos were playing on the telescreen.*

On May 2, I wrote: *I hope you enjoyed my diary.*

V. Green, how I want you green

My last name is Green. Briefly, my mother was Beverly Rabinowitz-Green, but then her marriage to my father, Richard Green, fell apart. He left after a few years because he wanted to pursue his goal of becoming a famous movie star. He moved out to Los Angeles. He had parts in three different television pilots, all of which were unsuccessful. He did commercials too, and when I think of him, I often picture a man coughing and then getting out of bed and taking NyQuil. His leading role in that commercial was the one thing I always mentioned when I told people my father was an actor.

My parents must have been on drugs or something. They got divorced and *then* they had my sister. It was an accident, of course, although my mother likes to say there are no accidents. One result of all this post-divorce stupidity is that my sister's last name is Rabinowitz. I'd always wondered when she'd switch to her real name, Roxanne, but at age thirteen she was still not convinced that Rocky Rabinowitz sounded like a cartoon mobster, though I'd suggested this many times. Meanwhile, I had no choice but to endure the years of people calling me things like Greenpeace, Jen of Green Gables (I'd say "That's Jennifer of Green Gables to you"), and Soylent Green. But my father, who after going on the lam for a few years began forging a relationship with me when I was six or so, had tried to convince me that it was a good name. He would say, "Green, how I want you green," which was a line from a poem by Federico García Lorca. During the summer when I visited him after my junior year of high school, he dragged me out to an all-night Truffaut marathon at a hip little theater in Santa Monica, and during an intermission, as I was lauding the actress Nathalie Baye, he'd mentioned that if I wanted to be an actress, Green was a better name than Rabinowitz. I asked him if he was a self-hating Jew. He laughed and said he thought that perhaps I would be better suited for directing. I'd pushed the question though, and finally he said, "Look, my little Green bean, you should be proud of your faith and heritage, but in the entertainment world it's sometimes easier not to have a name that doubles as a billboard for the Hebrew nation." He'd said his girlfriend at the time was Jewish. She was an actress and her name was Leah Davis. It sounded good, much better than her real name. What was her real name? I asked, and he said, "Bloomstein. Not a bad name, but not a name people can fall for."

Kind of like Goldstein, enemy of the Party in *1984*. On the day Kananbaum was going to return our diaries, he was recalling aloud my erratic entry of three weeks before and asking the class if we understood that Orwell's choice to give the bleating, reviled traitor the name Goldstein had created a clear subtext that pertained to anti-Semitism.

Peter Stamey, dumb as he was, was also capable of idiotic insights. He said, "But if it's supposed to be a subtext, doesn't that mean it isn't clear?"

Someone said, "Why did Goldstein turn into a sheep during that video?"

"Is it a thoughtcrime," Alison Belle droned, "to sit here thinking that most of you are *much* dumber than sheep?"

I had to admit that I was nervous. I was wondering what in the world Kananbaum's response would be to the manic entries in my diary. On his desk he had the diaries stacked in two neat rectangular pillars, and throughout class I stared at those pillars as if they were some sort of occult prop for a soon-to-be-enacted death ritual. Finally he began to call our names out, one by one. People walked up, received their diaries, and then headed to the door. Alison Belle was called first, which seemed to make sense, alphabetically. But it was soon clear that the order was not alphabetical. By the time Peter received his diary—he'd been called fifth—I was aware that I'd be called last.

And so it was. Everyone gone. Just me and Kananbaum. He

didn't bother calling my name. He said, "In case you're worried, I didn't read it."

"You didn't read it?"

He said, "I knew you didn't want me to."

"Maybe I did," I said.

"Then you've got me fooled."

"Did you read everyone else's diary?"

He told me, "Yes. Including Alison's."

"Your point being?"

He said, "I wondered whether you were aware of certain things Alison wrote."

I said, "Which things?"

"You're not aware of them?"

I didn't know where this was going, so it seemed prudent to say, "Possibly, I am."

He told me, "I would suggest you talk with Alison and discuss it. I also want you to know that it's all right. You can keep on writing whatever you want to in your diary. I won't read it."

"What if I want you to?"

He smiled a vaguely smarmy smile and then said, "Well, you can let me know."

And just like that, there was the question of when and how to talk with Alison, who appeared to have me at her mercy just because she had made some devious allusion to my character and perhaps had mentioned that it was me who'd first suggested blowing up Mrs. Turner's mailbox. You would have thought that after Mrs. Turner's class, the school principal, Vincent Luongo, would have made sure that Alison and I never again wound up in a class together. But no—instead Luongo had called a private meeting between Alison, me, and Mr. Kananbaum, during which Kananbaum told us that he'd heard about *the incident*, said that it sounded like things had gone a little further than we'd intended, and that he'd love to have us both in his spring class so long as we had no intentions of replicating past events. We said we didn't, of course, and thanked him very much for his understanding. Then he led both of us back to the principal's office, where he told Luongo everything was settled.

Later the same day, Alison had found me and said, "When do you want to do his mailbox?"

I said, "That's funny," and then Alison said, "I'm serious."

I said, "Never. Never again will I go near you and your certifiable boyfriend."

She said, "I broke up with Raymond long ago."

I told her, "Great. I guess that means you're a better person now. And through this difficult experience you have passed through growth and change."

Alison's lips curled up like Angie Dickinson's when she robbed banks in *Big Bad Mama*. "Want to be enemies?" she said.

Since there was nothing else to say, I told her, "Sure."

That was in March. Now it was May. We had not spoken directly in all that time. I found her out in the senior garden after eighth period, and I said, "Alison, can we talk?"

She had been standing with two sophomore girls, more than likely because she'd bummed a cigarette. She said, "Bored Genius Girl to speak with *moi?*"

I said, "Excuse us," to the girls, and they walked away.

"Kananbaum spoke to me," I said.

"Did he?"

"He asked me if I was aware of what you'd written in your diary."

"That's very interesting," she said. "I'd say that's interesting and relevant."

"What did you write?" I asked.

"A lot of things. But I am guessing he's alluding to the part where I said you'd like to fuck him."

"You *what?* You wrote that I want to fuck him?"

"I didn't say it in those words. What I said was that you and I were still so very grateful to be in his class and that we often talk about him and that you've recently been suggesting that we ask him to have us both over for dinner. I said that you were too shy to ask, but as for me, I'm not so shy, and I knew any such invitation he might make would always stay between the three of us, regardless of what happened, and that ever since his cute little wife left him he has probably been starved for company. Or I said something along those lines. You get the gist of it."

I said, "You're absolutely crazy."

"No, I'm not," Alison said, and I was thinking that suddenly she looked not so much like Angie Dickinson as the Snow Queen in that very weird children's fairy tale.

"Why are you doing this?" I asked.

"Being enemies is a job," said Alison. "And as O'Brien explains to Winston, while he's torturing him, the object of persecution is persecution. The object of power is, you know, power."

I said, "You've gotten ahead on the reading."

"It will be fun," Alison said. "The best part is we'll get away with it. No way he'd tell because we'd ruin him. A single man who teaches high school English and pays child support doesn't really have the option of getting fired. Turn to the dark side again, Green. I know you like it."

"You're an orc," I said.

She screwed her eyes up and said, "Interesting comment."

I said, "I'm done with this, and you."

Alison shrugged. Her wavy hair blew across her face, and as she moved it away she said, "I set it up for Saturday at six. Gave him a date and a time. I made it easy. I said to tell you no directly if that was his answer. Did Mr. Kananbaum tell you no?"

I was stumped. I said, "I have no clue what drug you're on or what you're asking."

She said, "In class, when he gave you back your diary. I assumed that's why he gave it to you last. So did he tell you no or what?"

I shook my head.

"Well, there you go," Alison said, and I could feel the part of me that was chaotic, though I could not yet tell whether this was chaotic good or evil. "I know what I'm doing that night, anyway," said Alison. "Whether you're there or not, it's going to be some fun. Then four more weeks of class, whoopee. Hard to know what he'll have us do with *A Clockwork Orange*."

"You really think we'd get away with it?"

"Did Bored Girl Genius just utter the word *we*?"

I walked away from her. I was shaking. I went and found my shitty car and punched the steering wheel and screamed. When I got home that day I discovered acceptance letters from Yale, Brown, UCLA, and Colgate. My own four letters. I thought, Jackpot. Then I went up to my room and cried. It didn't seem to me that Alison's proposal could be happening. It didn't seem to me that Alison could be this much of a mastermind. Nor did it seem to me that Mr. Kananbaum could be this much of a patsy. Still, I allowed myself, just for the moment, to consider it. Would it be worth it, one more time, to feel so reckless, to feel such power?

VI. Kananbaum o Kananbaum

On May 11, I wrote: *Because you will never read this I can say anything. I can say yes, I've thought about it. It would be interesting to see how you'd behave if Alison and I enacted your wild fantasies. I think you'd want us to be mean. That's what would thrill you at first. Meanness the way Alison can do it. Then you'd want me. You'd want more vision and more depth. Maybe you'd want me to tell you a hundred stories, one of which might approximate the single actual story of the Five Hundred Jewish Men. Maybe you'd want me to describe it, how I'll save them, how I'll save you. How I could shoot you and then save you. How I could shoot you but still know how I was saving you, that I did not aim to kill, that when you fell into the trench with the other men, you would be able to crawl out. What should we do, Mr. Bruce Kananbaum? Me on my knees? Alison standing on a table with your face inside her crotch? She'll make you beg. You know she will. And then she'll ask you. She'll say, Which one of us? She'll say, Who do you really want?*

VII. In the end I am a leopard, maybe

Now that I think about the whole thing, it was ludicrous. Me thinking I could stop it. Me even thinking that I knew what was going on. All week in class I watched his eyes, watched him avoiding mine and Alison's. Watched him allowing me to say nothing. Watched him allowing Alison to groan and cackle. Watched him pretending that Peter Stamey's diary entries were intelligent and that whatever people said about the torture scenes with Winston was insightful. Watched as he shook his head and summed the novel up as a "dark vision that hits eerily close to home" and concluded by saying, "Maybe it's 1984 and always will be." When the bell rang after Friday's class, I walked out into the hallway, stood there a moment, then went back in. The room was empty. I shut the door and said, "Don't do it."

"Don't do what?" Kananbaum said.

I took a breath before I answered.

"It," I said.

He took his glasses off and wiped them on his sleeve. He put them on again and said, "Jennifer, I have no plans to fail you. I have the sense that this trimester has been a difficult time for you. I am aware that you did not enjoy reading *1984*. I plan to give you an A, not that you need it. As for what Alison wrote, I spoke to her. She said you talked and that the two of you patched things up."

I shook my head and I said, "Really, Mr. Kananbaum. Don't do it."

He smiled quizzically. He said, "Jennifer, is everything all right?"

"Everything's *fine*," I said.

"Then what is it that you're trying to discuss with me?"

I said, "I'm trying to discuss Alison and myself."

"Have you two spoken, as she claims?"

I told him, "Yes!"

"Then would you like to share anything else?"

I was confused. Something was off. Either Kananbaum was playing it straight or Kananbaum was clueless.

I said, "I'd like to share that Alison is crazy."

"She's a bit wild," said Mr. Kananbaum. "It's true."

I said, "I don't know what she wrote in her diary. Will you please tell me?"

"I thought you talked."

I said, "We did. She didn't tell me what she wrote."

"Really," he said.

I told him, "Really."

"Alison wrote that you were angry with me," said Kananbaum. "She also wrote that you had plans to destroy my mailbox."

"And you believed her?"

He said, "It wouldn't be the first time that you vandalized someone's mailbox."

"And about Saturday?" I continued. "As in tomorrow? Tomorrow evening?"

Kananbaum stared at me, confused. Except he looked confused in the way a guilty person looks when he gets caught. His mouth opened to speak. No words came out.

I said, "Don't do it."

He said, "Do what?"

I said, "Big Brother is watching you."

Kananbaum smiled and then was able to collect himself.

He said, "Don't you have AP Spanish with Mr. Gregory right now?"

It was remarkable. The man still believed he had me fooled.

Saturday morning I ate Cheerios and watched MTV with Rocky. Saturday afternoon my mother went to her boyfriend David's in Piscataway. I knew she'd call at some point, and that, as always, she'd leave a message saying to call if we wanted her or needed her at home. If we didn't call, she'd return very early the next morning. In all the time she'd been dating David, we'd never called.

Saturday evening, I drove Rocky to her friend's house. Then I drove home, sat in my dying 1971 Subaru, which several years before, my mother purchased for a few hundred dollars and had fixed up by a mechanic she was friends with, so that I'd have a car to drive when I got my license. I'd briefly wondered why she hadn't just bought me a Honda Civic or some cheap car that was new and likely to last more than a few years. Then I'd stopped wondering because I understood that there were certain things about my mother that I would never figure out.

But what I *had* figured out was the thing that Alison Belle, my enemy, had concocted. In certain ways, she truly was a mastermind. Somehow she'd seen that, one way or another, I would show up. I wondered if she still believed that I might go for it. Appear at Kananbaum's door in slutty clothing. Then wouldn't Kananbaum be surprised? And what would I have felt when I got there? Would I have run away in shame when Mr. Kananbaum asked me why I was standing on his doorstep in a miniskirt? Or would I wing it, make it work? Would I ally myself with Alison and discover what unfathomable things might happen?

I played the radio in my driveway. I heard Van Halen and Phil Collins. I went to AM and listened to an inning of a ballgame. I waited until eight. Then I drove over to Mr. Kananbaum's small ranch house. Alison's red Chevy Cavalier Type-10 was parked right in his driveway. All as expected except that I had thought she'd be less brazen. I had expected that she'd at least park out on the street.

The house was dark. Kananbaum's car, a green Toyota, was next to Alison's. I sat there idling by the curb, looking for movement in the bedroom. I saw none. Then I got out with my ancient baseball bat, still saved from Bat Day at Shea sometime in 1973. The bat had an engraved autograph, *Ed Kranepool*, who, according to my father, had been a productive member of the team. I took my biggest swing at Mr. Kananbaum's cheap mailbox. It didn't make all that much noise, but the dent was large enough. No light went on. I drove away.

When I got back home, I called out-of-state information and was able to find Derek Hottel's number. It wasn't hard. There were no other people named Hottel in the town of St. Clairsville, Ohio. I thought I'd probably just hang up, but Derek answered on one ring. I said, "Hello, Derek," and told him who it was. Derek said, "Whoa."

"Whoa what?" I said.

"Whoa, as in you're not a person I expected to be hearing from in this lifetime," Derek said.

"Why did you get so mad?" I asked.

"I didn't get mad. I got even."

"Even for what? For not allowing you to do it without a condom? I would have let you if you had a fucking condom."

"I'm bad with condoms," he said. "I lose my focus."

"You were a virgin."

"Not anymore."

"So was it really just about the condom?"

He said, "No."

I said, "Then what was it about?"

"No one can touch you," he said. "No one can get anywhere near you."

"And what the hell do you mean by that?"

He said, "One look at you and a guy like me says, 'Wow. There's a hot babe. Not only that, this girl has clearly got a thing or two to say. The girl's no puppy dog. Girl looks more like a leopard.'"

"And what's your point?"

He said, "The thing is, when I'm with you I don't get it. Everything's fine. Your life is fine. The world is fine. But you keep acting as if everything's a disaster. As if the world is about to end. Like it's all a big mess, you know, when it's just fine."

I said, "It isn't fine."

"You see? That's what I mean."

"What if I drove there right now, to Ohio? It would take maybe eight hours. I could be there before you woke up in the morning. What would you do?"

He said, "I'd cheer."

"That's good to know."

"But I doubt your car would even make it as far as Allentown, Pennsylvania."

"My car or me?"

He said, "That's tricky." Then he said, "Both."

"You're not so nice yourself," I said.

"At least I'm honest."

"Then tell me honestly. What do you think of Alison?"

"Alison who?" Derek said.

"Belle."

"Oh, Psycho Kitty. That is one seriously messed-up girl."

"Is she a leopard?"

He said, "No."

"But I'm a leopard."

He said, "You're starting to sound desperate."

"What if I am desperate?" I asked.

"It's a long time coming."

"What do I do?"

He said, "Stop trying to save the world."

"You're full of wisdom," I said.

"That's why you liked me in the first place."

"Why did you like me?"

He said, "I don't really know."

That was about enough of Derek Hottel for a while. For a good long while, I thought, though speaking to him had been useful. I said good-bye to him and thanked him for his time and called my father. When he picked up, I said, "I got into UCLA. I'm coming out there. I want to stay with you in July."

He said, "Go west, young woman!"

I said, "Hey, Dad. Don't be a superficial asshole."

He said, "I'm thrilled, Jennifer. Really. But you should think a little harder before you go and turn down Yale."

"How did you know I got into Yale?"

"You'd get in anywhere."

It was probably the best thing he could say. Our conversations were never long, so I said good-bye before he could beat me to it. Then I went upstairs and waited for my mother's call from Piscataway. On this occasion, when she called to check, I asked her to come home.

It was ten-thirty when she walked in, demure as ever. She wore a thin cotton sweater and black jeans. I wondered if she'd just had sex. The world of sex was still a thing I had not experienced, and it upset me, just a little, to think that for my mother sex was such a regular occurrence. But this was not a thing I planned to ask her about, ever.

Instead I yelled out what I had been waiting to ask her for the last two months. I yelled, "Mom, tell me the story of the five hundred Jewish men!" She looked surprised and I said, "I read all the letters. I even copied them in a diary, word for word. I'm not weird. I'm just confused. Why did you suddenly start to look for him?"

She put her bag down, hung her keys up on the key hook. She said, "I got the urge, that's all. Sometime this winter I was remembering my father. For many years, since I was a little girl, I've known that story."

"*What* story?" I said. "And why haven't you ever told us?"

She said, "I didn't think it would concern you."

I said, "I'm eighteen years old. I want to know something about the world you came from. I want to know more than the names of a few people you wrote letters to."

"That world is ruined," my mother said.

"Then resurrect it for ten minutes!"

She said, "There is no resurrection there. Just ruin."

VIII. *Five hundred Jewish men*

This was the story my mother told me. It was not much different than what I had inferred from reading her four letters, but it relieved me just to hear it, brief as it was.

In the midst of the mass executions that were taking place in the summer of 1941 in Kovno, just before the Jews were to be relocated to a newly established ghetto, a special program was announced for which five hundred Jewish men would be selected. A college degree was necessary. All applicants were required to speak two of the three languages Russian, Lithuanian, and German. Those who were chosen were to be given paid positions as researchers in the city archive. It seemed a way to avoid the persecution, so all the best and brightest Jews in the city hoped to be selected. The competition was fierce, so anyone who was owed any kind of favor did what he could to cash it in. The men were doctors, lawyers, teachers, scholars, poets, architects, engineers, philosophers. Along with my grandfather Jonah, my aunt Doris and her husband, Pinchas, were also refugees in Kovno. Both my grandfather and uncle Pinchas had been secondary school teachers in Warsaw. They spoke fluent German, and they had picked up enough Lithuanian to get by. They had applied under false names, with forged documents, in hopes of passing themselves off as Lithuanian. When they received their two letters of acceptance, they celebrated as if it were a miracle.

They made a plan to wait out the violence. They had forged

contacts with an underground resistance group. They believed that after this burst of violence, things would grow stable, and that when the time came they would flee to the woods and try to make their way south, through the Ukraine, to Odessa, where they would try to gain passage to Palestine. On the appointed day, the five hundred men gathered in Kovno and awaited their instructions. Soon they were marched out to one of the nineteenth-century Russian forts that surrounded the city. Then all five hundred of these Jewish intellectuals had been shot.

But as the story went, two escaped. There was no description of how they did it, my mother said. Just the belief that two of these five hundred did not die. That they were hiding somewhere safely and that when the war ended it would be discovered who they were. It was a fairy tale, she said, after she told me. None of those five hundred men was ever seen again.

When she was finished, she said, "Jennifer, come upstairs." It was late. I went up with her to her bedroom. From a place I'd somehow missed, she removed a locket, opened it up, and showed me a picture of her father. His hair was dark and he was smiling. She said, "That's him. I don't have anything more to show you."

"But are you sure?" I asked my mother.

"Sure about what?"

"That he died."

She said, "The story is sentimental. As my father himself would have said, *Drek ahf a shpendel*. But people want to believe these things. Sometimes it helps if you can keep your ghosts alive."

"Is he a ghost for you?"

"Yes."

"Are you still looking?"

She said, "No."

"Why do you keep the letters?"

"You can have them."

Then she walked over to her drawer. She took the letters out. She placed them into my hands and asked, "What else is wrong?"

I said, "A lot."

"Such as?"

I said, "A lot but at the same time it's not anything. Just stupid high school stuff with teachers and, of course, Alison. I think I'm trying to avoid falling apart. I want to go away, to California, and live with Dad. I want to go to UCLA next fall."

She said, "That's fine, if he's okay with it."

I said, "He is. We spoke tonight. I need a change, but it's me, not you. So just don't disappear, okay?"

She said okay. I mumbled, "Thanks." Then she reached out and moved some hair off of my face and touched my cheek. "I'll be right here," my mother said, but I could feel her moving through me. I could feel my mother running across those beet fields. Bad men were after her but soon they would be torn apart by dogs.

5

Little Wolf

THIS ACCORDING TO Novalis: "The greatest magician would be the one who would cast over himself a spell so complete that he would take his own phantasmagorias as autonomous appearances. Would not this be our case?"

I recognize that we are all magicians in some way. We are complicit in all we see and comprehend that what we see will never coincide with absolute reality.

As a result, the human brain must make a narrative. This I can say with certainty, and yet each narrative we choose will reach a point at which it no longer suffices. One narrative must inevitably be abandoned for another. In this way, any narrative sequence defers meaning, even beyond the point at which it appears to end.

— — —

Now, to set this down. I recognized her just as soon as she removed her head scarf and her sunglasses. How could I not? I had briefly been part of the Movement in the sixties, though what had happened was that my involvement lasted only as long as it took me to complete an extended trip to San Francisco in early spring of 1969 and fall deeply in love with a woman who while performing as a puppeteer referred to herself as Midnight although while puppetless, which was not often, went by the name of Katie and yet preferred, it seemed to me, that I did not say her name at all. I stayed with her and her fellow guerrilla puppeteers for two months, partook in the free love that was part of this time and place, but even in a situation such as one in which I fondly recall hours of entwinement with both her and a lithe, curvaceous brunette called Marybeth Faith Angelina, the thing I wished for and looked forward to were my moments alone with Katie in our tent at night, in which we caressed and talked in a vast way that I will not go on about for fear that I will soon begin to sound like a romantic poet. I myself had begun to learn the art of puppeteering but was no good because I was not capable of the seeming simultaneity required in the flux between puppet master and puppet. Either I thought too hard and then the puppet, for all its apparent movement and my dexterity, would seem inanimate and flaccid, or else I didn't think enough and the result was that I could not control the puppet. Meanwhile Katie would perform with any one of her seven puppets, and the manner in which she pulled the strings always seemed effortless, sublime. I thought that I would learn from her, that I myself could achieve such gracefulness and fluidity, but then one day she announced to me abruptly that she was leaving her seven puppets behind, was in fact leaving that very afternoon for Florence, Italy, with a rich man she had met the week before. As quick as that, and without sentiment, she was gone, and shortly after that I was gone as well.

How do I explain this aspect of my story? My story was that I changed stories. I lost all interest in puppeteering, scoffed at the talent I did not possess regarding puppets in the first place, and went so far as to decide that I had no interest whatsoever in the liberal causes with which I'd aligned myself, despite being a second-generation Greek American whose father built a home in the hills of northern California and believed that this country was indeed the promised land. Suddenly I did not care about Vietnam or any of the U.S.-sponsored acts of global persecution. Suddenly, I wanted out of everything right or wrong.

I had majored in biology at USC. In May of 1969 I applied to medical school. I spent the ensuing years becoming a neurologist and then ultimately a neuroscientist, and fifteen years later I'm standing in my lab in Palo Alto, California, I am standing right in the middle of the eighties, in May of 1984 to be precise, and she appears again, Katie aka Midnight, who by now I know is Katherine Clay Goldman, and who was neither puppeteer nor radical nor any of the various things she told me, though as for what she is, even now I cannot say.

She knew of my work—my studies of the physical human body's mantle of electromagnetic energy, as well as my work with "preparation sets," distinctive patterns of brain waves that exist for every mechanical gesture or position a body takes. She knew of my more far-fetched ideas, which ranged from electromagnetic field effects that suggest the possibility of extradimensional space, as well as my speculation regarding an electromagnetic basis for what the indigenous Alaskan Koyukon people know as "Distant Time" and the Australian Aboriginal people call "Dream Time," both of which are thought to be extradimensional locuses accessible in altered mind states, including but not limited to dreams. She knew of my popular lay essay, published in *Smithsonian*, on "rapid-eye-movement art," the notion that an individual both actively and through access to some collective sea of energetic impulse creates dreams as we would any work of art. Perhaps this made up for my ineptitude with regard to puppeteering, but conversation regarding my scientific inquiries did not go on nearly as long as I would have liked it to, as what she wanted from me was far simpler, in many ways, than any of the topics I have mentioned. Far simpler on my end, anyway, although that which she was dealing with was anything but simple. In any event, I will now attempt to describe the events that took place during the interval of time in which I briefly renewed contact with a woman who had, for fifteen years, all theoretical models or clever assertions about REM sleep notwithstanding, haunted my dreams.

— — —

As she explained to me before I saw him, she was traveling with a twenty-one-year-old boy who'd been in coma for two months. To be exact, he'd been in coma sixty-three days. In early March of that year he'd crashed a motorcycle at high speed and had not been wearing a protective helmet. In her opinion, however, his was not an ordinary coma.

For one thing, she said, the boy had not gone into a vegetative state. Usually coma will last several days to several weeks, and only rarely more than five weeks. Within this time frame, victims can be expected to emerge gradually to consciousness, progress to a vegetative state, or die. But she claimed that the boy still had his eyes closed, that his limbs moved from time to time, that he would murmur an occasional unintelligible phrase, all of which were indicative of coma and not a vegetative state. Was there another thing? I asked, and she said there was. She wished to bring the boy into my lab. She said that after I examined him, she would explain.

She waited until darkness, at which point she wheeled him in. For reasons that were not clear at that moment, she provided me with certain details of his history. She mentioned that the crash had occurred in Israel, that he'd been transported back to his home in Utah, and that his older sister, who lived in Florida, had recently paid a visit. She explained that she herself had taken the boy from his family because his family was tied in with a ritual cult whose members included a wealthy oil magnate, several attorneys, two state officials, one former CIA operative, as well as a lot of run-of-the-mill lunatics.

What she wanted from me, first, was that I perform an electroencephalograph, or EEG. In other words, what she wanted was a measurement of his brain wave activity. I complied with her request, performed the EEG, and was surprised to find that his EM brain function was consistently in the range of 2 to 5 hertz. I expected his EM field intensity to be in the range of 6 to 20 hertz, based on the literature I had read as well as data from certain scientific inquiries of my own. It seemed that this atypically low brain wave frequency was what had enabled him to remain in coma rather than a vegetative state. Given the severity of his head trauma, it seemed probable that this was what had enabled him to stay alive in the first place.

Katie Goldman, however, did not appear to be surprised at all by this finding. She asked me whether I was familiar with the studies that had been published on calcium efflux events, through which an efflux or release of calcium ions can be induced in brain tissue with microwaves of a certain frequency, thereby interfering with normal brain chemistry and inducing confusion in the subject. I said I was. She asked me whether I was also familiar with the experiments that had shown that inducing lower than normal brain wave frequency could cause the opposite: a decrease in the normal levels of calcium efflux and thus a subject whose brain chemistry operated at levels of far greater potential and efficiency than normal. I said I was, although what I had read was inconclusive. She asked me whether his low EEG would suggest that calcium efflux events in his brain chemistry were continually lower than normal, and I told her that I had no idea nor the equipment to determine if they were.

Then she asked me if I had encountered literature on the phenomenon of multiple personality disorder. I said I hadn't read anything more than a textbook description in an abnormal psych class back in the sixties, that I had seen *The Three Faces of Eve* and found the movie schlocky, and that from what I understood multiple personality disorder was at best a controversial subject, not recognized as its own disorder in the 1982 revision of the *Diagnostic and Statistical Manual of Mental Disorders* and not something you'd want to research before being granted tenure. At worst, it was thought to be outright fiction.

And what did I think? she asked. My answer was that, intuitively speaking, I regarded multiple personality disorder to be a plausible phenomenon but was sufficiently uninformed about the topic as not to be able to say much more than this. Then she produced from her bag a letter that she claimed had been written by the older sister of the comatose boy and which, if nothing else, she believed would enable me to intuit what I will describe here, in my own words, as the mechanics of multiple personality disorder as a product of ritualistic programming by means of intentional inducement of extreme trauma states in young children, something analogous in certain ways to the Chinese methods of brainwashing prisoners during the Korean War but more pervasive because in dealing with young children, including infants, the substrate is a far less differentiated neuronal network. I read the letter, which was horrific and yet logical, given what I knew of neurophysiological development and differentiation.

— — —

I want to note here, as I read over these notations, that I do not always speak this way. In fact, I do not believe I ever speak this way, but when notating a case study, this is the narrative voice that of its own accord seems to emerge.

— — —

I gave Katie back the letter. I looked at the boy in the wheelchair, who had just kicked twice with one leg at nothing. I made the obvious inference that he, being the sibling of the letter's author, had been programmed in a similar manner. Before I could reflect for very long on this, however, Katie asked me something that pertained to a certain psychopharmacological anomaly about which she should not have had the faintest inkling, as there was no official research on the topic. All that existed were my own findings, about which I had been warned by both the FDA and some higher-ups in the federal government. I had been warned that all research in this area must be discontinued and that these findings were not to be made public. What I had observed was that some property intrinsic to a certain highly controlled sleeping pill, referred to in even the most classified FDA literature only as ZH, appeared to counteract the neurochemical gamma-aminobutyric acid, known as GABA, which, being a natural depressant, takes hold of brain cells in coma patients and shuts down brain functions in order to conserve energy and help brain cells to survive. The almost inconceivable result of ZH, however, is that it seems to break the hold of GABA and enable coma patients, for brief periods, usually ranging between forty and sixty minutes, to wake up. What Katie asked me was did I have in my possession any sample of the sleeping pill known as ZH, and if so, did I know what the correct dosage would be for a roughly 110-pound boy who'd been in coma for two months?

— — —

Am I the narrator of this story? I ask this as a narrator, but much like puppetry, the flux of narrative is such that I can simply say *presto!* and now you can see me standing in a room with Katie Goldman, who will undoubtedly soon vanish once again, and as I attempt to listen to what she says, all I can think are things like how can such a beautiful, tall woman hide so well, how is it that I feel as if she's always been right here, why does it seem that almost no time at all has passed since I shared a tent with her and discussed monologues for the puppet she called Jaguar God and the puppet she called the Centaur Pinocchio and the small, cute wolf puppet Loopdy Lupe, which in my mind has now merged with the small, cute wolf mascot Vučko from the recent Winter Olympic Games in Sarajevo, in which no repeat of the "Miracle on Ice" was to occur, no great sport narrative other than, it seemed to me, as I watched it on ABC, the constant reappearance in the form of Vučko of Loopdy Lupe, who in our puppet shows would, at a certain point, metamorphose into another, much larger wolf puppet called Big Bad.

If I am remembering correctly, the other finalists in the contest held to decide the mascot for the Winter Olympic Games in Sarajevo were a chipmunk, a lamb, a mountain goat, a porcupine, and a snowball. Do not ask me to explain why I would construe this as something relevant enough to include in this narrative. Nor should you ask me when the sleeping pill ZH will become available to the public or whether it seems like a good idea or a bad one to be able to wake coma and/or vegetative patients for periods of forty to sixty minutes, especially given that the sedative nature of the sleeping pill requires that the dose be given intermittently and sparingly lest the patient die from an overdose of sleeping pills. What I suspect is that ZH in some form or another will be discovered somewhere else and, as is the case with so many things, we in the almighty U.S.A. will unveil that we discovered it years ago once it is clear that there is a substantial profit to be made in the pharmaceutical industry. As this is the year 1984, we have been inundated with references to the 1949 novel of the same title, as well as articles and commentary on the Orwellian notion of *thoughtcrime*, not to mention the constant "Big Brother is watching you" refrain. What I will suggest is that the world is both very far from and very near to the fictional 1984 and one's relative position within this spectrum is a function of geography as well as the depths of understanding you choose to occupy. It is quite possible that I am guilty of what would be considered thoughtcrime, though perhaps not in these words, by one or another malevolent reader, possibly a member of the FDA, or a member of the aforementioned cult that the boy in coma's parents are allegedly a part of, or simply one who finds it wrong that I did not call the police the moment Katie Goldman took off her head scarf, though it is unlikely that such objections will be raised at present because of my intention of deferring the transmission of this information. The maverick scientist Wilhelm Reich invented what he called the orgone machine in the thirties as well as other machines that were thought to harness the primordial energy of the universe. Reich's work was discredited to such an extent that he left orders in his will to seal up all his writings and have them kept under lock and key for fifty years after his death as a means of safeguarding all that he'd discovered until such time when, optimistically speaking, our society would be ready to embrace them. As Wilhelm Reich died in 1957, while in prison, no less, it still remains to be seen whether the world's opinion of his work will be revised. I do not claim to be an innovator such as Reich, but I suspect that the world in 2007 will resemble the Orwellian dystopia to a greater extent than it will resemble whatever Wilhelm Reich may have envisioned. Here I have noticed that I am rambling, and perhaps it is simply my intention to sustain the presence of Katie Goldman for as long as is reasonably possible by protracting and augmenting this notation, which in retrospect I fear will not be believed whenever it so happens that it is read.

— — —

We woke the boy. I crushed up two tablets of the sleeping pill ZH, mixed it with water, and then watched as Katie administered the solution, taking care to make sure that he had swallowed after each teaspoon. Within a span of seven minutes, the gray pallor of his face disappeared and his cheeks flushed. Another ten minutes passed and his eyes opened. Then immediately the boy began to scream.

This I was not prepared for. The boy screamed, and the screaming was so loud that I turned the stereo in my office on at full blast, something I never do, and Katie sat beside him, stroking his face and squeezing his hand and trying to calm him down, but he kept screaming, endlessly screaming, for, by my watch, forty-seven minutes. Finally the effect of the ZH began to wane and then the screaming transitioned into a softer moan, and then, after fifty-three minutes, he was gone again, back inside his coma. I did another EEG and the same low-frequency brain waves presented themselves. I explained to Katie that in the six other instances in which I had administered ZH to coma patients, each of them afflicted with varying degrees of brain damage, none had screamed and in fact five out of six had smiled or laughed. All six had spoken, though in each case speech was impaired as a result of sustained brain damage, but all six had exhibited signs of knowing who they were and what had happened. I said the screaming, more than it was frightening, was to me incomprehensible. Then she said, "Zeno," which was my name as a puppeteer, "let me explain."

What she explained was that I had just witnessed one of the multiple personalities that lived inside the dormant boy. She said that these were not really personalities. Rather, they were "parts," and each part had been created to hold, as described in the letter from his sister, a particular horror that he had experienced. While the horrors themselves were perpetrated, on one hand, as both an exercise in the wielding of sadistic power and the enactment of sociopathic compulsion, what was inflicted was also a systematic means of inducing what Katie, from this point onward, would refer to as multiplicity. Most of the perpetrators, though not all, had been abused through a similar program as young children, and there were silent parts in each that carried on the legacy that enabled them to pass the training protocol down through the generations. Katie suggested that there was much, much more to say about the metaphysical nature of abuse, but that the relevant issue pertaining to Dillon Morley—this was the first time she had uttered the boy's name—was that she believed a part had been created at the moment of his injury, that whether this injury was accidental or an intended act of suicide, a part of the boy was holding what should have been, in a normal person, death.

——— ——— ———

By what mechanism could such a thing be possible? By the mechanism described in the sister's letter? By the mechanism described by Katie Goldman? By the enigma of life and its origins? By a freak of nature or by the hand of God? This much said, all that I have written here is either reiteration or speculation. There was no way for me to confirm Katie's supposition, no way for her, perhaps, to confirm it either. Many people have told me that even when I am speaking in my normal voice I seem faraway and sometimes like an automaton, and probably they are correct that I look for mechanisms, logic, and design more than I look for things like love or a good restaurant. I don't know what to say to this nor what to say about the fact that my notation, with all its wanderings, does not address my emotional response to the boy in coma or the ghastly origin of his current situation. Perhaps I believe that sentiment clouds reason. What I can say is that the boy, even while screaming, possessed what I would describe as strength.

She could release him, Katie said. She could release him from this limbo. When I asked how, all she would say was that there were ways to integrate the screaming part that we'd awoken. She said this part could be integrated into a group of other parts. Once it was integrated, however, she could not be sure which way the boy would go. Possibly the part would release death into the body. Possibly the continued life inside the body would override the death that was being held (and in which case, it occurred to me, though I did not say so, the boy might simply proceed to a less atypical coma). But what she needed from me, if possible, was enough ZH to wake the boy again. If possible, she would need to wake him several times. I gave her what I had, three vials' worth. It was illegal for me to use, and I did not foresee that I would have need for the pills again. She slipped the vials into her pocket, and at that moment I thought again of Loopdy Lupe but decided that a remembered wolf puppet and its coincidental correspondence to a recent Olympic Games mascot would be a ludicrous thing to mention.

Instead I asked her if I could kiss her. Katie smiled at me. She said, "Zeno. That's very sweet." Then, with the boy sitting beside us in his wheelchair, she placed her palms on both my cheeks. She pressed her lips to mine and this was not a soft kiss. Nothing about her was soft, but still I did not expect her to kiss me in the way she did. There is no point in describing the contortions of our lips and tongues or our breath and bodies, other than to say, as I have said before, that time seemed to protract, as it does in stories. Time seemed to move forward and back or else it was gone entirely because stories, though they appear to unfold in time, are really spatial things, which means you can go anywhere you want. For instance, with sufficient time or with sufficient imagination I could recall for you the future of Dillon Morley, though such a thing would be at least as ludicrous as any extension of my discussion of the similarities between the Olympic mascot Vučko and the puppet Loopdy Lupe.

Perhaps more relevant, I can recall a time when the puppeteer known as Midnight brought out Big Bad and began growling. This was the way she always began his monologues, but then strangely, before speaking a Big Bad word, she stepped behind the hanging tapestry that served as her backdrop, abandoned Big Bad, and abruptly reappeared with Loopdy Lupe. I can recall this moment in a puppet show in Golden Gate Park on a cool spring afternoon when Marybeth Faith Angelina stood beside me with her arm around my shoulder and Loopdy Lupe was saying all of us are part of a big story. It is a story that is much bigger than we know. Do not confuse the life you live with the story, says Loopdy Lupe. Do not be afraid to leave the story. You may get scared sometimes because you fail to understand that what is scared is not you. It's the story. The story looks for a way to travel. The story is afraid you will let it go.

6

The Ocean

Early that summer, Dara and I were sitting on the rocky, volcanic tip of Yawzi Point. We were out there spying on Dara's mother, who was diving with a graduate student, Charles, on a reef that was a hundred feet below us. Charles had his own research, on gorgonian sea fans, but he sometimes helped professors gather data. Dara thought Charles and her mother might be having an affair.

She asked me whether my father ever dated his students. "Sometimes," I said, "although that was before he met Beverly."

"Were they voluptuous?" she asked.

I said that one was.

"My mother says older men like younger women to be voluptuous."

I said, "They weren't all voluptuous," and then the sky rumbled with thunder. The rain came in over the bay, changing the color of the water from turquoise to dark blue. Dara yelled, "Mangos!" and we ran back to the grove.

There were some students from the School for Field Studies playing volleyball in the rainstorm. Two boys and a girl were wildly soaping up their hair so they could wash it. As the rain fell we waited by a mango tree. Picking the mangos was forbidden because everything in that part of St. John was national park land. Nothing could be disturbed. That meant the mangos, iguanas, conches, and all the coral on the reef. But we found ways around the rules—ways such as rainstorms that knocked mangos from the mango tree. I glanced at Dara. She smiled mischievously. I tried winking but could never really do this. It always looked more like both of my eyes were squinting. "Whoops," Dara said, and hit a tree limb with her shoulder. "Oops," I said, and shook it. We used our dripping wet shirts as pouches to hold the mangos and quickly took them to Dara's bungalow.

I was thirteen. Dara was fourteen. She was from Utah and she knew how to get a moray eel to eat out of her hand. Her mother was doing research on the territoriality of damselfish. She was tenured at a university in Salt Lake City. Like my father, she was teaching marine biology at the School for Field Studies that summer. Unlike my father, she wasn't in remission from leukemia.

Dara had blond hair that the Caribbean sun turned white. I loved the way her face looked underwater. Her eyes would seem very expressive, but with her mouth around her regulator, she smiled in a way that my father said was "languid." I also liked the way she would point to barracudas and then nervously give me the okay sign. Dara was constantly giving me the okay sign underwater.

Once, we buddy-breathed at fifty feet, and that night Dara said that it was almost like we had been kissing underwater. On another dive we landed on a stingray. When our fins touched on the seafloor, the sand moved and we both kicked up as a giant stingray flapped away. Dara turned quickly and gave me the okay sign. I took my underwater slate, wrote "Holy fuck!" and held it before her eyes. She smiled and wrote "Holy fucking fuck!" on her slate. I was about to write "Holy fucking fucking fuck" when Dara swam up close and pressed her mask to mine. For a few seconds we stared with our eyes an inch apart. Then Dara pulled her head back and gave me the okay sign.

— — —

The soldier crabs always traveled in the moonlight. From Dara's bungalow we could hear them—a loud *whooshing* that sounded more like wind than crabs. We were on Dara's bed, playing

Mastermind, the only game other than Chutes and Ladders that we could find in the recreation hut. Across the room, her mother was sitting on her bed with Charles, playing gin rummy, and eating the stolen mangos. Charles was talking about himself, as usual, going on about all the exotic places he had lived. He made a joke that I assumed was Monty Python because he said it with a funny British accent. I didn't hear the joke since Dara kept on whispering things like "Charles is such an asshole." Then Charles took a cigarette out and lit it, maybe because he knew that Dara and I would leave.

Outside we caught two soldier crabs, which was easy, though this obviously went against park rules. We took the crabs to my bungalow, but my father was there, sitting at his small desk with a pile of slates. "Professor Kahn, what are you doing?" Dara asked him. He told Dara he was grading the underwater identification quiz he'd given to his students that afternoon. He said that no one had correctly identified the tunicate *Ascidia nigra,* which is a black piece of slime that lives on rocks. My father often pointed it out while we were snorkeling. He liked informing people that *Ascidia nigra* was, evolutionarily, our closest existent relative on the reef.

My father's hair had grown back after he had been bald for three months, from chemotherapy. He'd grown a beard for the first time and it made him look like Grizzly Adams. He said, "Ten points if you can tell me the taxonomic classification for those land crabs?" Dara guessed *Uca,* which was wrong. That was the fiddler crab. I said, "It's *Coenobita clypeatus.*" He said, "Ten points! Now please go set Mr. and Mrs. Clypeatus free."

The crabs had ducked inside their borrowed whelk shells. We took them back to the woods behind Dara's bungalow, where Dara's mother and Charles were still playing gin rummy. Charles was telling another joke, and I was thinking about Monty Python's Flying Circus. "It's my mist-aaaake!" I sang to Dara, but she had no idea what I was referring to. "That's Monty Python," I said.

"One of their gag lines." Dara had never even heard of Monty Python.

We took turns lying down and letting Mr. and Mrs. Clypeatus walk around on our backs and stomachs. This got us both all sandy, so we decided to go swimming in the bay called Little Lameshur. It's pronounced *la-muh-shoor* and we sometimes liked to joke about this name. I'd say, "You sure?" and Dara would say, "Lameshur."

At the beach we took our shirts off. I wondered whether Dara would also take her bra off. I wondered why she wore a bra at all. We heard hooves clomping and we turned in time to see the herd of feral donkeys. In the moonlight they seemed like phantom creatures. They trotted into the eucalyptus forest behind the road.

I told Dara that my father thought the donkeys could be studied by a biologist who was interested in the behavioral ecology of equids. They had harem groups, I explained, which meant the males had groups of females that they either guarded territory for or fought for.

Dara said, "Hey, you know, there's an opening at the college where my mother works. My mom's on the committee doing searches. Maybe your father could apply."

"What's the course load?"

This was a question that my father would have asked.

"I don't know," Dara said. "All I know is that they've been searching since last fall."

"He might apply," I said, "although he likes his job at Rutgers. He'd also have to make sure that he was better."

"Better than who?" she asked.

I hadn't told her yet about my father's illness.

I said, "Just better. He had leukemia last winter."

She pressed her balled-up shirt against her chin and seemed embarrassed.

"He doesn't seem sick," she said.

"Right now he's not. He was treated with chemotherapy."

Dara said, "Oh," and stopped talking about the job opening in Utah. That always happened when I mentioned my father's illness. People stopped talking.

I said, "He's been in remission ever since last winter."

Dara nodded.

I told her, "People don't always die from it."

Dara said, "Oh."

"Should we go swimming?"

She dropped her shirt in the sand and took her bra off. I could tell she was still thinking about my father, which was too bad since I'd been thinking that I wanted to try and kiss her. I knew it wasn't the right time, and so I waited. "It's my mist-aaaake!" I sang again, but Dara clearly wasn't the type who enjoyed Monty Python humor. She looked at me as if I was insane.

It was low tide and part of Little Lameshur was a sandbar. We had to walk out a good distance before we got to water that was deep enough to swim. I took her hand while we were walking. She seemed okay with it. "I found a sand dollar here," she said, "but it disintegrated." I said, "That always happens with sand dollars." I considered this our first official conversation while holding hands.

We both dove in when we got to chest-high water. After we swam around a bit, I got the nerve up to ask Dara if I could kiss her. She said yes, so I slid my arms around her waist. "Are you all right?" she asked, because I'd started shivering. "A little cold," I said. Our lips touched. Dara tasted like salt water. "Do that again," she said. I did. "A little harder, please," she said, and I leaned forward, my hands pressing on her shoulders. We continued kissing for a while and then just hugged as we stood there in the ocean. I started noticing other things. A rising half-moon and all around us stars reflecting in the blue-black surface of the water. Over Dara's shoulder I could see the darker water where the reef was. There were no boats, no other islands, no other light except the moon. I was afraid for a few seconds, and then I wasn't. When we were back on the beach, kissing again, I wondered what I'd been so scared of.

— — —

On the Fourth of July, my father took me snorkeling in the mangroves, which smell disgusting—like very rotten eggs. But the mangrove swamp functions like a nursery. It's where all sorts of juvenile creatures live before they're big enough to survive out on the reef. My father said he had seen lemon sharks and nurse sharks the size of lobsters. He had seen lobsters that were only slightly bigger than his thumb. While we were walking there, I told him about the job opening in Utah. I said I didn't know the course load but that Dara's mom could probably pull strings for him. I said that Utah might be nicer than Piscataway, where we lived, that there'd be ski mountains nearby and maybe lots of beautiful blond people like Dara and her mother. My father said he had no plans to change jobs right now and certainly no plans ever to live in Utah.

"What's wrong with Utah?" I asked.

We had stopped walking because we'd reached the mangroves. He seemed flustered and said, "Nothing's wrong with Utah. Except it's far away and right now it's the last..."

He put both hands on his head, the same way football coaches do when their kicker misses an easy field goal.

"It's the last what?"

"The last thing I have time to think about," he said.

"Why?"

He took his hands down and said, "Jordan, we need to talk about some things. Let's take our snorkel and then we'll have a conversation."

Once we were actually swimming in the mangroves, I stopped noticing the sulfury rotten egg smell. Swimming was tricky because the roots made an underwater maze. They were encrusted with assortments of algae, sponges, anemones, and barnacles. Schools of young reef fish swam around them. We also saw some tiny crabs and lobsters, but no sharks. Each time I picked up my head and looked around, I was reminded that we were swimming under a forest. Above the water the mangrove roots made giant chairlike shapes that you could sit on. After we snorkeled for a while, we climbed up onto one to have our conversation.

He began by mentioning that a few months ago he wasn't even sure if he'd be well enough to teach a class this summer. Did I understand that his health was still a thing he had to be concerned about? I said I did. After that he started talking about Beverly, his girlfriend. She'd be arriving on St. John in about three weeks. He said he wanted to discuss something hypothetical. "About Beverly?" I asked, and he said yes, it had to do with Beverly. Then he asked whether, in the event that his illness recurred and he was not able to get better, it would be okay if Beverly adopted me.

"If you were dead, you mean?" I asked.

"That's what I mean," my father said.

He'd been with Beverly three years, ever since we moved from Rhode Island to New Jersey. She was a pediatrician who had two daughters but was divorced. I'd been to her house in East Brunswick a few times and I liked Rocky, her younger daughter, who was in the same grade as me. Her older daughter, Jennifer, always seemed angry and I hadn't ever talked to her.

I said, "I guess it would be fine."

"I'm glad to hear that," he said. "Beverly loves you."

We had our masks on our heads and our fins rested against the long roots of the mangrove. My father's beard was all wet. It had a gray patch that reminded me of coral. His wavy, sun-bleached hair was all bunched up and sticking above his mask. This also reminded me of coral.

"Hey, Jordo," he said. "I'd like to tell you something about your mother."

"That would be great," I said, though I felt nervous. My mother died when I was six, when she was driving home from a supermarket in Providence. She had been hit by someone going the wrong way on the highway's off-ramp. Whenever Dad talked about Mom, it made me anxious and I sometimes didn't sleep well. She was a dancer and she'd opened her own dance school. After she died I sometimes lay in bed for hours and hours, picturing her dancing.

He said, "I once brought her down here for the summer. That was in 1964, when I first began studying long-spined urchins."

I said, "They're black. *Diadema antillarum*."

He said, "That's right. But I'm not talking about sea urchins."

I said, "You're talking about Mom."

"Right."

I said, "So what do you want to tell me?"

He said, "Your mother and I, we once sat right here in these mangroves."

"This exact tree?"

He said, "Maybe."

"It would be neat if it was actually this tree."

He said, "It might have been." He looked at me. "Your mother and I were young and very happy. We were just sitting in these mangroves."

"You mean this tree?"

"I just mean *here*."

I said, "Okay," and nodded, trying to act like I was getting what he was saying. Then I said, "Dad, can I ask a question?"

"Yes."

"Do you think you *will* die?"

He said, "It's possible."

"But you said people survive leukemia."

"Some people do," he said. "More often, it comes back."

"You don't seem sick anymore," I said. "Not like when you were doing chemotherapy."

He said, "Jordan, do you remember why I brought you with me to St. John?"

"Because you thought it might be your last summer?"

He said, "That's right."

"I hope it's not."

"Me too," he said.

The breeze picked up and the surface of the swamp began to ripple. A lone pelican swam in through the entrance to the mangroves, and in a low voice my father said, "The ocean." He and I sometimes said this to each other. It was a code, although we'd never really said what it was code for. I nodded and watched the pelican. For a short while we sat in silence. Then we jumped back into the smelly water and kept looking for juvenile sharks.

— — —

On a moonless night, Dara and I walked out to Yawzi Point. A hundred years before, a colony of lepers had been living there. The donkeys always seemed to hang around the unmarked graveyard that had recently been discovered by archaeologists. As we walked past the spot, we saw the donkeys, but even though we were talking loudly, they didn't run.

Charles had left the island that morning. He had a wedding to attend in New Hampshire. He didn't know when he'd return, so Dara thought we should celebrate the remote possibility of never having to see his weaselly face again. She'd brought a bottle of Cruzan Rum, which she had stolen from Matt Daniels, a student in her mother's reef ecology class. Matt had twelve bottles, which he'd purchased when a group of students went into Cruz Bay for July Fourth. He'd stashed them out in the woods behind his bungalow. I worried about stealing, but Dara said it would be fine. We could always blackmail him, she said. Students could be sent home if a professor caught them with liquor.

We passed the bottle back and forth, and after three or four gulps I felt like I was floating. Dara took another sip and started gagging. I thought she was going to throw up.

When she stopped gagging, she said, "I'm drunk, Jordan. Are you?"

I said, "I think so."

"Close your eyes," she said. "You'll know."

I closed my eyes and the world was spinning. I said, "I'm definitely drunk."

Dara said, "Thought so. You're a lightweight."

She pulled my shirt up. I kept my eyes closed and everything stayed spinning. She started kissing me on my chest. Her touch felt cold with all the wind. She started licking me and then she started biting me. I said, "Stop."

"Stop what?" she said.

"Stop biting me."

Dara said, "Why? You taste so good."

My eyes were open. I said, "I don't really like when people bite me."

She started laughing and said, "You're strange."

After that she kissed me without biting me. I closed my eyes again. The world still spun, and I felt like I could spin to anything I wanted.

Later, in the bungalow, I woke up yelling after a nightmare about lepers. In the nightmare, my mother had been turned into a leper. My father woke, and I told him I'd been dreaming about Mom.

He grabbed the windup clock beside his bed and held it to his eyes. "It's almost two," he said. "How do you feel about going down to Big Lameshur for a night dive? We could be back here by four and sleep for a few more hours."

I said, "Okay," and asked him if we could use Cyalume sticks. They have a liquid inside that glows fluorescent green when you hit them. He said we'd wear them on our weight belts.

We only went down thirty feet, but even at that depth we saw things that you usually can't see during the day. A spotted moray was moving along the bottom. A queen angelfish seemed to be resting in the space beneath a head of brain coral. Its eyes were open but the angelfish wasn't moving. It was as if it was just sitting in the water. Then as we swam around the head of coral, I saw a shark-shaped shadow lying on the seafloor. My father shined his underwater light on it. A nurse shark. Full grown. It was yellowish brown, with spots. It had two dorsal fins and barbels hanging from its nostrils, like a catfish. I knew that nurse sharks weren't aggressive, but I was panicking and I pointed to the surface. My father gave me the okay sign, took my arm, and we started our ascent.

One of the Seven Rules of Diving was "Go up slowly." "Stop, think, then act" was another. We went up slowly, but I definitely didn't think before I acted. When we broke through the water's surface, I started kicking madly with my flippers. I didn't stop until I reached the shallow water by the dock. When Dad caught up, I was crouching in the water.

"It was a nurse shark," he said. "They aren't dangerous."

I said, "I know."

He said, "Then what were you afraid of?"

"It was so big."

He said, "You swam with manatees in Florida. They're much bigger."

I told him, "Manatees aren't sharks."

He crouched next to me. A damselfish was nipping at my ankle. My father liked to tell his students that the damselfish were by far the most aggressive fish on the reef.

He said, "You know, I've swum with mako sharks and tiger sharks in Australia. I've seen hammerheads and bull sharks. I once swam right through fifty or more blue sharks that had gathered near a sandbar in Bermuda. Even the great white shark I saw in the South Seas left me alone."

"Weren't you ever scared?" I asked.

He shook his head and said, "Whenever I'm in the water, I feel safe."

"Why do you feel so safe?" I asked.

"Because I'm part of it. I'm just another creature in the ocean."

We climbed up onto the dock, took off our tanks and our BCs, and sat there calming down and listening to the water. The knot inside my stomach slowly came loose, and in the faint light I looked out toward the spot where we'd been diving. The funny thing was that I'd always wanted to see a nurse shark.

— — —

I made a necklace for Dara. It was a Cyalume stick on a piece of string. The night she wore it we walked out to the sugar-mill ruins to see Sammy, the old mongoose who lived under the foundation. She wore it backwards. When I let Dara walk ahead of me, all I could see was the greenish-yellow glow.

We drank the rum again that night, but we got caught. Dara's mom smelled it on her breath when she got back to the bungalow. She slapped her face, Dara said—twice. At breakfast she tried to show me how her cheeks were red. I couldn't see any marks. She said her mother had slapped so hard that her bottom lip had started bleeding. She pulled her lip down to show me where the cut was.

Before classes that morning, Dara, me, her mom, and my dad had a talk. My father didn't yell but Dara's mother did. I worried she'd slap my face, but she just yelled a lot. We promised not to drink any more rum. Then we all sat there. Both of our parents were drinking coffee. They started talking about their work in marine biology. After a while they let us leave, but they still sat there. At lunch that day they sat together, all alone at the end of the long table.

That afternoon the four of us went snorkeling on the reef below Yawzi Point. Throughout that summer, my father had been searching for the emerald green St. Thomas false coral, *Rhodactis sanctithomae.* He had a theory that *Rhodactis* could kill corals and anemones with its tentacles. Then the *Rhodactis* could expand and take up more space on the reef. He had told Dara's mom about his theory and she was interested, so our goal that afternoon was to take data on *Rhodactis.* We found eleven different patches, and all but two bordered on dead coral or dead anemones.

Our parents sat together during dinner. I sat with Dara at a different table, and she told me that our parents would soon be having an affair. I said I doubted it since my father had a girlfriend and was in remission from leukemia. Dara said no, I was wrong. She said her mother understood how to make men want her.

— — —

We spied on them from Yawzi Point when they went back to map the patches of *Rhodactis.* From that vantage, a hundred feet above, it was strange to think the two of them were down there, thirty or forty feet underwater. Of course, we knew they weren't doing anything sexual underwater. But still it seemed like they were having an affair.

That night I asked my dad if he was falling in love with Dara's mother, whose name was Julia. He said he wasn't. I said they seemed like a nice couple. He said he was already a nice couple with Beverly.

I said, "I saw you in the water. Dara and me were at Yawzi Point."

"We were just diving," he said. "We're going to be co-authors on a study of *Rhodactis.*"

"But it was your idea first."

He said, "She's helping me. She's published a lot. Julia's also very, very smart."

"She's also mean," I said. "The other night, when she caught Dara, she slapped her face so hard her lip was bleeding."

"She's a good scientist," he said.

"You think it's all right to give Dara a bloody lip?"

"She didn't mean to," he said. "She told me she felt guilty."

"So does she know you were sick?"

He said, "I told her."

I was trying to hate Julia, but I couldn't. For one thing, she looked a lot like Dara. For another, she was making my dad feel good. They sat together at every meal and always talked about *Rhodactis*. They started leading dives together with their two classes.

One afternoon they took a group of students to a reef in Europa Bay. Dara and I got to go. We had to go there in the skiffs, and as usual, Dara and I were dive buddies. It was the deepest dive we took that summer. According to my father's depth gauge, we were down seventy-two feet. The water was much darker and there wasn't as much reef to see. In certain places we swam between giant rocks that rose alongside us like walls. Dara was nervous, I could tell, maybe because we kept seeing barracudas. She kept on looking at me and always stayed right next to me. She was so close that we could just make the okay sign with our eyes.

As we were coming out from between those massive rocks we saw a sea turtle. Dara stopped swimming for a second. Then we were holding hands and swimming toward this gigantic creature. It had a polished black-and-caramel-colored shell and a curved beak. It swam away very fast, flapping its legs like it was flying. Later that night, lying in bed, I kept imagining us holding hands and following the turtle.

——— —— ——

They were screwing, Dara said. And it was possible. I'd seen my father telephone Beverly after dinner, like he always did. Then he and Julia had vanished. We checked the bungalows and every one of the classrooms. They weren't anywhere.

I said, "They might be just sitting on the beach somewhere. They could be talking about *Rhodactis*."

"My mom's a slut," Dara said. She walked away from me and bent down on the volleyball court. She was picking up a stone. She said, "My mother will screw anyone she can."

"What does your father say?" I asked.

"He does it too. It's not such a good marriage."

She kept on picking up stones and throwing them through the volleyball net. I heard them hitting the ground somewhere on the other side.

"Let's get a mango," I said.

"Sometimes I hate my mother's guts."

"She doesn't seem so bad," I said.

"Do you hate your father?"

I said, "No."

Dara stared at me, as if it was so strange that I liked my father.

I said, "How come your parents aren't seeing a therapist?"

"It wouldn't help much."

"How do you know?"

She said, "I know."

"My dad and his girlfriend, Beverly, see a therapist. They started going when he got sick."

"My parents aren't sick," said Dara. "Their only problem is that they're idiots."

"But still a therapist could help them with their marriage—"

"Just leave me alone!" she yelled. "You stupid boy."

She walked away and went into her bungalow.

I yelled, "You're weird!" but followed after her. There were no locks on the doors, so I walked right in. Dara was sitting on the foot of her bed, her arms crossed, looking as if she was in pain.

I said, "Let's not talk any more about our parents."

She said, "You're right, I'm weird like you. I'm also angry."

"At who?"

"What?"

"Who are you angry at? You just said that you're angry."

"God, you're so dense," Dara said. She took my arm and pulled me down so I was sitting right beside her. I tried to kiss her, but she suddenly started crying. I asked, "What's wrong?" and she said, "My life." I asked her what was so bad about her life. She said her boyfriend Kyle had dumped her for an anorexic cheerleader. She said her father had spent the last six months in Texas and that her parents had been talking about getting a divorce. She said her mother wanted to leave Utah and go somewhere extremely far away, such as Australia. She said my father shouldn't apply for the job in Utah because even if he'd never had leukemia, her mother wouldn't pull strings for him or anyone.

When she stopped crying we went outside. It was dusk. We walked for a long time—past Little Lameshur, and all the way down the path that led to Europa Bay. I'd never been to Europa Bay, except by boat, and was surprised that its beach was so unlike the sandy coastline by Big and Little Lameshur. The surf was rougher and the beach was densely covered with bits of coral and rocks and shells and sea urchin tests and other dried-out reef things. We walked along it, holding hands, and I saw something very big, another shark shadow, lying ahead of us on the rocks. A jolt went through my chest, and my first instinct was to run. "Oh, that poor dolphin," Dara said, and I felt calmer for some reason when I realized that it wasn't a dead shark.

"PU, it stinks," Dara said, as we went closer.

Its dorsal fin was sticking up and looking rotted. Insects were flying all around it. It had probably been lying there for days. Dara picked up a piece of branch coral and threw it into the choppy water. I found some driftwood and poked the dolphin's tail with it.

"Everything's dead here," Dara said.

— — —

Beverly arrived on St. John during the last week of July. She planned to stay through August. To my surprise, Dara adored her.

She liked to sit near Beverly at meals. One night she told me, "Beverly's strong. I want to be her." Beverly was strong, in fact. And she was big. She was five foot nine, though she looked taller. She had broad shoulders, strong arms, and a full chest, all of which made Dara's mom look shrimpy.

Two days after Beverly arrived, she had a loud fight with my father. They screamed and yelled, like they sometimes did. She called my father irresponsible and pathetic. She called Dara's mother "the blond bitch." Everyone heard them, since the bungalows had screen windows. After the fight they didn't talk for half a day and I thought Beverly might leave.

But then they sat together during dinner. Dara's mother wasn't there. Neither was Dara. I later found out that they went in to Cruz Bay to go shopping and eat dinner at a restaurant. Dara told me that her mother had started crying during dinner and that she drank so many piña coladas that afterward she threw up behind the taxi stand. For a few days, I barely saw Dara's mother. She avoided Beverly and my father, and sometimes walked the other way when she saw me. But the fight blew over. Beverly hadn't left St. John. Julia started coming to meals again and no longer walked away from me or anyone. One evening at dinner, she sat down across from Beverly and my father. They chatted like old pals, and in the days that followed, they sat together at every meal. "Adults are strange," Dara said on a night the three of them had gone to Little Lameshur for a night dive.

"Maybe my father and your mother never slept together," I suggested.

She shook her head and said, "They did."

I said, "You're positive?"

She said, "My mother spews out everything when she's drunk."

Beverly, Julia, and my father started to go out diving during the afternoons to look for more *Rhodactis*. Sometimes Dara and

I went with them, and one afternoon my father got a nosebleed underwater. I didn't know why he'd gone up until I got back to the boat. He had his head tipped back and Beverly was pressing a bloody T-shirt against his nose.

After two more nosebleeds the next day, he decided he should stop diving for a while. He said he needed to heal his nasal vessels. Almost incredibly, Julia and Beverly continued going out, the two of them, in search of more patches of *Rhodactis*. "Adults are strange" became Dara's recurring comment about everything.

At night they'd all sit in the classroom and go over the new data. Dara called this their "*Rhodactis* ménage à trois." Once we snuck up to the window and crouched there listening for incriminating evidence. We heard them talk about their data. We heard them talk about the poor campaigning tactics of Walter Mondale. We heard my father ask a riddle. What did one vulture say to the other? He told the answer — "Carry on" — and then Julia asked my father how he was feeling. He said, "Not bad. So far there isn't any reason to leave the island."

A few days later, I caught my father holding hands with Julia. I'd gone to look for him in his classroom after his students had come out. When I walked in I saw them standing with their hands clasped. They pulled their hands apart but didn't seem concerned that I had caught them. I considered telling Dara, but I decided not to risk making her angry. Dara was in a good mood that day. She'd gone out snorkeling in Big Lameshur by herself, although you technically should always have a buddy. She had discovered a small inlet full of fanworms, which look like colorful fans or feathers and stick out of the little holes they bore in coral. If you touch them, fanworms instantly pull their feathers in. After five minutes or so, they'll put them out again.

Later that afternoon, Dara took me out to her secret inlet. We snorkeled over the fanworms, and we kept diving down to make them pull their feathers in. One type of fanworm looks just like a tiny Christmas tree. I started thinking about Christmas and wondered whether or not my father would be alive then. That he could die was still a thing that seemed impossible, but I suspected that I should, at least, imagine it. I also had a thought that didn't make much sense but still seemed logical. I thought that somehow, in the ocean, we stay connected to everything that's dead.

It was a very hot day and very muggy. We both swam back behind some rocks in the small cove, where it was shallow. Dara unzipped her shorty wetsuit and peeled it down to her waist. She had a bathing suit underneath and slid the straps down off her shoulders. The suit was white and almost see-through and it looked sexy. She said, "Hey, big boy," and pulled her bathing suit down too.

We took our masks and fins and all our clothes off. We piled everything up on one big rock. There was another rock that was even bigger, so we lay down on it and listened to that soft noise you can only hear when you're lying naked on giant rocks in a calm inlet beside an ocean.

For a long time we didn't speak. Then I said, "Sometimes I wish that we were older."

I thought that Dara would say, "Me too," but she said nothing. She took my hand and kissed me on the knuckles.

I said, "I think we're in love, don't you?"

She kissed my hand again but did not speak.

"If we were older we could run away and live on some island just like this one."

Dara sat up after that, breathed deeply, and said, "Please don't make me cry."

"I wasn't trying to."

She kissed me and said, "You always act so serious."

I said, "I'm serious and brooding. My mother used to say that I was *sullen*."

Dara just smiled and said, "Fine, so we're in love a little, maybe.

But I live in stupid Utah. And I don't plan to move to any islands. Don't get too mushy on me, okay?"

I said, "Okay."

After dinner that night there was a movie, but it was still so hot that Dara and I decided we would skip it and go swimming. I went to the bungalow for a flashlight. My dad and Beverly were there, standing between my bed and theirs and passionately kissing. I quickly took two steps backwards and snuck away.

We went out swimming off the dock at Big Lameshur. We swam too close to a shallow reef and I hit fire coral. It stung me all over my left arm and chest. It didn't hurt that much at first, though this was probably because I was in the water. When I told Dara, she touched the welt but couldn't see it in the dark. "Feels like a nice one," she said. "I guess you really pissed that patch of coral off." Once we were back on the dock, she pulled a flashlight from our pile of towels and clothes and said, "Okay, let's see the damage." She shined the light onto my chest and her first words were "Holy fucking fuck."

It was late when I got back to the bungalow. My father and Beverly were sleeping on twin beds they'd pushed together. I wasn't sure who to wake, but I woke Beverly because she was a doctor. I showed her the big welt and whispered, "Fire coral." She took one look and slid out of bed.

She brought me over to the School for Field Studies infirmary. When she turned the light on, the welt look scary. It was all blistery and red and not like any injury that I had ever seen. She washed it off and rubbed some cream on it. She said the welt on my chest would hurt for a few days, but that the one on my arm wasn't so bad.

Before we left the bright light of the infirmary, I looked at Beverly and figured I should say something. I said, "Dad told me that if he dies you're going to adopt me."

She pursed her lips like she often did. She said, "I'd like to."

I said, "I'm glad."

Beverly smiled. Somehow her smile was full of happiness and sadness, both at once.

I said, "So how do you think he is?"

"I've seen him better."

"I think he's happy now," I said. "He likes the research he's been doing on *Rhodactis*."

Beverly nodded to me, cautiously. She said, "Yes, I think he's enjoyed the summer."

"Things are okay then?" I asked.

"Right now they're fine. But I still need you to do me a big favor."

"What?" I asked.

She said, "The thing is, I need you to get ready. Things may change soon."

I said, "How soon?"

Beverly stared at me. Her eyes were aqua blue.

"I don't know. That's why I need you to get ready."

"Ready for what?"

She said, "Your father hasn't been completely well. He's very tired. There are other symptoms."

"Of leukemia?"

She said, "Jordan."

"What?"

"Your father's going to be sick again."

She slid her hands under my arms and picked me up off the table where I was sitting. This amazed me. Beverly picked me up no problem, like I was five. She set me down on my feet and crouched so that our eyes were exactly level. She said, "This year might be very, very hard."

"I should get ready."

"That's right."

"How?"

"You'll need to talk to him," she said. "You can also talk to me."

She wrapped her arms around my shoulders. She didn't say anything else, but she kept holding me. And though it hurt my chest a little, due to the fire coral, I stayed there. No one had ever held me like that. Even my mother didn't hold me. She just danced.

— — —

The next morning I woke at first light to the sound of braying donkeys. One of them stood right outside, looking at me through the screen. "Someone please kill that thing," said Beverly. I had to pee, so I went outside and shooed him. He took two steps back and proceeded to bray his head off once again.

I felt awake, and so I told my dad and Beverly I was going to walk down to Little Lameshur. Dad mumbled, "Fine," though he was already half-asleep again. It must have been about six o'clock, but the sun seemed hot, so I wore my tank top. I wandered out toward Little Lameshur and decided to walk the path to Yawzi Point.

It was the first time I'd been out there without Dara. I went as far as I could and sat down on a rock that jutted out above the reef. The fire coral welt on my chest still burned and I took my top off so the cool breeze would soothe it. A group of pelicans swam below me. They were fishing around the reef, and every now and then one of them would dive under. They sometimes twisted their necks so far that when they surfaced they would be swimming in the opposite direction. I watched one tilt back its head to swallow a fish that was still alive and flapping inside its throat pouch.

Two other pelicans crashed down and joined the others. I thought about the talk I'd had with Beverly, and somehow watching this group of pelicans seemed to be a way of getting ready. So did looking at the turquoise surface of the water. So did imagining everything beneath it. All of the trumpetfish and damselfish and angelfish. The spotted moray eels and sea cucumbers and stingrays and barracudas. Ten feet beneath the water's surface, there were sea sponges in every different color you could imagine. There were bright yellow and pink anemones and the emerald green false coral *Rhodactis*. The more I thought, the more I realized I could go on and on and on with all the things that lived inside the ocean.

Another pelican smashed into the water, and then I noticed a place where I could climb down. It was a steep slope, formed by rockslides, and one stretch was almost vertical. When I got down, I wondered what I had been thinking. I wasn't going to be able to climb back up.

So I leapt onto a big rock with a plan of swimming to the sandy beach in Little Lameshur. Beyond the rock there was a cavern of deep water. I dove in. Without a mask, everything was blurry. I kept my eyes open, and I could see vague shapes that were coral mounds and sponge formations ten or fifteen feet below me. It was slow going with my sneakers, but I kept swimming out to where it was too deep to see the bottom. I knew that nurse sharks and lemon sharks might be swimming underneath me. For all I knew a great white shark was down there, but I kept holding my breath and kicking through the water, now and then looking up to see where the group of pelicans had gone.

7

Shadow

In a secret part of my life I have served, unofficially, as the archivist for everything that Beverly Rabinowitz has ever given to me, including poems, drawings, photographs, and transcripts of her dreams. Why I do this, I cannot say. I grew up with Beverly in Brooklyn. When we were children, I would make fun of her by telling her that her American name meant "near the meadow where the beavers live." Possibly, this was because I was jealous since my own American name, Miriam, is thought to mean "sea of bitterness" and sounded virtually the same as it did before my parents found a way to send my older brother, Simon, and me across the Atlantic Ocean by boat in 1937, after the Nuremberg Laws, but still more than two years before the siege on Gdańsk started the war. I was five in 1937. Simon was eight. We lived near Kraków, and then we lived in Crown Heights with our aunt Malka and uncle Fishel, who'd immigrated before the First World War. In 1938 my parents and grandfather joined us, and as a result we all escaped, as my *zayde* used to say, not having quite mastered this idiomatic expression, "by our skins and teeth." Beverly arrived in Brooklyn in late 1940 with her mother. In Poland their names had been Bejla, which means "beautiful," and Chana, which means "grace," though I preferred to focus on the silliness of "near the meadow where the beavers live."

She and her family had fled Poland to Lithuania. From there she and her mother had journeyed over half the world. First a train across Siberia; second a steamer from Vladivostok, Russia, to Tsuruga, Japan; third a train from Tsuruga to Kobe, Japan;

and then, after weeks of pounding on the doors of consulates in Kobe, Tokyo, and Yokohama, they succeeded in obtaining visas to the United States. They had been lucky, even blessed to get those visas, as many Polish-Jewish refugees would spend the next four to five years living in a squalid ghetto in Japanese-occupied Shanghai. Bejla and Chana boarded a boat in Kobe. After the trip across the ocean, they spent two weeks in October of 1940 at Angel Island, an immigration station that had been set up at a military outpost off the coast of San Francisco. During their time there they decided — having heard someone on the boat speak fervently, if inaccurately, about the need to choose American names if they wished not to be turned back — that they would call themselves Beverly and Hanna. Eventually they reached San Francisco, where they were met by representatives from the state department, who interviewed them and delayed them, until Beverly's mother was able to get in touch with a second cousin of hers, Isaac, who interceded. He lied and said that Beverly's mother was his sister. He explained that they were to come to live with him in Brooklyn, which was true, and with the help of the Hebrew Immigrant Aid Society, he was able to support them.

When Beverly and I played together, we often went up on the rooftop. Beverly would call me Queen Miriam and I called her my princess. I was two years older than she, which made me queen, though on occasion I would allow her to be queen, although the rule under these circumstances was that she would be called Queen Bejla and I was to be called Princess Mirela, which was the name that both my father and my *zayde,* who was his father, always called me and the name that I loved best. Simon was, of course, in love with her. Everyone was in love with Beverly, but no one ever got very far and this has been true for her whole life. She was always introverted, distant, and for Simon, it is sad to say, unapproachable. I blame myself, at least in part. When she was seven and I was nine and he was twelve, I once invited him to come up on the roof and play with us. I became Princess Mirela and I called him King Szymon, and he didn't know what to say to his Queen Bejla. He did his usual thing, joked like a nudnik. He said things like "I am the king who is also secretly a poodle." Then he began to bark. Poor Simon. I should have told him that she missed her father. Maybe if he had this context. Maybe he would have thought, I must be helpful to this girl who has lost her father. Maybe if *I* had known how much she missed her father, they would be married today, Beverly and Simon.

She was nine when she told me about her shadow dream. She described it to me one afternoon up on the rooftop, and later, I don't know why, I wrote it down. For me this was the beginning of my vocation. For Beverly it was just a confusing dream. What she had dreamed was that she had awoken in the small room she shared with her two cousins Ruth and Dinah, who were asleep. They shared a mattress with no box spring. Beverly dreamed that she had woken and tried to step around their sleeping bodies. She'd accidentally stepped on Dinah's leg but did not feel it, and this frightened her. She tried to shake the sleeping girls, but soon she realized that her hand was passing through their bodies. It was as if she had turned into a shadow. She left the room, went down the hall. She did the same thing with her mother. She tried to wake her but no longer had a body. That was her dream.

"How very interesting," I had said, and I pretended to be Freud although much later I would understand that my temperament and proclivities were in alignment with Carl Jung. "How very interesting," I said. "This dream of yours. Now you will pay me twenty American dollars." I had been trying to make a joke, but she wasn't laughing.

I wrote the dream down that night, and when I saw her next, I told her I was sorry I had laughed about it. She said, "Oh, Mirela, there's nothing to be sorry for." I said, "I have an interpretation," and she smiled at me, her patient smile. I cleared my throat and then suggested that the shadow was a symbol of a fear of not belonging, which was natural to someone who'd been born in another country. She said, "That's smart of you. You're *so* smart." I asked her what she had dreamed last night. Beverly smiled again, although this time it was her silly-me smile. She said she'd dreamed about her uncle's dogs and her rural village outside of Warsaw. She proceeded to describe the dream in detail. I wrote the dog dream down as well, and after that we stopped playing queen and princess. Instead she told me about her dreams.

One day, as a joke, she said she'd dreamed of seven cows, and I was so used to her earnestness that it took me a few seconds to catch on. When I did, I said, "This dream of yours. The cows. Did any one of them look like my brother, Simon?" She said, "The truth is, Mirela, I dreamed again that I turned into a shadow."

A few weeks after that she wrote a poem entitled "Shadow," which she gave to me. I think this was what began our tacit contract under which I would be the keeper of whatever she decided to entrust to me. I think I did it because I loved her, though I suspected I did it also because I wanted myself to matter, to be the confidante of none other than Beverly Rabinowitz. Those were the two sides of it. I sensed it then, when we were the two brightest girls at the Yeshiva of Flatbush, and by the time we had become two of just a handful of Brooklyn teenagers at Ramaz, a private Jewish school in Manhattan, I understood that both were true. Like I've said, everyone I knew was in love with Beverly. Boys, girls, teachers, rabbis, janitors, people who passed by her on the street all seemed to love her. We both took babysitting jobs and would run errands to pay for school clothes and the subway. Those who employed us always preferred Beverly. She didn't notice this and would tell me it was my imagination. But she kept giving me her poems. One day she gave me a charcoal sketch in which the sky is gray and the earth is black and two big blurry dogs are streaking across a field. I asked her what the sketch was called and she said,

"Shadow." Eventually I began to put all of these items into a box that I labeled BEVERLY RABINOWITZ on one side and QUEEN BEJLA on the other. By then it was becoming clear to me that the difference in our ages no longer mattered. Beverly was the queen and I had become the princess.

I graduated from Ramaz a year ahead of her, and after that I did not see Beverly as often as I wished. But when we met, she would shout "Mirela!" the moment she laid eyes on me. Now there were three, I would think. Three in the world who called me Mirela. Then *Zayde* died of congestive heart failure and once again there were two.

I went to Brooklyn College and Beverly went to Barnard on full scholarship. During the years that ensued she sometimes wrote me letters, and not only would she tell me about dreams, she would describe her life as a college student and her confusion about her purpose in the world. In one letter, she wrote: *I think of the white storks, the bocian. There was a pair who built their twig nest on our roof and my father told me the white stork was a sign of luck. I'd hear the clattering of their bills. I'd go outside and look up, just to see that they were there. I'd see their bills, which are bright red, and when I heard them from my bedroom, I'd think that this was a special clattering, made only by the bright red bill of a mating stork. We thought they'd come again next spring, but by then we had gone to Lithuania. I think of those storks now and they seem like something that was real. And how excited my father was about them. In many ways what I'm doing here, in my whole life after leaving Poland, does not seem real.*

Still she got straight As and went to medical school. I began to see that she was like her father, Yonah, or at least like what everybody *said* about her father. She had a gift that could seem enchanted. Whatever you might do with great effort, she seemed to do without any effort at all. She would become a doctor, but she could have been a lawyer or a scientist or an engineer. She could make time stand on its head, my *zayde* used to say. But there was always the ennui, always the distance, always the sad and queenly poise that could be mistaken for a sense of superiority. And always the quiet boys who were filled with longing. There was once a boy called Reuben who loved her so much that he could no longer see things when she stepped into the room. He became a *tzaddik* and dedicated his life to studying the Talmud, and in this way (he once confided to me, years later), he taught himself not to think of her.

Once my youngest child was in school, I began my years of training to become a Jungian psychoanalyst, and for at least two decades I did not see Beverly at all. During this time, among other things, I learned about the shadow self. Within Jungian psycho-analytic framework, it is common to say that someone who seems kind may have a very violent shadow self. Likewise, a violent or sadistic person's shadow may be very kind. Jung emphasized the importance of integrating destructive aspects of the shadow self into one's consciousness, lest these shadow aspects be projected onto others or denied. He claimed that *projection, denial,* and *integration* represent three of the four primary ways people respond to the reality of the shadow. The fourth primary way is *transmutation.* Naturally, I thought of Beverly's dreams about the shadow, about the archetypes rising out from the psychic reservoir that Jung referred to as the human collective unconscious. I wrote a letter to her once, in response to a dream she sent about a tall shadowy woman she was following down a trail through the tall oaks in the ancient forests near Białystok in Poland. I wrote: *The shadow is an unconscious complex that Carl Jung defined as the repressed and suppressed aspects of the conscious self. He claimed that the shadow self will appear in dreams as a dark figure of the same gender as the dreamer. If I were your analyst, I would ask you if this shadow woman seems destructive. If so, perhaps she represents something you do not wish to know about yourself. On the other hand, if she seems constructive, perhaps she represents a secret purpose, a part of you that can help the world.*

She wrote back: *You are a very gifted thinker, but I don't want you to be my analyst. I only want you to be my witness because I worry that one day something unexpected will occur. I don't know if this occurrence will be constructive or destructive, but I would like it, with your help, Mirela, to seem real.*

Gradually, her letters to me grew more infrequent. Sometime when we were both in our late thirties, they stopped completely. This was toward the end of the time during which Beverly was involved with her short-lived husband, Richard, a flunky who she once described as "a gifted actor with no actual talent" and another time as "a man who would not allow himself to be rescued." Their story was confusing. They had a daughter, got divorced, and then they had a second daughter. She wrote to tell of the birth of her second daughter, and shortly after that she wrote to say that she had dreamed of a forest filled with trees that were laced together by a meshwork of dark, shadowy netting that could only be seen if you wore special glasses, though to all insects this dark netting glowed bright blue.

It was more than ten years later, in the fall of 1984, that our relationship was renewed. She lived in East Brunswick, New Jersey. She and Richard were long divorced. She would soon turn fifty and I was fifty-two. I was married to my husband of twenty-nine years and the youngest of my three children, my little soccer star, Aaron, was in twelfth grade. My oldest son, Tobias, was in his second year of law school. My daughter, Libby, was in her junior year of college. We lived in Suffern, New York, and I commuted into Manhattan three days a week. I shared an office on West 76th Street with another analyst. I also worked one day a week from home.

I ran into her accidentally on the Upper West Side, where she had been to the Museum of Natural History with her daughter Roxanne and a boy named Jordan, who I took at first to be her daughter's boyfriend. I was out walking in Central Park. I saw her holding her daughter's hand while the boy, Jordan, who was talking and gesticulating, walked beside them. I called out, "Beverly, is it you?" When she looked up she recognized my face immediately. "My Princess Mirela!" she exclaimed. Then we went into a café and ate a quick lunch with the two thirteen-year-old children. We exchanged kisses and set another date to meet.

Only two weeks later she came again into New York, this time alone. We found a restaurant near my office. We exchanged chit-chat. I had been giving her the rundown on my three children when I saw that she was smiling in a way that expressed something more like sadness. I asked her what was wrong. She said, "Oh, Mirela. I think there's a *klipe* that has burrowed its way inside me." I asked her what she meant. She shook her head and did not really answer the question. She said, "Sometimes I catch a glimpse of a thing beyond all this, a world where the things I see don't seem broken." I said, "A *klipe?*" and she laughed. She said, "I'm being hyperbolic. Or maybe not. I don't know how I got so tired."

Klipe is Yiddish for a husk or shell that has encased a spark of holiness, imprisoning its light and beauty. *Klipe* can also be a sort of demon or evil spirit. Either way, she was still talking about a shadow. But as my thoughts raced to the metaphysical, through all the Jungian constructs regarding shadows and far beyond, to the ways in which I might finally be of help to her, years later, more than I had while I was spewing off textbook theories, more than I'd helped her during those afternoons on a Brooklyn rooftop long ago, she said, "Oh, Mirela, the man I love is dying."

Then she began to tell me of her boyfriend, a marine biologist named David, who had been diagnosed with leukemia. She explained that Jordan, the boy I'd met, was David's son and that she soon would become Jordan's adoptive mother. She said that David had gone through treatment a year ago, was in remission for almost nine months, but since late August had relapsed and seemed to have reached a point of no return. I took her hand and I listened as she told me about David. She seemed to love this man a lot, more than what I ever would have thought possible. She described him as a cuddly bear of a man whose wife died years ago and who'd spent much of his adult life studying sea urchins, trying to prove that the population dynamics of certain species correlated directly with what he called the "health quotient" of an entire reef. He'd had affairs with a few of his pretty grad students. He hated board games but still played them with Jordan, his board game–loving son. Jordan was wiry and skinny like his mother. Sometimes Beverly worried because the boy could be obsessive. Meanwhile her younger daughter, Roxanne, was dyslexic, and her brilliant older daughter, Jennifer, had gone to UCLA and in recent months had threatened never to come home again.

"It still feels good," Beverly said, when we were parting. "To tell it all to you, who knows much more about me than any other living person. You'll always be my Mirela. I'm just sorry I talked this much. It's as if you're the only person in the world who I feel able to just talk to. What was I doing so far away from you all these years? It seems so crazy."

I said, "Let's do this again. Let's stay in touch. Sometime I'll visit you in New Jersey, if you'd like."

"That would be nice," she said. "I'd like that."

I said, "I still have your box of dreams. Now I'm an expert, as you know."

"Yes, you're an expert," she said. "Someday I'll give you a Technicolor dreamcoat."

Why did this make me feel such love?

I said, "I mean what I'm about to say, sincerely. You should still feel free to write your dreams down. I will still keep them."

"And you'll decode them?"

I told her, "Maybe." I was careful. "Unless the dreams are too ingenious to decode."

"But you'll still keep them," she said, "if I give them to you?"
I said, "Always."

She looked bemused, and I looked lovingly into her eyes, which
are a watery blue, unlike any blue eyes that I have ever seen. We
stared and smiled at each other for several seconds. I could feel the
perplexing wonder of our proximity, and when I searched for it, I
also could sense the *klipe*. I wondered if she had noticed that there
was a *klipe* inside me too.

— — —

Only a week or so had passed when I received a letter in the mail
from Beverly. She'd sent a short note along with transcripts of
two dreams. I had not been expecting this. Despite our promises,
I had doubted I would hear from her again for a long while. So
much for my logic and intuition. Neither had ever been much use
with Beverly. I briefly wondered how she'd changed over the years
during which we had not spoken. But then I read her note and
smiled.

Dear Mirela,

*I'm still dreaming about the shadows. There is no need
to interpret and not because my dreams are ingenious. The
shadow dream is the same dream, always. Do you have clients
who for all their lives have the same dream, over and over? If
it is true that you still keep my box of things, then please deposit
these. Also, I've enclosed a photo taken, I believe, in Poland
before the war. This is my father, my aunt Doris, and my uncle
Pinchas. I can't be sure but I assume my mother took the photo,
since the date on the back is written in her handwriting. A very
ordinary photo. Still there is something strange and dreamlike
about the picture, though I don't know what it is. Of course,
you know the story about my father and Uncle Pinchas. The*

five hundred Jewish intellectuals killed in Kovno as well as the fable my aunt Doris likes to tell about the two men who survived. I often look for those two men in my dreams, as seems to be the case in both Exhibit A and Exhibit B. I sometimes do have dreams without the shadow, but they seem lifeless, even pale—such funny words to use—in comparison. Thank you, my Mirela, for receiving these.

Yours,

Bejla

The photo was, as she'd suggested, ordinary. A glossy black-and-white of three people. Both her father and her uncle with gallant smiles and her aunt looking at something above the camera. Much more interesting and surprising than the photo, I thought, was how she had signed the note. Not "Queen Bejla" and not "Beverly." Just "Bejla." I did not know if she was aware that she had done this.

The first dream she had transcribed was the following:

The two men run together, swim together, fly together. The men will sometimes take the form of animals, such as wolves. I try to follow. I am trying to see their faces and thinking I can intercept them. Soon I turn into a dark wolf, but then the men have disappeared and I am stuck inside their shadow. It is as if I have switched places with the men.

The second dream:

I'm very old and I've come to an island in the far north of the world. It should be arctic but it's not. It's always dark there, except for a daily interval of twilight. I'm there in this strange light with a woman I don't know, though I'm aware that I have been to this same island with her before. A dark green canvas duffel bag holds our clothes. We've left it near the shoreline, but soon a shadowy wave breaks over it and the duffel is underwater. I run out to it, dive under, save our duffel bag. I bring it onto dry land, empty the contents. A pair of sea snakes tumble out with the pile of clothes.

I did as Beverly requested and did not try to interpret. I folded the letter up and slipped both it and the photograph into the envelope. Then I stepped out of my bedroom. I pulled the rope that was attached to the cutout square in the ceiling of our upstairs hallway. When it was angled down, I unfolded the wooden stairs and climbed up into that little triangle, with its unstable plywood floor and exposed fiberglass insulation. It took some time, but I was able to locate the box marked BEVERLY RABINOWITZ and QUEEN BEJLA. I dropped the envelope into the box and stood there looking all around the dusty attic, a place my husband and children rarely went, but which I ventured up to frequently. It was filled with cardboard boxes, most of them marked and most of them boxes of things I've kept for my three children.

"You'll want these odds and ends someday," I had told my middle child, Libby, who'd recently announced her plans to become a Peace Corps volunteer. Libby seemed to find what I said funny. She'd said, "And why would I want report cards from fourth grade? Why would I ever want to see pictures of me with that sleazebag I dated all through high school, Evan Stein? Why, for God's sake, would I want to remember that I was on the track team?" I almost said, "You were good at hurdles." It was her specialty, the one-hundred- and four-hundred-meter hurdles. I thought, One day you will tell your children that in high school you ran around a track and jumped these hurdles. And they will think of you this way. They will remember this as if they had watched a race. Maybe they'll dream it, dream of you running around a track and jumping all these hurdles. She would have laughed at me and then she would have said, "If I have children at all, they can dream of me living in Sri Lanka or Botswana or Niger." And I would have said, "You are lucky to have the luxury of forgetting. And you are very, very lucky that you can go anywhere in this world. And one day you will feel lucky that I've saved for you the trinkets of your own history." Naturally we did not go anywhere near this conversation. I put her things in the cardboard box that was marked LIBBY.

I had my own box, of course. My own history. My own shadows. It was all in there, and I didn't have to look. I could still see myself as a college junior. The exact same age as Libby. The year was 1953. I had long straight hair, a big nose, very full lips. To certain people, I suppose I seemed exotic, an eastern European Jew who on occasion could be heard speaking Yiddish with her parents. What I discovered that year was that I could observe men in an aggressive way that still allowed me to seem passive. The whole thing came like a revelation. I could stand waiting and men would come to proposition me. Always the drunk ones, the adventuresome ones, college men who were not yet busy looking for their wives. I slept with seven different partners in a period of roughly one and a half years. But the seventh of these men was Philip Downing, my professor of modern European history. I had run into him at the college bookstore. I told him I was in his class for that semester. He asked me questions about myself. He seemed to think I was something special, a living part of the history he studied and wrote books about. The more we spoke, the more I realized that I could lure him the same way I'd learned to do it with my classmates. It was much easier, in fact, to reel him in.

He liked me to tell him things in Yiddish. The funny sayings, the Yiddish doublespeak, which he called "apotropaic" and which, depending on my mood, I called either superstition or precaution. *Zol dir nisht tsebrokhn vern a fus!* May you not break your leg. I would say this to him, half-joking. He would laugh and say, amazedly, "By this you mean the opposite? By this you mean you hope I have an injury to my leg?" I told him that in Yiddish the cemetery is often called *beys khayim* or "house of life." I explained that certain Talmudic tractates that pertain to mourning are referred to as *Semakhos* or "happy times." His favorite thing of all was the ritual of not-counting that occurs when Jewish men gather for a *minyen*. A quorum of ten is required before the group can begin to pray. The men will point at each other and not-count. *Nisht eyns, nisht tsvey, nisht dray,* etc. As I explained to Philip Downing, the counting of Jews was considered dangerous. He told me, "You Jews are *farblondjet,*" and seemed pleased with himself.

He had a Yiddish fetish, he said, this Protestant man, Professor Philip Downing. He went so far as to joke that if he had been a Nazi soldier he would have found a way to have a lot of sex with imprisoned Jews. That was where I began to lose my appetite for him, where I began to notice that this affair—Downing was married—was not all right, that it was moving toward depravity. But I did not leave, not just yet.

One day he asked me to come with him to a hotel downtown. As we drank cheap champagne and took our clothes off, there was a knock and Downing opened the door. A prostitute he'd hired entered. She was a great big blond Brunhild, and Downing said that he'd brought me there to play a game. He said together we would abuse a Nazi whore. I should have run, but I stayed. I did it. The woman got down on all fours, rolling her eyes as Downing, over and over, yelled out, *"Schweinehund!"* I helped him into her and then I stood in front of her with my arms crossed. It made her laugh at me and leer. At some point in the whole proceeding, she abruptly put a finger up inside me. It was awful and in some way it aroused me. But then the spell broke and I slapped her. The woman shouted and called me anti-Semitic names. At first Downing seemed to think that we were playing, but I said, "Pay her and take me home."

He did not understand, I told him later. The Yiddish language has its apotropaic speech because the language is not thought to be symbolic. In a world that was created by God's words, words are not symbols. They are things. You call a demon, you *make* a demon. You curse at God and you risk dying. I told him, "We have called a demon and cursed God at the same time," and he said, "Why don't you tell me that my head should become an onion?" I didn't bother to explain the correct version of this expression.

I broke things off and I did not speak to him again. For nearly a year after that, I stayed away from men altogether. But shortly after my college graduation I met Howard. He was in law school. I did things right, I believed. For weeks and weeks all I did was kiss him. After five months he proposed and after ten months we were married. Another two and I was pregnant. Still, it was a long time before I did not feel haunted by my memories of Professor Philip Downing and that prostitute, a long time before I stopped worrying that a demon had taken hold of my soul. It helped that Howard could be forceful, a bit rough in bed, a little spiteful. It was just enough to keep my shadow self appeased. Then the children came and eventually I grew absorbed in my dual life as a mother and student at the C. G. Jung Institute of New York. Soon Howard lost his edge and it seemed all right. I believed that I'd passed through a little tunnel and come out the other side.

———   ———   ———

To my surprise, before I'd even had the time to respond to her note, Beverly called me at my home. I had just stepped out of the bathroom. My son Aaron answered the phone. After a moment he looked up and said, "For you, Mom." I took the phone, said, "Hello?" and she said, "Mirela, it's me."

She sounded mournful and distraught. I said, "What is it?" She said, "Have you put my two new dreams inside the box?" I said I had. "I have a strange request," she said. "I trust that you'll tell me if it's too inconvenient or just not possible, but I'd like to see the box." I said, "Of course you can see the box," and asked her when she would like to come. She said, "Anytime that's good," and I said, "How about tomorrow?" It was a Thursday, my day off. She said tomorrow worked just fine. She had to see a few patients in the morning, but she could leave by noon and be at my house no later than two o'clock. I gave her the directions. It was strange to think I'd lived in this house so long and Beverly had never come to see me. Most of the ride would be very simple, up the parkway. Early the next afternoon, she was pulling into my driveway.

And so I took Beverly up into my attic. I'd thought of bringing the box down, but it was heavy and I worried it could break. She climbed up the wooden ladder after me. Unlike three days before, I knew exactly where to find her box. She said, "So this is where you keep me." I said, "It's there," and then I pointed to the side marked QUEEN BEJLA. She approached and pulled the lid up. She looked down at the thick pile of multimedia that was easily the most comprehensive record of her existence. She dipped her hand inside and when it reappeared she held the letter she'd sent that week. She opened up the envelope, took out the picture of her father, aunt, and uncle. "Such an odd photo," she said, just as she'd written in her letter. "So normal-looking and still so odd."

Less than a minute passed. She put the photo into the envelope. She put the envelope back into the box and closed the lid. I said, "It's okay to look through it." She shook her head and said, "It may seem funny to you, Mirela. I just wanted to see that it existed. It's not that I didn't believe you, but there was something, some compulsion. I just wanted to see this box, the place you keep it, and that it's here."

"Did something happen?" I asked.

Beverly nodded. "I had to bring him in," she said. "Yesterday morning, to pain management. That's the euphemism for going to the hospital, getting injected continually with morphine, and then dying. I really thought he would last a little longer."

"I'm so sorry," I said.

She said, "This summer he was fine. It's ironic. I went to stay with him down in the Caribbean. A few weeks later, he starts to die. I have the fear that it was my shadow."

I told her, "Hush. You're talking nonsense." This was the only thing I knew to say.

"I thought you'd meet him," Beverly said. "I thought we'd have enough time. I would have liked you to get to know him."

This seemed a curious thought coming from my Queen Bejla. She'd never once, of course, wanted me to meet her husband, Richard. She'd never wanted me to meet the boyfriend, Alan, she had in college. I touched her arm as we stood there in my dusty attic, amid my private little archive, more than halfway beyond the time frame that would most likely constitute our lives. I told her, "I will come tomorrow. I'll come to see him in the hospital."

"Oh," she said. "No, that isn't necessary."

I said, "It's not up for debate."

The next morning, having canceled two of my clients, I drove down to a hospital in New Brunswick where David Kahn was undergoing "pain management." Beverly met me in the lobby. As we rode the elevator up to his floor, she said, "I'm afraid that David won't be much fun." But he was more alert than I had been expecting. He smiled at me when I walked in and clearly knew just who I was. He had his hair, mustache, and beard, so I surmised that he had forgone treatment after the relapse or that he had not been doing the latest round for very long. He said, "So this is the famous Mirela!" and then I laughed to myself. Now, for a brief time, there were again three in the world who called me Mirela.

My visit with David lasted perhaps an hour. He asked me questions about my work. He thanked me for being such an important friend to Beverly. He told me silly jokes and he made me laugh. I said good-bye when it was time for his next injection. I went down into the lobby, waited for Beverly. She stayed with him, held his hand, until the painkiller took effect. "I'm glad you met my

Princess Mirela," she told David. This I am sure of, even though I was not there.

Then she came down and we ate some food at the café. She seemed serene, but all at once, it was as if her watery blue eyes had looked inside me. I said, "What is it?" She said, "Mirela, I'm sorry. All of this time and I don't think I've asked you how you are."

I said, "Not bad."

Beverly nodded.

I said, "Not great."

Then I was troubled because I knew she had seen the *klipe* that lurked inside me. And I was tempted to say a lot, because she'd asked. I was tempted to explain that I had a shadow self as well. Nothing so bad, I believed. Nothing resembling my sordid fling with Philip Downing. But it was late enough already and I needed to get back home.

— — —

This was not a dream. Seventeen years old and suddenly my son Aaron was a soccer star, *keynehore*. It didn't make much sense since his older brother, Tobias, was skinny and uncoordinated, like Howard. But there's a gene somewhere, the gene that enabled Libby to do the hurdles, and little Aaron, with his small compact frame, seemed to be a holy man with a soccer ball. He was good enough that for the last year he'd been playing on a traveling team in the Eastern Coast Premier League, and on any given weekend, he could wind up playing soccer games in New York State, Long Island, southern Connecticut, or New Jersey. One weekend every month or two, it was my turn to drive three or four boys to an *away* game in our station wagon. And when it was my turn to drive, I would sit and watch the game with Gerhardt Ullman, whose son Fritz was also on the team.

The Ullmans lived in Nanuet and Gerhardt went to every game. Together these facts explained why I never drove his son and why I would always see him there. Both Fritz and Aaron played in the midfield. They seemed to be the two players on the team who never rested. They ran and ran, and the coach would never put in a substitute for either one of them. What Gerhardt Ullman said was that Aaron and Fritz both had high *fitness levels*. More important, he said, they had *good touch*. Each time I came to a game and we sat together, he would explain to me the more subtle rules and strategies and soccer terminology.

It was the parity between Fritz and Aaron, the obvious fact that they were the team's two most important players, the respect that the rest of the team displayed for these two boys, that seemed to create the affinity between Gerhardt Ullman and myself. Possibly it was just mutual pride, or possibly, in some subconscious manner, we were mirroring the on-the-field alliance of our sons. Or, possibly, it was just weirdly exhilarating for me to sit next to a man named Gerhardt and listen to his thick German accent. Both he and Fritz were tall and blond. They could have been part of Hitler's master race. That was my joke for a while with Aaron. He didn't like it, and eventually I stopped saying it.

One weekend in the spring of Aaron's junior year of high school, I drove the carpool to a game against a team called Farcher's Grove in the town of Union, New Jersey. Farcher's Grove, as it turned out, was a German sports club. A bar and grill sat adjacent to the field. I watched the game, and at halftime I was wandering around inside the bar, seeking a bathroom, and on the walls I saw team photos of many soccer teams. I was looking at these photos. Gerhardt walked in and I heard him speaking German with some employee of the bar and grill. Then he was heading for the bathroom. I felt uncomfortable. I was suddenly afraid of him.

Later, as we watched Aaron and Fritz make *wall passes* and *crosses* and *diagonal runs*, all of which Gerhardt was explaining in his methodical way, I asked him, and God only knows what I was thinking, if his parents had been members of the Nazi Party. For the first time in the ten or fifteen games I'd sat beside him, he seemed uncomfortable. He fidgeted for a moment, and to my utter surprise, he said, "They were." So unexpected was this response that I was tempted to run away from him. But then I gathered myself and put things in perspective. Our two sons were on a soccer team. They played together in the midfield. Aaron was number eight and Fritz was number six. "And you are Jewish?" said Gerhardt Ullman. I said I was. "You are the first Jewish woman that I speak with in my life," said Gerhardt Ullman. "This is not because I have a dislike for the Jews." Down on the field, there was a *corner kick*. I watched as Aaron ran in little circles and then made a hard, fast sprint in the direction of the goal. The ball was kicked into the air, and he leapt high and seemed to sail right over one of the defender's shoulders. The ball caromed off his forehead and flew into the top corner of the net. There were some cheers. The timing of it all seemed eerie. Gerhardt said, "Your boy sure can get up in the air for one his size." I knew it was a compliment. I knew it was Gerhardt Ullman's broken English. But I just heard it wrong. *For one his size.* For one what? I thought. One Jew?

How do these things happen? After the game, I was resolved never to speak with the man again. A month passed and naturally, having not been to a game, I had not exchanged another word with him. But then it was my turn to drive the carpool. Maybe he knew this. For the first time in all the games I'd been to, Gerhardt Ullman wasn't there. It was the final game of the spring season. On a play similar to the one on which Aaron had scored that goal with a *glancing header*, Fritz Ullman leapt high in the air to head the ball but instead smacked foreheads with the opposing team's defender. Then Fritz Ullman, for close to a full minute, was out cold. When he came to, there were several coaches and players standing around him. He sat up holding his left wrist in his right hand. I made my way down from the bleachers. His wrist was swollen and I guessed that he had broken it in the fall. What came over me, I don't know.

I told the coach that I knew his father and would take Fritz to the hospital. I found rides for the three boys I had driven to the game. We were in Englewood, New Jersey. After the game, Aaron, Fritz, and I went to an Englewood hospital's emergency room. I had Fritz give me his home number, and from the hospital I called the Ullmans' home in Nanuet. His mother answered. I gave instructions. An hour later, Gerhardt Ullman arrived in Englewood. The broken wrist was a simple matter, I explained to him. The concussion was more complex and they would need to do more tests. We stayed a little while longer. After that, Aaron and I left the Ullmans at the hospital. A few days later, Fritz's mother called to thank me. Then it was summer. There would be no more Eastern Coast Premier League soccer until the fall.

In September I did not know what to expect—not only regarding how I would react to Gerhardt, but whether, after more than three months, he would want to speak to me. He was there, of course, with Fritz before the game, talking in German. I saw him pat Fritz on the shoulder. We were in Tarrytown, New York, and this particular field had only one small section of bleachers. For the first few minutes Gerhardt walked the sidelines. Then he looked up at me. Before I was aware of what I was doing, I waved. He came to sit with me. At first, we acted as if everything was the same. I noticed that tall Fritz had filled out during the summer months, and that despite his double injury in May, he played with confidence. I did not think I had ever seen him play so well. He scored a goal late in the game, on a *full volley*, Gerhardt excitedly explained. As we parted he asked me if, after the next game, which was in Suffern, Aaron and I would like to go with him and Fritz for hamburgers. I said I'd need to check my schedule. He said, "We see you at the game, and so you tell us. If you will come, we will do nothing very fancy." All week I laughed at myself for feeling anxious, for feeling morally capricious, for feeling sneaky, for feeling clear that I was interested in going. Usually I didn't even go to the home games. But still I went, and I sat with Gerhardt, and sometime during the first half, he turned to me in the way he would when he was going to explain something about soccer. But what he said was "I must speak this. I must tell you that my parents went to Nazi parades during the time of Adolf Hitler, and they were neither of them doing things so terrible, except they lived their lives without thinking too much about anything. This is what they have told me. We lived in Stuttgart until 1947. I was born there, in 1940. They live close by to us now, in Nanuet. This is all I know to tell you." I thanked him. For several minutes we sat in silence. I thought, Either he is lying about his parents' naïveté or he is absurdly naïve himself. Then Aaron made a good play, a strong *tackle* followed by a *through ball* that allowed one of the forwards to run by the defense and shoot directly at the goalie. The goalie saved it, but still Gerhardt yelled out, "Very good ball, Aaron!" After the game we all went to a restaurant. We ate hamburgers and hot dogs. We analyzed the game until we had determined exactly why our team had lost. When I got home that night, I said hello to Howard. I went upstairs and took a shower. I wondered whether my episode with Gerhardt Ullman was just beginning or if the game and postgame dinner I'd just attended had been, more or less, its moment of completion. Sometimes in these situations, you cannot know where you are. As I was drying myself off, the phone rang. I stepped out into the hall, where Aaron, still in his uniform, had just answered it. He said, "For you, Mom." I took the phone. "Hello?" I had said, and Beverly said, "Mirela, it's me."

— — —

All this I reviewed on my drive home from the hospital in New Brunswick. Soon I was more than halfway up the parkway. I thought of David Kahn and wondered if a photo of him would find its way into the box in my attic. Then as I wondered for the twentieth time that hour if I'd been right not to tell Beverly a single word about Gerhardt Ullman, I felt the *klipe* I'd been carrying inside me. I felt it wiggling. The *klipe* literally started wiggling. I was passing by an abandoned warehouse with smashed windows somewhere in Irvington, New Jersey. Perhaps the *klipe* thought it looked inviting. Then it was gone.

— — —

For a long time I have wondered whether I still love my husband, Howard. We are both sweet to each other, always, kind and considerate. We share a bed and this will never change. I go to sleep later than he does. I do not need much sleep and get into bed at midnight. Howard is always in bed by nine and up by five. Sometimes, when I get into bed, I feel something for Howard that I cannot feel at the times when we are both awake. I feel the way we are entwined, forever, in this lifetime. I feel that we were always right to be together. I feel the love that is the echo or the glow of our love from years ago, and who am I to wonder, really, about our love?

When I returned home from my jaunt down to New Brunswick, Howard was waiting. He had met Beverly very briefly the night before. We had been sitting at the kitchen table when he walked in and he'd assumed she was a client. Later, I told him who she was and suddenly he was full of questions and curiosity. I told him that as girls we'd played together on my rooftop, but that even as a young girl, she was very, very old. "Was she a beauty?" Howard asked, and I said, *"Mayne sonim zoln zayn azoy miyes."* My enemies should be as ugly. What this implies, in Yiddish doublespeak, is that my enemies should be as ugly as she is beautiful.

Then I said, "Did you find her attractive?"

Howard said, "Feh." I rolled my eyes. He said, "There is something about her. What can I say?"

That night, for the first time in three years, Howard made love to me. "What did she bring out?" I asked afterward. Howard said, "You. I don't know why." I told him, "Try. Try to know why." He told me, "Seeing your old friend helped me to see you." I said, "In what way did you see me?" He said, "I saw that there are things that I've stopped bothering to see." "Such as what?" I asked, and he said, "You've been a good mother to our children." I said, "What else?" and he said, "You have always guarded me, watched over me. Without you I would not sleep." I said, "What else?" and he said, "When I first met you I had hidden anger at the world and I would direct this anger to you in bed and you seemed to like this." I said, "Go on." He said, "One day I didn't want to be so angry. I was afraid you would no longer respond because I wanted to be soft." I said, "What else?" and he said, "I believe that we can be soft and that we have not lost things. I believe this because I wake up every morning and when I make the coffee I still love you." I said, "What else?" He said, "Seeing this woman, your friend Beverly, I thought to myself that if I had met her when I was young I'd want to love her in a difficult way that would not suit me. If I met her when I was young, I would have tried to be what I am not. I would have failed because what I am is a man who should be with you. You are much happier by far than this Beverly." I told him, "This is because she has never been like other people. This is because there are things about her that defy a rational understanding. Sometimes I believe that I can help her and sometimes I think it's always been the other way around. She helps people. She does not even mean to. There are also some people who she hurts. She does not mean to do this either."

When we stopped talking, Howard fell asleep in an instant, the way he always does, and I got up and went into the bathroom. I was still naked. I looked at myself in the mirror. I tried to see if the *klipe* had returned, but I did not see or even feel it. It seemed the *klipe* was still gone.

— — —

I spoke to Beverly for only a few minutes at the *shiva* call I made with Howard two days after I'd attended David's funeral. We brought a *kugel*. We stayed an hour. I told her Aaron had been accepted early decision to Brandeis College. I said the coach of the soccer team had scouted him. He was going to be one of their star players. I didn't tell her that Fritz Ullman had banged his head again and suffered an even worse concussion, bad enough that he was told not to play soccer for a while. I was glad that there was no reason to tell her this. I was glad that in this whole endeavor my own shadow had stayed shadowy and alone.

A few months later I received a manila envelope by mail. She had sent me a thick packet. I expected there would be pictures of her lost love, David Kahn. But she had not sent me pictures of David for the box up in my attic. As far as boyfriends or husbands went, I began to suspect that there would never be any pictures to be placed in the box at all.

In her note dated January 20, she'd written:

Mirela,

> *First, I miss you. Second, I've been meaning to send these copies of some letters I received last winter. I xeroxed them all back then and thought to send them, although this was at least six months before I happened to run into you in Central Park! There's a long story I meant to tell you about a trip I took with David. While he was well, we went to Florida with Jordan and we all snorkeled in a river filled with manatees. That night I watched the manatees swimming under the light of a full moon. I was reminded of our river back in Poland and I felt as if my father, in some literal way, had been close by.*
>
> *I never told you this, but when I was sixteen my mother went to see a psychic who determined for three dollars that my father was alive and well and living in an apartment that*

*looked out on the same canal in Delft that the Dutch artist
Johannes Vermeer painted in the seventeenth century. Of
course, my mother decided it was true and then did nothing.
And now years later I thought, Why not? It's something like
that old joke about the woman who wants to give her dead
mother-in-law an enema and when her husband asks why she
says, "It couldn't hurt." It couldn't hurt, I thought, so I made
inquiries. I found someone in the town of Delft to write to.
Someone in Amsterdam as well. The man in Amsterdam was
supposed to be a scholar of the Holocaust. I wrote to someone at
Yad Vashem and I wrote to someone at an agency in Kovno.
After I sent out those four letters, I understood that it was silly.
It seemed more silly after I received these four extremely useless
responses. Still, in a strange way, it was as if I was in touch
with him, my father. That's why I've sent you these silly letters
and will appreciate it if you can place them upstairs in the box.*

*Lately, I've been dreaming of the shadow again. I have
enclosed a recent dream for the box as well. This is a strange
dream, a recurring one, but very hard to describe. I don't think
that I've ever tried to describe it. In certain ways, I don't think
that I really can, though I have made an attempt here.*

*Needless to say, I have also been thinking about David,
about death, about his absence, and I've realized that despite
whatever people want to say about life and death, or light
and dark, these are not separate things at all. To use a cliché,
they are two sides of the same coin. Maybe it's only a trick of
language, but the word "life" or "death" alone could not be
understood without awareness of the other. It is the same for
light and dark, for day and night, for good and evil.*

*But words are just words, and there is more to this. My
thought about the dream I have enclosed and cannot seem to
describe with anything approaching accuracy is that the shadow
is not made of light and dark. It is not something that exists*

halfway between the day and night. Instead I think the shadow is what lies behind these oppositions. Perhaps the shadow is a good way to describe the mind of God. Maybe the shadow is the origin. It's where we go or maybe it's where we are. Now David has died and the coin has flipped to the other side and it can flip again, I think, at least in theory. Why wouldn't this also be true about my father? Now I am losing my train of thought because this doesn't work like logic. So I will end this by just saying that I love you, my dearest Mirela, and leave you with my dream.

Yours,
Bejla

I looked for the transcript of her dream and at first I could not find it. I sifted through the xeroxed copies of the letters she had sent me. I read one of the responses to her letters, and then I wondered if I should call her to let her know that she'd accidentally left the dream out of the packet. Then it slipped out from within the pages. All very shadowy and dreamlike. The words were scribbled on the back of an old envelope that had been pressed between two of the xeroxed sheets. I imagined her in her room, alone, writing the dream down. I imagined it was dawn, that her shades were drawn, and that she'd fallen back to sleep almost as soon as she wrote these words. I tell my clients to write their dreams down without thinking, without imposing secondary elaboration, to let the dream speak in its own language. Sometimes, as Beverly suggested, a dream remains beyond description, but in such cases what you write will often show you something far beyond the things that you think you know.

Beverly's dream:

I am inside all this, again. A certain angle in a dark place. Climbing up. That's what I try for. When I go into this place

I must do it right. There is a woman who is me. Shadowy woman. She has been around forever. When I am sleeping I am her inside this dream. I walk through Poland, through Lithuania, through the Ukraine, through Romania. I walk through Hungary, through Slovakia, through the Netherlands, through Greece. I walk through countries without names as well as countries I've never heard of. Everywhere I go I am choosing shadows. A few here. A few there. It's just enough to get us through. This is survival, in a dream. This is me when I am not me but still here as if by accident. It is this slipping through the cracks. It is this knowing how to do it.

Soon I will put this all into the box, after which I will stop trying to organize these letters, photographs, and dreams into something like a coherent narrative. It is a danger, said Carl Jung—who was himself, I should note, believed by some to have been sympathetic to the Nazis, although most evidence suggests this is unlikely—it is a danger to be unyielding in our belief that all things must be coherent. It is a danger not to question the worldview, the blind accord with all the dominant norms, etc. It is important to pay attention to what sneaks up on us, those silly things that, for no reason, we imagine or remember.

Once when Beverly and I were playing on the rooftop, she said, "Mirela, we could jump," and I said, "Then we would die," and she said, "Maybe." Then she said, "Why don't we pretend it's something else?" I said, "Like flying?" She said, "Flossing!" This seemed whimsical and funny. I said, "Flowering!" She said, "Fluffing!" Then my brother came out onto the roof and I said, "Look, it's the king of all the poodles." He began barking and she said, "Mirela, he's really a good dog." I could go on with this and possibly these words would come to life, or possibly the truest thing will be the silence that will come when I stop speaking. How do we know the difference? Maybe this is like asking how to love. Or maybe this is like asking how to understand the shadow. At any rate, this concludes at least one portion of my thoughts and recollections regarding my dear friend Beverly, once called Bejla. My enemies should be as ugly.

8

Many Colors

In HINDSIGHT, THERE were many different reasons that I should have broken the deal. The seller turned out to be a crotchety man who'd just retired from twenty-five years of teaching algebra. He smoked imported cigars and the house smelled of them. I assumed the smell would go away once the house aired out, but this was just the first of what would prove to be a catalogue of poor assumptions. With the help of my anxiety-provoking realtor, Madeline, I spent close to two months arguing with the seller about things like rotted clapboards, missing storm windows, a broken bathroom fan, carpenter ants, and other items that were to have been taken care of as part of the purchase and sale agreement. I spent these weeks feeling sure this was not worth it, thinking that at any moment I'd make one phone call to my lawyer and walk away from the whole thing.

But it was always like this, said my father. It was always like this, said the people who I worked with at the Berkshire Hills Veterinary Clinic in Lenox. It was always like this, said my newspaper photographer boyfriend, Luke, who I caught flirting with a busty redhead in advertising when I stopped by his office to pick him up and bring him with me to the closing. There was a fire, Luke said. A fire that had just come through on the scanner. A fire out in the town of Otis and he needed to go shoot it. He was sorry, Luke said, and I went by myself to my lawyer's office for the closing, signed all the papers, and wrote a check for the down payment. The seller wasn't at the closing. He'd sent his lawyer somehow as proxy. After the seller's lawyer left, I told my lawyer that this whole process had been hellish. My lawyer said, and I quote, "It's always like this." Always like what? I thought. Like people turning into monsters? Like people thinking they can say one thing and do another? I said, "I'd prefer to think that buying a house *isn't* always like this." The lawyer shrugged and said, "The seller probably hates you too."

So much for sympathy. I peremptorily shook hands with my lawyer and left his office with my new house keys. Then it was done, so I went home to the beat-up farmhouse that Luke and I had been renting. When I arrived I was greeted by Henderson and Sadie, my bluetick coonhounds, both of whom we had rescued through an adoption program from an overcrowded shelter in Mississippi. They were long-legged pack hounds, trained as hunting dogs. When they walked they seemed to swagger. Mostly, what they loved to do was run and run. I put my running sneakers on, hooked up their leashes, and took them out to the trail where I went jogging in the evenings. When we were deep into the trail I took their leashes off. The dogs stayed with me. I had determined in the two years since adopting them that so long as they were with me, the alpha member of their pack, they wouldn't take off for the hills. But this was risky, I knew, because those dogs wanted to run.

After my three-mile loop with Henderson and Sadie, I returned home and found Luke sitting in the kitchen with our cat, Charlie, on his lap. "How was the fire?" I asked, but then it wasn't a fire. As Luke explained, with his absurd belief in honesty, what he had done while I was closing on the house was fool around with that busty redhead in the darkroom. "Who the hell is she?" I asked, and he said Stephania was a former stripper who was trying to go straight but having a hard time with it. I said I didn't want her biography. I meant who was she to him. She wasn't anyone, he said. She was engaged to an older man, a senior editor at the paper. He said that really what he'd done in the last three hours did not have anything to do with Stephania. Really what he had done was to determine that he needed to break up with me.

I was too nervous, Luke said, and I was stressing him out more than he could tolerate. Also, I wasn't letting him have equal say in things. Just because the house was being paid for with my money didn't mean that he was not part of the whole ordeal. Just because I was a veterinary doctor, just because I was making three times as much as he was, it didn't mean I had the right to get all pissy every day and then expect that he would be there to soothe me. He wanted Charlie, he said. I told him no. Then he said what about our set of World Book encyclopedias. I was in shock, I think, and mostly I was speechless. I told him fine, he could take the encyclopedias. He asked to give me a good-bye kiss and what I did was walk over to the bookshelf, pull out one volume of the encyclopedias I'd just given him, and fling it at his head. I said, "Set foot in here with your girlfriend and I won't miss next time I throw an encyclopedia." He tried again to say that she was nothing, just a catalyst. He said the part again about her being engaged to the senior editor. "Luke, you are absolutely clueless," I said. "It's like some person I don't know is standing here with your body." Then I sat down on the floor and began shaking. When Luke walked over to me and crouched down, I said, "Go away!" He wouldn't. He tried to hug me, so I kicked him in the face with both my sneakers. "Why all the rage?" he said, incredibly, then went to get a paper towel and some ice for his bloody lip.

I moved into my new house. I stripped the wallpaper, had the house ozoned, and mopped all of the floors with Murphy's oil soap. I called in an exterminator and had him put down ant poison. I had the furnace checked, the ducts cleaned. I painted the kitchen walls. At night the dogs would curl up on the floor of the bedroom and Charlie would climb onto what used to be Luke's pillow. All in all, it should have been okay this way, but it was not.

On the second day I lived in the new house, I woke up

wheezing. Also, my sinuses were clogged, though I had never before had allergies. I vacuumed and mopped again. Throughout the day I kept the windows open. At night I closed them and I smelled the smell of ocean, which was actually the residue of the ozone. In a week or two that smell was gone, and the smoky sweet cigar smell had returned.

By that time I had begun to feel a strange pressure on my sternum. It went away when I was at the clinic. I started bringing Henderson and Sadie to work with me, leaving them out in my Chevy Blazer if the sun was not too strong. That way I could walk them without going home and going inside the house that I'd just purchased with the combined savings of bat mitzvah gifts, graduation gifts, and twenty thousand dollars that my late grandfather had left me in his will. I made a doctor's appointment, just to make sure I hadn't come down with pneumonia. I had my lungs x-rayed and I was tested for pneumonia and TB. A nurse asked questions. Did I smoke? Did I have asthma? Might I be pregnant? No was the answer to all these questions, so she asked others. She asked me if the house had mold. I told her that I hadn't seen any. She asked if, on a scale of one to ten, I could approximate my stress level. "Ten is the highest?" I asked, and the nurse nodded. I said, "Twelve."

Tests came back negative and the doctor's diagnosis was that I had inhaled too many chemicals. Too many floor cleaners and wallpaper glues and paint fumes. Just take it easy, they said. Spend time outdoors. I took it easy. I let the paint dry. I bought fragrance-free cat litter and a three-hundred-dollar air purifier for my bedroom. I stopped wearing perfume on weekends, not that I had anything to do on weekends. I bought fragrance-free laundry detergent, body lotion, and hand soap. My jogging loops with Henderson and Sadie got much longer.

But now, at the doctor's recommendation, I made the animals sleep downstairs, and when it started to get hot in early June, I had to leave the dogs at home during the day. I hired a dog walker, a teenage girl named Nora who advertised her dog-walking services on a flyer that I found on our clinic's bulletin board. Roughly two weeks after I'd hired her, I came home to find Nora sitting on the floor of the front hallway, her face puffy. She looked miserable and terrified. They got away from her, she said. Right when she opened the door the dogs had burst outside. They had been waiting behind the door. They ran and ran, and for an hour she had chased them on her bicycle. They kept appearing, then disappearing, but eventually she lost them. Nora had called the police and every animal shelter in western Massachusetts, several in New York State, as well as several in northwestern Connecticut. "I'm sure we'll find them," I told Nora, and sent her home with a check for the last week. But these were scent hounds, bluetick coonhounds. They had been bred to run forever. I went to sleep that night and dreamed that they were downstairs in the kitchen, jumping up on me the way they had when I first brought them home. I don't know why, but when I woke I was sure this dream had been their way of telling me they were gone.

I called perhaps three dozen different animal shelters, spent weeks hoping the dogs would turn up, but I never saw them again. Things got much worse after that, it seemed. I would wake up and feel the pressure on my sternum and was reminded of the play *The Crucible*, the scene where all the alleged witches are being killed by the punishment known as "pressing." Lying supine, they're immobilized and rocks are piled on top of them. As the weight increases, they are continually asked to confess to witchcraft. As Giles Corey is about to die, they listen for his confession and two words come out. "More weight." That was how I felt each morning and I would say it, say it to Charlie, when he climbed onto my chest. It was a joke at first because I still assumed I would get better. I still assumed it was all the stress and all the chemicals I had breathed. I assumed the loss of Henderson and Sadie had interrupted any progress I had been making. A few days later I walked into a department store and fainted.

I went to see another doctor. I now had asthma, it was decided. Late-onset asthma. It often happened at my age. Did I smoke? I was asked. TB? Was there a chance that the house had mold? I was given the name of someone I could call to have the house checked for things like mold, gas leaks, asbestos, and other horrifying substances. I was given a sample of a steroidal inhaler and a prescription for the anti-anxiety medication Ativan. I was told that the dog and cat hair I breathed in all day at the clinic was most likely aggravating my symptoms. It was suggested that I take some time off work, but I said no. At least not yet. I said the only place I actually felt *well* was at the clinic.

I left the doctor, went to a pharmacy for the prescription, took an Ativan, and decided to see a movie. Halfway through, I got a migraine, and a full third of the movie screen went blank. So I went home and called my parents in Philadelphia. They had been worried. I tried to tell them things were fine. I took more Ativan, went to sleep. At the vet clinic the next morning, the migraine returned while I was neutering a wire-haired fox terrier. My next client after that was my friend Lillian. She came in with her Maine coon cat, Allagash, who had some sort of anal rash he'd aggravated by continually licking it. I gave the cat a cortisone injection to stop the itching, prescribed the antibiotic Bactrim, and then threw up into one of the metal pans we used to collect urine samples. Lillian was still there. She was a nurse herself. She took me outside and said, "Vicki, tell me what's happening." I said that my life was falling apart and that all the stress appeared to have been affecting my immune system. Lillian said, "Stress can do weird things, but it might not be stress." Then she asked questions. Smoking? TB? Gas leaks? Asbestos? Mold?

The Healthy Homes tester people came eventually in their white Tyvek suits and spent the better part of a day crawling around my attic. They left with air samples from every room as well as hundreds of tape-lift samples from floors, walls, ceilings, windowsills, and beams. They pointed out that my bathroom fan was not working, which was a good thing, since it vented into the attic. They said my soffit vents were terrible (whatever that meant), the chimney cap was cracked, and there was evidence of a substantial roof leak. They said they'd found black mold in a roughly ten-by-fifteen-foot section of drywall under the fiberglass insulation in the attic. They charged me more than five hundred dollars, and two weeks later their results confirmed the nightmare I'd been hoping I wasn't having. The mold was dangerous, they said. Spore counts in every room qualified as "hazardous." The recommendation of the experts was to evacuate.

I called up Luke, and when he answered, he said, "Vicki, is that you?" I said it was and he said, "Your voice sounds different." I said I had a sore throat and asked him if he would take Charlie. There was some work I was getting done on the house, I said. For the time being I was staying with my friend Lillian, who, unfortunately, had a large and extremely territorial cat.

Luke said, "You know, I've really missed him, Charlie."

"I'm sure you have," I said. "So how's the redhead?"

"Her name's Stephania," he said. "She's fine."

"Are her breasts real?" I said. "They're going to give her back problems."

I didn't think he would respond. But this was Luke. He told me, "No. She had them done three years ago. Back when she was, you know, still a stripper. She says she thought about the back issues. She chose the regular D cup over the double Ds with that in mind. Pretty good boob job, all in all."

I hung up on him.

I called back.

I said, "I'm sorry, Luke. I'm feeling kind of wound up, and I know I walked right into that, but maybe we shouldn't talk about

Stephania. So, as for my question. Will you take Charlie while I'm staying over at Lillian's?"

He said, "I'll take him. But I think that I should keep him. You got the dogs."

I hadn't told him about the dogs. I said, "Don't do this."

"I was the one who picked him out," he said.

I said, "And I've been the one who buys his food, feeds him, brushes him, changes his litter box. I could go on."

"I rub his belly more," Luke said.

I said, "Since when did you become sixteen again?"

"Take it or leave it," Luke said. "I have to go because Stephania's here."

I looked at Charlie, who at that moment was asleep on the couch, his belly exposed, and so far had not exhibited any symptoms from the mold. I had the premonition that things in my life were going to get stranger than they were already. I breathed in, muffled a sob, coughed, and told him, "Yes, okay. Take Charlie." I thought that soon I would have nothing else to lose.

The next afternoon I drove Charlie to Luke's new one-bedroom apartment. I spoke to Charlie in the car. I said good-bye to him, apologized, and promised that he'd be okay with Luke. I brought him to Luke's door. Luke was alone, and when he let me inside, I started to feel light-headed. I smelled ammonia. I knew I'd faint if I didn't get right out of there. So I left Charlie there in his cat carrier on the linoleum floor of Luke's front entryway. "Did you bring his litter box?" Luke asked. I said, "I have it in the car. I'm going to leave it in the driveway." "Did you bring food? What about litter?" By then I was walking briskly out the door.

I read the thirty-eight-page mold report. There were extremely high levels of airborne *Penicillium* and *Aspergillus* in the basement. There was evidence that the basement, although dry now, had been flooded many times. All of the rooms in the house had significant levels of these two types of mold as well. More disturbing was the black mold under the insulation in the attic. The *Aspergillus* and *Penicillium* were allergenic molds, but this black mold, called *Stachybotrys*, was a toxigen. *Stachybotrys* should not be confused with *Cladosporium*, the report explained to me. *Cladosporium*, also known as *Hormodendrum*, was a common black allergenic mold that grew in bathrooms and was what people tended to call mildew. *Stachybotrys*, however, grew in hidden places. It required a steady water source, such as a roof leak. *Stachybotrys* had been linked to sudden infant death syndrome, emphysema, and just about every other pulmonary condition imaginable. When Lillian returned home that night, I showed her the report, and as she read she exhaled loudly and shook her head a few times and then told me that although most allopathic doctors would not acknowledge the reality—just as they would not acknowledge fibromyalgia— exposure to toxigenic mold was often linked to a condition known as "ecologic" or "environmental" illness. She said that molds like *Stachybotrys* sensitized the immune system. Prolonged exposure broke the immune system down and gradually sensitized you to everything. She recommended that I have the mold cleaned up professionally and then put the house back on the market.

I paid contractors four thousand dollars to remove the moldy insulation, cut out the moldy drywall, and then patch it. I spent another two thousand dollars on a new roof. I spent six hundred on new insulation. I had the basement steam-cleaned, the ducts and furnace blown out again. I rented a large machine called an air scrubber at a rate of fifty dollars a day. I had the Healthy Homes people come again and it took three visits, as well as three more rounds of cleaning, before they signed a certificate of clearance. I thought that maybe I'd move back in, that with the house clean things would naturally be fine now. I tried to spend a night in my own bed but woke up wheezing and had to drive over to Lillian's at two o'clock in the morning. "You're too sensitized," Lillian said. "It's an old house. God only knows what's in the wall cavities." It was July by then. I'd owned the house for less than three months when I signed on with a new realtor. It took only a week to sell and, amazingly, mold disclosure and all, the sale price was fifteen thousand dollars more than I had paid for it.

I was relieved that the buyer seemed to be experienced. That way I wasn't afraid that I might be doing something morally problematic. I'd cleaned the mold, after all. I'd given the buyer the final clearance testing report. I'd even put in a new, properly exhausting bathroom fan. Lillian said I could stay with her until I found a place, and I started looking. But then my symptoms at work grew so bad that I could barely set foot inside the clinic. I had developed, it seemed, an ability to smell smells that were so subtle that one co-worker jokingly suggested that I was having olfactory hallucinations. And it wasn't the dog or cat hair. I could smell fumes from paint or oil-based stains that had dried years ago. I could smell shampoo fumes emanating from a beagle whose owner claimed he had not been bathed for several months. I could smell cinnamon, then sandalwood, then green apple on our receptionist, and eventually I determined that at home each night she lit scented candles. I talked to Lillian about it. She said, "Oh yes, when you get sensitized like you have, you develop something like a bionic nose."

"Your life's not working," Lillian told me a few days later, when I fainted shortly after excising several lipomas from an elderly Saint Bernard. She said, "I've seen it before. You have to change things. Very daringly, I might add. I don't mean that you should start doing acupuncture and taking Chinese herbal supplements. I mean that you need to get away from here."

I saw a doctor the next morning. He said that there was no recognized medical condition that accounted for all my symptoms. It was clear that I'd developed allergies and problematic respiratory issues, but the rest — for instance, I'd informed him that I got sick at the smell of cooking fumes — was in my head. He recommended a medical leave from work and said a change of climate would be a good idea. He had known patients with bad asthma who couldn't live in the northeastern U.S. climate, and he suggested that I consider moving to Arizona, where the dry desert air would have less mold.

Meanwhile, Lillian, whose house seemed to be the only indoor space in all of the Berkshires where I could still breathe normally, suggested that it might be more restorative to go live on a kibbutz in Israel. There were at least five that she knew of in the desert. There would be people there to talk to. There would be lots of Jews, like me. Lillian said that she herself had done it years ago, just after she finished college. Then she went on and on about the fig trees, acacias, pear trees, the fronds of date palms — *lulav* in Hebrew, she said dreamily — and pomegranate juice and a grape vineyard and any minute I thought that Lillian would burst into the Song of Songs. But all in all, it seemed a better option than Arizona. Over the next week, I wrote five letters of inquiry. I received only one response, from Kibbutz Ein Gedi, situated on the western shore of the Dead Sea. If I could work in the gardens or with the livestock, there was currently a place available. I wrote back the next day and I said I would be there as soon as possible. It seemed a reckless, radical gesture, and only Lillian applauded.

— — —

The Dead Sea basin is the lowest place on earth, but you feel lower. You feel as if you have almost reached the underlayer, the sea beneath all seas, beneath all time. The air is hot, sluggish, anesthetizing, hazy, torpid, miraculous. The sea is really just a lake that is filled with so much salt that you can sit on the surface of the water holding a boulder on your lap and you won't sink. For reasons I don't understand the water glows a shade of blue that is like no other color in the world. As I described it in a letter I wrote to Lillian, the color I saw each day when I awoke in my tiny room at Kibbutz Ein Gedi and went outside was a deep dead blue.

At first, I did not know how long I would leave my life for. I did not know if I would ever start feeling better. I could feel the desert air inside my body, inside my stomach, inside the sockets of my eyes. But within weeks of living in the desert wilderness called Judea, my allergy symptoms began waning. After a month I began to feel the tightness in my chest move from my sternum to my bronchioles, which seemed better. Soon after that it localized to the upper left part of my chest, where even now, all these years later, it comes and goes.

But it was clear that the desert air was helping, that in some way that I did not question, the air was drying out the mold that had grown inside me. I cultivated soil and watered plants in the kibbutz's botanical garden. I milked the goats, something I happened to learn to do while in vet school. I was twenty-nine years old, with all those years of veterinary education, the years of training. Now I milked goats. The strange thing was that I felt fine about it. I was perhaps the best goat milker among all those who lived at Kibbutz Ein Gedi. Soon I was no longer gardening, and my work with the kibbutz livestock had expanded to feeding chickens.

That was how I met the Israeli graduate student, Moti. Moti was doing his dissertation on the leopard population around Ein Gedi. He was twenty-five years old or so, olive-skinned, and very shy. He spoke poor English but liked to talk to me because I was curious about the leopards. Mostly what Moti did was collect leopard scats, note the locations of each sample, and then dissect them to see what these leopards had been eating. He came by each day to see if any leopards had been prowling around at night outside the livestock cages. Often he found leopard prints, as well as the tracks of wolves, hyenas, foxes, and the spiral-horned goats known as ibexes. He collected the scats in little baggies. He would say, "Shalom, Vee-kee," and he would show me the things he'd found inside the scats. In his poor English, he'd say, "Try you guess what this is." I'd shake my head and Moti would say, "Is fur from ibex he is eating." Or he'd say, "This is teeth from mouth of, how you say him, heerax?" I said, "The hyrax"—a brown, rabbit-size mammal that lived around the Ein Gedi oasis. Moti said, "Heerax is cousin of the ellyfone." This was true, I knew from a mammalian genetics class I'd taken long ago. The little critter's claim to fame was that it shared numerous features with the elephant, including hooves, sensitive foot pads, and tusks. I let Moti tell me all about the hyrax, their social structure, and how they warned each other about leopards and other predators, such as eagles. I assumed I was the only woman he'd ever met in his whole life who found this interesting.

Quite possibly, Moti also had a crush on me. For a time, I worried that he would try to ask me on a date. Some sort of nature hike, or worse, a gondola ride up to see the hilltop ruins of Masada. I didn't know what I would say. I guessed that at some point I really should go see Masada. But soon it became apparent that he was far too shy ever to do more than show me bits of ibex fur or hyrax teeth he'd found inside a leopard scat.

I grew restless, began to feel a strange alacrity. I took long hikes around Ein Gedi. I saw the ibexes and hyraxes all over the place. I thought of my bluetick coonhounds. Gradually, I began considering what to do with myself. Some days I'd smell the acidic smell of chicken poop and notice it didn't bother me. One day I noticed a bloom of bright green mold that was growing out of a pile of goat shit. I wondered how it could grow in the desert heat, but there it was. I was elated as I stood over it because I had no reaction whatsoever.

But after two months, I still got dizzy spells sometimes in the cafeteria. I'd also learned that it was necessary to keep my distance from a woman named Ya'el who used a strong-scented shampoo and fragrant underarm deodorant. So I decided that I would keep on milking goats and feeding chickens. I wrote my parents to say that things were fine and that I was feeling better. Sometime that

October, I took a bus to the hotel that was near Masada and bought a gift box of Dead Sea salts and Dead Sea mud to send them. As it turned out, I never sent the Dead Sea salt and mud, which was undoubtedly the result of meeting Dillon.

He was a young man, American, twenty-one when I first laid eyes on him. He'd come with Moti, and I learned that he was Moti's roommate at the field school. He seemed so young that I did not imagine that what I felt could possibly have consequence. He was the age of a college junior. I would turn thirty in two months. Still I took one look at his messy blond hair, his round face, his skinny arms, and I thought maybe I had traveled far enough away from who I was that nothing I said or did would matter. I thought that possibly, if given the opportunity, I might do something truly strange or reckless. That night, for the first time in God knew how long, I examined myself in a full-length mirror. My wavy hair was much longer and much frizzier than I had ever seen it. The desert sun had turned my face and arms and legs to a golden brown. But my bottom lip was cracked, and it looked as if I'd put on ten pounds since I'd last weighed myself. I turned around, looked at my ass, and it seemed larger. I'm an old maid, I thought. Later I cried myself to sleep.

He came again with Moti two days later. This time he spoke to me. He told me his name. When I asked where he was from, he said he'd grown up in Salt Lake City. He'd lived in Holland and then in Greece and had been living in Israel since late spring. Did I like motorcycles? he asked, because he had one, a Suzuki that he purchased in Tel Aviv when he arrived here. I said I'd never even been on a motorcycle. I said that I was not the motorcycle type. "I think you could be," he said, and that night I looked again into the mirror. I had a thought, which was something like *I have a crush on a blond-haired boy from Utah*. I turned to look at my ass again and then I bumped into the shelf on top of which I had left the jars of Dead Sea salt and Dead Sea mud. Both jars fell to the floor and smashed. I got a broom and swept the mess up.

To buy more Dead Sea salts and Dead Sea mud I would need to go to the hotel again. I had already written my parents a short letter to accompany the gift. I had just milked the goats and fed the chickens, and I was walking down to the bus station on the road by a public beach that was part of the Ein Gedi Nature Reserve and was filled with tourists, some of whom read newspapers as they floated atop the deep dead blue water. Others had covered themselves with Dead Sea mud. I planned to take a bus down to the hotel. I had just cut across the driveway that led up to the Ein Gedi Field School when I saw him on his motorcycle. He rode to me, stopped the bike, and then, as if I had forgotten who he was, he introduced himself. Before he finished, I said, "I know. We met the other day, with Moti."

"Then are you interested in seeing if I'm right?"

"Right about what?" I asked.

"About you on a motorcycle."

I said, "And what do you think I'll like about a motorcycle?"

He said, "I think that you'll like going very fast." He said, "I mean that you'll like speed." He shook his head and rolled his eyes at himself. He said, "I'm going to stop talking before you run away and warn all the kibbutzniks."

But I was not running away. I said, "I'll warn them about what?"

Dillon crossed his skinny arms. He said, "My sister, back in Utah, used to say that people think I'm mysterious. Then I start talking and the mystery goes away. She used to say that when in doubt I should shut the hell up and just act pretty."

"That's what you're doing now?" I said. "You're acting pretty?"

He said, "I think that what I'm doing is acting stupid because I like you and I'm worried you might say no to me."

Dillon was possibly worse at flirting than my ex-boyfriend, Honest Luke. But he was different than Luke. I could see that clearly. Another blond-haired *goy* but completely different. Completely beautiful. I climbed on.

He wore no helmet and he didn't offer me one. I wrapped my arms around his waist. We did not speak for the next hour. He drove at speeds in excess of ninety miles per hour, a hundred forty or more kilometers per hour on his speedometer. I watched the deep dead blue of the Dead Sea, and then we were beyond the Judean Desert, into the dull beige plateau of the Negev. We headed south and I held him tighter. I wasn't sure if I liked speed, but I was sure that I never wanted to let him go.

— — —

Once upon a time there was the Hai Bar Yotvata Nature Reserve. Located near Eilat in the southern Negev, the park had a two-part mission. The first was the preservation of endangered desert wildlife. Uncommon predators such as caracals, striped hyenas, steppe wolves, and various types of raptors were kept in cages. Most had been injured in some way or had caused problems along the lines of raiding garbage cans or getting too close to people who were afraid of them. This component of Hai Bar was simple. It was in essence a roadside zoo.

The more complicated aspect of Hai Bar was its breeding park, which had been founded for the purpose of reintroducing populations of certain animals to the Negev. This was its so-called program of biblical wildlife restoration. The idea was that any animal cited in the Bible had theoretically once roamed the Israeli wilderness. Therefore, if a breeding stock could be established using animals that had been captured or purchased elsewhere, then these biblical wildlife species could be reintroduced.

In certain cases the existence of biblical wildlife could be documented. Jeremiah 2:24: *A wild ass used to the wilderness, that snuffeth up the wind at her pleasure; in her occasion, who can turn her away? All they that seek her will not weary themselves; in her month they shall find her.* The corresponding animal was considered to be a majestic species of wild ass known as the Syrian onager, *Equus hemionus hemippus*. It had been hunted to extinction in the Middle East, with the last sightings having been recorded in 1936. The founders of Hai Bar had acquired a stock of the closely related subspecies *Equus hemionus onager*, also known as the Persian onager. Some had been captured with loop-and-snare traps in Iran's Khorason Desert. Some had been purchased from the Artis Zoo in Amsterdam. Since the seventies they'd been bred in a four-thousand-acre enclosure in the Arava Rift Valley, and the first reintroduction of eighteen stallions and eighteen mares into the wilds of Negev Desert had occurred in 1982, right about the time I was asking Luke to move with me to western Massachusetts.

Some of the other correlations were much fuzzier. The park was also breeding a herd of Arabian oryxes, which are white, desert-adapted antelopes with long straight horns. In profile it can look as if an oryx possesses only one horn, and in the Bible there are references to unicorns. The idea was that the oryx was the corresponding animal. I learned all of this eventually from Dillon, who worked at Hai Bar for a man named Amnon Grossman. A taciturn, blue-eyed man in his early forties, Amnon was an Israeli Nature Reserves Authority biologist who served as curator for the breeding park. Amnon was tall, with curly black hair that was always very dusty. He had a staff of four, which included Dillon and would eventually expand to include me.

It took just over an hour to get there on Dillon's motorcycle. I still recall the feeling I had when Dillon pulled into the Hai Bar parking lot, stopped his motorcycle, and killed the engine. I didn't know where I was. For all I knew, he was about to sell me into slavery. I recall thinking that I needed to bring myself back to reality, to acknowledge that I'd just traveled at reckless speed without a helmet with a young man I didn't know and that we appeared to be, as they say, right smack in the middle of fucking nowhere. I looked around, saw several people. This reassured me that I was not in danger. Dillon turned to me and said, "This is the place I

work. I think you'll like it at least as much as you like motorcycles."
Then he reached out, touched my arm, and said, "You see? You
liked the speed."

When I climbed off of the leather seat that I'd been straddling,
my legs felt wobbly. I started walking, just to walk, and then the
feeling I had was one of lightness, literally. It seemed as if my feet
were barely touching the ground, and I expected to faint at any
moment. Dillon called out to the people I had noticed, two men
with official-looking shirts who were leaning against a jeep, talking and smoking. They spoke in Hebrew. They both wore tan,
circular-brimmed hats with drawstrings. They looked like rang-
ers or park employees. The older one was large and stocky, and
he spoke loudly. The younger man was roughly the same height
but thinner, with darker skin. Both men had automatic rifles slung
over their shoulders. I saw a woman there as well, though she was
inside, behind a screen door, looking out at us. Then I could feel
the lightness dissipate and I wondered what had just happened. It
felt as if I had just gone somewhere, invisibly, and returned.

Dillon introduced me to the two men. The younger one's name
was Yotam. The older one called himself by his last name, Berstein. He said, "You call me this but do not say what Mr. Blondy
like to call me."

Dillon said, "I like to call him Mr. Great Big Ugly Bear."

Berstein laughed loudly and said, "So, what is your name?"

I said, "I'm Vicki."

"Ah, Vee-kee," he said. "You have face like movie star."

I thanked him, though I guessed this was a line he used a lot.

"Where you come to us from?" said Berstein.

I said, "I live at Kibbutz Ein Gedi. Before that I lived in Massachusetts."

"And you are movie star?"

I said, "I'm trained as a veterinarian."

"A veterinarian!" Berstein boomed. "You speak to Salzman

when he come here. He is also veterinarian. He drink his tea without the sugar. He is from Sfat, up in the north. He come some time next month to meet with Amnon about the possible translocation of new *pra'im* to the Makhtesh Ramon crater."

Then he said, "So, Mr. Blondy Boy. You take her in. You show her the Hai Bar." He looked at me and said, "Hai Bar is park with animals. Is like a zoo, except you no have cages. You go in jeep with Mr. Blondy Boy from United States and then you tell me what you think of the *pra'im* if they come near you. Then if you are still in love with Blondy Boy, you stay with him and he will ask you to shovel ostrich shit."

Berstein laughed loudly at his joke, then stubbed his cigarette out against the front hood of the jeep he had been leaning on. So far the smoke had not been bothering me. Neither had quiet Yotam's cologne.

We took a jeep and drove in through the gate, and then I got my first look at the animals in the enclosure. A group of ostriches approached us. With their large wedge-shaped beaks, several began pecking at the windshield. This startled me although Dillon found it hilarious. I saw two different species of oryx, as well as long-horned wild sheep known as addaxes. The *pra'im* turned out to be the Persian onagers. They were the only animals we could not get near. They had bright white rumps, legs, and bellies. The color of their flanks ranged from light tan to creamy beige. We drove around within the fences of the park for half an hour and then returned to the main building, after which Dillon said, "I really do have to shovel ostrich shit."

I helped him shovel. Five hours later, having eaten at a restaurant in Eilat, we raced back north at crazy speeds on the road through the Arava Rift Valley. I held him tightly. I was cold. There was a wind that blew east across the valley. The sky was dark and there was no moon and the stars glowed in the sky ahead of us. At some point I closed my eyes and thought that if I died right now I would die happy. Soon we began to see the lights of the Dead Sea Salt Works factory. Then we were driving along the shore of the Dead Sea. To our left were the craggy hills of Judea and to our right the smooth surface of the water held the reflections of the stars. I closed my eyes again and then I felt the lightness taking hold of me. The same lightness I'd felt before, but now much lighter. I held one hand out to the wind, felt the air streaming between my fingers. All my disasters, I thought, and suddenly I was no longer afraid of anything.

— — —

What Dillon's sister had said was true, however. You could look into Dillon's eyes and see a colossal mystery, but then he would start talking about which new decal to put on his motorcycle. Or he might want to analyze the lyrics to a Cheap Trick song. Or he would want to discuss episodes of *In Search of...* as if these television programs had been gospel about everything from the Loch Ness Monster to King Tut. Once he asked me if I thought Lee Harvey Oswald acted alone, and when I said, "No, of course not," his face brightened with a Cheshire cat–like grin and Dillon hugged me as if we were the only two people in the world who felt this way. I say all this, and yet, there was still that look in his eyes when he was quiet, that eerie stillness around which a hurricane seemed, invisibly, to swirl. I knew enough to know that what I saw of Dillon's surface was not the same as what I felt emanating from the depths of him. I knew that Dillon, in some hidden way, was extraordinary, that whatever I could sense lurking within him was neither my own projection nor a mirage.

I expected that things would gradually reveal themselves, that I would gradually discern what might or might not be possible. Then Dillon asked me to accompany him on his weekly jaunt to monitor the onagers that had been released in Makhtesh Ramon, a desert crater in the central Negev. This single day together caused things between us to accelerate in a manner akin to Dillon's habits on his motorcycle. As I would learn, Dillon's role at Hai Bar included a day or two a week of monitoring the movements and home ranges of these animals. As I would also learn, he possessed an almost extrasensory intuition, which was as useful for finding onagers as it appeared to be for guiding him through his life. Possibly what I saw that day with Dillon was my first glimpse of the extraordinary things I had been sensing. Or possibly—and I do have to consider this, all of my hard-boiled predilections notwithstanding—my path with Dillon had been decided long ago.

Formed by erosion when an ancient sea receded, Makhtesh Ramon was a two-hundred-square-kilometer depression, the floor of which was a rich array of earth tones—reds and yellows and browns that glowed with the setting sun. The introduction site for the onagers had been the Saharonim oasis, a natural spring near the crater's southern wall. Since the release, there had been a steady stream of field technicians monitoring the movements and behavior of the onagers. Or rather, I should say, attempting to. Among those who had tried in earnest was a postdoc from the United States who'd been attempting to test his own predictive model for equid social structure as a function of ecological habitat. He'd conducted research on several herd animals within the family Equidae, including mountain zebras in South Africa and feral horses in the Nevada section of the Great Basin Desert. He'd thought the onagers would become a perfect facet to his study. As an introduced population, the onagers could be viewed as a controlled experimental situation, in which the arid-adapted equid sociality would evolve. But after six futile months, he'd filed a one-page report with the Israeli Nature Reserves Authority, the final lines of which were the following: *Despite the novelty of this situation, I have determined that the onagers cannot be studied. I had an easier time tracking the wild ass species Equus kiang in the Himalayan foothills of Nepal.* In fact, the only person who had been able to locate the onagers with regularity was Amnon Grossman, who'd overseen the translocation of the animals from Hai Bar two years before. But the Makhtesh was a two-hour drive from the park, and Amnon had neither the time nor the inclination to keep tabs on them.

And then along came Dillon Morley. He spent a few days out with Amnon, and after learning to navigate the area both within and around the crater, he had acquired all of Amnon's skill and more. Because Dillon lived at Ein Gedi, it was a shorter drive to get there. One night a week, he left his motorcycle at the Hai Bar park and returned to Ein Gedi with one of the green Nature Reserves Authority jeeps. He would wake early, ascend the winding highway that led up out of Judea, through Dimona, and then south to the small desert town called Mitzpe Ramon, from which he could access a paved road that led down to the crater floor.

And so, two weeks after our first meeting, Dillon asked me to go with him. I can recall the first time we coasted through the pass known as Ma'ale Ha'atzmaut and wound our way through four switchbacks along the crater's inner wall. A herd of ibexes skipped up the limestone cliffs as we descended. A Griffon vulture soared in a patch of sky that was beneath us, then at eye level, then high above. When we had reached the crater floor, he took a turn off of the paved road, followed a dirt track along the northern side of a long, craggy limestone outcrop. He navigated the jeep across several of the dry riverbeds called wadis. He headed east across a smooth basaltic plain toward a cluster of dark black lava hills, known collectively as Giv'at Ga'ash. We found three mares grazing together in a wadi between those lava hills. By means of subtle field marks he had memorized—patterns of small black dots on their rumps, scars on their flanks, one mangled ear—Dillon identified them as Zilpah, Hagar, and Esther. Silly as it might seem, all of the onagers were required to have biblical names. This had been the official edict from bigwig nature officials in Jerusalem. Supposedly, it helped with funding.

It was six-thirty in the morning. I had been taking in the quiet, austere beauty of the desert when in his guileless manner Dillon said, "I'm wondering. Would you like it if things between the two of us moved quickly?"

I said, "What things are you referring to?"

He said, "Everything."

"To be honest," I said, "I'm trying not to think about things too hard."

He said, "Well, I have."

"You have what?"

"I've thought about things very hard."

I laughed at first, but soon I realized he was serious.

I said, "I guess you should tell me more."

"Not much to tell," Dillon said. "I'm pretty sure that you're the woman I've been looking for."

"You're twenty-one."

He said, "At some point I'll be older."

For lack of anything else to say, I asked him, "Where else have you looked?"

Then Dillon told me, for the first time, about his travels. He said that shortly after his nineteenth birthday, he had begun to feel an urgent need to go somewhere and, in his own words, to get beyond the equation he was part of. He used his trust fund, moved to Holland. He lived in Amsterdam for a while and then The Hague. He stared at paintings in museums and wandered around old churches. He saw the first wave of tulips blooming at the Keukenhof Gardens. He had a brief affair with an arty, chain-smoking girl from France. One afternoon he took a trolley ride from The Hague to a nearby coastal town called Scheveningen, where he visited what was quite possibly, in his mind, the worst aquarium in the world. While he was staring at an unhealthy-looking ray—its underside possessed a faintly greenish tint, he said—he understood that it was time to make another change. The next morning he began planning a move to Greece.

He lived on Naxos, Crete, and Mykonos, in that order. He spent much of that time in isolation, reading. He read three Dostoyevsky novels, Heidegger's *Being and Time*, and every poem by Ezra Pound or T. S. Eliot he could find. He explained that Dostoyevsky, Pound, and Eliot had all been anti-Semites. Martin Heidegger had literally been a member of the Nazi Party. Dillon had read their work with the hope of understanding how these men could be at once both visionary and morally illiterate. I asked him if he had found an answer and he said no.

He moved to Israel after finishing *Crime and Punishment*. He settled first in a small flat in Jerusalem, where he immediately immersed himself within the horrors catalogued at the Yad Vashem Holocaust memorial. After that, he paid a guide to show him all the stations of the Via Dolorosa. He spent days sitting inside the Church of the Redeemer, staring at what, supposedly, was the site of Jesus Christ's crucifixion.

He explained all of this as we sat inside the jeep, within those lava hills, and watched the three mares graze on broombushes and two other plants that Dillon called by their Latin names, *Astragalus* and *Echinops*. When Zilpah climbed out of the wadi and headed east across the jet-black plain of lava, Dillon spent five or ten minutes writing in his notebook. I sat in silence and I wondered why his story did not seem strange, but it did not.

Then I did something so precarious that it amazes me, even now. I blurted out that I had cried myself to sleep on the day I met him. I said that my heart had raced with a wild desire after one look at him, but I had assumed nothing could ever come of it.

He said, "Well, I loved you before that."

"You didn't know me."

He said, "I watched you milk your goats. It took me weeks to get the nerve up to ask Moti to introduce us."

I said, "You loved me?"

Dillon said, "Yes, I did. I do."

"You're twenty-one," I said.

Again he said, "At some point I'll be older."

"And what?" I said. "We're going to get married?"

He said, "I hope so."

I said, "Okay then. Thanks for laying all your cards out on the table. Can we slow down now?"

He said, "Sure."

Hagar and Esther climbed up out of the wadi and followed Zilpah across the lava plain. Dillon looked again at his notebook. He resumed writing, now and then glancing up to smile impishly. Finally I smiled back and understood that "going slowly" had been bypassed, that likewise any attempt at slowing down would be merely a formality.

For the next ten hours, we crossed wadis, climbed over outcroppings, and glided across plains of limestone rubble. We startled bustards, gazelles, puff adders, and agamas, and he continually found the tracks and dung of onagers. When they were fresh, he would scan the wide expanse of desert with his binoculars, locate vague shadows that would turn out to be equine silhouettes. We found one large group—seven mares, five with foals—grazing within a sandstone plain that resembled Mars and was known as the Red Valley. We found two bachelor stallions, Samson and Noah, skulking behind a table rock known as Har Katum. We caught up with the alpha stallion, Abraham, as he patrolled a dirt path that was once the Nabatean spice merchants' route between Petra and Gaza. Based on the manner of Abraham's patrol—a constant zigzag, with frequent stops to expose the scent glands in his gums—Dillon predicted that the stallion known as Zebulon was nearby. Ten minutes later Zebulon climbed out from a wadi just ahead of us, glanced once at Abraham, and fled at a full gallop. The way that Dillon located these animals seemed so methodical, so matter-of-fact, that if I hadn't known better, I would have assumed that hundreds of wild onagers roamed the area.

Near dusk, as the winds came up, Dillon navigated his way back to the paved highway. We ascended the crater's northern wall, and when we reached the plateau above, it was as if we had emerged from an ancient world. We ate falafel at a small pub near the Mitzpe Ramon bus station. We climbed back into the jeep and Dillon drove with his crazy speed to Kibbutz Ein Gedi. I did my best to hide my lingering sense of awe as I made love to him with unprecedented ferocity, after which I fell into a deep slumber. Later I woke to find him transcribing the day's data while he listened and sang along with the song "Too Shy" by Kajagoogoo on his Walkman. And just like that, it was back to the nonmysterious, almost adolescent Dillon, who played his music so loudly that I wondered if he had problems with his hearing; the twenty-one-year-old who'd traveled between Holland, Greece, and Israel with a hodgepodge of cassette tapes that included the Velvet Underground, Duran Duran, and the full soundtrack from *The Muppet Movie*.

But soon enough I grew used to Dillon's quirks and eccentricities. Soon enough my only fear was something akin to a red-haired former stripper with breast implants — that someday blond, beautiful Dillon would meet a reformed stripper or whoever and that this wouldn't bode well for his much older girlfriend, me. One evening, as we sat watching the deep dead blue of the Dead Sea water, I explained all this and Dillon told me, firmly, not to worry. I asked if he had any fears, and he said no, he could already see our future. Shortly after this conversation, he learned from Amnon that there was a spare room at Hai Bar. He asked me if I could be persuaded to move in with him, although the room was even smaller than my room at the kibbutz. We had been standing near the kibbutz chicken cage when he asked, and I said, "Will you catch me if I jump?" When Dillon nodded, bemused, I said, "I've always wanted to do this." Then I leapt into his outstretched arms and said, "I'm yours."

I had been gradually losing touch with Lillian. Now and then she wrote a letter, but it took me weeks to write her back, and soon her letters had stopped coming. My parents continued writing. One of my co-workers at the veterinary clinic sent me a wedding invitation. But I did something strange. I left Kibbutz Ein Gedi and gave no forwarding address. I wrote my parents a single letter to say that I had left the kibbutz and would be out of touch for a while. I told them not to worry. I told them that I was getting better. It was December, I said, and it was colder, although nowhere near the temperatures at this time of year in western Massachusetts. I don't know why, but I considered this to be a sufficient update. I also did not give them my address at the Hai Bar Nature Reserve.

We moved into the room at Hai Bar and it seemed as if my body had forgotten things. For instance, it had forgotten that mold could hurt it. It forgot to react to things like scented soaps and cooking smells and all varieties of biblical wildlife excrement. One night when Dillon came back from running errands in Eilat, he crawled in bed with me and said, "Let's make a baby." I said, "A baby?" He said, "A baby. It will be easy." And I thought yes, it would be easy to make a baby. We'd have a baby just like the baby gazelle whose mother had died and who we had been feeding from a bottle. Except that our baby would not be an orphan. "Let's make a baby," I said, and I'd repeat this every time Dillon climbed onto me and flexed the sinewy muscles in his skinny legs and made noises unlike anyone I'd ever gone to bed with. Sometimes he'd coo, sometimes he'd howl, sometimes he'd roar at me. Some nights he'd fall asleep immediately, almost collapsing when we finished. I'd lie awake, allowing wave after wave of memory to wash over me.

I saw myself as a high school senior at a basketball game. I had been wearing one of those big foam fingers, cheering wildly, turning to make out with my boyfriend, Neil. I recalled taking LSD on a warm spring night during college, dancing around with Mardi Gras beads, and later breaking into a lecture hall, where I lectured to a pair of tripping boys who laughed hysterically at every word I said. I recalled meeting Luke in Ithaca while I worked at the raptor rehabilitation clinic at Cornell Vet School. He'd come to photograph an injured golden eagle. I'd thought immediately that Luke would look much better once he shaved off his goatee. I recalled *2001: A Space Odyssey,* a movie I loved and Luke hated, particularly the scene where the man is alone and old in a room somewhere beyond the outer reaches of the universe. I recalled the eerie silence in that place outside of everything, so hypnotic and so alarming that I rewound and replayed this final sequence after Luke had gone to sleep. But soon these memories no longer made me wistful or nostalgic. Soon all these memories were starting to float away.

— — —

I had been pregnant for two months when she appeared again, the woman I had glimpsed through the screen door on my first day at Hai Bar. I asked her name and she said that it was Helen-Ariadne. She was tall and had blond hair. Later, when I asked about her name, she would tell me that her father had been a classics professor at Harvard and that she had been named after his two favorite mythological heroines. Still later, she would tell me many other things, but on that day in early March of 1984, she'd come to Hai Bar to tell me about Dillon.

He'd crashed his motorcycle as he was heading north past Ein Gedi. He had been driving more than a hundred miles an hour, and as always, he had not been wearing a helmet. He had veered off the road near the Dead Sea beach and he had flown through the air and crashed into a rocky hill and no one in the universe could have been expected to survive.

Except he had survived, she said. She'd been a witness. She had been standing at a nearby bus stop when it happened. She'd been the one to call the ambulance. He had been taken to a hospital in Jerusalem. He was unconscious and, at least for the time being, in a coma. But he was breathing. There had been several operations.

I went to see him. I saw his disfigured face, his bruises, the wires connected to his body. I went to see him for six straight days, and then his parents flew in from Salt Lake City. His parents frightened me, made me nervous, made me think Dillon would die soon. I said I knew their son from the field school in Ein Gedi. I didn't tell them I was pregnant with his baby. Then he was gone, flown to his home in Salt Lake City. I stayed in our little room at the Hai Bar breeding park. I was consoled by Yotam, Berstein, and another park ranger, Natan. I worked for Amnon, who came and went. I waited for my belly to start growing. Twice in that week I was visited by Helen-Ariadne. She warned me not to follow Dillon. She said his family was powerful and dangerous, that I'd been right not to tell them about the baby. She said that she would soon go after him. She had a reason to, she said, and I was too overcome with despair to wonder why. Eventually she would return, she said, and then I would know what happened. She could not say how long she would be gone.

— — —

One of the onagers who still lived at the breeding park was called Joseph. He could be recognized very easily because his coat was colorful. Reddish beige and a bit of tan and a patch of creamy mustard brown. His rump and legs and belly were bright white, like all the others. But because of his so-called coat of many colors, he was one of the few onagers at the park who you could always pick out of the herd. Joseph had always been Dillon's favorite, and he preferred to call him Mr. Rainbow.

Though it was far simpler than trying to locate the reintroduced onagers in the Makhtesh Ramon crater, the only way you
could get anywhere near the Hai Bar herd was to take a jeep and
follow them around the enclosure at low speed. They would eventually habituate and allow the jeep to get as close as twenty or
thirty meters before they'd run. I liked to go out looking for the
onagers, to stare at Joseph through binoculars, and in some way
I can't explain, this simple act helped keep me going despite the
lack of any word from Helen-Ariadne. I don't know how I stayed
so calm during those weeks, which turned to months as the baby
grew inside me. Finally, I broke down and wrote a letter to my
parents. I wrote to say that I was pregnant, that I was living at a
nature park near Israel's southernmost city of Eilat and had been
thinking of returning to the U.S. at some point in the near future.
But then I ripped the letter up, and for the first time in the months
since Dillon's accident, I felt something like desolation. I wrote to
Lillian instead. I told her everything. How all my ailments had
resolved. How I'd believed I had found Shangri-la in the desert
with a twenty-one-year-old boy from Utah. How I'd been so sure
everything would turn out right that I'd stayed calm for three
whole months after Dillon's accident, but that this certainty was
rapidly eroding. Should I come home? I asked Lillian in the letter.
Was it possible that symptoms would return if I came home? How
long did people need to remain in the desert for when dealing with
these symptoms? Listen to this, I wrote, and described the onager
named Joseph. I wrote that, if nothing else, I still had Joseph and
his coat of many colors. But suddenly the entire letter seemed foolish and I ripped it up as well.

At this point, I entered what is easily the strangest part of my
story. It began that very night, just a few hours after I ripped those
letters up. I began having what seemed to be a conversation with
the tall blond woman, Helen-Ariadne. Almost like dreaming but
more like half-dreams. Inside my head I told her I was still healthy.

Inside my head I said, I'm five months pregnant and I'm no longer throwing up my breakfast. Inside my head I asked the tall blond woman, Should I go home?

I still had debts to pay from vet school. I had applied for and received a medical deferral, but after one year I would have to resume paying my student loan. I still had money from the sale of the house, but that was money I would need when I had the baby. I didn't know how long my free room and board at Hai Bar would last, and eventually I would also need to renew my visa. That or attempt to become a citizen of Israel. I said these things to Helen-Ariadne in my head, and she replied.

She said, The best thing you can do for yourself is stay right where you are.

I said, The mold ruined my life. All of my plans. I was on track.

She said, There is no track except for one you cannot see.

I said, Who sees it then, you?

She said, The track that you imagine is a ghost that cannot be followed.

Am I a ghost as well? I asked.

She answered, No.

— — —

There was an oryx at the park who was known as Hermes. Unlike the onagers, the oryxes had not been given biblical names. Ares, Nero, Ferdinand, Attila, Napoleon, Elizabeth, Hera, and Isis were among two dozen or so oryxes. A mix of emperors, gods, goddesses, kings, and queens.

Hermes had been gored by a younger oryx. It was July, and the hot ionized winds called the *hamsin* had been blowing across the Negev. The hot winds seemed to make the animals more violent. We had Hermes harnessed in a stall. Beside me the vet from Sfat, Yeheskel Salzman, was observing as I cleaned and stitched

235

the wound. He was impressed with my skills, he said, over and over. I was dressing the wound when a car pulled into the Hai Bar parking lot. I didn't listen very hard. I was too focused on the oryx. Soon we were wrapping gauze around his body, taping the wound so that Hermes wouldn't chew the stitches off. Then I looked up and she was standing right beside me. Her hair was dark now. It was Helen-Ariadne. By then I'd seen her so many times inside my head that at first I could not be sure it was really her.

"Dillon is back," she said. "He's here. Before you see him, I'd like to talk to you."

Then I was happy and I was frightened and I was thankful. I said I'd be done with the oryx in a minute. Yeheskel Salzman said, "Go on. I'll finish up." Then I walked out of the stall and began to cry.

Dillon was conscious, the woman said, after a moment. He was alive. He'd been up and walking for six weeks. She was still working with him, though. He was much better than he'd been when she began with him in May. It would take time, she said, before he would remember me.

She led me to our little room, where she had brought him. Dillon was sitting on the chair. There were two curving seams of scars from where the stitches had sewn his face up. He had lost thirty pounds, at least. His head had been shaved, so his blond hair was now a little tuft. When he looked up at me, Helen-Ariadne said, "This is Vicki. She is the woman who is carrying the child you made together." Dillon smiled at me and said, "You're very beautiful." I said, "Thank you." He said, "Hello."

She took him somewhere at night, but in the days she would return with him. She would sit with him for hours while I tended to the animals. He was alert and very talkative, though the woman hardly spoke. Now and then, when I walked by, Dillon would look up at me and smile. Once he walked past me in the paddock and he was singing: *Getting to know you. Getting to know all about you.*

Another time I caught him singing *The Muppet Movie* theme song to Joseph, who he had recently resumed calling Mr. Rainbow.

A day came when the tall woman took me aside and said, "He's starting to remember you. Even so, you need to understand, this isn't the same Dillon. Or not entirely. Once he is well enough and feels comfortable, I'll leave it to him to explain."

Another day she said, "He wants to touch you. Touch your belly."

I let him touch me.

Another day she said, "He'd like you to tell him all about the mold."

Sometimes I watched her, the tall woman. Sometimes it looked to me as if she were shimmering or rippling. Sometimes I told myself that this was just the rippling of the heat haze. Sometimes I thought, This woman isn't real. At other times I decided that she was part real and part shadow. Still other times I had the feeling that she had come from outer space. Sooner or later, I would call my parents, as well as Lillian. What would I tell them? Would I say people can dissolve? People can be erased or disappear right in front of you? People can travel to strange places that you can't follow? On rare occasions, people actually return?

One morning in late August the woman named Helen-Ariadne shaved all her formerly blond and recently dark hair off. Being bald, she still looked beautiful. Maybe more so.

She said, "He'd like to spend a night with you, beside you. He wants to do it in a few days, if you're ready."

I said, "I'd like that very much."

"Good," the woman said. "Now I have something else to tell you."

I said, "I'm listening."

She said, "Dillon has been through a long ordeal, much of which he will not remember. But he will tell you bits and pieces, and you must not be afraid."

I said, "I thought he was all right."

She said, "He is."

"What if his parents come?"

"They won't."

"Do they know he's here?"

"It doesn't matter. Now please listen. I am going to give you some instructions."

I expected these instructions to pertain to Dillon, his recent injuries, his coma. I prepared myself for whatever it was that I was about to hear. I guessed that maybe she was going to teach me some of the techniques that she had used in her rehabilitation work with him. But her instructions were both simpler and more expansive, and these instructions were for me.

She said, "Someday, years from now, you will need to write all of this down. You must recount your version of what has happened. You won't remember everything, but what you do remember will be important."

I asked her why it would be important. The woman said that it would help me to make sense of things. It would help me as well as others to see the ways in which this chain of events that I was part of would resolve. I asked her if she meant the mold and my decision to come to Israel and meeting Dillon — was this the chain she was referring to?

She said, "That's part of it, but this chain is much longer."

I said, "How long?"

"I do not know," she said.

I waited for more instructions, but there were none.

Apparently, our conversation was concluding, so I asked Helen-Ariadne one more question. I asked her if she recalled speaking to me on that evening about two and a half months ago. She said no.

"In early June," I said, but all she did was look at me.

Then she leaned down. She kissed my cheek and she said, "You are a strong woman. Soon I will leave you on your own."

— — —

When Dillon returned that evening he seemed quiet. He moved with his pleasant, gangly strides across the parking lot. He raised his hands above his head, wiggled his fingers. He said, "Shalom." It was the first time I had ever heard him speak a word of Hebrew. It was the first time I considered the idea that our unborn child, if we stayed in Israel, would learn to speak the Hebrew language. It was the first time, I believe, that I began to visualize this desert as my home.

Soon after, I would hear many things. For instance, he would tell me of his rescue from his parents' mountain chalet in Utah, the details of which were sparse, as Dillon's knowledge of the incident had been limited to the skeletal account that Helen-Ariadne had provided. I would hear him describe waking up in one place, then another, always with Helen-Ariadne there beside him, explaining that she had administered a drug that could temporarily override the brain chemistry responsible for maintaining his coma. Each time he woke it had seemed like teletransportation or else time travel, Dillon said. It took him weeks to understand what she was doing.

I know about a parking lot in Kalamazoo, Michigan, where for the first time since his accident, Dillon woke briefly on his own. I know about a drive through the Badlands of South Dakota, where Dillon first began to speak to her. About a drive through the Pawnee Grasslands in north-central Colorado, where Dillon listened as Helen-Ariadne taught him the names of birds. McCown's longspur, horned lark, burrowing owl, lark bunting, mountain plover. These are the birds of the western prairie, Dillon would tell me, as if the names were a sort of code.

About an island off the coast of Maine where Dillon realized that he was no longer slipping back into his coma. About the sound of barking seals. About wild blueberry bushes growing on spongy bogs.

About the dark secrets of his family, which in themselves could fill an encyclopedia and yet still might not be believed. About the things that seemed to me so preposterous that at times I had to ask him to stop talking and leave the room and wonder whether one or both of us was crazy.

About the ways Dillon had changed. How the techniques employed by Helen-Ariadne had caused, in Dillon's words, a reintegration of his mind. He still possessed his extrasensory intuition, could still find onagers as if tracking them with the help of a crystal ball. But the hurricane that I had seen inside him was much quieter, and it was only now and then that I would notice it at all.

In October of that year, our daughter, Arava, was born on a windy morning at the Hadassah hospital in Jerusalem. On the first day of her life, we took her into the hospital's famous synagogue, where we sat gazing at the Chagall windows for some time.

Six months later, Dillon and I were married at Ein Gedi, which marked the first time I laid eyes on any members of Dillon's family besides his parents. His sister, Dee, had flown in. So had his aunt Julia and teenage cousin Dara. The three blond sirens, I sometimes called them as a joke.

That spring was also the time in which an attempt was made on the life of the park's curator, Amnon Grossman. The shooting took place after he'd returned from the Gaza Strip, where he'd been stationed during *miluim*, which is the Hebrew word for the month of active military duty that all Israeli men must serve until the age of fifty-four. I didn't see the shooting, but I heard it. Then I ran out and saw him lying there, his shirt and trousers soaked with his own blood.

Amnon spent five weeks in the hospital and survived. In the following year his wife, Shoshanna, gave birth to their son Yakov, who they called Yaki. He and Arava grew up together almost as siblings, or so we thought, until their teenage years. Then something changed, although perhaps it was always there, and suddenly it became clear that they did not think of each other as two siblings. Why do I find myself believing that Helen-Ariadne saw all this coming? Was it so obvious that these two children would be born and would fall in love?

Dillon and I did what we needed to become citizens of Israel. He took Judaism classes and formally converted. He served three years of mandatory service in the army. Every year since then, he leaves to serve his month of active duty. Arava also served in the military. For the two years required of Israeli women, she served as a desert guide in the Negev. Yaki served as part of a telecommunications unit at a base up near Tiberias, and when he had completed his three years, they took a trip together to New Zealand. Upon their return, Yaki entered the Hebrew University in Jerusalem, where Arava was enrolled already. They lived together in Jerusalem and not long ago were married. It almost feels as if I've conjured up a spell, foretold a future that is also my own past, as I record this. Yaki and Arava. They seem to be the resolution to this story.

Dillon once told me that he felt as if he'd traveled across many worlds in order to return to ours, and that when he had made it back he was astonished at what he saw. He was astonished, as well, he said, that what he would see from that point onward would for the most part be the things we saw together. Now I am fifty-four years old and Dillon is forty-six and he still listens to loud music through his headphones and I still wonder if Helen-Ariadne will reappear. I still wonder about all I do not know, and I wonder why it is that what I do know seems to matter. Why I keep watching Dillon move across the Hai Bar parking lot. Why I go back to this one moment as if being pulled there by the force of gravity.

I was outside, holding my belly. I waved to Dillon and looked around for a tall, bald woman. When Dillon reached me, I said, "Where is she?" and he told me she was gone. I said I'd spoken with Helen-Ariadne just that morning. He said he knew this. He was sorry. He had been nervous and he'd sent her as a messenger. If it was okay, he said, he wished to lie beside me that same night. He said he wanted to tell me everything, all at once, but she'd instructed him to do it slowly because certain things might seem impossible. "Don't underestimate me," I said, and then the baby kicked inside me. I took his hand and we started walking, just to walk, to go wherever we would go.

9

The Ancient Forest

In a tale written by the Argentinean writer Jorge Luis Borges, an imprisoned magician called Tzinacán states the following: "The god, foreseeing that at the end of time there would be devastation and ruin, wrote on the first day of Creation a magical sentence with the power to ward off those evils." The magician's cell sits adjacent to a cage that holds a jaguar. His narrative arises from his conviction that the one magical sentence he has alluded to may be deciphered from the pattern of the jaguar's spots. After years of staring at the jaguar, he deduces a series of fourteen seemingly random words that if spoken aloud will make him equal to the Creator. But he chooses not to state these words, and instead he quietly awaits his own death and oblivion.

My wife, Doris, read this story to me long ago. "*Nu*, it's a puzzle," she said, when she had finished. "He solves the puzzle but won't tell us the solution."

I agreed, and so at first the question seemed to be that of whether this magician had decided he was not qualified to read the text aloud and ward off evil or if the story's implication was that the fate of the human race, despite the god's foresight, would be devastation and ruin. Only later did I realize that the question the story caused me to ponder more than any other was that of what it takes to find a thing that's hidden, a thing that lurks within whatever it is you're staring at each day. Perhaps the meaning of the story is that you must look deep rather than far if you want to unlock any of the secrets of the universe, that once unlocked a secret loses its power unless a part of it is withheld. I've read the story again perhaps a dozen times in the years since Doris passed away, and in my daydreams I imagine that I have recognized the god's magical sentence. I imagine that I've inferred its secret words from the shapes of clouds or have deduced it from the angles of the branches of an oak tree out my window. And I have wondered what to do. I have imagined speaking the words aloud and equally I have considered the many reasons to stay silent. Needless to say, these represent the fantastic wishes of a man who has read far too much literature and philosophy. More to the point, these are the thoughts of an old man who must wear diapers to bed and who, on certain mornings, can barely move his arms or legs.

— — —

My name is Maximilian Rubin, and by the time you read all this, I may be dead. I very well may be alive, however, as I am planning on it. But at my age life becomes tenuous. I have angina and a heart murmur and, of late, diabetes. My arthritis has been plaguing my every move for the last ten years. I have been married twice, and just this week I've come to know the first of my great-grandchildren. You might be tempted to think that I am "ready." In certain ways, I suppose I am. Yet by no means have I grown tired of life. Like some, though not all, I would like to live forever. Inside my head I feel as if I am still twenty-five, and ten, and sixty, and my age, which is ninety-four. No wonder Descartes wanted to keep the mind and body separate. Though he was wrong, of course, it feels like the two are separate. And if tomorrow I were to learn that I had only a month to live I would be outraged, bewildered, and for some period incapable of engaging in my daily habits and rituals. But when the shock wore off I would go back to it all, and I believe I would be able to accept death, make a plan for it, and apprehend why, especially at my age, death is not something to be feared.

It might amuse you—or not—that, at present, I am living in the Charles Bierman Home, a Jewish assisted-living facility located in the town of Montclair, New Jersey. I have lived here for ten years, having moved after my former residence, the Pine Manor Home for the Elderly, in South Orange, closed due to bankruptcy in 1985, shortly after the death of my beloved Doris and the events that I intend to transcribe here. I am writing all this longhand on a small wooden desk that does not have room for a computer of any kind. My bedroom is roughly two hundred square feet, and my wall has a lone poster of Bavtah, a leopard who once roamed wild in Israel's Dead Sea basin but spent the final portion of her life as a zoo exhibit at the Hai Bar Yotvata Nature Reserve, near Eilat. Naturally, I have looked hard at the leopard's spots.

By way of other introductory information, I should also mention that I was married to my first wife, Natalie Rubin (née Weinberger), for thirty-seven years, until her death in the fall of 1973. Our son Michael lives in the nearby town of Livingston, where he works as a physician. Our younger son, Daniel, died at age fourteen of leukemia, an incident that is recounted, much to my amazement now, with unblinking detail in the one book I have ever written, *The Invisible World*, published in 1963 by the long-defunct Temple Beth El Press of Hawthorne, New Jersey. In the book, I have described in detail my practice of speaking to Daniel, whose presence I continue to feel so strongly that at times I've wondered why he does not speak back. I met Doris in the spring of 1982, shortly after she became a resident at Pine Manor. Born in Austrian-ruled Galicia in 1911, which became part of the Second Polish Republic in 1918, she survived the Holocaust and immigrated to the U.S. in 1945. We eloped in August of 1982, to Las Vegas.

Had you told me that I would find my truest love at the age of eighty-one I would have doubted you. Had you told me I'd still be alive right now I might have laughed but then believed you in my heart. It seems uncanny and in certain ways alarming that almost thirteen years have passed since the spring morning when I met

Doris. Even now, I still wake with the expectation that I will look up and find her sitting or sleeping in my armchair.

As for Doris, she was seventy-one years old when we married, which was quite young as the range of ages went at the Pine Manor Home for the Elderly. But her children lived far away and in recent years she had developed a sort of vertigo, which had resulted in several falls, including one that broke her hip. She came to Pine Manor following her rehabilitation, and, lest you mistake my attraction to Doris as something quaint, I'd like to note that from the first time I laid eyes on her I felt what I had never felt with Natalie. I felt attraction that bordered on longing. I felt the crazy sense that I would do anything she asked of me. I was drawn to her hard demeanor, which also seemed to be imbued with vulnerability. Not to mention that her full figure corresponded exactly to what has always been my type despite having married Natalie, who was all bones. I recognized that, like most of us, she'd been deeply wounded. I sensed that, unlike most, she was aware of it. I understood that I was witnessing both inner and outer beauty of great proportions, that at age forty this woman had still caused heads to turn, that at age thirty her eyes alone would have rendered most men useless. But aside from all this I could feel a certain resonance between us. I could feel it during our first conversation, and I could feel it when she first mentioned her late husband Victor Schulman, a bank executive who died in 1977. Though she remembered Victor fondly, I suspected she did not miss him. I sensed that Victor's inner nature was not expansive enough for Doris, and I dared to believe mine was.

I quickly learned about Doris's activities as a Holocaust survivor. She would give talks at local synagogues. I attended two of these programs, in which she and other Holocaust authorities gave short presentations and then served as a question-and-answer panel. Doris could speak matter-of-factly about Nazis tossing babies in the air and shooting them, about sets of twins who simultaneously had their arms sawed off in Josef Mengele's infamous experiments, about a famous Polish singer who was assaulted by four men and then killed because she proved unable to sing clearly with a horse bit in her mouth. Once I asked her how it was that she could speak with such detachment about incidents that on more than one occasion had caused fragile audience members to leave the room. Doris's answer to my question was straightforward. She said, "I tell these same stories, over and over, so I grow used to them, as stories. I also never speak about the worst things I have known."

In late winter of 1983, about six months after we were married, she was contacted by a man from Arlington, Virginia, who expressed interest in gathering the stories of Doris and a group of her friends who also survived the death camps. This was to be for archival purposes geared toward the planned Holocaust museum to be located in Washington, D.C. Most of these other survivors with whom Doris retained contact lived in the Catskills. After what seemed to me an overly drawn-out period of planning, we took a bus up to the Catskills in order to get on a chartered bus the next morning with this group and travel back down to Arlington. There each survivor was to take a turn giving testimony about the Holocaust on videotape. We were all to stay in a fancy hotel, complete with kosher dining option, where plans included a gala fund-raiser in which Doris and company were to be the guests of honor.

It was during this trip that I heard, for the first and only time, the full account of Doris's survival. I sat in the room with her while she was taping, and the words that came out of her mouth were the kinds of things I had only read in history books or watched in epic movies. It is not possible to recount her entire testimony here, as it required more than three full hours of taping. But I will try to recount what struck me as most memorable, not that any single word of her testimony seemed to me anything less than miraculous. I will also note that, as we went into the studio, she said, "It's good of you to come, Max, but I fear that you will not like me if you listen to my whole story." I thought about this for a moment and tried to gauge what I was made of. I decided that there was no part of Doris I was afraid of. And I will tell you right now that I was correct in my assumption. There was nothing in her testimony that disillusioned me.

— — —

She fled Warsaw in the fall of 1939, after the Nazi siege began. Her first husband, Pinchas, a mathematics teacher and prominent Warsaw citizen, feared that the Germans would take him prisoner if he did not escape to politically independent Lithuania. She and Pinchas went first to stay with relatives in Wyszków, which was then bombed by the Germans, so they fled through the woods to the town of Jadów. Jadów was bombed as well and they went north. Two days after the Soviet invasion, they were intercepted by Red Army soldiers, and after explaining — through a mix of Polish and bits of Russian and frenzied gesturing with their arms and legs — that they were running from the Germans, they were placed on a cargo train to Białystok, where they were given half a loaf of bread and allowed by the town committee to spend a night on a crowded floor inside a synagogue. The next day they were able to hitch a ride in a farmer's horse-drawn cart as far as Grodno. From there they traveled north and crossed the border into Lithuania, which was still free. Eventually they made their way to Kovno, where they were soon among thousands of Polish-Jewish refugees.

Two weeks after their arrival, with the Soviets having fully occupied eastern Poland, they were joined in Kovno by Doris's sister Hanna, Hanna's husband Jonah, and the couple's five-year-old daughter. Pinchas had known Jonah in Warsaw, where they had been teachers at the same gymnasium. Jonah had left the city two years before, in 1937, at which time he had taken his family to live on his brother's farm in a tiny village on the northern banks of the Bug River. He and his family had run away in the night when Russian soldiers came for his brother. He'd had no more than forty seconds to send his wife and daughter out to hide in a barn, grab his emergency pack of food, water, tools, American dollars, and Polish złotys, and run out after them. Within ten minutes, his brother, Lejb, and sister-in-law, Idel, were being marched away at gunpoint. He assumed they had been deported to a work camp in Siberia and that the Russians had taken ownership of the farm.

Between Pinchas and Jonah, the men were carrying enough currency to rent a tiny room for the five of them, in a flat that housed, in all, twenty-seven Polish-Jewish refugees. They were able to find a small amount of work as tutors. Both men also possessed rudimentary carpentry skills and could find work this way as well. They survived through their own resourcefulness. Doris noted that her sister's husband, Jonah, was extremely charismatic, which helped a great deal when they needed things like blankets or new shoes. They received support from the local Jewish community as well as several charitable organizations, which provided soup kitchens and other resources while assisting refugees who sought passage out of war-torn Europe. Sooner or later Lithuania would be swallowed up by Germany or the USSR, and everyone in Kovno understood this.

Pinchas and Jonah were both attempting to get visas and secure passage to the Western Hemisphere or Palestine. But in the end, only Jonah had been able to succeed. In late July of 1940, a month or so after the Soviets occupied Kovno, he secured a single-family visa for transit across the Far East, through Japan. But all the months as refugees had long used up what little savings he or Pinchas had arrived with. He applied for funding from the American Jewish Joint Distribution Committee, which was able to grant him two but not three tickets for the trans-Siberian railway. The tickets were to be used by Jonah's wife and daughter. Doris, Pinchas, and Jonah would stay behind, though they believed they would obtain more funding and follow soon. Subsequent months passed by with no success, however, and by late 1940, escape from Soviet-occupied Lithuania had become extremely difficult. All of the charitable organizations and sympathetic foreign consulates had been forced out by the Russians, and there was mounting pressure for all refugees to declare Soviet citizenship, through which the right to emigrate would be forfeited. Jonah and Pinchas had developed contacts with the Kovno underground and were considering fleeing south with a vague plan of finding their way to Palestine. Simultaneously they were working on securing false identities, through which they might pass as Lithuanians and circumvent the need to declare Soviet citizenship. Thanks to the underground connections they had forged, this latter plan succeeded, which seemed to make the need to escape less urgent.

The Germans seized control of Lithuania in late June of 1941. Within a day of the invasion, anti-Semitic Lithuanian extremists calling themselves freedom fighters accused the Kovno Jews of handing Lithuania over to the Soviets and then used the excuse to terrorize and kill. Countless atrocities were committed over two days of nonstop violence. Others were arrested, and throughout that summer, the Kovno Jews were taken by the thousands to the Seventh Fort, one of the nineteenth-century Russian fortresses that surrounded the city, where eventually an estimated seven thousand men were killed and buried in mass grave sites. Somehow or other, Doris claimed, she'd remained hopeful. She, Pinchas, and Jonah had believed that after this initial burst of violence things would calm down. During this time, Pinchas and Jonah learned of and then applied for positions that were being offered to five hundred Jewish intellectuals. The jobs were to involve archival work in the city hall in Kovno. In hopes of finding a way onto this list, they had appealed to every person who they believed might have the slightest bit of influence. These were to be the five hundred best and brightest Jewish intellectuals in the city, and when they learned they were among the men who had been chosen, they considered themselves to be extremely lucky. The selection had been made by supposed Lithuanian nationalists, who on the eighth of August, 1941, met the throng of men in order to accompany them to their posts. Later that day, word came back that these supposed nationalists were just extremists and other armed criminals who'd been recruited by German security police to march the chosen men to one of the Russian fortresses outside the city and then shoot them. Doris concluded this part of her testimony by noting that every year since then, on this day in August, she'd woken in the morning, gone to the toilet, and thrown up.

Four days after Pinchas and Jonah had been murdered, Doris moved into the Kovno ghetto. She lived there from August 1941 through July of 1943. She described two more horrible massacres that took place in the fall of 1941. The first of these occurred in late September. A selection of about a thousand men, women, and children from the ghetto was made, after which these Jews were taken away and shot at the Ninth Fort. Three weeks later, the ghetto's Jewish Council received orders to assemble all inhabitants in the courtyard. This time more than ten thousand were marched out of town, taken in groups to be slaughtered by machine-gun fire, and then buried in large pits at the Ninth Fort. This was referred to by surviving Kovno Ghetto Jews as "the Big Action." No other large-scale executions took place there for the next two years.

I have glossed over these events for the sake of getting to what seems to me the most unlikely and miraculous parts of Doris's astounding testimony, which began with her years in the Kovno ghetto. While ghetto life was, in a word, horrific, there were some lesser-known and indeed surprising activities that took place there. These included an orchestra that performed in summer 1942 and in that same year the establishment of a vocational school. Doris, who had sung in a yeshiva choir in Warsaw as a girl, was recruited by the Jewish Council to lead a choir for ghetto children. She claimed that, relatively speaking, this was a happy time. Under the auspices of the vocational school, she taught these children to sing and led performances in which she sang as well. Then in late July of 1943, Nazi soldiers raided a performance and the next thing she knew, she and the fourteen children in the choir had been imprisoned and within two days were being loaded onto a train that went first to Vilna, then headed southwest through Grodno and into what had formerly been Poland. Perhaps because she felt herself to be the chaperone of these children, she kept her head and did not suffer a nervous breakdown like many other adults in the overcrowded train car, which, after the war, she determined had been headed to Treblinka. Meanwhile, the children, being children, were not as fearful as the adults. One of the older boys had informed her that the train car door had been left unlocked, and then she recognized the *puszcza*, the primeval forest that extended north and east and south of Białystok. As the train passed through those ancient woods, she asked the boy to choose five children he believed would have a good chance of surviving in the forest. By that summer, the Nazi policies were no secret, and so she knew, to some degree, what was in store for all the prisoners on that train.

Doris was thirty-one years old. Although she was significantly underweight by then, she was still relatively fit, as were the children. Still, she had wondered if any of them were fit enough to jump from a moving train. She claimed, in her testimony, that she almost failed to give the signal, that when she saw a patch of dark, thick forest, which seemed to her the best of the spots she had considered, the thought occurred to her that maybe it would be better for these children to die quickly, rather than to starve out in the woods. But then she thought about the atrocities she had witnessed in the ghetto, as well as the horrors that had been recounted to her by those who believed it better not to live in ignorance of what was happening. And then she gave it. She gave the signal. Five children jumped and then another five and it became clear that all fourteen children were in on it. She was the last to jump and by then guns were firing. After hitting the hard ground and somersaulting with her momentum, she quickly sprang up and looked around. Three of the children who had jumped seconds before her had been cut down by a spray of bullets, but there were two boys who were sprinting toward the cover of the woods. She followed the boys into the *puszcza*, Doris said. This was the only remaining part of the immense forest that once spread across the entire European plain. Just inside the trees, she ran along the woods' edge in hopes of finding other children. They found one girl, who said that none of the other children she had jumped with had been able to reach the woods. Doris told the children that they were inside the *puszcza*, an ancient forest that once upon a time had been a private hunting reserve for Russian czars who would hunt deer, elk, wild boar, and the European bison known as wisents. She explained, in her testimony, that she had not mentioned the bears and lynx and wolves and other predators to the children. She said that long ago she'd come to think of the place as sacred, and she believed that the sacred animals who lived there would not dare hurt them.

She led the trio of children deeper into the forest. It occurred to her that possibly she was merely leading them to starvation, as she'd feared. She also knew that these forests would be searched by teams of German soldiers with trained dogs when word came back of the escape. It wouldn't be very hard to locate the exact spots where the children jumped, since most of them lay dead or dying beside the train tracks.

They walked for hours, and as the sky began to lighten, they found a giant fallen oak, the roots of which had formed a natural depression in the earth. They gathered branches from evergreens and used them to cover the depression while they hid there and slept most of the day. When darkness fell, they walked again. Still Doris did not know where she was going. Her only plan was to walk deep into the forest. On the third day, at dawn, as she and the three children searched for a resting place, they heard voices speaking in Russian. They all took cover and sent Rivka, the most lightfooted of their group, to steal ahead to see who these Russian voices belonged to. When she returned, she announced that there were three men who appeared to be members of a partisan group.

She had the children hide while she went forward. She knew that Jewish women often were assaulted by groups of partisans, and she did not know what became of children. As she approached, she saw the three men and called out in her best Russian. She said she had escaped from a Nazi train with three others and would like to join the partisan resistance. One of the men laughed at her. Another man said, "Dobrusz?" This was Doris's given name in Polish. She recognized Jankiel Fischman and his younger brother, Anszel, who smiled at her. Then the man who had laughed spoke to her in Polish. "Do you have weapons?" he asked, and Jankiel Fischman said, "This is Dobrusz Werblonsky, married to Pinchas, who taught at the gymnasium in Warsaw." The other man said, "If they do not have weapons, they cannot join us. Certainly they cannot join if it is only she and some other skinny girls."

Doris explained that she was hiding with three children. They were all quick and fit and nimble. They could be trained to be good spies. The man said, "You do not have weapons and you do not have food and you are traveling with three children?" He turned to Jankiel and said, "I'm sorry, this will not happen." Then the man pointed his gun at Doris, but before he could shoot, if indeed he would have wasted a precious bullet, Jankiel brought the butt of his rifle down on the man's head. As Doris watched in amazement, Jankiel repeatedly struck the man's head with the rifle butt, until his skull was smashed and he was clearly dead. "Go get the children," Jankiel said. "We'll bury this Belorussian pig and you can take his two guns and his knives and we'll return to the camp and say that you and the children are armed with weapons. We will say that we have separated from Alexy and we expect him to return by nightfall." When Doris turned around, she saw that the three children were already approaching.

Doris lived in the forest through that winter. She cut her hair so that she looked like a man, and she learned to fire a gun and run like the wind and hide perfectly at any sign of German soldiers or Russian peasants who might turn them in. The two boys fared well, though she lost track of them. The girl, Rivka, who was fifteen, did not survive long. Less than a month after the chance encounter with Jankiel and Anszel, Rivka was raped by Russian partisans, stabbed through her belly, and left to die. She blocked it out, Doris said. She blocked it out that this girl, whose voice was a beautiful soprano, had been one of her favorites among the choir children. She blocked it out that she had told the girl to be strong and to trust the ancient forest, that the *puszcza* would enable her to survive.

In May of 1944, Doris was captured by German soldiers. She'd been informed on by a villager whom she had believed to be her ally. The capture came two weeks after her resistance group attacked and killed three soldiers who had been hunting deer in the forest. As a result a special unit, aided by dogs and anti-Jewish peasants, had been formed to "clean" the ancient forest. Doris was caught alone in a village. She denied being part of the resistance, but even so, she was astounded that she was not executed on the spot. She began to fear that an even worse fate was in store for her. She had heard stories of sadistic abuse and torture by German soldiers in the area. But within a day she had been loaded into a cattle car and deported with other able-bodied men and women, mostly non-Jews, to Auschwitz-Birkenau.

Doris claimed in her testimony that her memory of the eight months she spent at Auschwitz was very poor. Something had happened to her brain. It was as if her brain refused to take in more. Or, it was as if a single memory had blocked out all the others. This was her memory of what Doris called "the audition," which took place several weeks after she had arrived. An SS officer had put the word out that any women who could sing well were to come to this audition, and that if it was discovered that any woman with experience as a singer failed to attend, she would be hanged. Doris was one of six women who had come forward for the audition. A well-known opera singer from Warsaw was among them, and the officers had recognized her. Possibly the discovery of the famous Jewish woman at the camp was what had motivated these auditions in the first place. The fate of this woman I have described already. She was asked to audition first, and as she stepped forward, she was ordered to remove all of her clothes. One of the SS officers produced a bridle. The bit was fitted into her mouth and then an officer commanded her to sing. They jeered and taunted the naked woman, and finally one of the men took a stick and smacked her backside so hard that she fell down. The men assaulted her and raped her with sticks and rifles, and then one of them fired a bullet through her anus and joked that this was how to give a famous Jewess a good hard screwing. They let her scream and writhe for several minutes before she was shot a second time and killed. When the next woman was asked to sing, a similar sequence followed, although this one did not involve the horse bit. Rather, she was to sing while an SS officer pressed the barrel of a rifle down her throat. As had quickly become clear, Doris said, the audition was simply a game these officers had invented for a bit of what they considered fun.

Doris, as it turned out, was the last of the six women to "audition." The other five—three of them dead, two critically injured—had been dragged to the infirmary. When the SS officer commanded her to sing, Doris replied that she would not. She had braced herself for whatever sadistic assault would be inflicted. But none had come and the SS officer again commanded her to sing. He said that if she did not, he would have every third woman in her barracks hung that evening. So Doris sang and what came out was the part that Rivka, the teenage girl she'd led into the forest, had sung when the choir did "Shalom Alechem." The other women had sung in German or else Polish. She sang in Hebrew and assumed that one of the officers would put a bullet through her throat. But she sang until the officer ordered her to stop, and then he looked at another officer, made a face, and burst out laughing. "The Jewess sings us a Jewish song!" he said. "I do not think I have seen anything so funny!" Clearly the officer was the highest-ranking Nazi in the room, because the others began laughing. "Sing it again!" he shouted. Doris envisioned Rivka in the forest, sleeping within the shade and shelter of a giant fallen oak. And then she sang it again. She sang louder and the officer said, "This is a Jewess who wants to die, and so we keep her alive and singing." The other officers again burst into laughter. "We will not let you die, or not for now," said the SS officer. "Congratulations," he continued. "You have succeeded in your audition. Now we will feed you, make you bloom again. Then we will find a satisfying way to kill you." More laughter followed. She was given a drink of water and a small piece of a smoked sausage. She was sent back to her barracks without harm. For the next seven months, until the liberation of the camp, the SS officer provided her with protection. Now and then she was called back for a new "audition," and each time she assumed she'd be killed for sport. She claimed the irony was that her attitude to this officer remained consistently disdainful. At more than one of these auditions, she had said, "Do you plan to shoot me today? If so, I will appreciate the gesture." Sometime after the war, she learned that this particular SS officer was believed to have escaped with Mengele and others to Brazil. She claimed that more than any other Nazi, including Hitler, this was the man she would have wanted to see dead. As Doris said this, she winced. She closed her eyes. Then she said, "My God, I've been talking for so long." She was asked if there was any more that she would like to put on record, and without shedding a single tear, Doris said, "No. I've said enough."

— — —

Outside of the trip to Arlington, nothing during that first year of our betrothal deviated from the regular routine at Pine Manor. We would play Scrabble and listen to the programs on National Public Radio. We would eat meals with Hiram Merlinman, who was my closest friend and only worthy chess opponent. My son Michael would come to visit weekly. Once every month or two, one or both of my grandchildren would come with him. More frequently, it was Anthony, as his older sister, Dani, had started college.

Except for our two nights in Las Vegas, we slept in separate beds, in our separate rooms, though sometimes, on nights when Doris was at the mercy of her incurable malady, insomnia, she would tiptoe into my room and seat herself in my armchair until dawn. Despite her heaviness, Doris was quiet as a mouse and I would never hear her enter. But at times, when I would find myself in that state halfway between sleep and waking, my eyes would open to find the shape of Doris's face and body, which at first would seem like a fantastic apparition, but which would slowly coalesce into her living, breathing presence. Sometimes I'd fall back to sleep and Doris would become part of a dream. More often, I would feel myself slipping back from whatever galaxy I had occupied. I'd say good morning, and then Doris would smile and tell me I had been snoring or perhaps talking in my sleep or that it looked as if I'd been sleeping peacefully and soundly. Sometimes I'd tell her about my dreams. Sometimes we'd listen to the radio. This intimacy was far beyond all that I had known with my first wife, Natalie, and if anyone should ever ask me to describe happiness, I would simply repeat what I've just recounted.

Perhaps the only complexity I was facing at this juncture was philosophical—that inasmuch as my love for Doris was as ebullient, if not more so, than it had ever been, I was grappling with that most modern of conundrums; namely, that having married my beloved Doris, I was conscious of having moved into the great mystery of what would take place *after* we had, by all appearances, lived happily ever after. Let me say this. There is no happily ever after. Neither is there always a reversion to bleak reality. In the most basic of summations, what occurs is, simply, life in whatever form it takes. But oddly enough, that form can sometimes shape itself into yet another story.

— — —

It was January of 1985. We were sitting together downstairs, watching the news in the common room at the Pine Manor Home for the Elderly. I recall a report on AIDS, which was still relatively new. Then there was something about a woman who had used cyanide to kill squirrels in her attic and inadvertently wound up killing her two children. It was the usual gloom and doom, and I had started to doze off when I felt Doris clench my thigh so tightly that I almost fell off my chair. She gripped my arm after that. Doris's hands were very strong. I'd always noticed this but never had I felt anything like the power of her grip as she grasped the back of my wrist and stared at the TV.

The screen showed a photograph of the face of a man who looked to be approximately forty. It took a moment for me to figure out the context, but I soon learned that this man was a soldier in the Israeli army. Then the news segment showed some grainy gray-green footage taken in Rafiah, a Palestinian city located on the western end of the Gaza Strip, which had been captured in the Six-Day War and occupied by Israeli troops since 1967. I saw a grainy gray-green human figure leaning out over the edge of a rooftop. Then the camera zoomed in, and I could see that it was two people intertwined and then untwining, and then one of these two people became a fifteen-year-old Palestinian boy who was falling from the rooftop. Filmed from below, it was hard to tell how high up the roof was. It appeared to be about three stories. The boy passed out of the frame, but as I quickly learned, he landed on concrete and died on impact.

You may have seen this segment on the news. It was aired repeatedly throughout that week in January, and if you saw it you most certainly would have wondered, as I did, which one of two possible interpretations of this grainy gray-green film was correct. Was the Israeli soldier on the rooftop a barbaric criminal who had just thrown a teenage boy to his death? Or was it the exact opposite? Had the boy been intentionally jumping, and had this soldier been attempting to grab him out of the air before he fell? You could have watched the film, which lasted all of about ten seconds, as many times as you wished and still you would not have been able to know for sure. The problem was that the film was taken from below, and although you could hear faintly the sound of the boy screaming *"Allah-a-akbar,"* an invocation of his god, you could not hear much else besides the discussion taking place between the American camerawoman and whoever stood beside her, a discussion that consisted mostly of phrases such as "Oh my God, Lorraine, are you getting this?" The problem was that the film quality was as bad as that of the supposed film of Bigfoot taken by someone on a bucking horse. And finally, the problem was that the soldier, identified as a forty-two-year-old Israeli man named Amnon Grossman, refused to make any comment to the press about the incident.

There was, of course, a statement issued by a spokesperson for the Israel Defense Forces, who provided details of the Israeli mission in Rafiah. The soldier seen in the film was described as having been part of a unit that had broken into a house in order to arrest a known terrorist and leader of a fundamentalist group called the Islamic Jihad. The Palestinian boy was said to have slammed a plank full of rusty nails into the face of an Israeli soldier who was now blind in one eye. Amnon Grossman and another soldier had been ordered to pursue the boy, and the soldier who'd stepped onto the roof with Grossman had made a statement under oath that what he witnessed was Grossman throwing his gun down and trying to grab hold of the boy and save him as he jumped. Indeed, if you watch the film, you can see that initially the soldier is practically falling as well, that at a certain point his hands appear to grab and take hold of the boy's shirt. But then the hands release and this is either because the soldier's final reflex was to save himself rather than go down with the boy or because the solider had been throwing the boy down. The camerawoman, identified as a New Yorker by the name of Lorraine Williams, said that she believed the teenage boy had been murdered, as did the members of the Palestinian family she happened to be interviewing when the raid began. But the more you watch the film, the more indecipherable the event appears. All in all, the occurrence was intriguing as a flashpoint of almost geometrically perfect ambiguity. Apparently there were tires being burned in protest all over Gaza. There were demands that Amnon Grossman be tried for murder, but the Israelis were treating Palestinian claims as fiction.

As mentioned, Doris had clenched my arm, and this continued throughout the fifteen minutes or so of news coverage we watched when the story was aired in the U.S. on that first evening. Then, when the news had moved on to something else, Doris released my arm and took hold of the cane she used to get around Pine Manor. She turned to me and said she needed some time alone up in her room.

"Is something wrong?" I asked.

She shook her head and said, "It's nothing."

I said, "You squeezed me pretty hard for a thing that's nothing."

"I had a spasm in my back," she said. "A little spasm. I should lie down now."

She kissed my cheek, rose, and headed toward the elevator. I knew by the way she walked that her back, in fact, was not in spasm. I stayed downstairs for a while longer and waited in a mild state of confusion for the basketball and hockey scores.

Over the next few days, Doris continued following this news piece. She read the newspaper, which was something that she rarely found the time for. She went so far as to cut out a photo printed in the *New York Times* of Amnon Grossman. The man was pictured in the uniform of a park ranger, which apparently was his job. She also read me editorials supporting each side of the argument, including one that pointed out the obvious—that the incident had been turned into pure media hype.

From time to time, she would surprise me by saying things like "I think he did it. What an awful thing. It's unforgivable." Yet other times she would claim that she did not blame him if he had thrown the boy down. "Given the chance," she said, "that Palestinian boy would surely have done the same." And yet another time she said, "This soldier, Amnon Grossman, he is not the type who would throw a boy off a rooftop. He was trying to save the boy, undoubtedly. I've watched the film a dozen times and it's clear as day. After all, this boy is calling to his god. He believes himself to be a martyr and that his soul will fly straight to heaven." And yet another time she said, "I understand it. This heart of darkness. This is what brings you to throw a boy off of a rooftop. It's clear as day."

Overall, I was perplexed by her ongoing rumination but was afraid to broach the subject. She did not seem aware of just how preoccupied she had become. I was relieved when the news item grew less topical, and within three weeks it seemed to have all but passed.

But then sometime in mid-February of that same year, Hiram Merlinman knocked on the door to my room, where I was reading an article about the Greek mathematician and philosopher Zeno of Elea and Doris was snoozing in my armchair. Hy announced that he and several residents had been watching TV in the common room. A nature program had come on about a special breeding park for rare wildlife in the southern Negev Desert, Israel. Amazingly, the soldier Amnon Grossman had been interviewed. Apparently he was curator of the park. The segment was a rerun, filmed sometime before the incident in Gaza, but PBS seemed not to have made the connection. He explained this as Doris woke, and I felt relieved that we had missed the broadcast of this program. But Hy, who the month before had been the one to come up with the idea of using the Pine Manor VCR to tape the news clip of the falling boy so that we could watch the grainy sequence over and over, announced to us that he had taped the final portion of this nature program. Doris stood up immediately. She said, "Where is this tape? Downstairs?" Hy said it was.

Reluctantly, I accompanied her downstairs to watch whatever Hy had taped. I sat with Doris on the couch. I looked at Hy, as well as Ada Kupritz, who was knitting in an armchair. I considered asking them to leave the room, but I did not. Then Hy rewound the tape, which interrupted an episode of the game show *Wheel of Fortune*, abruptly moving from the frantically superficial faces of three *Wheel of Fortune* contestants to the intent face of a white, medium-size antelope. The antelope had long, pointed horns, and the beast was sparring with none other than Amnon Grossman, who held a bamboo pole and was continually smacking the antelope on the horns. "Oh, this is horrible," Doris said, but as we watched we learned the white antelope, a species known as the Arabian oryx, was named Hermes, that he was old and recently had been getting gored by other oryxes because he would pick fights with younger, stronger males, all of whom roamed within the fences of the four-thousand-acre expanse of the breeding park, the aforementioned Hai Bar Yotvata Nature Reserve. Hermes had to be stitched up after each injury, and they'd decided it would be better to keep him enclosed in a pen. But Hermes continually found ways to escape. He'd pick another fight and again lose badly. After his third breakout, Amnon Grossman had devised a clever plan. He realized that the old oryx wanted to be dominant, and so each morning Grossman would go into the pen with a bamboo pole, rap Hermes on the horns and stage combat, and then retreat so that the oryx believed he'd driven the man away. Once this daily ritual had been instituted, with Hermes always the victor, the oryx never again broke out of his pen.

After the scenes with Hermes, we watched and listened as Amnon Grossman, the man who may or may not have thrown a boy off a rooftop, discussed the conservationist mission of the park. At the time the program had been filmed, breeding stocks included herds of Arabian oryxes, scimitar-horned oryxes, ostriches, Nubian ibexes, wild sheep called addaxes, Somalian wild asses, and a species of wild ass called the onager. Herds of the onagers had already been released and future plans called for release of the Arabian oryxes and the ostriches. All three were believed to have roamed the Negev during biblical times. "Lots of good Scrabble words," I commented to Doris, but by then Doris seemed to be in her own world and was not listening. She rose without comment and headed for the elevator. When I called after her, she shouted, "Max, you stay here. You stay with Hy."

I would have gone upstairs sooner, except that Michael was coming by that evening with Dani, my granddaughter, not to mention that whatever was upsetting Doris with regard to Amnon Grossman did not seem like it could be anything too dangerous or inherently problematic. I would soon learn that on this account I was egregiously underestimating the fact that Doris was more agitated than I had ever witnessed in what was nearing three years since I'd first laid eyes on her. I sat with Michael and Dani when they arrived. I played a game of chess with Dani, in which I mostly gave her instructions. While Dani was not a natural, she was far better than her father and had a sharp enough mind that with some coaching, I believed, she would soon become a competitive opponent. Dani and Michael stayed for dinner. At around eight I walked them out to Michael's car, said my good-byes, and headed upstairs to see what was what with Doris.

We had our rooms on the same floor, one concession that had been made after our marriage, since the two floors at Pine Manor were not supposed to be mixed gender. Doris's room, with its private bathroom, was located on the far end of the hall. As I approached it, I could hear her muffled sobbing. This was, I believe, the first time I had ever heard her sobbing. I knocked lightly and said, "Dori, you okay in there?"

Between her sobs, she said, "Come in. The door is open."

I found her sitting on her bed, her eyes all puffy and red, her glasses on the night table.

"Was it the program?" I said. "Something to do with the Israeli man?"

Doris said, "Maybe," and exploded into tears.

I took her hand. When she calmed down, I said, "Please tell me what's going on."

Doris said, "I'm not sure you want to know."

"I want to know," I said. "Anything that concerns you, I want to know."

She said, "Okay. This may be silly, though I don't think so. The Israeli man, Amnon Grossman. You may have noticed he has a very Polish face. But what you could not notice, what only my sister Hanna or her daughter Beverly could notice, is that this man looks just like my first husband. It is as if he is Pinchas's double. The resemblance is so strong that it is frightening or else magical. It's doing something to me, bringing out feelings that are buried inside so deep that now I'm barely in control of myself."

I said, "Your husband died over forty years ago."

Doris breathed deeply and said, "I haven't become delusional. Don't worry."

It seemed to make sense after that. After all, why wouldn't her feelings about a man she loved and married, a man murdered for being Jewish, be overpowering when faced with this strange revenant. "It must be shocking," I said to Doris. "I understand exactly why you would have these feelings."

Doris said, "No, Maxi, you don't. Because there's more to this."

"How much more?"

She said, "Oh, Maxi, this is not such a simple thing as talking to your son who died in 1958, though it might seem so at first. I'm sorry."

"That isn't simple," I said.

She said, "I know." She rubbed my arm apologetically. Then she said, "I've never told you much about my first husband. You heard the story of his death when I gave testimony, but even then there were many things I did not see the point of telling. I was just twenty-eight years old when we fled to Kovno. I thought I was smart but I was stupid. I also thought that I was pretty. I thought this would make me safe. Now I am babbling. I must stop babbling. What I can tell you is that there was a story about those five hundred Jewish intellectuals murdered in Kovno. One of those stories people tell. The story claims that two of the men escaped and did not die. This was a way, I have always thought, to provide hope for those who knew some of these men who were killed for being smart and talented. But not one of these men has ever resurfaced, until now."

"Until now?" I repeated.

"Yes."

I said the obvious — "How could that Israeli man be your husband?"

She said, "The Israeli man, Amnon Grossman, may be his son."

I said the obvious once again. There was no way she could be sure.

She said, "They have identical posture and their noses are the same. I recognized these things when I watched the nature program. This is not proof, I know. I'm sorry. What I am doing now is telling myself a story. That he survived and had a son. And what to do with it, this story? I am not even sure I *want* it to be true."

"What if it is true?" I asked. "What would you do?"

"I have no idea!" she yelled. "This is the stupid thing about being human. You want to find things. Then you find them. You can solve them. And so what? There is that saying, you know? Why fix the sole of an old shoe if you've lost the other one?"

I said, "I've never heard that saying."

"It's from the Yiddish. Or it may be that my mother made it up. She would do that. Make up sayings. Sayings that no one will remember. Here is another one. She said mystery is a carrot. You can peel it but you still put it in soup! Those were her stupid sayings. And what I found when I first came to the U.S. is that I would make up sayings too. A book is just like a king. Did you know that, Max? If you cannot understand, maybe you should ask your long-dead son. Or possibly I can ask my long-dead mother. I can also ask her if she enjoyed living in Warsaw Ghetto. I can ask if she enjoyed the liquidation. Then I can ask whether my husband survived his death sentence. And why this word anyway, *sentence*? Is it like someone saying a sentence? Now you will die. Is this the sentence? How is this different from the sentence we are born with? Why not a birth sentence, Max? Have you considered this? And what if it is true that he lived? Does this make things any different, if he lived? I do not think it does and I also think it does. Oh, Max, I am so sorry. This is tiring. There are so many strange things happening in my head. I will stop babbling on and on. I need to quiet myself. I need to sit here and be quiet and still with you, Max. I am so sorry. Now I am going to be quiet."

I stayed with Doris for an hour. She was not quiet for very long. But gradually she calmed down. Eventually she began laughing at her outburst. She said, "I must seem like a person of unsound mind, so please ignore me." I said that if she was of unsound mind, then I might qualify as a certifiable lunatic. She laughed again, and she agreed. Then she said, "Max, you are a good man and I love you. It is good that I have ended up here, beside you, after the years I spent with Victor. It is good because you remind me of what I used to feel like before everything that happened in the war. I do not mean to be dwelling on my first husband. It is just that this man's face conjures it. It is just that we all wish sometimes that stories could be true."

I left her room soon after that, and as I walked down the hall I felt a ludicrous pang of jealousy. I imagined saying something to her in the morning such as "You are my wife. Why should you care about the past if we're together?" But then I caught myself and said to myself, "Max, you are not such a small, pathetic man as this." Then I stepped into my room, closed the door, sat on the toilet, and concentrated on my bowels. I realized that in the excitement of the day I'd skipped my afternoon glass of water mixed with orange-flavored Metamucil. It took some time, but when I finished, I sat down on my bed and closed my eyes and spoke to my son Daniel. I said, "A book is like a king." I said, "I have to admit that I don't understand this." I said, "I realize she has seen things. She has done things that I cannot fathom." I said, "For a man who taught high school English in New Jersey, a man whose family made it out of Russia by the end of the nineteenth century, this is unsettling, and this is also why I love her."

I got in bed that night and continued reading the article I had started that afternoon about Zeno of Elea, which naturally discussed Zeno's eight paradoxes, a set of problems he devised to support the theory that contrary to our senses, all plurality and change and even motion is an illusion. All of the paradoxes are similar, the simplest being the one known as the "dichotomy paradox," which argues that in any act of locomotion we must first arrive halfway before we reach our goal. But then we must cover half the remaining distance, then half of that, and so on. Looked at this way, we can never reach our goal. I'd learned of Zeno long ago, but I'd been interested to see if there was anything new to learn about him in this article. I didn't get very far before I drifted off to sleep. Thinking about Zeno, it now occurs to me, is not unlike the exercise of counting sheep.

I woke at dawn with renewed anxiety, however. I shifted over, off of my badly arthritic right shoulder. I lay on my back and kept my eyes closed in hopes of falling back to sleep. Soon I gave up, opened my eyes, and I found Doris sitting in my armchair, walker in front of her. She seemed calm but very tired. When she saw my eyes open, she smiled gently and said, "Maxi, you were talking in your sleep again."

"What was I saying?"

She said, "It sounded like 'Poor, poor Edgar Linton.' Who is he?"

"He's from a book, *Wuthering Heights*. I used to teach it."

"Did you like Edgar?"

"I thought I hated him most of all."

"Maybe you liked him but don't know it," she said playfully.

I sat up and I could feel my body letting go of whatever it had been holding through the night. I looked at Doris. I wondered when she had come in, and as always, how she'd managed to be so silent.

"How are you feeling?" I asked.

"I didn't sleep a single minute."

"I had a rough night too," I said.

She said, "I know. You tossed and turned. You were like a pancake."

I said, "A pancake?"

"It was like someone with a spatula kept flipping you."

She stretched her hand out and touched my leg as I was pondering this metaphor. She said she'd been reading the magazine article about Zeno of Elea.

I said, "I've already tried twice to read that article, but I haven't gotten past the second page."

"He must be right then," Doris said. "That it's impossible for anyone to get anywhere."

I said, "We'll get somewhere."

She laughed. Then she sat up and, very carefully, she climbed into the bed. It was a full-size bed and we fit snugly. She put her arm around my back and kissed my cheek. Then she said, "No, Maxi, we won't. We are too old. Most of the forest is behind us."

For half an hour I fell back to sleep, beside her.

— — —

"A man becomes confused, gradually, with the form of his own destiny." These are the words of Borges's imprisoned magician, Tzinacán. These are his words just before his narrative launches into an account of his communion with the divine, through which he comes to understand the script of the jaguar's spots. But for this moment, we are not sure if he will decode it. Nor are we sure that the jaguar's spots are the true script. All we can know is that the story must continue. We know that something will be narrated in the paragraphs that remain. So, we read these paragraphs. The tale becomes whole, and suddenly it is as if we have been staring at a hologram. The entire tale has been there all along. It took me years to understand that this is why I enjoy reading stories. That every story, in this sense, is like the god's magical sentence. In the years since her death, I have explained all of this to Doris. But as I write this now I wonder who I am speaking to. There is a feeling I get sometimes. The funny feeling that I am speaking to myself.

— — —

On the morning of February 20th, Doris leaned her cane against the couch so she could fasten the top button of her cardigan. As she was reaching for her cane afterward, she had a spell of vertigo and fell. One of the Pine Manor aides called 911 and I went to her. She was in pain. As I got down on the floor beside her, she said, "Maxi, I'm sorry. Something is broken."

I said, "You don't have to be sorry."

"I want this year to be like last year," Doris said. "Both of us healthy and nothing crazy. But I don't think it will be like last year."

"You'll be just fine," I said. "Broken bones heal."

"It may be more than that," she said. She moved her leg slightly and winced. "I think this look-alike man, this Amnon Grossman, he has shown me that my heart is also broken."

"You have a beautiful heart," I said. "Your heart is valiant and heroic."

She said, "That's good of you to say. And it's okay, Maxi, for you to say this, because there is no way for you to know who I really am."

Two days later Doris had surgery on her hip at Saint Barnabas Hospital in Livingston, where my son Michael worked, and in the days that followed the operation, I spent much of my time in her hospital room, reading while she slept, watching television, and playing Scrabble with her whenever she felt like thinking. When visiting hours were over, Michael or Anthony drove me back to Pine Manor. There wasn't anything to be worried about. As I'd assumed, the prognosis was that Doris would be fine in a few months. She would need outpatient rehab. She would need to use her walker at all times now to protect herself from falling when she had dizzy spells. She had more pins in her hip, which possibly, I joked, would cause her to beep next time she needed to go through airport security.

But then one morning I arrived and I was told by a hospital administrator that in the last twelve hours Doris had made more than two hundred dollars' worth of phone calls. I was told that her phone had been removed and asked if I knew whether she could pay for the calls she'd made. I said she could and to give her back her phone before I filed a written complaint. Then I went up to her room and found her looking pale and very agitated.

"They took my phone!" Doris yelled, and I assured her I'd taken care of it. I asked who she had been calling. She said, "My sons in California." I said the bill was over two hundred dollars. I asked if she had been speaking with her sons the entire night. "Yes, all night," she said, and I said nothing. I supposed that it was possible that she'd been having important conversations with her sons. When I sat next to her, she said, "Okay, Maxi. Listen. I've been making calls to Israel. Mostly to Yad Vashem, which is the Holocaust memorial in Jerusalem. I spoke to many people there, and every one of them told me the same thing, which was nothing. Then I found someone who could give me the phone number for the nature park in the desert. I called it twenty times before they brought him, Amnon Grossman. I asked him if his father fled from Poland to Lithuania in the war and he said no but I can tell that he is lying. I called again but I was told he is not available. Someone must go there, fly to Israel as soon as possible. Someone must talk to Amnon Grossman. Maybe your son Michael would be willing?"

"He won't have time. I can assure you."

She said, "Can you go?"

I told her, "Maybe I could do it. What would I be going there to ask?"

She yelled, "Goddamn this! I must go myself because I am the only one who knows why I would go. I have to go there but I can't with a broken hip, and Amnon Grossman, for all I know, will vanish."

"He won't vanish," I said.

"Why not!"

"Your hip will heal," I said. "Then I'll go with you."

She said, "You can't go, Max."

"But you just asked me to."

She said, "I know, but I am acting very crazy."

"Should I get help? Should I call a nurse in?"

Doris screamed, "No!" and then one of her eyes twitched and half her face seemed to go limp and I said, "Doris, oh my God." I pressed the button for a nurse and I felt the despair of knowing I was not capable of running down the hall. Nor was I capable of lifting Doris in my arms and carrying her to safety. I was not capable of anything at all. I pushed and pushed the button with one hand and I held Doris's with the other. It took almost five minutes for the nurse to appear, at which point, I yelled, "Hurry and get a doctor!"

— — —

A hemorrhagic stroke was what I'd witnessed. Apparently, this explained why the symptoms came on so fast. She spent three days in critical condition, and though the stroke had paralyzed the left side of her body, she lived through it. Neither her speech nor her vision had been affected, but for a week she had barely spoken. For that whole week I had come to see her every day and held her nonparalyzed hand and sat beside her. For that whole week I was unsure if she was moving toward death or away from it.

I was relieved when Michael told me that she'd been transferred from CCU to her own room. He'd been to see her, Michael said, and she seemed to be in better spirits. That day he picked me up himself instead of sending a taxi, and as he drove me to the hospital, I began to feel optimistic. I thought to myself that Doris, beyond anyone's comprehension, was a survivor. I thought to myself that there would be ample time for us to laugh at silly things and be together.

When I arrived at her new room, the TV was on and my first thought was that things had gotten better. I said hello, and the nonparalyzed side of her mouth curled into a soft smile. She switched the television off and I sat down in the chair beside her bed. I said, "How are you?" I said, "I've missed you at Pine Manor."

Then her eyes filled with a hazy desperation and, without a word, Doris began to cry.

As I have mentioned, I had never seen her cry before that day we had watched the program that had featured Amnon Grossman. I'd been surprised then, and I was equally surprised to see her cry so quickly upon my arrival in her new room at the hospital. I held her hand and I watched as the right side of her face contorted while the other side stayed motionless. She cried and cried. It seemed as if it might never stop. When Michael returned me to Pine Manor late that afternoon, I asked him if the protracted crying I had witnessed was something commonly seen in hemorrhagic stroke victims. He said no.

At my next visit, we talked some and played Scrabble. But at a certain point, she asked me to close the door and then proceeded to weep, on and off, for at least two hours. The day after that, she asked me to close the door the moment I walked in. She turned the TV off and for the next three hours, she cried and cried. What was inside there, I did not know, but in these half-contortions of her body, many years of grief seemed to be emerging. Doris would thank me whenever she had finished crying. Then I would sit with her until, in her exhaustion, she fell asleep.

Eventually I met her sons, who had flown in together from California. Their names were Benny and Andrew Schulman, both in their thirties. They had made plans to stay for a long weekend. They both seemed nice enough and Doris seemed glad to see them, although I knew she had not been close with her sons for many years. Benny did the majority of the talking, telling his mother of his life in a town north of San Francisco. Andrew read magazines and periodically left the room to go outside and smoke a cigarette in the cold. On each of the first two days of their visit, the sons departed half an hour before visiting hours had ended. They ate together at a nearby diner and headed off to wherever it was they were staying. Doris had animated herself, as much as possible, throughout these visits. But just as soon as the sons left, she would request that I close the door. Before I had even returned to her bedside, she would erupt again into her weeping.

A Sunday morning arrived when her sons left early so that they could catch their flight home from Newark Airport. Doris kissed them both good-bye and watched them go. She waited possibly five minutes before she asked me to close the door. I expected her, as usual, to launch right into her fit of crying, but she did not. Instead what she said was "Maxi. Did you tell him? Did you tell Daniel that a book is like a king?" I said I did. She said, "I tricked you because this is not a saying. This is a riddle. They both have subjects. That's one answer. They both have pages is another. They deal with plots. The list goes on. When I first thought of this, I thought I was very clever."

"They both have spines," I said.

She smiled her half-smile and said, "Good one." Then she said, "Maxi, I am going to be dead soon."

"No, Dori," I said. "You're doing fine here. You're not in critical care. All this crying must be good..."

She said, "Hush, Maxi."

I hushed.

"I have seen the *mise-meshune kolir*, the strange death color," Doris said. "I have seen it and this means that I will die in a way that is not soothing. Before I do, I have to tell you something difficult. I am so sorry to be telling this. After so much time, and being this close to death, I need to tell. This is the last thing that I will ever ask of you. It is not fair that it must be you who will hear what it is that I have tried so hard never to reveal to anyone. But you have listened to so much. You've been my witness, and for this I am always grateful. Now I will tell you this thing, if it's okay."

I said it was and I prepared myself for more atrocities, including anything that she might say about her dealings with the SS officer who'd made her sing at Auschwitz.

But what she said was "Maxi, listen. The Israeli man, Amnon Grossman, he does *not* resemble Pinchas, my first husband."

Naturally, I was confused. For a moment I was concerned that she had entered into a delirium, especially because this admission caused her to cry. I thought that possibly this was all she'd tell me, that she would cry for an hour or two and I'd go home. But she stopped crying after a few minutes. She said, "Okay, now I will say this thing that may cause you to despise me. It is my sister's husband, Jonah, who he resembles. My sister's husband. He was my love."

I took her hand and I said nothing. She said his name. *Yonah Rabinovitz.* She said that Pinchas was a good man, but that Jonah was like a dream, a burst of color. He'd left his job at the gymnasium after the school would not expel a gang of boys who had badly beaten a Jewish teacher. He took his family to live on his brother's farm. There he had planned to become a writer, to write a big important novel about Poland. To include everything. All of the border realignments. The way a place can be part of one country, then another, and then not be a place at all. She said he wanted to write of the lynx and wolves and wisents in the *puszcza*. She said that all the time she lived inside the forest, she had believed she was inside him, inside his book, even though this book was supposed to be about his daughter, Bejla. His ingenious and charmed daughter, who would ask questions such as whether the wind was made of spirits who passed through you when you walked across a meadow. He'd told his daughter that someday she would be the hero of a story. That she would have to fight the lynx and wolves and ride on the backs of wisents. That in the story, she would always save the world.

Doris explained that she had fallen in love with Jonah during the time they lived in Kovno. It was from the fall of 1940 through the spring of 1941, soon after his wife and daughter had departed, that she and Jonah commenced their secret love affair.

Right behind Pinchas's back, and somehow Pinchas did not notice or did not want to, as he had not even kissed her in all the time since they'd left Warsaw. Then suddenly *both* were gone. Here she'd been trying to choose which man she would stay with after they had escaped from Lithuania and were safe again. Here she'd been thinking how hard it would be to tell Pinchas that she loved Jonah. Here she'd been wondering if Jonah would still love her if he was not alone in Kovno. Jonah and Pinchas. Both gone. Both of them marched away and killed. Finally Doris paused in her story, and I expected her to burst back into tears at any moment. But this was not what happened. She took a breath and she said, "Now, Max, I will tell you the worst part."

And what was the worst part? What could be worse than all of the calamity she had been part of, worse than the losses she had endured? The *worst* part, she claimed, was that she had heard a story. She'd heard a story about those five hundred Jewish intellectuals killed in Kovno. According to this story, two of the five hundred had survived. And naturally, at first, she had believed those two to be Pinchas and Jonah. She prayed each day for their survival. Like other widows in Kovno, she prayed and prayed, but soon she started to lose hope. And then, Doris said, she began to bargain. In her mind, she began to say that she would take one of them, one man. And slowly it became clear to her that she was praying that her husband had died and Jonah had survived. She prayed to God that he would live and return and then with Pinchas dead and Jonah's family in America, it would be okay for the two of them to love.

She said, "I prayed, Maxi. I prayed. I prayed that my sister's husband was alive and prayed to make it so by giving up a prayer for my own husband. This is the hardest part of the war for me, and not because of guilt to Hanna or any shame about what I was feeling. This is the deepest pain for me because it is *still* what I would pray for."

She said, "In Auschwitz, in my delusions, I could see him. I would be singing for that officer. I would be naked. Jonah would flicker in the corner of the room. And on my bunk at night, I would see him standing on the floor below me. For a moment I would feel my love for him and then I would realize my mind was playing a cruel trick. I believed that I received what I deserved for my selfish prayers. I did not care if I lived or died. I did not care about anything that was done to me. I did not care, at a certain point, what was done to others. I didn't live because I was virtuous. I am called a survivor, but I survived only because I did not care. Because this made it harder for them to torture me. Because they knew that living was my torture. This is the dark corner of my soul and I do not think, if there is heaven, I will go to it. But you must never tell my sister. You must not tell her. Hanna must never hear of this while she still lives."

Again, I thought she would weep. But this time Doris squeezed my hand. She squeezed so hard that it was difficult to resist yelling out in pain. She said, "Thank you, Max, for hearing this. Thank you for being a man who loves so well." Then she said, "Jonah used to speak of the Jewish mystics who believe all living creatures are surrounded by an aura of glowing colors. I feel this aura from you, Max. Sometimes I have imagined these colors bathing you in your sleep. I can feel Jonah's aura too, which is not logical, but still, I could feel Jonah the first time I saw Amnon Grossman on TV. There is a wonder in this, Maxi. Such great wonder. I have seen it. Do not ask me to explain more."

Finally, she began weeping, perhaps allowing herself, for a brief moment, to feel the love that for years she had believed she was not entitled to. I understood this, with resignation. I also wished there had been some way to explain that what she felt for Jonah was not horrible, that her secret prayers were forgivable, that possibly her husband Pinchas, after so many years, would have been able to understand. But I did not think she would believe me. Regardless,

I knew she would not want to hear it. And I believed, for the first time, what she had told me shortly after her sons' departure. More than believed, I understood that she would die soon. I knew that Doris would not survive another week.

She died that night, as it turned out. When the call came from my son early the next morning, I took the news with equanimity. I had spent the better part of the night crying my eyes out. And I had already come to understand the small part that I would play in this account. A man certainly does become confused, gradually, with the form of his own destiny. Often this is because the form it takes is less extraordinary than what he has hoped for. In my life I intended to be larger, more heroic. But a man must take the part that he is given, and when it's done he must do his best to speak of it with dignity.

— — —

There was a funeral for Doris in South Orange. Michael arranged it. Her sons flew in again. This time they were accompanied by their families. I gave a short eulogy. So did her sister and her son Benny. In keeping with Doris's wishes, she would be cremated. The ashes were to be entrusted to her sister, who would call me, she said, when she determined a good date to go and scatter them that spring. There was an outdoor sculpture gallery, the Storm King Art Center, up in the Hudson Valley. Hanna said this was the place she was considering because Doris always liked it there. I knew of this place, with its five hundred acres of sweeping fields and modern sculpture, because Doris had taken me there by limo on my eighty-second birthday. I told Hanna that this location sounded fine and then I thought to myself, A book is like a king.

After the funeral, we sat *shiva* at Pine Manor. Her sons came, as did several women Doris knew from the local synagogue. I let the rabbi rip my lapel. I covered the mirror in my room. And when the time was right, I approached Bejla Rabinowitz, who until

Doris's final confession I had known only as Beverly. She herself had recently been in mourning after a boyfriend died of leukemia. I was tempted to mention Daniel and his illness all those years ago. But I could see that she was like Doris in some ways. She did not want sentiment, nor would she have wanted to hear my thoughts about speaking with the dead.

I gave her the video recording Hiram had made of Amnon Grossman on the nature show. I also gave her some of the newspaper clippings Doris had saved after the incident in Gaza. Then I did something that might seem strange. I told her all that Doris had told me regarding Jonah, including her wish that Hanna never know. I relayed everything because, after prolonged contemplation, I had decided this was neither a breach of trust nor a breach of what had happened. I told her everything because it seemed that this was the last moment in my life that I would do anything of import or significance. When I'd finished speaking, I recognized that I was no longer this story's keeper. Then it was over. I had nothing else to say.

10

This World

About stories

For most of my life I have believed that words are the ruins left by those compelled to record their thoughts as the result of their addiction to this world, and just as ancient pottery must break into shards and ancient buildings are reduced to their foundations and dinosaurs have left behind their skeletons, all of our scribblings and notations, even our books, must eventually lose their meaning. I say this to you, and yet I will attempt to describe, at least this once, my own experience, though I promise you that nothing, in the end, will seem conclusive. Stories are like dreams in this way. They happen. They do not happen. They are right here. They exist in some other place entirely.

About rooftops

Listen. I was stationed with two men on a rooftop in Gaza City. I stared through binoculars and scanned the streets beneath me. I stared at garbage because the street below me was deserted. I stared at the steel curtains covering the storefronts, at the metal painted with graffiti, colorful Arabic, slogans on top of slogans. By then the letters had been covered up so many times that all the storefronts looked like murals. The colors filled the lenses of my binoculars, explosions of red, black, green. Each time another Palestinian boy was dragged out to paint over the graffiti, they covered it with more red, more black, more green, so that the colors on the storefronts just grew darker, until each facade formed a shapeless flag of Palestine.

I didn't want to be there, except at night, when I watched for barn owls. After the sun went down I watched the garbage in the alleys through a nightscope. The Palestinians left their garbage out in the alleys for their goats. The barn owls fed on the rats that feasted on the garbage in the darkness. I would listen for the screeches, hisses, and maniacal shrieks of barn owls. Occasionally I would see one, silent, mothlike, flying through the alley.

One of the men with me on the rooftop was called Uri. I spoke to Uri about the barn owls and Uri liked to talk about the sea. In the daytime the Mediterranean was our background and from that height the deep blue was bewitching. Uri would tell me that he had been to the United States and learned to surf. He said that sometimes he thought of going back there, to California, with his children. He knew I'd gone to graduate school in New Mexico and he asked if I ever thought of leaving Israel and I shrugged at him. I said no.

Uri had seen barn owls. He had seen their heart-shaped faces through the nightscope, which made all things look green, or he had seen them flickering past like shadows in the twilight. He'd never seen their true colors, though I had told him that they are golden above, spotted with blue-gray, black, and white; their breasts are white or sometimes a pale cinnamon; the face is white — two white auricles, each with a jet-black eye at its center.

The other soldier on the rooftop was Meir and he did not care about the owls. He spent most of his time smoking and writing letters and complaining about being stuck on a rooftop. He would have preferred to be patrolling the refugee camp or else searching cars at the Erez checkpoint, like he did during his first week of *miluim*. Meir told us of how, a week before, he had fooled a Palestinian into thinking he had killed him. At the checkpoint, he had searched a car and found a hammer. Then he informed the driver and his family that carrying a hammer was grounds for execution. He ordered the driver to step outside and to remain standing. Meir stepped behind a truck and loaded his M16 with the filter from a cigarette. When he returned the man was down on his knees, crying about his two sons and three daughters. The man was praying for his life when Meir stepped up to him, pointed the rifle, and fired the cigarette filter at his chest. Disturbing laughter came from Meir as he recounted this. He described how the Palestinian man clutched at the place where the filter struck him, how he dropped down to the ground, leaned on his forehead, and was afraid to lift his hands. How he believed he was dead until Meir had yelled, in Arabic, "You're a spirit now, get up!" In shock, the Palestinian rose. When he moved his hands, he saw that his chest had not been harmed. Then he burst into tears and fell to his knees once more. Meir told us how he kicked him and how the Palestinian had curled up like an insect. I told Meir that he deserved to be in prison. Meir had laughed and said, "An Arab is not a man."

About monsters

I tell you of Meir because I want you to understand that in this world there are good people and there are bad people and there are many in between. I tell you of Meir because I want you to understand how easy it is to turn Meir into a monster. What you must understand is that he turns himself into a monster, but that to me and to you he is, like the Palestinian, a man.

I have raised many animals and I am good at this and maybe this is why I am not afraid to become a father. But there are times when I am aware that I do not know what this world will have in store for you. There are days when I feel sure the world will end, and there are days when I know it will go on regardless of whether or not I wish to be a part of it. This is also why I tell you of Meir.

About lunging

After ten days of manning this same post and two more days until *miluim* was over, we were ordered off the rooftop and I was disappointed not to be able to watch for the owls that evening. We followed a small convoy of vehicles through the marketplace. We pushed through people as if moving through water. The vehicles ahead parted the crowd, but the space filled in once the vehicles had passed and all these women and children, even the goats, acted as if they did not see us. Several times a person bumped into my rifle. Several times I heard Meir behind me, shouting at people in his way. Then I saw Uri recoil ahead of me because twenty or thirty stones had been thrown from behind a concrete wall. A jeep that trailed us came roaring forward, missing one fleeing Palestinian boy by centimeters. Then rubber bullets were being fired by Israeli soldiers. Storefronts slammed down and I heard screams. Uri began to run and I ran after him. Another rain of stones pelted my helmet. I felt the point of a stone strike beneath my eye. I made a leap for the truck's bed, twisted around, and watched the crowd receding. I turned to Uri, who let me know that I was bleeding.

At a base in Khan Yunis, I had my face stitched. We were allowed to sleep that night for several hours but were awoken by our commander, Hershel Cohen, sometime past midnight and given orders. We were to arrest a Palestinian radical, a leader of the Islamic Jihad, who recently had abducted and murdered two young Israeli soldiers. Shehadeh was the man's name. He had been sighted near his home in Rafiah during a riot that afternoon. We went in jeeps to Rafiah. When we arrived at the house, it looked to be abandoned. The front door was bolted shut, so we set explosives. When the door blew we rushed in. I find it strange to recount this. Most of my days were spent caring for animals, cleaning out cages, and managing a nature park. Now I was running through the splinters of what had recently been a door.

Meir was in the lead, Uri behind him, and then myself. Meir was ambushed by a boy, who struck his face with a wooden plank full of rusty nails. Meir's neck and cheek were ripped wide open. He fired bullets into the ceiling and began screaming. The young boy dropped the plank and vanished up a stairway. Uri and I were ordered to pursue.

The boy had run up to the rooftop. A full moon hung in the sky above the sea and by its light I could see the boy. On the far side of the roof he stood atop a ledge, and as Uri and I approached, the boy began to scream, *"Allah-a-akbar."* His hands were empty. There was no danger of being killed by him. Uri pointed his rifle and then ordered the young boy to step down.

But the boy kept screaming to Allah. I saw it coming. His legs tensed. The boy sprang up and gave a final, piercing shout. I dropped my rifle, lunged, and for a moment I was gripping the boy's shirt. For a moment I felt as if I were floating, as if I would fall forever with this boy. Then Uri's hands clutched the collar of my uniform. I lost my grip on the boy's shirt, and as Uri yanked me toward the rooftop, I faced downward as if hovering above the falling boy. His face was pointed to the sky. His eyes were closed and it seemed that the earth below was rising up to meet him. When the boy crashed against the concrete, there was hardly any sound.

Our commander had watched it all. He had been standing in the doorway to the rooftop, his weapon ready in case the boy turned out to be a decoy. When Uri let me go, I stood. Cohen reprimanded me for jeopardizing my life and Uri's. What was I doing? Cohen yelled. Was I a lunatic? I almost died trying to save a jumping boy who'd driven a plank of nails into Meir. I was assessing what to say, what to explain, but Hershel Cohen just shook his head and waved his hand to say that I should not bother answering.

We left the rooftop. A pool of blood lay in the hallway where Meir had been attacked. I saw a handcuffed Palestinian man and I determined that this was Shehadeh. I saw a woman and six children held against a wall at gunpoint. They slipped a blindfold on Shehadeh and led him out to an idling IDF truck. I could hear Meir screaming, and I will say this to you: A part of me did not mind that he'd been injured. Another part was thinking, Now it is less than two days until I return to the Negev. I tried to shrug all of this off, to remind myself that I was just a soldier following orders. But as the jeep raced back to the base in darkness, I saw the boy in my mind, over and over. I watched him fall and could not tell what I was feeling. I did not know why I had risked my life to try and save him.

About the consequences of lunging

There was a video, I soon learned. Someone had filmed the falling boy from below, and when I returned from *miluim*, an entirely new situation had just begun. Your mother ran her finger along my stitches and did not ask if I had thrown the boy off of the rooftop, but I told her anyway that I had not. She'd seen the news and seen the video, coverage of which was being exaggerated in the manner of a tabloid story, although due to the nature of the short video, it was impossible to tell by watching what had happened. The footage was so blurry and inconclusive that even I could not interpret what I was seeing.

One pro-Israeli American television station, I would learn, had entitled their coverage "Leaping into Another World" and focused extensively on the Palestinians' rejection of the United Nations Partition Plan, under which Palestine was to have been divided in 1948 between the Palestinians and Jews. At the other extreme, one Jordanian station gave the story a title that translated roughly to "The Jews Have Become the Persecuting Nazis." This same station reported my name, my age, my place of work. I asked your mother if she thought we should take a trip somewhere. Shoshanna rolled her eyes at me and said, "The animals."

I was asked, at least two dozen times, to make a statement, but I chose not to. I was told by Avner Kornblum, an official at the Nature Reserves Authority offices in Jerusalem, that two threats had been received there from unnamed callers representing the Islamic Jihad, one of whom promised to kill me, chop up my body, fill a bag with my body parts, and bring it to that same rooftop in Rafiah, where he would throw me down piece by piece. The other had, more simply, vowed to fill my heart with bullets. Kornblum suggested I reconsider my decision, but I told him that my position was unchanged. You may wonder, should you ever see the footage of the falling boy, why I would elect to make no comment. The first part of my answer is that I knew anything I might say would be taken out of context, used to suit the spin selected by the interviewer. That is to say, I felt sure any comment I might make would appease no one, except for perhaps Avner Kornblum. The other reason for my silence was more perplexing. I knew I had tried to save the boy. I knew that this boy would have been happy to kill me. I knew that the Palestinians had rejected the Partition Plan. I knew that six million Jews were murdered in the Holocaust and that for many Palestinians as well as many Arab nations this was not nearly enough. And yet, there was some part of me that still wondered at my own actions. There was a part of me that did not entirely know what I was doing there on that rooftop.

I spoke hourly, it seemed, to the officials at the Nature Reserves Authority office in Jerusalem, and after two more days of news coverage, Kornblum suggested I stay away from Hai Bar during hours of operation. I woke early each day that week, went there at five to begin the rounds of feeding and other chores. I left at eight and gave instruction to my staff. I fielded calls from home and wondered when the story would go away. I stayed at home with your mother, who gave art lessons to groups of local children after school. I surrounded myself with our animals, all of whom you will come to know. Do not be fooled into thinking that I am anywhere near normal or even rational when it comes to animals. These are our pets: Logo (a dog), Nachman (a hyrax), Zviya (a gazelle), Jojo and Avigail (fennec foxes), Lester (a three-legged striped hyena).

About the sudden desire to know me

A week passed. Then another week. According to the Hai Bar staff, the parade of reporters seeking me out had all but ceased, so I called Kornblum to tell him I thought it okay that I return to the park during its regular operating hours. Kornblum had not received any more death threats, so he agreed, and I returned. All was fine until the fluke event of a rerun of a nature program. It was a segment for the show *Animals Around the World.* It had been filmed at Hai Bar during the past summer. It had aired during the fall, and for no reason whatsoever it aired again in February. Suddenly people around the world were reminded of my existence and of the murder I may or may not have committed. Now that a month had passed, there was no footage to watch and declare ambiguous, no editorials to read, no "smoking gun" clues to search for or make up (one absurd American tabloid had reported that my father had been a vicious kapo at Auschwitz, a veritable right-hand man of Hoess and Mengele). Instead there were people, most of them elderly, who watched nature programs and had recognized me as the man identified in that news footage from the Gaza Strip in which a boy had either jumped or been pushed off of a rooftop. Given this chance link, they found themselves compelled to write me letters and mail these letters off to Hai Bar. During the two weeks that followed the nature program, I received notes of appreciation for my attempted rescue, letters of condemnation for my brutal act of murder, letters consoling me for having become a victim of the media, and letters offering forgiveness. One letter in particular I recall because it began with the sentence *After I watched you talk about the oryx you call Hermes, I was overcome by a sudden desire to know you.* I do not understand what it is about seeing a person portrayed by a narrative that is simultaneously visual, but it can cause reactions that we do not think about very much. It can cause us to worship movie actors, and it can cause us to feel intimacy with a person who is not so much a person as an illusion. Had I accidentally become an illusion?

I read each letter. I parsed the sentences. One of the Hai Bar staff members, an American veterinarian named Vicki, who lived at Hai Bar with her husband-to-be and their four-month-old daughter, who they called Arava, asked me why I did not throw all of these letters into the garbage. I told her it was merely curiosity, but the reason I read all of these letters, if I am honest, is that I was amazed by their arrival. I did not want them, and yet I could not help but marvel that I had become, however briefly and/or illusorily, a point of focus for so many different people. I did not answer any of these letters, but I felt obligated, at the very least, to complete the transaction by reading the words that were intended as a medium between the writer of the letter and myself. I thought that this would, in some way, help tip the scales back to where I had been before the chance circumstances that had resulted in this unexpected notoriety.

Early one afternoon I even received a phone call. The caller was a woman in New Jersey. She'd called Hai Bar and asked for me, and without any preamble she asked me if my father had died in Kovno, Lithuania. My first thought was that this woman was a reporter, but her voice labored with every word, as if the woman had summoned all of her physical strength to make this call. I began with the assumption that the woman had been overcome with a sudden desire to know me, but very quickly I was overcome by the desire to know her. I told her yes, my father had died in Kovno, Lithuania. The woman immediately began crying. Then she hung up but called again an hour later. Again she asked me if my father had died in Kovno, Lithuania. I told her yes, this was what I had been told. The woman burst into tears and hung the phone up. She called a third time, just before I went home that evening. She asked me the same question. As she spoke I experienced an odd sensation, as if at any moment my physical body might dissolve.

Again, I told her yes. Then I said, "Tell me who you are." But the woman had already begun crying and hung up on me soon after. I waited for her to call again. All the next day at work I stayed near the phone and waited, but the woman did not call.

About the desire to kill me

When I told your mother about the phone calls from the woman in New Jersey, her response was to kiss the scar where I had recently had my stitches taken out. She asked me why I didn't think the woman would contact me again and I said I didn't know nor did I know why she had contacted me in the first place. It was early on a Friday morning. I went to sit out in the yard, where our gazelle, Zviya, pranced around and occasionally danced up to me. Soon your mother stuck her head out the door and told me that it was Vicki calling from Hai Bar. I went back inside with the hope that Vicki had taken a message from the woman in New Jersey, but instead I learned that Samson, one of the thirty-six Persian onagers we had released into the Makhtesh Ramon crater, had wandered back to Hai Bar and was at that moment standing outside the northern fence. He seemed to want to come in, Vicki explained. I found this laughable, and yet this was something that I knew I would have to manage carefully if I did not want a visit from Avner Kornblum. So I called Kornblum in Jerusalem, explained that Samson had found his way back to the Hai Bar fence, and that I was seeking consultation before I made the choice of whether to let him inside the enclosure or leave him out in hope that he would wander the hundred and twenty kilometers back to Makhtesh Ramon. I was not at Hai Bar at present, I said, but would go there promptly. Kornblum said, "Will you recognize his field marks?" I said I would. "And you will be sure this is Samson?" I assured him that I would confirm the onager's identity, a fairly ludicrous consideration, given that whether this was Samson or not, it was obviously one of the onagers we'd released, and so our actions would be the same regardless of which onager it was. "What do you expect you will do?" he asked, and I said, "I expect we'll let him in. Then we'll evaluate to see if he is injured, with the goal of assessing whether he should eventually be retranslocated to Makhtesh Ramon." "I do not think another translocation of Samson will be advisable," Kornblum said smugly, as if I hadn't already determined this. "How is the tide?" Kornblum asked. "The tide of what?" I asked, confused, and he said, "The tide of reporters seeking to turn you into a villain of celebrity." His English was not particularly good, and for this reason I generally spoke to him in English. It tended to keep our conversations short. I said, "The tide is getting lower, but things still wash up now and then." This metaphoric banter seemed to please him and he said, "Good, very well. Keep me informed of your operations."

I took Logo in my jeep and drove the twenty minutes from our flat in Eilat up to Hai Bar. When I arrived I saw the onager. Now he was standing directly outside the main gate. Vicki was sitting on the steps to the front office. Dillon, her fiancé, stood beside her and held the baby. Berstein was also standing there and when he saw me he smiled and pointed a thumb at the soon-to-be-no-longer-wild onager. "Now we let Eeyore back inside?" Berstein asked, and I said, "Yes, of course." I got out of the jeep. I asked Vicki when she had first sighted him and she said, "Right before I called you." And so I opened up the gate. I looked at Samson, who looked back at me, then lowered his head and leisurely strolled back in.

Vicki, Dillon, and the baby went in after him. I closed the gate and conversed with Berstein.

He said, "The leopard, Bavtah, seems unhappy. She's peeing blood again. We might need to call in Salzman."

I said, "Did you sedate her and have Vicki take a look?"

He said, "Yes, of course, but she does not know how to treat a leopard."

"Neither does Salzman," I said.

"This is true," Berstein said. "Also it is true that it is nice to look at Vicki's ass when she is leaning down to examine a sick leopard."

Then Berstein laughed at his tasteless joke. I am sorry to have included this, but you will soon know Berstein and perhaps this will prepare you.

I wandered off to check on the leopard, Bavtah, who'd been with us for several years, ever since the Ein Gedi kibbutzniks trapped her mistakenly after a different leopard, Hoordus, had killed and eaten one of their goats. I had pleaded with the kibbutzniks to set her free, but it is difficult to reason with kibbutzniks. Bavtah was the third female trapped or killed, and now the sex ratio of the leopard population around Ein Gedi is badly skewed, possibly beyond repair.

I had taken about ten steps across the parking lot when a car pulled up. Out stepped a tall man wearing what Berstein liked to refer to as the clothing of someone who had blacked out. In other words, a Hasid, with his long black coat and black hat. I saw thin, wavy strands of hair dangling from each side of his face, which appeared to confirm my assumption. I asked the man if I could help him and he said no. He said he'd come there to help me. He said that for this very purpose he'd driven down from Gush Katif, which was a block of Jewish settlements in Gaza. He said he'd seen me on TV and that if I was not careful someone would kill me. Then the man reached inside his long black coat, took out a rifle, aimed, and fired.

About Mordechai Akiva

His bullet hit me in the belly and punctured part of my small intestine. He fired only one shot. An instant later Berstein put a bullet through his head. As to why this man, who was identified as Mordechai Binyamin Akiva, age thirty-seven, meant to kill me, there was never an explanation. No one from his particular settlement nor any of the settlements in Gush Katif claimed knowledge of his actions. There were theories thrown out by newspapers, the main one being that Akiva had believed I deserved to die for my attempt to save the Palestinian boy and had assumed that with so oblique a motive he could get away with driving down to Hai Bar and shooting me. Another theory was that the man believed he'd been obeying a command issued by God.

I tell you this, and yet I don't entirely blame Mordechai Akiva. Things were rushing at me from all directions. I had opened, however briefly, a doorway through which anything might have come. I was relieved, in certain ways, as I was being flown by helicopter to a hospital in Jerusalem. Despite losing a lot of blood, I was alive, and I thought maybe this would at last balance whatever needed to be balanced. I thought that possibly this incident would close the portal I had opened inadvertently when I reached out for the Palestinian boy as he began to jump.

Berstein and your mother were with me in the helicopter. They were both handling themselves admirably under the circumstances. If they were worried for me, they did not show it. There is a saying. You'll come to know it. We say, "Israelis are mean people. Israelis say what they mean and mean what they are saying." Perhaps this was not always true in Berstein's case, but it was true for Shoshanna. Your mother held my hand and said, "Amnon, you must survive this." I told her I would. Then I began slipping out of consciousness.

About being unconscious

I heard voices, all around. They were all my voice. They were not. I tried to move outside of me, to the next voice, but when I got there I was still inside my own voice. It was as if I were somehow gathering these voices. It was as if I could, by speaking, let them rest and also give these voices something to move through.

About time moving strangely

Then I was lying in a hospital bed, the bullet removed, machines attached to me, a lot of stitches in my belly.

Then I was back in the Negev Desert. The hot ionized wind known as the *hamsin* was blowing.

Then I was parachuting into the Golan Heights on June 9, 1967, and there was golden grass growing everywhere, purple thistles, wide blue sky, a pair of storks nesting atop a telephone pole, and somewhere there was gunfire but the bullets did not touch me.

Then I was feeling better, my stitches gone, another scar, your mother somewhere in the house, my dog and my hyena lying beside the bed, my disgruntled hyrax plodding across the floor.

Then your mother and I were kissing.

Then I was standing in my yard on a starry, moonless night, with the *hamsin* blowing, and I could hear what seemed like wind-voices, sounds that if you are not focused in your listening sound like meaningful words, but if you listen closely sound like the husks of words that ghostlily float around you, such that finally you give up and hear wind. Which then repeats, of course, the cycle, and you hear words that you half hear, half make up to fill the space that surrounds the bluntness where an edge should be. I stood outside for a long time. I heard the wind and watched the stars. Patches of cloud moved underneath the constellations, at times erasing them, until these clouds would pass and the patterns of the stars could be restored, over and over, as if repaired by the endless spinning of a relentless, unseen spider.

About the people at the wedding in Ein Gedi

On the Sunday afternoon when I attended the wedding ceremony for my two American employees, Vicki and Dillon, I saw Shoshanna holding the baby, Arava, for some time. Arava had big cheeks and she would open her mouth and smile and sometimes point at things. We were all standing beside the spring of David in Ein Gedi. I watched this beautiful girl and thought to myself that I would like to have a child of my own.

Besides the rabbi, Shoshanna, myself, and the baby, the small guest list consisted of Vicki's parents, her American friend Lillian, Dillon's aunt Julia, his cousin Dara, and his sister, Gwendine, who introduced herself as Dee. At the reception after the ceremony, I spoke at length with Julia, who struck me as the type of woman that young Israeli men tend to imagine when they fantasize about pretty blond American girls. We talked about the coral reefs off the coast of the Sinai peninsula, where she and Dara planned to scuba dive after their stay in the southern Negev. Julia was a marine biologist, and she had arranged for lodging in Sharm el-Sheikh for several weeks so that she could collect data on various species of false coral that lived in the Red Sea. All this was pleasant chitchat with an interesting woman. I expected my impressions of the five other guests to be more or less the same, but that was only until Vicki clanged her wine glass with a spoon because apparently Dillon's sister was going to comply with a request to sing.

I had heard Julia refer wryly to her niece as "the enchantress," but when Dee Morley first stood up at the table, she seemed shy. She made a short speech regarding her delight in finding "Dilly" so happy here in Israel. She took a breath after that and began to sing. Without a microphone or accompaniment, she sang "Blackbird," but the song was nothing like the version that had been recorded by the Beatles, nothing like anything that I had ever heard. Her voice was full and sweet and liquid, yet there was more to it than beauty. Something about the song was quietly ecstatic, as if her voice was traveling beyond us, into another world.

After the reception, Dillon and Vicki went to a hotel in Eilat while Shoshanna and I took Arava and had the six guests from the

U.S. over to our flat. We tried to keep the animals in our bedroom, but Logo managed to get the door open, and for a short time all the animals were milling around the kitchen and the living room. The guests were amused, and so after I had identified each animal by name, I gathered Nachman, Jojo, and Avigail in my arms while Shoshanna herded Logo and Lester back into our bedroom. I tied some twine around the door handle. This was as much to preserve harmony as it was to keep Nachman, Jojo, and Avigail from escaping out our front door.

A short while later I stepped out into the yard to check on Zviya and I found Dee there. She was drinking a Kinley soda. We introduced ourselves, as we had not yet spoken. I asked her why she was out there all alone, and Dee told me that she had been afraid of Lester. I said, "He's tame," and she said, "I know, but it still scares me to be near a hyena." "You would get used to him," I said, and then suggested that, eventually, she would come to see that Lester was even more docile than Logo. "I'm sure I will," she said, but added that there was, simply, a part of her that worried about being near a hyena. Then in the same shy voice she had used when she'd first spoken at the wedding, she said, "It might help if you could tell me why he's tame."

I said that Lester had been abandoned as a pup and that a gangrenous rear leg had required amputation, but he was still so young that he'd adjusted to the loss of the leg quite easily. I said that Lester liked to sleep on the floor adjacent to my side of the bed, and after years of this, the sound of Lester's snoring tended to soothe me and to help me fall asleep. I explained that Lester had never learned that he was wild and had imprinted on me, more or less, as his mother. Dee smiled faintly and said, "Thank you. That helps put things into context." Since she did not appear to need any more information regarding Lester, I changed the topic and asked where she had learned to sing.

She'd been in church choir, she said, and then her school choir.

At a young age she had noticed that when she performed any kind of solo, people clapped loudly. I told her that she sang beautifully, and Dee thanked me but then apologized for her song that afternoon. It was too forceful, Dee said. She had been nervous with both Dillon and his new wife there. I asked her if she could explain more fully what she meant.

Dee said, "When I sing, I do something to the people who are listening. I do something that makes people pay attention."

"I'd call that talent," I suggested.

Dee shook her head and said, "It's more, or it's less, depending on your perspective. It's something I do to protect myself, though I'm not totally sure how."

I said, "Well, I enjoyed your song."

"At least, you think you did," she said, and laughed in an incongruously derisive manner. She rolled her eyes like a young girl and then she let out a long sigh. She said, "You really liked my singing?" I assumed that she must be speaking with further irony or sarcasm, but when I looked at her, I realized that the edge I had felt a moment before was gone. I smiled and repeated my assertion of her talent. I said I wouldn't be surprised if she went on to achieve a great deal of success. After a pause in which her expression seemed again to be one of shyness, she said that this was something that she was still trying to work out, both the success part and whether or not she wanted it. In the meantime, she explained, she had recently broken up her band of the last three years and had moved by herself from Florida to New York, where she was working as a waitress and singing at a club in Greenwich Village. I asked if "Blackbird" was a part of her standard repertoire. She said it was, except that usually she sang the first line of the song four or five times before moving on to the next. In this way she could assess the potency of her voice on a given night. During the pause after each repetition, the room tended to grow quiet. When she moved on to the second line, people exhaled and she could feel what she had done to them. As she explained this, I did not have the sense that she was bragging and that, if anything, she was not entirely comfortable with the phenomenon. Then I said something that even now surprises me. I told Dee to keep her guard up. I told her to watch out for people lurking in the corners of the room. This made her smile, and it seemed, strangely, like a perfect thing to say to her.

I had assumed that this conversation would conclude my interactions with Dee Morley for the evening, but later, when I was cleaning up the kitchen, she sought me out and asked if she could speak with me again. She said there was something else she wished to tell me. I asked her what, and Dee explained that she and Dillon came from a family with many problems, that consequently there were very important reasons for the two of them to stay far away from their home in Utah. When I asked what these reasons were, she would not elaborate. She said, "I'm sorry to be so cryptic. I barely know how to describe the things I speak of. I think that mostly I'm just hoping you'll watch over my little brother. I know he's safe here, and I'd like that to continue. As for me, I have the sense that I have more to do, much harder things than trying to become a famous pop star. Though it would help, I suppose, to be a pop star." She smiled again—her shy smile—and removed something from her purse. "This is my demo tape," she said. "You might enjoy it." I thanked her for the tape and promised I would watch over her brother. She said, "I know you will," and quickly left the room.

It was your mother who first suggested that I write to you because I have stayed up late many nights wondering how to explain this world. A futile gesture, and yet what I write here is as much an act of faith as it is one of defiance. I am aware that this is not a document, not in the strictest sense. I will not seal this in an envelope with instructions to open on your thirteenth, twenty-first, fortieth, or sixty-fifth birthday. I will not place this in an envelope at all. I am not even sure you will read this, though you may. But

I have tried to include the things that seem most relevant. This includes Dee, whom I suspect will come again to visit. One day you'll meet her, and by then she will not be as afraid of Lester. I also mention her because she seems the type of person who may experience, at some point in her life, a situation resembling that which I recount here. Of course, I do not mean that she will try to save a boy in Gaza or that a man from Gush Katif will attempt to kill her. I mean that she is someone who, for whatever reason, may find that she has become a focal point of considerable attention. That she may open up a doorway of her own.

About a letter sent from New Jersey

There was another pile of letters waiting for me at Hai Bar when I returned to work later that spring, having received permission from my doctor and from Kornblum and from a voice in some nether region of my body, which suggested that the time of Mordechai Akiva and other would-be assassins was past although it wouldn't hurt to keep an eye on whoever happened to be loitering in the parking lot. Vicki had saved the letters in a box, assuming, as had been my habit, that I would want to read them all. But I was done with reading letters. I was done feeling as if I were a radio receiver picking up the varied signals of human beings across the entire world. She said, "You want me to throw them out?" and I said, "No, why don't you read them. Screen them for death threats. Screen them for anything that looks interesting."

A day later she handed me two unsealed envelopes. The first contained a typed and verbose letter that had been dictated to a secretary by a Hollywood producer offering to buy my "life rights" in hopes of developing a movie script about the events I've described here, possible titles for which included "The Holy Land," "The Land of Solomon," "The Land of Milk and Honey," and just "The Land." I read all five typed pages and then ripped the letter up.

The second letter, however, gave me pause even before I opened it. I stared for several minutes at the return address in the upper left corner of the envelope. My correspondent's name was Beverly Rabinowitz. When Vicki walked into the office, I said, "I'm staring at the name Beverly Rabinowitz. What kind of name is that? Some midwestern girl who married a New York Jew?" She shook her head and said, "I don't think she's midwestern." As Vicki said this I first noticed that the letter had a postmark from New Jersey. Vicki said, "You might want to read that one at home."

I did as Vicki suggested. I took it home, and sometime after your mother had gone to sleep, I sat down at the kitchen table, pulled the letter out, and with Jojo and Avigail scurrying about, playing their usual nocturnal chasing games, I read what Beverly Rabinowitz had written. She had seen my photograph in the newspaper and she had seen me on the segment of *Animals Around the World*. She was a fifty-year-old pediatrician who lived in East Brunswick, New Jersey, with a teenage daughter and teenage son. Another daughter was in college. She had written me because I bore such a striking resemblance to her father that she could not help wondering if we shared a lineage of some kind. With the letter, she had enclosed a photograph of two men and a woman. As she explained, the attractive woman in the middle was her aunt Doris, who survived the war and had died only two months ago. She said the man on the left was her uncle Pinchas and the other man was her father, Jonah Rabinowitz. Both men were believed to have been killed during the execution of five hundred Jewish intellectuals in August 1941. In certain ways, it was a very simple letter. She asked me whether I might write back with information about my parents. Had they by any chance lived in Poland or Lithuania? Were they survivors of the Holocaust? Were they alive? When I finished reading the letter, I stared for a long time at the photo she had sent me. The man on the right side looked so much like me that at first I thought this must be a false impression.

About me

I will tell you now that my own origin remains, at least in part, a mystery. I was born in March of 1942 in the Kovno ghetto in Nazi-occupied Lithuania. That a woman could sustain a pregnancy through a winter during those times is a thought that boggles the imagination. More boggling yet, my mother knew me for an hour. Then I was whisked away by the Jewish underground, through Belarus and the Ukraine, through Romania, Bulgaria, Greece, eventually to Palestine. I was carried in bags, in suitcases, inside cabinets, beneath the shirts of women. I was given sedatives so that I would remain silent. In one instance I almost drowned. It took three months to reach the Jewish settlement on the outskirts of the desert city of Be'er Sheva, where my adoptive parents, Ehud and Naomi Grossman, waited. I was told all this when I was seven. It still confounds me to think that I made this journey and that my life was saved by many people I do not know.

My adoptive grandfather Rachmil lived in the Pale settlements of Russia and immigrated by boat to Sydney, Australia, in the late 1800s. My adoptive parents came to Palestine from Sydney in 1933. I do not think of myself as having a first language because at home my parents spoke a mixture of English and poorly accented Hebrew and ultimately these languages for me are not separate. You will come to know your grandfather Ehud and your grandmother Naomi, and I believe that you will love them as I do. Your great-grandfather Rachmil and great-grandmother Etka have been dead for many years.

About my biological mother in Kovno, there were stories. No one knew her name, but it was said that she eventually was able to escape the ghetto, live in the forests, and become a part of the resistance. It was said that she killed a German soldier once, stole up on the man while he was sitting on a stump, smoking, hoping the deer he had been tracking would reappear soon, though he was there in that forest for the purpose of hunting Jews. She put her rifle to his head and she said, "Life. Death. How are these different, Nazi pig?" When the man turned, she fired a bullet between his eyes. How can I know this? I have most likely made it up.

And yet, I have considered her question carefully. What I will tell you is that there are connections between the thing you are while living and what you are when you are dead. We are linked with ourselves, always.

As for my father, he was supposed to have died in Kovno. That was the only thing I had ever been told.

After I showed the letter to Shoshanna, she suggested I call my parents and ask whether they knew any more than what they'd told me. Both were amazed when I told them about the photo and read the letter, but neither could tell me anything new. We spoke of other things, such as my bullet wound and a recent change in the bus route to the town where they lived together in the Golan. Ever since my brother Ariel, also adopted, died in the Six-Day War, I have spoken to my parents at least once a week, without fail, even during the time that I was completing my Ph.D. in desert ecology at New Mexico State University in Las Cruces. I too fought in the Six-Day War. I began my doctorate in September of that same year. I returned to Israel in 1974 and a year later I was married to your mother. I was thirty-two and she was twenty-seven. I mention these things here because I included all this information in my response to Beverly Rabinowitz, which I sent off to her the next morning.

About the second letter from Beverly Rabinowitz

It came in a padded manila envelope, which also contained five cassette tapes. For a multitude of reasons, I do not think I can ever describe the feelings I experienced as I began to read this letter. She'd written:

Dear Amnon,

Thank you for your reply. I have spent many hours considering the handful of details you were able to provide. As you will see it has turned out to be quite a handful, though I mean this in the best possible way.

To be truthful, I felt silly as I was writing my first letter. I was almost sure that it was a waste of time. I had shown my mother the video of "Animals Around the World" sometime after it was given to me by my late aunt Doris's widower, Max Rubin, who she lived with at a home for the elderly in New Jersey. My mother, who has just turned seventy-eight, sighed repeatedly as we watched. Then she told me to be careful, lest you prove to be some sort of dybbuk or other tricky spirit that was playing a sort of game with us.

For some it is easy to think in mystical terms. I am not one of those people. Much of the information I will share was reported to me by Max Rubin, who in 1982 married my late aunt Doris. She was the woman in the photo that I sent you. Max was her third husband, and although he is eccentric in certain ways, Max has always seemed reliable and honest to a fault. It was Max who provided me with the VCR tape of "Animals Around the World" and at that time informed me of several confessions that Doris made to him on her deathbed, one of which was that she had loved my father, Jonah Rabinowitz, who remained in Kovno after securing visas and transit funds for my mother and myself, through which we were able to get to Japan and eventually to the United States. I was five then and my memory of that period is quite fragmented. However, according to the account provided by Max Rubin of the information my aunt Doris revealed to him only days before she died of stroke, my aunt and my father, deplorable as this may seem, had an affair while they were refugees in Kovno and this affair is likely to have continued up to the day that both my father and my uncle Pinchas disappeared. They were two of five hundred Jewish men who were marched out of town on August 8, 1941, believing that they had secured jobs working in the city archives. There is a story about these men that has been passed on among those who knew them. It was said that two of these five hundred found a way to survive, but I have made several inquiries and it seems likely that all five hundred men were killed.

Aunt Doris, incidentally, recorded three-plus hours of testimony about her survival, which has been incorporated into a growing archive developed for a planned Holocaust museum in Washington, D.C. I have recently listened to this testimony and I have enclosed tapes of her testimony here. In the testimony she does not mention her affair or for that matter any specific feelings for my father. She does, however, describe in detail a period from summer 1941 to summer 1943 in which she lived in the Kovno ghetto, until her arrest and intended deportation to Treblinka, from which she escaped by jumping from a train and after which she became part of the armed resistance in the forests around Białystok, Poland. She was later captured and imprisoned at Auschwitz, where she remained until the camp was liberated.

I am suggesting that Doris is your biological mother and that my father, Jonah Rabinowitz, is your father. I suggest this despite a lack of any testimony even hinting that she might have become pregnant by my father or given birth to a child during the time she lived in the Kovno ghetto and also despite a lack of any such revelation to Max Rubin on her deathbed. I am suggesting this because, upon reading your letter and learning that you, my father's look-alike, were born in March of 1942 in the Kovno ghetto to a mother you never knew, the only precise detail about whom you can provide is that

*she was believed to have been part of the resistance, it seems
likely. The timing of her pregnancy works mathematically so
long as Doris became pregnant in those last weeks before my
father's disappearance. Naturally, what remains unclear in this
scenario was how Aunt Doris, in both her recorded testimony
and her confessions to Max Rubin, could have left out the
prolonged and remarkable event of being pregnant while living
in the ghetto and giving birth to a child who was whisked
away by underground philanthropists, a child who she perhaps
never even held in her own arms. Possibly she intentionally
withheld this information or possibly she repressed the memory,
in which case, when Doris saw your face on television, she
would not have been conscious of the fact that she was looking
at her son. Or, it is possible that all these correlations are
happenstance and the conclusions I have drawn represent only
a compulsion on my part to find a story that fits together. I
have considered this final possibility carefully and continue to
dismiss it. Perhaps this is a place where I am not being perfectly
rational. If I may be so bold, I am interested in speaking with
you by telephone. I include my work and home telephone
numbers here and welcome you to call me at any time.*

Yours,
Beverly

About speaking with my long-lost sister

I called her after I had listened to those five cassette tapes, on
which I'd heard the voice of her aunt Doris, a voice that seemed to
me uncannily familiar. Following a period of somewhat nervous
greetings and introductions, I described to her the phone calls I'd
received from the woman in New Jersey. She said that Max Rubin
had indeed mentioned a significant phone bill from the hospital

and that Doris had revealed to him that she'd been making calls to Israel, including one in which she spoke to me, although she claimed that I had been evasive. Despite the discrepancy between Doris's account and my recollection of not one but three short conversations, not to mention that I had been anything but evasive during these phone calls, there seemed no point in exploring the matter further. The confirmation that the woman who'd called Hai Bar had almost certainly been Doris only solidified my conclusion that she was in fact my biological mother and that Beverly was my sister. Perhaps I too was not being perfectly rational, but to me all this astounding if wholly circumstantial evidence seemed sufficient beyond a reasonable doubt.

We spoke a second time and then she proposed making a trip to Israel with her three children. I warned her that of late I had been under public scrutiny and that this scrutiny had included death threats as well as one attempted murder. She said she'd sleep on it, and when she called again she said she was not afraid and wondered if she could come for ten days at the end of August. I warned her that it would be hot, but this did not bother her much either. She said she would book a flight on El Al and then she asked me to suggest an Eilat hotel.

Three months later she appeared with her two biological daughters, Jennifer and Rocky, and her son, Jordan, whom she had recently adopted. How beautiful they all were. I quickly fell in love with all of them. Rocky and Jordan wore matching pendants of what looked to me like malachite or tourmaline, the green stones dangling from thin black cords around their necks. They were delighted with all the animals. They were delighted, as well, by a private joke they developed about the rockiness of the country Jordan, which they could see each time we drove on the road between Eilat and Hai Bar. The older daughter, Jennifer, was not as playful, although she did announce, at one point, that while we were all in the spirit of claiming kin, she wanted to adopt Berstein as her father. This tickled Berstein, who told her, "Anytime you want, I sign the papers." By the end of the visit Berstein had taught her how to load and fire an M16. She liked the photograph we took of her holding the rifle. There were also photos of her, Rocky, and Jordan holding a baby wolf that recently had been left at Hai Bar by a Bedouin who said the mother had been killed. The little wolf was quite a character, always snorting and making other funny sounds through his nostrils. He drank his formula with gusto from a baby bottle, and it was Jordan, more than anyone, who enjoyed bottle-feeding this wolf.

I took Beverly and the children on a hike down in the Sinai, the culmination of which was an afternoon of snorkeling in the Red Sea at Sharm el-Sheikh. Back in Israel, I toured them around the Timna Valley and took them up to Makhtesh Ramon. I tried to show them the many colors of the desert. When time allowed, I took walks with Beverly, just the two of us. She seemed to me more like an Israeli than an American. Beverly's poise and repose filled me with quiet wonder, and when she spoke, she was direct. She always said what she meant and meant what she was saying.

On one of our walks, on a trail near Timna, I asked her what else she could tell me about our father. She reiterated that she was only five years old when she last saw him and that given the murky space he'd occupied inside her for close to a half a century, it was hard for her to know the difference between her memories and her dreams.

"Tell me the dreams then," I said.

She said, "That's funny. You sound just like my friend Miriam."

But then she told me things. She looked into my face, which was her father's face, and she said, "Here's what you should know."

He was a man who liked to use his imagination. He used to say that one day he would write a book that would fill a thousand pages and would have drawings of flowing rivers you could actually dive into. Under the water there would be fish that talked and plants you could wear as clothes. He taught science at a gymnasium in Warsaw. He used to claim that he knew all the trees and birds and rocks in all of Poland. He knew them personally. He loved them.

He collected feathers. He liked to swim. He once cut his thumb badly with a knife. He had blue eyes like mine and yours. He loved to sing. He loved the moon. When the moon was full, he often took me out to see it and we would walk along the fields and along the river. Even in winter, we would walk or sometimes run under the moon.

We ran all the way to Lithuania. That's what it felt like. Possibly we didn't actually run so far before we climbed into a train car, but in my mind we ran practically forever before the train station appeared across a field. We had to hide ourselves until the train arrived. In the field there were seven or eight dead cows and I did not understand this. Someone had shot them, he explained. There was no reason. Sometimes people will shoot cows. Some of the dead cows lay on top of one another, and I thought this was a thing that could be corrected, that all these cows would eventually return to life.

On the train we hid under bags of grain and there were rats who did not seem as scared as I was, so I liked them. There were tall trees as the train passed through the ancient forest. There were tall trees when I climbed off the train near Kovno. But there were so many things missing. So many things were lost already. Where were the two big dogs that had run away with us? Where were my uncle Lejb and my aunt Idel? Where was my friend Krajndla Brotman? Where were her dogs?

One night in 1940 there was the biggest, brightest moon that ever was and it was rising over Kovno, Lithuania. Then there was my father coming back from a day of waiting with a crowd of refugees. In his hand was a family visa to Japan and two tickets for train passage across Siberia. He said that I would cross the ocean to America. My mother was crying loudly and my father spoke in Yiddish, saying, "Very soon I'll follow." And then I asked my father, "What if you can't follow?" He said,

"A nechtiger tog." Impossible. Don't be silly. He picked me up, swung me around, and I believed that the whole thing was that simple.

About holding her

Just once, while Shoshanna was snorkeling with the children, Beverly asked if she could hold me. "I want to hold you in my arms," she said to me. We were in the living room. I stepped forward and I wrapped my arms around her and soon both of us were weeping like little children. Lester, Logo, and Nachman remained sacked out on the floor.

About stories that continue to open up

You would expect my story to end sooner than it does, and I would have expected this as well. But I was wrong, as it turned out, about the doorway being closed after the incident with Mordechai Akiva. It was still wide open and only seemed to be getting wider. If at some point in your life you should experience such a confluence of events as I experienced in the time of which I speak, it may seem as though you are a tuning fork or magnet, as if you've found your way into a lucid place where many things appear at once and you can see how close you are and have always been to all these things and then you'll wonder why it is that they have suddenly been revealed. Some of what you see in such a time will change your life and some of it will be forgotten. It is not my intention to speak in riddles, but I will suggest that it is very natural to see all of these things as a big puzzle you must assemble. I will suggest, as well, that certain pieces will not fit, not now or ever, and that you must learn to live with these ambiguities. You must also learn to trust these ambiguities. This is perhaps the most important thing I know.

The day before Beverly and her children were to fly home, two men appeared at Hai Bar, an Agent Sachs and an Agent

Witherspoon from the U.S. Federal Bureau of Investigation. I wasn't there when they drove up, but the men immediately found Dillon and began to ask him questions, at which point Vicki called me and I hurried to Hai Bar. When I arrived, I was questioned about Dillon and the woman who had helped him. Agent Sachs asked me what the woman's name was, and I confirmed that we had known her only as Helen-Ariadne. The man nodded and probed further with regard to my knowledge of Dillon, his motorcycle accident more than a year before, his reappearance in the Negev Desert, and his rehabilitation. The strangest thing was that for me to recall the woman we called Helen-Ariadne required a special kind of concentration. Even now my memories of this woman can be recalled only by holding her, for lack of a better description, very lightly in my thoughts. I was able to remember that she had shaved her head before she left. I recalled that I'd first seen her right around the time that Dillon Morley came to work for me. I noted that Helen-Ariadne had sometimes walked with me and assisted me as I would search for holes in or beneath the metal fence that surrounds the Hai Bar enclosure. I said that much of the time we did not speak as we walked. Then Agent Sachs said, "Where is Dr. Beverly Rabinowitz right now?"

At this point in the conversation, I gathered my wits and realized that I was under no legal obligation to answer questions for these agents from the United States. I wanted to call Beverly and warn her, but I did not know what I would be warning her about. Berstein walked into the room with Yotam. Dillon and Vicki remained quiet and sat behind the front desk, their baby sleeping in a portable crib beside them. I looked at Agent Sachs, a tall, lean man in his early fifties. I looked at his stockier and more physically intimidating partner, and then I said, "You'll need to explain to me exactly what it is that you're doing here."

Agent Sachs, who clearly did most of the talking, said, "We're tracking a fugitive whose real name is Katherine Clay Goldman.

We believe that the woman you knew as Helen-Ariadne was this same woman, operating under an alias, as has been her habit since the early seventies and possibly before then."

I said, "What does this have to do with Beverly and her children?"

Almost as I spoke her name, Beverly's car pulled into the Hai Bar parking lot. I watched the children emerge. Then Beverly stepped out.

"Is that her?" asked Agent Sachs. I nodded.

"Guess she's not Clay," said Agent Witherspoon, "or Helen-Ariadne."

Agent Sachs said, "No, she's not. At least so far as I can tell."

He shook his head and we all stared at the men, confused.

About the two U.S. agents

As Agent Sachs eventually revealed to us, he and his partner had been keeping tabs on Beverly for a year or so. Her name had come up during several interviews with a young man who played guitar and worked on boats in Florida. They had been following up with the young man, Timothy Birdsey, because he'd previously accompanied Dillon Morley's sister to Salt Lake City, where at the time Dillon lay in a coma, and through a series of events that Sachs did not explain, they had encountered Katherine Clay Goldman. More recently, they had heard about the wedding. They'd questioned both Dee and Julia when they learned that they had attended. They were incredulous when Dee told them that Dillon had made a full recovery with the help of a woman he called Helen-Ariadne, and they'd confirmed his state of health with the assistance of an agent stationed in Jerusalem. Since that time they had monitored commercial flights to Israel for suspects that might be Katherine Clay Goldman/Helen-Ariadne. Because her aliases tended to be nonrandom, their suspicion had been aroused when they discovered that Beverly Rabinowitz would be flying from JFK International Airport to Ben Gurion and then staying at a hotel in Eilat. For an American woman traveling to Israel with three children, a ten-day trip spent solely in Eilat seemed atypical, and so they were operating on the hunch that Beverly Rabinowitz might be Goldman's latest alias. Once Agent Sachs made all this clear, Beverly and I sat down in a room with the two men for at least an hour and we explained the precise circumstances of our first contact back in June as well as those of her current visit. The FBI men listened attentively and taped our conversation. In this way, we told these men most of the story that I am telling you.

The next day, we sent Beverly and the children off with T-shirts and posters from Hai Bar and a promise to visit them in New Jersey. Their flight on El Al did not leave until almost midnight, so they spent the afternoon and evening seeing sights and eating dinner in the old Jaffa Port section of Tel Aviv. Shortly after returning to her home, Beverly called me from New Jersey. They were back safely, without incident, other than the amusing fact, as Beverly put it, that those two FBI agents had been sitting in the row directly behind them. "What was that like?" I asked, and she said the presence of those men had been unnerving, to the point that she had not fallen asleep for a single minute. Nor had they, Beverly said. Nor had the ever-watchful Jennifer. She said that Jennifer had continually turned around and engaged the shadowy men in small talk. She said that even as we spoke she had the feeling these men were lurking somewhere close by.

About you

You were conceived shortly after the visit from Beverly and her children. I started to write to you six weeks later. At that time, I had no idea what I'd begun. When I first put pen to paper, I wrote: *Today, in a certain frame of reference, you are twenty-eight days old.*

*According to the pregnancy book your mother makes me read, you are
an embryo, soon to become a fetus. Each day the things that happen to
you are vast. Two days ago your arm buds appeared, as did the depres-
sions that will soon become the insides of your ears. Yesterday your liver
formed, along with the beginnings of your gallbladder, stomach, thy-
roid, intestines, pancreas, and lungs. Today, the buds of your two legs
appeared. So did the lenses of your eyes. Little did I know, you will go
through three sets of kidneys before your birth. The first set, which do not
ever become functional (so far as we know), appeared early this week
and have now been replaced by a second set, which will function only
briefly.*

When I began this I assumed I would complete it that same
night. Clearly the scope of what I thought to tell you has grown
larger.

I am moving toward the conclusion of this note to you, this
curious thing that seems to keep accreting, spiraling in on itself
and circling out again. I have debated whether or not to include
this document, which late last fall I received most unexpectedly
from U.S. Federal Agent Leopold Sachs. He wrote to say that he
had followed up on the story Beverly and I told him, the story I
have already recounted about my origins in Kovno, Lithuania, and
additionally, Beverly's tale of the five hundred Jewish intellectuals
executed in August 1941, with its legend of the two men who were
said to have survived. In his letter, Sachs described the xeroxed
pages he'd enclosed as "interesting, even tantalizing" but just as
likely "the delusions of a man experiencing suicidal ideation and
gradually losing sanity." What he had sent were six pages from
the handwritten journal of Georg Vogel, an alleged former Nazi
official, who changed his name to George Gunther Birdsey and
lived in Florida until his suicide in 1954. The journal entries, only
recently discovered, were in German, but Sachs had included
English translations. Why he had gone to all this trouble, I do
not know. I read his letter, and then I looked at the xeroxed copies

of the entries written in German. I picked out words I knew and noted that the alleged Nazi's handwriting was slanted to the left and that he made slashes rather than dots over his *i*'s and that there were places where his letters grew thick, indicating that he had been pressing very hard. When I had exhausted all possible methods of procrastination, I read the following translations.

3 October 54

There was one Jew I remember more than all others because he and another crawled out of the dirt in Lithuania and when we saw them we began to shoot and though the other was killed instantly this one Jew continued running and was not hit by our bullets. We chased him by jeep and he ran onto a bridge and when it was clear that he could not escape he jumped and I ran to see where he had fallen. I reached the guardrail and looked down and what I saw with great surprise was that the Jew was hanging from a girder. I felt a jolt in which I did not feel that I was in control of my own actions and in this moment I reflexively reached down. Before I knew what I had done I pulled the Jew to safety. The other soldiers were as confused as I was by my action, and to explain myself I told them that this man must be questioned before we disposed of him. Because of my rank they obeyed. Later I went to see the Jew. I meant to kill him but still the surprise I felt when I had clutched his arm was making the act of killing him impossible. Instead I stole the Jew and hid him in my basement. I gave him food and I killed others as compensation. In truth, I shot any Jew who resembled him on sight. I fired bullets into the heads of these replacement Jews and still I would not kill the Jew who I kept in my basement. When I recall him now, I think of his blue eyes.

6 October 54

The Jew told me that he had lived in Poland before fleeing to Lithuania with his family and he asked many times if he could leave and return to Kaunas and I explained to him that he would die if he went there and he asked me why this would concern me. I did not care if he was killed, but what I did know was that if the Jew was captured he would betray me. I was aware that it is best to kill a thing that you don't understand except that I still could not bring myself to kill him. Instead I hid the Jew with my family for more than three and a half years.

12 October 54

When the war ended the Jew vanished. I woke up one day to find that he had run. I knew that it was only a short time before what I had done at Stutthof and then Chelmno became known so I paid enormous sums for our visas and soon we left by boat from Riga. But somehow the Jew followed when I left Europe. I mean his letters did. He traced me. He would write to me and three times I wrote back. I wrote to Denmark, to Holland, and to Toronto. Eventually I would not write because I feared that my true identity would be discovered. Then he began to send me lists of names of Jews killed in the camps and I would quickly destroy the letters. I would burn them or chew the pages up and swallow them.

21 Oct 54

The Jew has sent me letters from Argentina to say that he is going back to the Old Country by which I start to think he means East Germany or Poland but it is hard to return to these places now and I am not sure what he means. Maybe by this Old Country he means Palestine. Possibly this is the Old Country but I think not. The Jew writes to say that he will put a shotgun in his mouth and he will die this way and maybe this is what he means by the Old Country. He writes to tell me that I will put a shotgun in my mouth as well and he is right, I plan to do it.

23 Oct 54

I cannot sleep this night and it is as if the Jew is talking in my ear and saying I should be as thankful for his charity as he should be for mine.

To stop the chatter in my ear I recall his letters. He wrote from Holland once to say that if you climb to the top of the New Church and stand very still you will feel it swaying in the wind. I did not know what he means by the New Church but thoughts of swaying this way causes my mind to race and now I am waiting anxiously for dawn.

24 October 54

Another time the Jew wrote of volcanoes he has visited in the South Seas and he said this was a place where the earth belches and where you will see more than what is known if you pay attention to the belching. He wrote it in block letters. PAY ATTENTION TO THE BELCHING. *I could not tell if the Jew is laughing behind these letters and it is also possible that he is crying and it is equally possible that he is belching.*

28 Oct 54

Possibly this Jew who haunts me is related to an ancient order of things that lives beneath the ground and inside air and this is why I could not kill him. There are two in every world, he told me once, while I was feeding him. Two in every world who will not die because the two are one and the one is neither. He laughed when he saw that I was interested and he said my little son had told him this having most likely read it in a storybook.

4 Nov 54

In the last letter I will read from the Jew he says that we will meet again in another place that is not this world but seems like it except that certain patterns will be different. What am I to make of this? He says that in this other world we must not kill Jews or whales or birds. I have begun to think I am a hero for saving this Jew even if I cannot understand what compelled me to grab his arm while he was hanging from a bridge. I have begun to think it is a good thing to leave the world with all its questions and information. Soon I will go outside and put a shotgun in my mouth and pull the trigger. I ask that my reflections if ever found be sent if possible to this one who climbed out of his grave, this necromancer or whatever this man was. If he cannot be found, this should be sent to the sons and daughters who survive him. Perhaps they will understand the actions that I speak of and will know if saving this one Jew when I killed thousands was any use.

I later consulted with a professor at the Hebrew University who spoke German and was able to confirm the accuracy of the translations. I spoke to Beverly, who had also received a copy of these pages from Agent Sachs. She said that all she had done was read the entries once to herself and once aloud to Jennifer by phone and then send them to her childhood friend Miriam, who for reasons that were symbolic and therapeutic and just a strange quirk of their friendship had placed the entire packet in a box up in her attic. I asked her if she believed the Nazi's words to be delusional. She said that she had not yet formulated an opinion and that at some point she'd look into the matter further. I still do not know what to make of all of this, if anything, but I include the rambling and highly suspect testimony of Georg Vogel here for the sake of suggesting that what we comprehend about this world may always be called into question.

About stories ending

As you can tell, I am preparing to stop speaking, for the moment. This is where stories cannot follow. This is where life and stories must diverge.

But I will tell you one more thing. I will tell you that on a recent afternoon, as I drove north along the road through the Arava Rift Valley, I saw the woman we called Helen-Ariadne. She had been walking along the western fence of the Hai Bar park. I pulled my jeep onto the roadside when I noticed her, and in that moment I did not stop to wonder what she was doing there.

I called, "Hello," and she looked up. She said, "Come over here," and so I stepped down out of the jeep and went to her. She pointed out a spot where the fence was loose and where some animal had dug a small depression that had enabled it to tunnel into the enclosure. I was surprised that I had missed it, as I had walked the perimeter of the enclosure that very morning.

"I've seen some others," she said. "Several."

I said, "It must be a persistent jackal or a fox."

She said, "It's neither."

I said, "What is it?"

She said, "Best not to find out."

I ran back to the jeep and got a shovel. I filled the hole in. I hadn't seen her car back at the lot by the main office, but when I mentioned this she said that her car was parked beside the cage where we kept our caracal, Dionysus, and I must not have noticed. We continued walking. She found another hole, somewhat larger, and once again I filled it in.

"Always new holes," I said, and she replied, "Always." I began telling her of Beverly Rabinowitz and our encounter with the U.S. agents, but before I had finished my third sentence, she said, "Don't worry. No one is after me today."

I said, "You know about those men?"

"I know them well," she said.

"Do you know what they wanted?"

"Hard to be sure," she said. "They seem to think that I'm a criminal, but sometimes things are deeper than they seem. Sometimes they're deeper than any one of us can know."

We reached the end of the fence and stopped. To the north lay an unbroken expanse of the Arava Rift Valley. Clumps of broom-bushes and the occasional acacia congregated in the wadis. Most of the valley was smooth sand and limestone rubble.

I said, "Who are you?"

She said, "The answer is always different."

"Who are you now?"

She said, "I'm someone who's here to tell you about these holes."

I said, "That's it?"

She said, "That's it. We need to walk the whole perimeter."

And so we walked, and when we'd finished, her car was there, exactly where she had said it was. She climbed inside and said, "It was good to see you again, Amnon." I waved good-bye, and as she drove away, I told myself that if I thought hard enough I'd come to understand her purpose. I thought and thought, until it felt as if my brain were melting, yet all I understood was that she had moved on to a different purpose.

This world escapes itself. Perhaps this is a simpler way of putting it. There are nights when I stay up almost till dawn, when I sit quietly in the living room while Shoshanna sleeps in our bed and you sleep inside her and Lester and Logo sleep on the floor beside the bed and the two foxes scamper about like the little tricksters that they are and Nachman waddles around this living room and wonders what I'm doing. There are days when I look at your mother, whose only outward sign of you to the untrained eye is that her breasts have swelled beyond their normal size, and what I think to myself is that what she holds inside her belly remains the strangest of all mysteries. There are days when I look at her, and what I feel is a joy so strong that it is frightening to consider that the future I imagine remains uncertain. Then I let go. I do what I can to prepare for your arrival. I put this down, step over Lester, and climb in bed with Shoshanna. I close my eyes although it feels as if a part of me is waking, as if a part of me is only just beginning to remember who I was.

Acknowledgments

I would like to express my appreciation to my wonderful editor, Reagan Arthur, and my miraculous literary agent, Gail Hochman. Thanks also to Jenny Parrott of Little, Brown UK and to Jaco Groot of De Harmonie in the Netherlands. For inspiration, feedback, and all varieties of assistance, I would also like to thank Virginia Barber, Joe Mangine, Murray Schwartz, Mako Yoshikawa, Richard Hoffman, Edison Santana, Dan Green, Meghan O'Rourke, Linda B. Swanson-Davies, David McGlynn, Andrea Walker, Oliver Haslegrave, Jody Klein, Jeff Gordinier, Michael D'Alessio, Herb Hartman, Doris Hartman, Ronnie Lambrou, and Randy Cole. Many thanks as well to Peggy Freudenthal, Ben Allen, and Tracy Roe for their efforts during the copyediting process. Thanks to the Senior Historians' Office at the U.S. Holocaust Memorial Museum, historians at the Lower East Side Tenement Museum, and staff members at the National Yiddish Book Museum. As always, thanks to my parents, whose recollections have been an essential resource during the writing of this book. Most of all, thanks to my wife, Cailin, first reader of all these pages—for your love, your patience, your excitement, your unwavering support.

The two Borges quotes in chapter nine are from "The God's Script" translated by L. A. Murillo. The quote used in the epigraph is from "The Garden of Forking Paths" translated by Helen Temple and Ruthven Todd. For Yiddish expressions used in chapter seven and elsewhere, I have used YIVO spellings except in instances in which I judged popular transliterations to be more recognizable.

Finally, I would like to acknowledge and remember the artist and poet Anne Krosby (1957–1993). The inception of this book dates back to several late-night moonlit walks we took in fall of 1992 in Cummington, Massachusetts.

About the Author

FREDERICK REIKEN is the author of two previous novels, and his short stories have appeared in publications including *The New Yorker*. His debut novel, *The Odd Sea*, won the Hackney Literary Award and was a finalist for the Barnes & Noble Discover Prize. His novel *The Lost Legends of New Jersey* was a national bestseller and a *New York Times* Notable Book. He lives with his wife and daughter in western Massachusetts, and he currently directs the graduate program in writing at Emerson College.